A Su... ...g

Chris Kelly

coronet

CORONET BOOKS
Hodder & Stoughton

First published in Great Britain in 2000
by Hodder and Stoughton
First published in paperback in 2001
by Hodder and Stoughton
A division of Hodder Headline

A Coronet Paperback

10 9 8 7 6 5 4 3 2 1

A CIP catalogue record for this title is available from
the British Library

ISBN 0 340 68214 0

Printed and bound in Great Britain by
Mackays of Chatham PLC, Chatham, Kent

Hodder and Stoughton
A division of Hodder Headline
338 Euston Road
London NW1 3BH

Chapter One

At first Hugh Severin had sensed her heart inside him like a pilgrim's offering. Something given with humility and tenderness; something slight and perishable, lodged in a niche, part of the whole and yet not belonging.

It hadn't been like that at all, of course. They'd harvested the heart. That was the word they used; harvested. Strange. When you harvested something you cut it off at the root. Killed it. But this was living. Cut off at the root, yes, but capable of attaching itself to new ones. A robust, dynamic muscle that might give service for a hundred years.

Not to Hugh. He was forty-nine already. There had been that French woman who'd remembered meeting van Gogh, and hadn't given up smoking until she reached three figures, but she hadn't been suffering from heart disease. As things stood, the longest-surviving transplant patient had managed sixteen years or so. That would take Hugh to his mid-sixties, and medical science was making amazing progress all the time. Or so they kept telling you. In any case, who could guarantee they had more than sixteen years left?

But that wasn't the point. What mattered was the way he felt now compared with the state of him before the operation. For weeks, unable to do much, he'd had the sensation of drowning from inside. That was the only way he could describe it. This great, flabby, expanding bag in his chest had made him feel awash. It had been both frightening and somehow repulsive; out of control, unnatural. Like the thing in *Alien*. And then one evening on his way back from Chalk Farm tube station, the thing had decided to strike. Falling as though in slow motion among the rush-hour crowds, he'd come round to find a Samaritan asking if he was all right. The man had hair like Bobby Charlton's, Hugh recalled. Later he discovered that a less altruistic passer-by had stolen his watch.

After the months with an oxygen cylinder by the bed, the tests at UCH, the ever-present bleeper, the call had come at ten twenty-five one Tuesday night. Pre-med. at Papworth, pushed to theatre in a wheelchair, three hours of carnage he'd rather not think about, coming round in Intensive Care with pipes in every orifice and his body's fluids draining. They'd brought a mirror. This face he saw reflected had changed colour. For four years it had been grey. Now it was pink. His own personal sunrise. And inside he was no longer drowning.

Friends had called: Charlie, Gary, Martha, Miles, and Tilly, who was much more than a friend. She and Hugh had been married for thirteen years, until she'd given up on him, at least as a husband. That had been a decade ago. In the end she'd found his constant absences, his lack of ambition, his heavy drinking with colleagues she regarded as worthless, plain dull; a life that invited, embraced, settled for disillusion. But they had remained necessary to each other. Released from the tension of a failing marriage, they had progressed to a tolerant, fond mutuality.

On one of Tilly's two visits, Hugh, still woozy and apt to drift off in mid-conversation, had woken to find her warm hand on his forehead. Often when callers had gone he couldn't remember anything, except weird Dali-esque sensations, like the clock seeming to move all over the wall. Gary had brought a blow-up rubber woman which he'd propped in the bedside chair. Nurse Killick hadn't been amused. Miles, a cavalier foreign correspondent whom Hugh had met in Manila, said the operation had improved Hugh's communication skills: now at least he was awake some of the time. Charlie, a cartoonist on the *Sunday Times*, had left a pile of books, three of them by Patrick O'Brian. Charlie had said he was that rarity, a writer who made you glad you were ill. And the travel editor of the *Telegraph* had sent him a note saying he should think himself lucky because the staff writer he'd sent to Colombia had been shot in the right buttock. Typical, Hugh thought. He wasn't at all sure that *Telegraph* men were allowed left anythings, including buttocks. That was the beauty of being a freelance. Equilibrium.

The one thing none of his visitors had asked him about was the donor. They had longed to, he saw that, but they'd felt it was taboo. So he'd told them. Not only

3

did he know who she was, but he knew their operations had been simultaneous. Her name was Siobhan; Siobhan Herbert. She was twenty-three; a victim of cystic fibrosis. After her heart had been harvested for him in an adjoining theatre, she'd been given the heart and lungs of another donor. The procedure was known as a domino transplant. Like an awesome game of musical chairs. 'When the music stops you'll have intimate bits of someone else inside you,' Siobhan had said. They had both wondered why, if her heart was healthy, she'd had to part with it. The surgeon, Scoular, had said that unlike their American colleagues, the British thought the lung/heart combination gave the cystic fibrosis patient the best chance.

As soon as they were encouraged to take exercise, Hugh and Siobhan had begun to talk often. Their sternums held together with steel wire, and their cuts from throat to navel knitting with dissolving stitches, they nevertheless found conversation easy. They had the curious sensation that, even though they'd never met before Papworth, they'd always had a lot to say to each other. The age difference had seemed unimportant. Or perhaps it had been important in the sense that they felt able to be friends; friends bound by an extraordinary common experience, without the complications of sex. Which, as Gary had pointed out, was just as well, since sex in their condition would have been like Frankenstein's monster shagging a mummy.

Not that Siobhan was unattractive. Though by no means a conventional beauty she was animated and instinctive, with large, dark eyes. The generator that powered her was the awesome ability to be bright in the face of spiky odds. There was, as yet, no cure for cystic fibrosis. Despite advances in research and treatment, maximum life expectancy was still little more than thirty. Ruling the calculation out of bounds, Siobhan was reading law at Downing, Cambridge, determined to become a barrister. And she would. Nothing was more certain. Hugh recognised in her the spirit that had borne Victorian women through the Empty Quarter, and other unimaginable hardships. He never heard her say she was tired, out of sorts, depressed, under the weather. She must feel these things, like any human being, but they were punctured before they could bubble to the surface. Maybe she was being brave for him, he thought. But he knew she wasn't. She was being brave because to be anything else was a waste of precious time.

They talked for hours. Sometimes he fell asleep as he listened. He didn't like waking up to find her no longer there. When she had visitors and he hadn't, he found it hard to read even O'Brian's tangy, wind-burned prose, with its main topgallants and pugnacious carronades. He would realise he was looking forward to seeing her again. In spite of their ages she seemed fascinated by what he had to say. She thirsted for information, and offered views and asides and observations with extraordinary confidence and maturity.

She liked best to hear about his life as a travel writer. Though he'd been to dozens of countries, some several times, few, in truth, remained vivid to him. And such memories as there were had too often been fogged by long nights on vodka and hair-raising local brews. Like John Crow Botty in Jamaica, a rum named for a vulture's backside, which was rumoured to dissolve granite. Or arrack in Beirut. Or poteen on remote nights in Connemara, where once he'd driven the hire car into a peat bog.

So he blended his recollections to make them more entertaining. He transposed, embroidered a little, peopled one place with characters from another. It was a technique he'd always used in his pieces for papers and magazines. Not lies, but a cocktail of several truths. Well, true-ish. The difference, he'd always told himself, between a painter and a photographer. By rearranging the human landscape, he maintained, he could often give a more accurate impression of a country's mood. In his account the graves of the missionaries were now not in Malawi, where they belonged, beside the vast lake with its dive-bombing fish eagles, but in the Aravalli mountains guarding Udaipur in Rajasthan. The maître d' who'd bitten the head off a living cobra, then swallowed its shiny gall bladder, had been relocated from Hong Kong to Beijing. The Italian skiing story, where he careered down the mountain dragging a startled beginner behind him, had adopted a new piste in Utah.

One day, as they strolled beside the duck pond, his walk still more tentative than hers, he came clean.

'I sometimes exaggerate,' he said.

'Good Lord,' she said.

'How come you're such a clever dick?' he said.

'Only child. Irish . . . well, a bit. And a woman.'

'So it's true what they say about women?'

'Some of it.'

'How Irish?' he said.

'My grandad, my mother's da, came from Westport. It's a little town in Mayo. I went there once. There's this column at the top of the main drag with no statue on it. A distinct absence of statue. I went into a newsagent's and asked the man behind the counter what the story was. He pointed to the bookie's across the road. "You'd better ask Jimmy," he said. "Jimmy's deadly at that sort of thing." '

Hugh laughed, aware of the stitches. 'Great word, "deadly",' he said.

They stopped at a patch of white flowers, puny but hopeful on a day pumiced of colour.

'There were times, last year,' he said, 'when I wasn't totally convinced I'd ever see these again.'

'Faint heart,' she said. Then, after a pause: 'Does it make you feel different, having a woman's?'

'I've thought about that.'

'And?'

'I do feel different but I don't think it's mostly because it's a woman's.'

'Why, then?'

'Hard to explain. Because it's someone else's, obviously. But in a funny way specifically because it's yours.'

'Just you take care of it.'

'Scoular says people get very proprietorial. They know their son's heart's gone to some middle-aged bloke, say, and they see him at check-up time and he's smoking and getting fat. They can be dead choked, apparently. Fingers wagged. Stiff letters written. "How dare you . . .?" *et cetera, et cetera.* Must be awful.'

'Deadly.'

'How about you? Are you curious about your donor?'

'No point. I know he wasn't much older than me. Motorbike smash. They don't tell you any more. I'm sorry for him and his parents, of course, but it just makes me want to get on with it, you know? For him as well as me. But mostly for me.'

Two days later, Hugh met Siobhan's mother. She was an anxious-looking woman, older than he'd imagined. Late fifties, perhaps. She must have been in her mid-thirties when she married and had Siobhan, Hugh thought. Her manner was polite when they were introduced but conversation wasn't easy. He had the feeling she disapproved of his comfortable way with her daughter; maybe also of the fact that in a sense they already shared a physical relationship. Then again she appeared to be a woman to whom disapproval was second nature. The Irish weren't supposed to be like that. Wherever Siobhan had got her buccaneer's outlook from, this was not the source. Miles, who had been with Hugh at the time, said all she needed was a touch less humour and she'd be Gerry Adams. As she was leaving, she disconcerted them with a sad smile.

And then, ten days after the operation, the father had at last made an appearance. Here was the answer. Tanned and disarranged, with a hint of dash despite his crumpled black jeans, scuffed suede brogues, old brown jacket and faded blue, open-necked shirt, he exuded the sense of self-possession that is not acquired in one gen-eration. He held Siobhan's hand, which at first she withdrew. In a few minutes she relented. The body lan-guage said here was a man who didn't visit very often, but who believed that a physical gesture bridged a chasm. But it was clear the bridge was made of reeds and swayed when you walked on it.

Later, when he'd left, Siobhan explained that he was an antiquarian bookseller and lived in Antigua.

'Much demand for antiquarian books, is there, in Antigua?' Hugh had an absurd image of an England fast bowler hurtling in between overs for a first edition of Thomas More's *Utopia*, followed by the gilded owner of a chain of Essex launderettes whose sojourn would be marred if he failed to find Newton's *Philosophiae Naturalis Principia Mathematica*.

'Apparently they've come up with something called the postal service,' Siobhan said.

'Look, it's none of my business but how come it's taken him so long to turn up?'

'You're right. It is none of your business.'

'Sorry.'

'He's a bit peculiar. He said he couldn't bear to see me with pipes sticking out. He's rung every day.' She paused. 'Up to now I've only ever met him in restau-rants. Practically.'

Hugh frowned. 'What, is he a waiter in his spare time?'

Siobhan shook her head. 'He bunked off when I was a kid. Then I got sent to boarding school at six. When he came to see me he used to take me out to tea.

Sussex. A little thatched tea-shop. He was living in Marrakesh at the time. He's lived all over the place. By the time I got to Mayfield he was in New Mexico. Then it was dinner when he came over. Very grown-up. Wine and everything. The other girls thought he was really sexy. Their dads were all boring old businessmen and solicitors and stuff. I was quite proud of him, in a funny sort of way. When you're that age any whiff of romance is infinitely better than some old suit with a Bentley and a briefcase. And he was so great to be with. Briefly. Interesting. Interested. Life isn't a ladder for him. It's like a huge . . . I don't know, game reserve or something. Playground. Library, maybe. But he's too absorbed with all that to have much time for duty. For dutiful relationships. The thing with him is, when you've got him you've got him completely, but when you haven't you've hardly got him at all. Mother says he's a throwback. He should have been around when it was all a big adventure. She can't stand his irresponsibility. I can't imagine how they ever got together.'

'Have you been out to Antigua to see him?'

'Once. No, twice. Once I stopped over on the way to Florida. He's living with some Chinese chick he didn't seem to want me to meet, so we ate at a place on the beach. The Foolish Fish.' She smiled.

'It's amazing you can take it all so . . . you know, casually.'

'I'm used to it. And I don't have a choice. He is what he is.'

When they were strong enough, they were moved to adjoining flats in the village. Half-way houses, was the idea. By now they were beginning to find Papworth Everard raw and dispiriting. 'Well wrapped up' became their catchphrase. It was a constant reminder from the staff. When he was alone now, Hugh sometimes found himself fighting depression. He tried to rationalise it as a reaction to the drugs, but it was more complicated than that. He envied Siobhan her apparent lightness of being. So young and yet so positive. So non-judgemental. Maybe that was a class thing. She'd inherited both her mother's down-to-earthness and her father's reckless assurance.

Hugh's father, a chartered surveyor from Northwich, had died on Hugh's twenty-third birthday. Heart-attack. He'd been a good man; a Freemason, a gardener. Well ordered. Well wrapped up. Unhappy. Not happy, at any rate, which wasn't quite the same thing. He'd spend the week saying, 'Roll on the weekend', but when it came he found it unendurable. Sometimes Hugh would find him slumped in a green leather chair, drumming his fingers on the arm, staring at the hedge. Not the flowers, the hedge. He seemed to be in an eternal waiting room. Worse, much worse, he didn't know what he was waiting for. And then, just as his son's birthday cake from Williamson's on Castle Hill was being carried in, bright with its twenty-three candles, he'd found out. He'd pulled the tablecloth with him as he fell. It was the best one, from Brown's of Chester; Irish linen with appliquéd pansies. Hugh and his mother had watched the tea-stain spread. His father's dead face, almost as white as the icing, had looked surprised.

You couldn't call those roots. Hugh's mother had

been more content since he'd gone. Less 'mithered'. 'Mither' was a word she used a lot. She'd joined the Northwich Historical Society; trips to stately homes; archaeological digs. Windsor had been the highlight so far. They'd spotted Princess Anne leaving in a Range Rover. Hugh's mother had thought she waved, but conceded that she might have been adjusting her head-scarf.

Hugh had been a mither to her. Still was. She had assumed journalism was something you grew out of, failing to grasp that in Hugh's case it was something you ran away to. For him travel wasn't so much a means of getting somewhere new and exciting. It was a way of escaping something sterile and inhibiting; giving yourself an outside chance of being different. It hadn't taken him long to realise that the difference had to be in your head, rather than your passport.

At first, when he was on the *Northwich Chronicle*, his mother had been quite proud. Later, when he turned freelance and his by-line was dispersed, she'd found it unsettling. When her friends asked who he was writing for these days, and she replied, 'Oh, all sorts,' she was aware that it sounded like 'Well, nobody at all, actually.' She'd been pleased when he published a slim collection of travel pieces, *Making Tracks*. She'd prayed that W. H. Smith's would stock it, have it in the window even: Local Author. In the event the only bookshop that carried it was a small one run by a German woman none of them liked. Hugh's mother had got her sister-in-law, Pat, to buy it for her. The review in the *Northwich Chronicle* said it was a valuable contribution to the genre, and showed 'a remarkable sensibillity' (*sic*). Nationwide, this remarkable sensibility had accounted for 543 sales in hardback.

On her first visit to Papworth, Hugh's mother had been much impressed by Scoular. She couldn't get over the fact that he was still in his thirties and 'such a gentleman'. For some reason she remarked on his teeth. In that respect he had something in common with the Royal Family, who also had excellent teeth, she said. When she saw Hugh's long red scar she was shocked. She called him a 'poor thing', but was unable to reach out for his hand. Hugh had the feeling that, for her, his condition was a sort of confirmation, the logical outcome of the way she thought his life was going. It wasn't his fault, poor lad. He just wasn't cut out for it. All part of an inevitable pattern; a pattern she'd lived through once already.

She hadn't known what to make of Siobhan at all. Though Siobhan had been pleasant to her, and talkative, she hadn't made any concessions. She had been forthright, stemming Hugh's mother's predilection for expressing pity. In many ways Siobhan had seemed the older woman of the two. They had met going in opposite directions. Siobhan only knew how to look ahead. Hugh's mother lived in a permanent state of semi-regret.

Hugh and Siobhan resumed their routine. A wing-beat of apprehension every morning as they weighed themselves and took their temperature. A rise on either scale might mean rejection. Dread word. Hugh feared that almost as much for her as for himself. Regular walks up the cheerless pavement to the clinic and the physiotherapist. The pleasure in pain from muscles, in Hugh's case, long idle. The daily dose of steroids, which left their faces puffy.

But the nights were more difficult. When they'd finished talking, Hugh would shut his door behind him and feel very alone. Patrick O'Brian. Television. A couple of telephone calls. A desultory attempt at keeping a diary. Anything to postpone the dark. When the light went out it was as though this stranger's heart in him was like a fragile thing cupped in his hands; like an egg-yolk he'd seen a television chef hold in his palm while the separated white ran through his fingers. He felt he was its host; its protector. His own, to which, while he was healthy, he hadn't given much thought, had seemed competent, integral, a tireless pump; until it failed. But this felt delicate and insubstantial. And, as time went on, feminine. That was the ridiculous thing. He told himself a woman's heart was just an organ like any other. Like a lump of calf's liver. It couldn't think, it couldn't empathise, it couldn't send Valentine cards. He'd reassured himself that the feeling would fade. A few days and it would seem just another part of him, no more distinctive than a car battery. But a few days had passed and the feeling had grown. The feeling that Siobhan's heart, lifted hot from her body, was still as much a part of her as it was of him; that it was a guest with an unknown past.

And then, when sleep did come, there were the weird dreams. They weren't frightening in any specific way, but they disturbed him and stayed with him, like a distant murmur, through the days. In them he was always alone, never so much as glimpsing a familiar face. And he was always conscious of being an onlooker; almost a voyeur, never a player. The images were imprecise, as though viewed through a prism. It was like dreaming a mood, rather than an event or a narrative. But it was apparent that the mood was not a contemporary one. It had the feel of a time revisited. In a way he longed for the focus to sharpen; for the hazy tones to coalesce into something recognisable. But part of him was apprehensive in case that obscure something was fearsome.

He tried to confide these thoughts to his notebook. There ought to be a piece in this: 'My Heart-swap Ordeal'. Sally Jex, the editor of *Cosmo*, had already suggested it, via Miles. 'No hurry,' Sally had said. 'Tell him to take his time, but the punters'd really go for that. Get the girl's angle. Brilliant.' And she was right. It was a great story. In its way the biggest story he could ever tell. A near-death experience with a happy ending. So far. Unique. Better still, there might even be a book in it: *Travels Inside Myself*. Great title. Make it a love story. Open it out. Best-seller. Serialisation. A film. Loadsamoney. Who could play him in the movie? Someone charismatic but real. Not too starry. Gene Hackman, maybe.

But within two minutes of getting excited he knew he couldn't do it. He couldn't do it for Siobhan's sake. She was an equal partner in this. He had no right to intrude on her privacy, to make it public. Nor did he have a right to fictionalise the story. That would still seem a betrayal. It would also mean revealing his feelings about her, about her heart, and he was certain she would find that ludicrous and despicable. No more chats. No more sharing the same wavelength. No more her. And afterwards, the knowledge that she would always be inside him; an inescapable reproach. He'd be worse than the patient who'd started smoking again and getting fat. Her father would find him, in a restaurant, and run him through with a swordstick. Or, more cutting still, ignore him in a patrician way. Get all the diners to do the same. Turn their faces to the wall, wherever he went. No, sorry, Mr Hackman, but we've thought this one through and to be frank it just isn't going to work.

Hugh felt relieved at his own instant decision. Congratulated himself on it, even. At the same time he recognised that instincts like these had hampered him as a journalist. More successful friends, like Miles, to say nothing of Wedge on the *National Enquirer*, would have knocked it off by now, and to hell with the consequences. Well, good for them. But he knew for sure he'd done the right thing when, one morning, he knocked on Siobhan's door and saw at once that she was paler than usual.

'What's up?' he said.

'Come in.' She closed the door behind him and sat on the arm of the sofa.

'What is it?' he said.

'Temperature's up. A hundred and one. And I've put on two pounds. I'm a bit scared.'

'Have you told anybody?'

She shook her head.

Hugh was touched by her sudden vulnerability. In a curious way it made him feel vulnerable too. He wanted to comfort her. Hold her hand. Put his arm round her. But he knew, or thought he knew, that she'd be more reassured by something practical.

'Do it. Now.' He was surprised by his own firmness.

She hesitated a moment.

'Now! It happens all the time. They can deal with it, no problem. It doesn't mean . . .'

'It means rejection,' she said.

'OK, it means rejection. But that's a normal part of the thing. They told us that. They can sort it quite easily with . . . you know, what d'you call it . . .?'

'Prednisolone.'

'Exactly. Sounds good, tastes good, and by golly it does you good. Now, pick up that phone. I'll come with you, if you like.'

She got up. 'As it happens, I would like,' she said.

'Good. And whatever you do, make sure you're well wrapped up.' His passable imitation of Nurse Killick's Solihull drone made her smile.

Scoular prescribed regular one-hour treatments on a prednisolone drip. Siobhan made mock complaint. 'It's pumping my face up so huge it won't fit in a mirror,' she said.

'Vanity is a terrible scourge,' Hugh said. 'Besides, it's a well-known fact that the bigger a barrister's face the bigger the fee. Michael Mansfield's was unacceptably small, which is why he grew his hair like General Custer to compensate. Quite sad, really.'

In due course the temperature came down. So did the weight. And the time to leave Papworth approached.

'What will you do? Go straight back to Cambridge?' His tone was light, as it had been throughout her treatment. But he found himself hoping she'd say she didn't want to leave.

'Can't wait,' she said. 'You?'

'Er, yes. Get stuck in. Take up the old quill. We're supposed to take it easy for a bit, aren't we?'

'Travel writing *is* taking it easy, isn't it?'

'More or less. Well, more actually.' He paused, unsure how to carry on. 'How about we meet now and again?' He didn't want to frighten her. Maybe he was pushing it too far. Better shut up.

'Great! When do we start?'

'Er . . . when do we start? We start . . .' Hugh thought fast '. . . we start in two weeks' time. Maybe we alternate. Say monthly. I come to Cambridge. You come to London. We have a club tie, which you may choose to wear round your waist, in the manner of Edwardian gentlemen cricketers. And we have a motto . . . Nina Baden Semper.'

'Meaning?'

'Absolutely nothing at all. I think she was on telly, long before you were born. Just sounds vaguely Latin.'

'That's cool.'

The morning they left, Hugh felt dry-mouthed. For a while Papworth had been his home, his carer, his routine, his saviour. Above all, it had been the place where he'd met Siobhan. As he said his goodbyes he realised he wasn't going back to the familiar. It was the familiar he was leaving behind. He'd been somewhere his friends and family could never imagine. It was an overwhelming experience he would never be able to share. At least, not with them. It had made a difference. It had put a distance between them.

And the only human being he could share it with was getting into a battered Ford Escort, driven by someone called Gareth, an undergraduate friend from Cambridge. Nice enough bloke. Easy manner. Ready charm. Bit like her dad. Hugh hated him. No, that was insane. Get a grip. Strange. It wasn't jealousy. Well, in a sense it was. But it was more a conviction that he, Hugh, belonged in that driving seat; that he and the passenger were . . . well, bound together in a way. But that was daft. A forty-nine-year-old man and a twenty-three-year-old girl . . . woman. Didn't make sense, of course. But then, what did in human relationships? Arranged marriages, he supposed. They made a sort of sense. Other than those, sense didn't have much to do with it.

His attempts at rationalisation were interrupted by Siobhan. She had second thoughts as she was ducking into the car and ran back to him. Despite the cool morning she was wearing a shirt with two buttons undone. Against her pale skin the top of the long, livid scar looked shocking; like a violation. Her arms round his neck, she hugged him tight.

'Thank you,' she said.

'I think you've got that the wrong way round. I think it's me thanking you.'

'Oh, all right then. Take care of yourself, Hugh. Great care.' She started back to the car.

'And you,' he said. 'Well wrapped up now, mind.'

She laughed and waved. 'See you in a fortnight.'

Gareth revved and gave him a thumbs-up sign. Hugh stood and watched them go. When they turned left at the gate and disappeared, the place at once lost its meaning for him. The twenty minutes until Gary arrived to pick him up seemed like an indefinite suspension.

For a while, as they headed for the M11, Hugh had little to say.

'You're a bit shtum for a man just back from the grave,' Gary said. 'You in love again?'

'Er, no.'

'Best thing. Easy on the old ticker.'

'It's not an old ticker, Gaz. It's a new one. One previous owner. Low mileage.'

'Just run in.'

'Exactly.'

'It'll go round the clock, mate. You'll see the lot of us out. Fancy a pint?'

'Still under doctor's orders. I'll get you one down the other end.'

Eighty minutes of relentless disregard for the speed limit saw them arrive in Willes Road, behind the St Pancras swimming baths, on the edge of Kentish Town. Hugh's ground-floor flat was in a once-handsome, peeling, nineteenth-century house, with a white, pillared porch and large windows overlooking small gardens front and back.

Thanks, Gaz. Swift half, then?' Hugh said.

'No time, mate. Got a session in half an hour. Leggy lovely. The Hon. Thingy Doodah.'

'Sounds exotic.'

'Not half. Apparently she's shagging a sword-handler.'

'What's the job description exactly?'

'That's what he does. There's this bullfighter from Hackney, Frank McGuffog, would you believe, and this geezer's, like, his sidekick. PA, whatever. Carries his swords and that.'

'Frank McGuffog? If you were a bull you wouldn't be too bothered would you, taking on a bloke called Frank McGuffog? Not like, say, Manolete. That sounds more the business somehow, doesn't it?'

'Well, you wouldn't know his name, would you? It's a well-known fact bulls can't read, Hugh. Except maybe the *Sun*. Anyway he calls himself El Franco. Goes down big in places like La Linea, apparently, that crappy little dump near Gibraltar.'

'Shrewd move, naming himself for a dead dictator. Well, well. Anyone done Señor McGuffog?'

'Bits and pieces. Not a ballsy one with colour pix and everything. If you fancy it, give me a bell. I could do with a spot of the old *pasodoble*. One of the glossies'd go for it, no probs.'

'Will do.'

'Welcome home, mate. I'll catch you later.'

Hugh took his time carrying his case through to the bedroom. Though he didn't feel like an invalid, he moved like one. Not so much because his legs were tired or reluctant, but because he still felt his chest contained something that couldn't quite fend for itself. Scoular had said that would soon pass. Hugh hoped he was right.

The flat was calm and ordered. Louisa, who came in once a week, had tidied the books into neat piles and put his mail in two tall bundles on the desk under the sitting-room window. Bills for the most part, he supposed; juicy wine merchants' lists; unsolicited catalogues for electric trouser presses, and kettles that played selections from *The Merry Widow*.

He sat on the red sofa. How empty it seemed. Since the end of his marriage he'd become used to his own company, but the events of the past few weeks had made him realise what he was missing. Not so much the physical warmth, though he did miss that, but talking in shorthand. Knowing that the other person didn't need telling everything; didn't need telling anything, in a way. That was the paradox. The best people to talk to were the ones to whom you didn't have to say much. You didn't come across many in a lifetime. Most men were too competitive. Most women were working to a hidden agenda; hidden from him anyway.

Tilly had been an exception. He'd always loved talking to her. He'd talked for thirteen years, much of the time in a half-drunk haze, articulate nonsense as insubstantial as cigarette smoke; self-pity, rage against obvious targets, on good nights seeded with humour. Talking hadn't been enough. When Tilly met Anthony Granger at a Writers' Guild award ceremony, she'd seen there was something else: a spirit of enquiry, an appreciation of small things, eyes open to every day and every experience. It was all there and you could either sharpen your appetite for it or shut it out. Tilly knew she'd been telling herself for years she wasn't hungry, and that now, before it was too late, she must eat.

Anthony Granger wrote plays. Witty plays about relationships. Successful plays. Worse than that, Hugh liked him. He was shy, kind, attentive, short, overweight; a bit preoccupied as a rule, but you had to make allowances. Hugh half expected, half dreaded turning up as a character in one of Anthony's witty, successful plays. Some dreadful old drunk who bored the arse off everyone. Stumbled on stage and snored in a corner while the rest of the cast said amusing things at his expense. In the light of the operation Anthony might have him enter with a large plastic heart pinned to his Fair Isle sweater, flashing on and off. But he knew Anthony had better things to write about. And he knew Anthony made Tilly happy.

He had also made her a mother at last, something Hugh hadn't succeeded in doing. Tests had shown it was Hugh's fault, although at the clinic they'd stressed that faults didn't come into it. Nevertheless he'd always thought of it that way. He and Tilly had talked about IVF but had somehow never got round to it. In any case there was no guarantee.

Tilly had encouraged Sam to include Hugh in his life. For a nine-year-old he was remarkable. Unlike most children he showed no interest in toys. Instead he'd devoted his obvious talents to a study of supermarket products, specialising in cleansing agents. There wasn't a single make whose price, properties and packaging design he didn't have at his fingertips. Many an elderly shopper in a quandary had reason to thank him for a cool appraisal of the options available. He'd also built up an impressive collection of fire extinguishers, whose beauty he alone appreciated. And far from being solemn about these rare preoccupations, if gentle fun was poked he would smile along with the poker, tolerant of their lack of imagination. Hugh loved him, and had taken to sending him wry postcards, with drawings in the margin, from every country he visited.

Siobhan should meet him. Maybe when it was her turn to come to London that could be arranged. Hugh was sure Tilly would like her, though unsure what she would make of their relationship. He was unsure himself. But whatever it was, Siobhan was never far from his thoughts. In the days after his homecoming, he often found himself on the verge of saying something to her. He wanted to ring her but was afraid of forcing the pace; of giving the wrong impression. The fact was, he missed her. Finding himself counting the days until his first trip to Cambridge, he told himself not to be silly. Concentrate instead on dredging up a few ideas he could flog to editors. Señor McGuffog, El Franco, maybe. Monitor the weight and the temperature. And think about coinciding Cambridge with the first check-up at Papworth.

Meanwhile his dreams, in which he remained a spectator rather than a participant, were still hazes of shifting colour from a time he couldn't identify. But little by little he began to hear faint accompanying sounds, and to be aware of smells. Foul and pungent smells. And then, on the fifth night of his return, in the small bedroom with the bright kelim under the window, the shifting colours cleared like a sea-fret dispersed by sun. For the first time shapes were sharp-edged, and the passing show was vivid.

It is evening. The cold streets are dark, but for the flickering of yellow candlelight in the small-paned windows. Far away there is the indistinct sound of voices, accompanied by a wind instrument. In the echoing church a pale hand cups font-water and anoints a baby's head. The infant, a boy, opens his eyes but does not cry. His christening dress is made of lace. His mother, her cloak trimmed with fur, inclines her head, her face obscured by a silk cowl. The father is dark, severe, his hair shoulder-length.

Now the darkness gives way to a broad, forested landscape. The horses, with ornate saddles and saddlecloths, are foamed with exertion. The hooded falcon lands on the young rider's glove. This is the infant grown to manhood. His older companion turns, approving. His face bears long scars that have become furrows with the years. The young man is dressed all in black. He is tall, slender, with an aquiline nose. When he speaks it is with a slight stammer.

He stands next in a cloister, holding the arm of another young man. This friend has been blinded, not by nature but in a deliberate, violent act. In the background a youth hangs from a makeshift gibbet. His face is calm, beautiful.

Now the principal actor in the drama, though not cured of his stammer, is rich. Wherever he walks, dressed in silks and velvets, trimmed with miniver, he is accompanied by fawning attendants. There are wolves at his side, and monkeys, their collars studded with precious stones. Three men, knights, bow low in his presence. A dwarf holds his horse while he mounts. He rides beside a younger man who outranks him but holds him in great affection. Speaking in a strange language, the younger man teases him about his scarlet cloak. Among the bystanders, awed by the long, dazzling procession, is a shivering beggar. The beggar holds out a filthy hand. The younger man urges his friend to give him his cloak. He refuses. Both dismount and wrestle in the mud and excrement, laughing as they struggle. The bystanders babble and hoot. A woman at a high window turns her back to the crowd and hoists her skirts. More laughter, like hounds growling. Menacing laughter. Laughter that would rape, maim if it could. The wrestlers roll, their clothes fouled, their faces streaked. The wearer of the scarlet cloak, the most charismatic figure in every tableau of which he forms a part, relents; hands the garment with mock deference to the beggar, who darts away with it. The crowd bay. The younger man offers his hand to his friend, saluting the woman at the window as they remount. They ride off side by side. There is a dangerous intensity about their closeness . . . .

Chapter Two

The boat had not been built for travel. Comprising a small office, a large gallery space, storeroom, and washroom, it had been designed for permanent mooring on the Cam. Visitors approached from Chesterton Lane via a short path and railed gangplank. Exhibitions changed every month, but all featured the work of local artists. Many tried to come to terms with the vast fen skies, serene or brooding, compressing the black earth. Ely Cathedral was often prominent; miraculous eruption on the dark plain, as though magicked into being by a wand of lightning. Flower paintings were also popular; careful primroses by gentle, self-effacing women. The striped awnings of Cambridge market, viewed from the top of Great St Mary's tower; broken-backed Clare Bridge; Parker's Piece, planted with cricketers; King's College Chapel, with the bicycle nesting in the giant chestnut tree, all made regular appearances, together with pale attempts at abstract harmonies.

Kate Mellanby knew they weren't great art. Nevertheless she cared about the artists who painted them. Seeing their reactions to a red sticker, the blushful symbol of success, gave her real and constant pleasure. It made them allies in the ongoing battle against indifference. Other galleries in town might consider themselves superior, with their Trinity Street status, but that didn't bother Kate. They didn't have the satisfaction of seeing a timid first-timer blossom in the warmth of her genuine enthusiasm. They didn't form links of friendship and mutual dependence with their artists.

What they did have, however, were sites in busy places and backers with money. The Crick Gallery had neither. Its present owner, Roger Crick, a King Street antique dealer, had opened it without much forethought. He'd heard the boat was going cheap and, on the strength of two good years in his existing business, had made an impetuous bid. Artistic policy had been left to Kate. As time went by Roger's enthusiasm appeared to wane, and Kate saw him less and less. Every three weeks or so he'd turn up to see how things were going, and at private views he still relished the role of Great Patron. On these occasions he wore what he imagined Great Patrons wore: pink bow-tie, baggy linen jacket, silk handkerchief spilling out of his breast pocket, spectacles attached to a black cord round his neck. When private viewers complimented him on the quality of the work, he thanked them with modesty worn like a blazer badge. Sometimes he paid faint tribute to Kate. He would concede that of course it couldn't have been done without her, in the tone a shipbuilder might use of a riveter.

Nevertheless she couldn't bring herself to dislike him. She was amused by his absurd chutzpah, his dated style, his ebullience. She rationalised the rarity of his appearances by telling herself that he had complete trust in her, and therefore saw no need to interfere. True, he had the reputation of a philanderer, but that was all of a piece with the rakish persona he'd invented for himself At least he wasn't a cautious bourgeois, only lured from his burrow by the promise of free wine, however unpalatable. Unlike most of the private viewers: glass clutched in white-knuckled fist, a cursory cruise of the paintings, occasional murmured appreciation, punctuated with thoughtful frowns; feet planted, endless comparisons of children's schools, and tut-tutting at the frightful liberties taken by the restaurateurs on Midsummer Common. Having observed the ritual, no need to trouble oneself further about Art.

In some ways Kate despaired of them, but had to be polite even as she despaired. She owed that to her artists. It must be that for these consistent non-buyers, private views slotted into their diaries and their supper-party conversations as Cultural Activities, though, in truth, only in the ersatz sense that a trip to a garden centre was communing with nature. It topped up their tiny Culture tank; the sort you keep in the boot for emergencies.

In a sense, however, they represented a real problem. The Puritan reluctance of Cambridge people to part with their money was notorious, and unless Kate could coax it out of them on a regular basis, Roger might lose heart altogether. At present, after overheads and her own salary, she was managing to clear fifteen thousand a year for him. This, together with the added value of prestige, seemed to keep him, if not content, at least uncomplaining; except in so far as it suited him to complain, along the lines of '. . . the Sisyphean burden one must bear in order to support the Arts'. But if the figure should ever dip below, say, eight thousand, Kate knew that Art's martyr might yield to an altogether less attractive, more pragmatic individual.

It wasn't just contact with the artists she enjoyed, and the adrenaline of selling. She loved the whole experience. She loved being captain of her own small world. She loved the solitude, in winter, when there weren't many tourists in town. She loved the slap of the water on the sides of the boat when punts glided by; the sound of the ice-cream van as it pulled up near the path. The Crick Gallery had given her calm purpose, and confidence, and a sense of achievement.

Shame there was no one to share them with, when she got back to her flat at night. Tell him about the child who'd said the portrait of the Provost of King's looked like Postman Pat. Or the Japanese who wanted to know where Lutherford had lived. (It had taken Kate several confused minutes to realise he was asking after the atom-cracker.) Or the woman from Exeter who broke down when she talked of her son in Hong Kong. But, since Peter, she'd slept alone, except for a one-night stand with an undergraduate actor from Peterhouse. At least, he'd said he was an actor. When she next went to the ADC theatre she'd spotted him as a friar who never uttered a line all night. And a week ago she'd thrown a small party to celebrate her twenty-eighth birthday.

Then, two days later, as she was still allowing herself one small slice of Marks & Spencer's birthday cake a day, she had met someone else. Quite by chance, in Dillon's. He'd seen her searching.

'Struggling?' he'd said, after a while.

'Not particularly.'

'Who're you after?'

'Ted Hughes. *Birthday Letters*. Bit late in the day but . . .'

'What does it matter, with a book? It's not like you're buying a Vivienne Westwood is it?'

For a moment Kate hadn't been able to think who Vivienne Westwood was, and then the penny had dropped. She'd felt herself blushing. 'No.'

'It's over there, I think.' He'd pointed to a nearby shelf.

'Thanks.'

'There's some about Cambridge in it. Eltisley Avenue! Imagine Milton, Blake, Byron writing about Eltisley Avenue.'

'Well, it's just a road with people in it.'

'But it's not a road, it's an avenue. I mean Freedom Road, great. Freedom Avenue? I don't think so.'

Too late it had occurred to Kate that great cities had important, even poetic sounding avenues: the Avenue of the Americas. And wasn't the Champs Elysées an avenue?

'Anyway,' he'd gone on, 'he seems to have got away with it. Be interesting to know if you think so.'

Kate wanted a man in a gorilla suit to walk into the

shop and divert his attention while she escaped. His persistence had just a shade too much of the lonely bed-sitter about it.

'Maybe we could compare notes,' he'd said.

She didn't answer.

'*Could* we?'

'Probably not. Anyway, I've got to . . .' She gestured in the direction of the door. Damn! He'd made her miss out on the Hughes.

Thinking about it, she'd come to no particular conclusion. He was a bit below medium height, slim, quite sharp features, with dark lines under his eyes. Not unintelligent. At any rate he seemed to be a reader. Bit pushy perhaps, bit nerdy, but not offensive. The streets of Cambridge were full of unremarkable blokes like him. Faces in the crowd. Oldish heads on young, stringy bodies. She had no reason to think she'd ever see him again.

But on the Sunday morning, during a private view of Susan Eveleigh's Venice watercolours and *papier-mâché* masks, as Kate was talking to the artist she'd become aware of a dark figure with his back to her, on the far side of the gallery. Isolated from the crowd, who by now were paying no attention whatsoever to Susan's work, he was looking at a mounted mask with the familiar long beak of the *commedia dell' arte*. A few moments later he'd turned and made his way over to Kate. Even then she'd wished he wouldn't.

'Hello again,' he'd said.

'Hello.' She'd kept it cold.

'Good turnout.'

'Not bad. Have you seen something you like?' Maybe she could embarrass him out of there.

'Not really my cup of tea.'

'Oh? What is, then?'

'Blake.'

'Ah, well. 'Fraid you've come to the wrong place.'

'Not necessarily.'

What had he meant by that? 'Anyway, you might as well have a glass of wine,' Kate had said, back in PR mode.

'I have.' He looked rueful.

'Best we can afford. It's called suffering for one's art.'

Just then Roger had called her across to deal with a potential sale.

'The boss,' she'd explained.

'Sure.' The dark young man had pretended not to be disappointed.

In the flush of selling an unprecedented seven paintings, as well as two masks, Kate had forgotten about him. But the following morning, as she began to plan the next exhibition, of paper collages by Terry Wolfendale, the telephone rang.

'Crick Gallery.'

'You really want to change that you know. Sounds a bit dry.'

For a moment she couldn't place the voice. 'Who's . . .?'

'It's me, the uninvited guest.'

'Oh . . .'

'How did it go in the end? Did you sell many?'

'Many by our standards, yes.'

'Great. Look, I was wondering what you were doing for lunch?'

This was so unexpected, so unwanted, that she had no excuse ready. 'Er . . . I'm going to . . .'

'Fancy a bite at the Eagle? Not in the Dracula sense, I hasten to add.'

'Look . . .' She realised she didn't know his name.

'It's Martin Taylor, by the way, in case you're wondering.'

'Look, I don't know you and I've got a lot to do.'

'I got you the Hughes, by the way. I felt bad it was me that made you not get it . . . You can tell I'm not reading English!'

'I'm perfectly capable of buying my own books, thanks.' Little Ms Up-tight. Why couldn't she be Ms Cool? Ms Witty Put-down, like they were in films?

'Obviously. It's just that I made you miss out on it and I'd like very much to give it you. Just a small present. Absolutely no strings. Make it a quick bite? Say one-ish?'

Kate felt trapped. Even if she refused, Cambridge was a small town. She might well bump into him again. Or he'd come round to the gallery with the bloody book. Maybe best to confront him and tell him she wasn't interested, face to face. That ought to shut him up. 'OK,' she said, and put the telephone down.

Deciding to go the pretty way rather than up Bridge Street, she took a brisk line along the Backs and cut over Garret Hostel Bridge. Cambridge was the way it looked on calendars: lawns as smooth as Georgian games tables; unfrivolous flowers in the privileged gardens of the Fellows; the handsome buildings wearing their age with the glamour of matinée idols; cyclists leisurely in the seductive sun; lunch smells and the clatter of pans from college kitchens. As she passed Trinity Hall and turned into Senate House Passage, she felt a pleasant, calming sense of optimism. The private view, their best yet, had left both artist and Great Patron beaming. It was the overture to summer.

The Eagle was packed: Round Tablers with gin and tonics; dons flaying reputations; beefy undergraduates unable to speak below a roar, flirting with the pretty barmaids; office girls ogled by monolithic oarsmen. Kate's sister said you could spot them a mile off because the backs of their hands faced forward. Kate tried to peer through the scrum but couldn't see Taylor. Since he wasn't much taller than her they might both spend the entire lunch-break separated by palisades of unyielding bodies. Not that she was prepared to stay that long. She was beginning to feel foolish and flustered when she felt a tap on the shoulder.

'Hi.'

She turned. 'Oh, hello.'

'What would you like? Then we'll grab some food.'

After a long, awkward wait when conversation was impossible, he got them each a glass of wine, and led the way to the cold table. They filled their plates, a salad for her, a Scotch egg with baked beans for him, and managed to find two seats in a corner.

'Madhouse,' he said. 'Anyway, cheers. It's Kate, isn't it?'

'How did you know?'

'It's on the board outside the gallery.'

'What do you do, then?'

'History. At Jesus. Colour of eyes, brown. You may want to verify that.' He widened them to a crazed stare. 'Shoe size, seven. Favourite sport, fencing. Prospects, excellent. Does that just about cover it?'

Kate took a sip of her wine. It over-covered it.

'Oh, here's the Hughes by the way.' From the pocket of his black jacket Taylor produced the book, precision-wrapped in gold paper.

Kate had no option but to take it. 'Thanks,' she said.

'My last year,' Taylor went on. 'Thank God.'

'Haven't you had a good time? Most people seem to.'

'It's been OK, but I want the real thing now. Grown-up stuff.'

In a nearby group a plump figure wearing a string vest and a Stetson was talking to a languid, olive-skinned girl who'd stepped out of a time when Rupert Brooke strode through Grantchester Meadows.

'Have you made many friends?' Kate found herself asking.

For a second Taylor seemed off-guard. 'Er . . . some. Does one make many? Have you?'

Kate wanted to say hundreds. 'Yes,' she lied.

He was looking at her now in a different way. It made her uncomfortable. As though he was seeing something in her she didn't know about; something behind her eyes. She took another sip of her wine, not wanting to start the salad because it would mark a small commitment.

'Good,' he said.

'So what happens next?' she said. 'To you?'

'I start my work.'

'Which is?'

'Justice.'

'The law?'

'Justice,' he repeated, his unblinking stare once more making her uneasy. 'How about you? You going to go on Cricking?'

'Certainly. I love it.'

'Isn't it a bit, you know, mediocre, not to put too fine a point on it?'

'What, the gallery?' Kate felt her cheeks colouring. 'No, I don't think so at all. It's people doing the best they can. And lots of people like it. I don't see anything wrong with that.'

'But if that's the best they can do what's the point in doing it? That's like making a – a fork with no prongs and saying that's the best you can do. In which case you'd be better off not making forks. No?'

'I don't see what forks have got to do with it. Are you saying only people like Matisse and van Gogh should be allowed to paint? That's rubbish.'

'I'm saying how can you respect people who put themselves up there and don't do it well? That's the English all over. Entertainers who can't sing, dance, tell jokes, we pay them millions. Boxers who'd be flattened by any of the greats within seconds, we make them national heroes. Lousy meals in restaurants, we simper and tell the waiter it was delicious. A House of Commons where boors and morons gibber and snipe we call the Mother of Parliaments. Middle class, middle of the road, middle England, for God's sake. We're in love with the second rate. It's the only thing we feel safe with. It's disgusting.'

Kate wasn't used to anger, but now it ambushed her and took hold. It wasn't his views on lack of aspiration she found offensive. To some extent she shared them. But to slag off the gallery, *her* gallery, and make out he was above it all, that was too much. 'And what exactly are you so perfect at that you can sit in judgement?'

'No, no, not perfect. Nowhere near. But I want to be. I will be. That's the difference.'

There was a moment's silence. His eyes were unwavering, confrontational, disturbing. Kate turned away, unable and unwilling to outstare him.

'I've got to be going,' she said, rising.

'Oh, please. I'm sorry if I . . .' Now there seemed genuine concern in his voice.

'Thanks for the drink.'

'Hang on, you've forgotten the book.'

'Give it to a perfectionist.'

When she got outside and felt the sun on her face, Kate thought there was something cold about Taylor, something older than he was. She sensed he was concealing a different, deeper self. In a room full of his contemporaries he seemed the only one who was unconnected. Disconnected, even. Maybe this wasn't a regular haunt. He might have suggested they meet here because he thought she'd like it, because it was central and lively. But still he seemed a man apart, and she felt he would wherever they'd met. There was no law saying you had to be gregarious, of course. She wasn't always very gregarious herself. That was part of the gallery's appeal. Nevertheless, however she reasoned it, there was something about him that made her flesh creep. His arrogance, his intensity, his unsettling, intrusive stare. She felt something that might wish her harm had entered her life.

All afternoon she half expected the slight, dark figure to materialise on the boat, but the only visitors had been a likeable, homesick New Zealander, and Gilbert. Famous in the neighbourhood, Gilbert was a tramp whose town address was Professor Bukovsky's garage. He brought in two new pictures on cardboard for Kate to see; small dreamscapes after Chagall, of whom Gilbert had never heard. Elongated angels hovered over flower gardens, giddy with pastel colours. Kate, who enjoyed his runic observations anyway, kept him talking as long as possible, as a form of protection. And too late she realised that Gilbert's work was a counter-argument she should have used in the pub. It was joyous, it was unique, it was his way of saying something that not even Ted Hughes could put into words. It was valid. Unable to resist, she bought the pastels for the asking price – ten pounds the pair. When Gilbert had left, whistling a tuneless anthem, she made several calls to keep her spirits up, the last of them to Hester, asking her round to the new Hertford Street flat that evening.

Hester was Scottish, round, feisty, and ironic. The two of them had met three years earlier at a grisly undergraduate party at Queen's. Kate had been struggling to fend off a boring mathematician and Hester had come to the rescue, convincing him that there was a woman

in the corner with bottomless cleavage who'd just con-
fessed she was in love with him; had always been in love
with him; wanted his babies – now. Kate and Hester
had watched, open-mouthed with anticipation, as the
man-eater in question, an Italian don with a well-
known penchant for boa-constrictors, had slapped the
mathematician with such force that he fell over the
back of a sofa, almost concussing the Dean of
Emmanuel. The bonding had been immediate. Kate
had found in Hester the forthrightness she often
lacked. Hester had found in her a willingness to share
her sense of the ridiculous. Both heterosexual, neither
with a meaningful mate, they had developed a closeness
both compensatory and uncomplicated. For much of
the time they loved each other's company more than
that of anyone else they knew.

Now, curled barefoot on Kate's purple Habitat sofa,
with her second glass of Chilean red on the go, Hester
was saying, 'Sounds a bit of a creep. And fencing's dead
weird, isn't it? Playing at running people through with
a sword. Mr Dodgy or what?' The assessment was all the
more uncompromising for being delivered with the
soaring inflections of Glasgow.

'I don't know what to make of him,' Kate said. 'Why
me?'

'That's what my auntie said when I told her I'd got a
job at the University Press. "Why you?" Great! Thanks
very much, Auntie. Ever thought of a career with the
diplomatic? You're an attractive young woman, for
Christ's sake. Why not you?'

'Thanks for the young.'

'Oh, come on. Women are having babies in their sixties. I mean the women are sixty, not the babies. Twenty-eight's the new twenty, like green's the new black.'

'I just wish I'd never met him. There's something about him that feels . . . I don't know. You just feel he's got reasons for being around that he's not saying. He can be quite . . . OK, I suppose, quite bright, and then he'll be all bossy. Laying down the law. That's what he says he wants to do.'

'What? A barrister? You want to watch men in wigs.'

'He just said justice.'

'Did he now? How old did you say he was?'

'Mid-twenties? Going on forty-two.'

'Look, it's probably the last you'll see of him. He's tried it on, it hasn't worked, and the next, please. Anyway, giving you a book's hardly Jack the Ripper, is it?'

'Hardly,' Kate agreed. As she crossed to refill Hester's glass, the telephone rang. She put the bottle on the table by the sofa, turned and lifted the receiver. Recognising the voice at once, she mouthed in exaggerated dumb-show, 'It's him.'

'So?' Hester mouthed back.

'I don't want to talk to him.'

'Neither do I.'

Kate held out the receiver. 'Please!'

Hester rolled her eyes, tutted and got up. 'Hello,' she said, into the mouthpiece. 'No, I'm a friend of hers. A huge friend with muscles you wouldn't believe.' Hester mimed a hearty laugh.

Kate looked apprehensive.

' . . . No, she's out. Gone to a poisoning class . . . Don't know. She might not come back at all. Who shall I say called, by the way? . . . Well, yes, it does matter, actually, otherwise I wouldn't have asked. I'm a very busy woman. Busy and huge . . . Hello? Hello? . . . Bloody cheek!' She put down the receiver. 'Cut me off.'

'How did he get my number?' Kate said. 'It won't even be in the book yet.'

'Maybe he rang Roger Prick.'

'Crick.'

'Crick, and said he desperately wanted to get in touch with you. He'd fallen in love with a picture and he just had to have it. Your boss has got your new number presumably?'

Kate nodded. 'I don't think Roger'd fall for that one, though.'

'Or he could have said he was your cousin, just over from Brussels, or . . . any old thing.'

'I suppose so.'

'Good. Now, lighten up for God's sake. You look as though you've just won William Hague in a raffle.'

Kate smiled.

'Anyway, probably all the poor bugger was going to say was he was sorry for being such a jerk.' Hester filled Kate's glass. 'Here, get this down your neck and relax.'

Before she joined Hester on the sofa, on impulse Kate pulled back the curtain and looked down into the street.

'What are you doing now, you silly old tart?'

'Come here a minute,' Kate said, her voice urgent.

'No.'

'Please, Hest.'

With elaborate reluctance, Hester complied.

'Isn't there somebody in that red car?'

'What if there is?'

'I'm sure it's him.'

'No you're not. It's probably just a bloke.'

'I am.'

'Well, say it is?'

'He must have rung on his mobile.'

'OK. Shut the curtain. If it is him, which I doubt, don't let him know you're interested.' Hester guided Kate away from the window, picked up the telephone, and tapped out one-four-seven-one, jotting a number on the pad as she listened. 'There,' she said. 'That's the caller's mobile number, but it doesn't make him Whatsisface or the man in the car.' She tapped out a further ten digits. 'Switched off,' she said. 'Doesn't get us very far does it?'

'Why would you want to make a phone call from outside somebody's house? Why not just use the phone in college? He said he's at Jesus.'

'Maybe he went out for a drink. Maybe, on impulse, he stops in this street, not even knowing it's yours, and thinks, I know what I'll do. I'll give her a buzz. No time like the present.'

'On the other hand maybe he's a stalker. He kept banging on about being perfect.'

'If it makes you happy I'll go and have a look. Anything for a quiet life.' Hester left her drink and went down the stairs to the front door. The hallway was lit only by the streetlight, which dappled the black and white floor with the reflected colours of the stained glass. Though she'd put on a brave face for Kate's sake, she too felt a surge of apprehension as she opened the door. There was a small but immediate sense of relief as she saw that the red car was no longer there.

'This,' she said, back in the warmth and comfort of Kate's sitting room, with its Bonnard prints, 'is what happens to spinster ladies when they drink too much of the old Red Infuriator. They hallucinate. Think they see men in cars. Next thing their hair falls out in fistfuls and they end up sleeping in cardboard boxes.'

Opening up the gallery the following morning, Kate had already begun to feel Hester had been right. Either she'd been mistaken about the driver, or there was a plausible explanation for Taylor's presence. She switched on the answering-machine: Roger, telling her the *Cambridge Evening News* had been in touch and wanted to interview Susan Eveleigh on the Bridge of Sighs at St Johns, to go with a review of her Venice paintings; the anxious man from Cottenham, Clive something, she still couldn't make out his second name, saying that after all he'd decided against the small gouache of San Giorgio Maggiore, on reflection ninety pounds was a little more than he wanted to pay; and her sister Jo, ringing from Leamington Spa, reminding her that Friday was their mother's birthday, and making sure they weren't giving her the same thing. As she listened, Kate made notes on a pad. There were no more messages, but after Jo there were three separate beeps, each followed by silence. Hester, perhaps. Or an artist. Or . . .? Could it be

Taylor, remorseful? Who cared? The less she heard from him the better. Reassured by Hester, she was pretty certain that by now he'd have decided to cut his losses.

And then the flowers arrived. White lilies. A large bunch, with a small envelope attached.

'Cost a few bob,' the lugubrious middle-aged man from the florist's said. He pronounced 'few' to rhyme with zoo. 'Must have it bad.'

Too surprised to smile, Kate thanked him. He was right. They must have cost a few bob. Two pounds a stem in the market. She laid them on her desk while she opened the envelope and drew out the plain white card, on which were written three words. 'Sorry. No offense.' They were uneven, dictated, she supposed, to an assistant in the shop. He or she hadn't quite been able to cope with 'offence'.

So it wasn't sinister after all. It was an apology, as Hester had predicted, and a generous one at that. If it had been Taylor in the car last night, maybe he'd called to say sorry in person, but thought better of it when he suspected she wasn't alone. As to how he'd found her address, there might be a simple explanation, though she couldn't think of one off-hand. Meanwhile she felt a little ashamed now of her behaviour in the Eagle. Perhaps he was just one of those people, lonely and a bit clumsy, who thought the best way to get things going was by being provocative. Her mistake had been to rise to the bait, instead of keeping it light; giving as good as she got. *Fencing* with him. That was it, of course! That was his sport; clashing swords, or whatever they called them, just for the fun of it. How humourless she'd been. How *middle*. She must have confirmed all his worst prejudices. And with his fastidiousness, his quest for perfection, how mortified he'd have been by the spelling on the card.

She wondered whether to ring the college and thank him, but supposed he'd be at lectures, in which case the mobile wouldn't be switched on either. And even though it was a thoughtful gesture, she had no desire to get involved. Quite the reverse. No, the simplest thing was to leave him a short note at the porters' lodge when she went for lunch at the Mill with Hester. Just a line; nothing too enthusiastic. She practised on the back of a used envelope, deciding, after several versions, on a plain 'Thanks. Kate.'

'Bad move,' Hester said, as they sat on the Mill bridge, surrounded by undergraduates enjoying the sun. 'You should have made the bugger sweat.'

'Well . . .'

'Well nothing. One minute he's got your knees knocking and the next you're all over him like a cheap suet.'

'Shouldn't that be suit?'

'I prefer suet. It sticks better. Anyway, don't change the subject. What did the porter say, "Ah, ho, ho, ho, another sucker"?'

'Didn't say anything. I just put it in the pigeonhole under T.'

'The guy might be an axe murderer for all you know.'

'I thought you were the one who said he was harmless . . . Oh, God . . .'

'What?'

'That's him. He's coming over.'

Slight and pale, in black jeans and white shirt, Taylor was threading his way towards them through the drinkers. Hands in pockets, he seemed at ease, smiling. 'Hi.'

'Hello . . .' Kate faltered. 'This is my friend Hester Edmond.'

Hester held out her hand. 'Good afternoon.'

Taylor shook it. 'Martin Taylor.'

'We spoke,' Hester said.

'We did?' Taylor's surprise sounded genuine enough.

'When you rang Kate last night. From the car. Outside her flat.'

With a slight shrug Taylor said, 'If you say so.'

'I do.'

'Did you . . . Have you been in college this morning?' Kate was aware how hesitant she sounded beside Hester.

'Yes. But I'm not permanently in college now. I live out.'

'Where's that?' Hester said.

Taylor smiled. 'Would you like me to fill in a questionnaire?'

'Not particularly.'

'How about you?'

'I'm not in college either.'

'Hester works for the CUP,' Kate explained.

'Good for Hester,' Taylor said. 'Can I get anyone a drink?'

'Large vodka and tonic,' Hester said. 'Ice and lemon.'

'I don't think you'll need the ice,' Taylor said, unblinking.

'On the contrary,' Hester said, 'you can never have enough.'

'Kate?'

'No . . . thank you. I'm fine.'

As Taylor turned towards the pub, Hester said, 'Aren't you going to thank her for the note?'

For an almost imperceptible moment Taylor appeared to hesitate, before looking back with a regretful smile. 'Sorry. Few things on my mind.'

When he was too far away to hear, Hester said, 'White man speak with forked tongue. And he is a very white man, isn't he?'

'How do you know?'

'Fatal hesitation.'

'Since when have you been into psychology?'

'Just you mark my words, young lady. Let's bunk off before he comes back.'

'I can't do that to him twice in a week.'

'Oh, all right then, we'll stay and be horrible to him.'

Hester was as good as her word. When Taylor brought the drinks, she went on at length about a new schools' edition of D. H. Lawrence she was working on, with particular reference to the more arcane footnotes. The strategy was successful. After a few punishing minutes, during which Taylor had asked three perfunctory questions while he sipped his half of lager, and Kate affected fascination, he had looked at his watch and remembered an important meeting with his tutor.

'Yesss!' As he left Hester made a small fist and

punched the air. 'Bored the arse off him.'

When they walked back across the bridge, arm in arm, Kate was aware of an animated couple sitting in a stationary punt below them. The man was middle-aged, the girl much younger, and striking. Kate noticed the thin line of a livid scar above the V of her white shirt. Father and daughter, perhaps? They seemed too intimate for that, as though they shared a comfortable conspiracy. Neither, she thought, were they lovers. Too much in urgent need of saying. Whatever their bond, it caused her a momentary pang of envy, soon dispelled, however, by Hester, who hadn't seen them.

'What do you call a man in a black shirt having breakfast?' she said.

'Don't know. What do you?'

'Oswald Muesli! Great, isn't it? Just came to me. Just like that. There's no doubt about it, I'm wasted on this town.' She went on to outline her ideas for a choice of weekend breaks, proposing either cycling in Southwold, or recycling in Etruria, a place in the Midlands she'd spotted from a train.

Another quiet afternoon at the gallery gave Kate time to reflect on the meeting at the Mill. To be fair, Taylor had seemed normal enough. True, he hadn't mentioned her note unprompted, but it could have slipped his mind. Or maybe he'd been into college before her. And he'd been generous with the drink, despite Hester's hostility. Perhaps the coincidence of his being there at all was a bit odd, but there weren't many pubs in Cambridge where you could drink outside. He'd been alone again, of course, alone and unrecognised by anyone, but in an undergraduate population of thousands there was nothing very remarkable about that. Anyway, all this speculation was exhausting. He might be a bit of an oddball, but on the whole he seemed innocuous.

Hester, however, remained intrigued by the lunchtime meeting with Taylor, and convinced that mention of the note had taken him by surprise. After work, before heading home for the Kite, she decided to cycle over to Jesus. The long path leading from Jesus Lane was loud with undergraduates coming back in time for Hall. She remembered that Coleridge had called this place 'the palace of the winds', and wondered if he'd been referring to the cuisine rather than the cold. Whenever she regretted not having been to university, she would summon up a vision of the more forbidding Cambridge colleges, like this one, in an attempt to persuade herself that she'd had a lucky escape.

The porter's lodge, polished and cosy, couldn't have changed much since the wild boy from Ottery St Mary had stood at the counter, talking himself to breathlessness. The duty porter, ruddy-faced with a severe haircut, was busy answering questions from two undergraduates. As she felt in the pigeonhole marked T, unnoticed for the moment, Hester tried to look as though she belonged. She drew out two pieces of paper. One, which was stapled, was addressed to Henry Tattersall. The other was Kate's note. Hester put them both back. It was possible, of course, that Taylor had read the message and left it where it was. Possible, but in view of his reaction, not probable. Best to ask about

Martin Taylor. See if anyone knew him.

She waited outside the porter's lodge. Two minutes later one of the two undergraduates emerged. Blond, well-built, firm of buttock, he looked like an American footballer. A bit spotty, but no one was perfect. Hester would relish describing him to Kate. 'Excuse me,' she said. 'I'm looking for Martin Taylor. You wouldn't happen to know him at all?'

The tall undergraduate shook his head. ''Fraid not,' he said, in a nondescript English accent.

How about a sweaty wrestle at the University Arms then, two falls and a submission? Hester thought. Just you, me and a crate of champagne? Oh, and something for those spots? When expressed, this translated as 'OK. Thanks.'

As she went back into the porter's lodge, the second undergraduate was on his way out.

'Hello,' Hester said to the porter.

'You're soon back,' he said.

'Yes, I am, aren't I? The thing is I'm just down from St Andrews for a few days and a friend told me to look up a relative of hers, Martin Taylor. She said he was here. She didn't seem to know what he was reading or anything.'

'He was here, that's correct.'

'But he's not now?'

'No, I'm afraid not.'

'What, he left?'

'He's passed on. Martin Taylor's dead.'

'Oh, God. How?'

'Hit and run, poor feller. End of last term, on the

Madingley road. Good-looking lad. Boxed for the college. Would have got a blue, most likely. Wanted to go in for a vicar.'

'How sad. And there's nobody else of that name here now? No other Martin Taylor?'

The porter shook his head. 'No, Miss.'

Hester turned to go. 'I'm very sorry,' she said. 'Thank you.'

As she once again took the path to Jesus Lane, heavy with the news, she called Kate on her mobile. 'Hi,' she said. 'Look, I don't want to worry you but there's something you need to know.'

Chapter Three

'Sorted?' Dacre leaned back from his keyboard. As he stretched his arms behind his head, elbows east and west, the sweat patches on his blue shirt looked like improvised Rorschach tests. Over the fourteen years Hugh had known, and worked for, the veteran travel editor of the *Mail on Sunday*, he'd had much to sweat about.

Resisting an impulse to interpret the dark blots, Hugh said, 'Feeling good, Daks.'

'Top man.' Dacre's attention wandered to the computer screen, while with his left hand he began to mine his ear. 'Where d'you fancy, then? Not too far for a kick-off, what with the old ticker.'

'It's a new ticker, Daks. That's the point of it.'

'I know, mate. Figure of speech.' Dacre's eyes stalked a young woman carrying two paper cups. 'Good God, you can't tell me that's not provocation.'

'What, carrying drinks?'

'That's not all she's carrying, Huge. She knows exactly what she's doing, don't you worry. Exactly.' He eased his feet off the desk. 'How's Paris sound?'

'Sounds great. Anything in particular?'

'Not really. Little present, Huge. Welcome-home type thing. Forgotten Paris. The Paris Nobody Knows. Have a shufti. Few little bars and bistros the punters haven't infested. Little-hotels-for-under-fifty-quid type thing. Christ, last time I was over it was a fiver for a cup of coffee. Bottle of wine at . . . where was it? some poncy dump . . . hundred and twenty quid! Daylight robbery, bloody Frogs.'

Hugh smiled. 'How long are we looking at, then?'

'Couple of thousand words, say. Nice pix. We'll get Gary on the case.'

'Gary was telling me about this bullfighter . . .'

'Not a top scorer with the punters, mate, poking swords in dumb animals. Not unless they happen to be foxes and it's in the *Telegraph*.'

'I know, but this bloke's a Brit apparently. Frank McGuffog! A native of Hackney. Well, a Geordie originally.'

Dacre's large face grew redder as he chuckled. 'Bugger me, Frank McGuffog! I think I'd have that changed if I wanted to pull the señoritas.'

'He has. He calls himself El Franco.'

'Oh, well, then, now you're talking. El Franco! Eat your heart out Leonardo DiCaprio.'

'Might make a fair colour piece. He's never been done, apparently. Just, you know, a couple of pars when he's been injured or whatever.'

'Go on, then. Schlep down there after Paris. But stick to the human angle. Not too much blood. The Pride and the Passion type thing. You know the form:

"Toreador from the Tyne," "From Hackney to a Hacienda". Could be average.' Dacre leaned forward with a slight frown of concern. 'You sure you're up for this, Huge?'

'Thanks, Daks, I'm better than I've been for years.'

'Wish I could say the same, mate. Well, fair enough.' He held out a meaty hand. 'Send us a saucy postcard.'

As he rode home on the bus through the afternoon traffic, pleased with his first commission since the transplant, Hugh found himself thinking of Siobhan. The fact that Papworth had been satisfied with their progress had turned their Cambridge rendezvous into a small celebration. At first, when she'd met him off the London train on that long platform that seemed to stretch all the way to the North Sea, he'd felt awkward. He hadn't known whether to go for a hug, a handshake, or a French-style kiss on both cheeks. Maybe their closeness of a short while ago hadn't survived their changed circumstances. In the end she'd taken the tricky decision out of his hands by flinging her arms round his neck, as she had when they parted on that last, grey morning. From then on they hadn't stopped talking.

The strange thing was that, in her company, Hugh had at once felt younger again. He didn't have to work at hitting a note she recognised. He didn't try to adopt a new, less articulate vocabulary. He'd often noticed people do that when they tried to match the borrowed street wisdom of middle-class youth. It was like the temptation to sound transatlantic when you talked to Americans. No, with Siobhan it had seemed easier to be himself than it was with some of his contemporaries. With her he felt no need to compete or impress. Instead he was calm, relaxed, confident. Perhaps that was something she'd transferred to him, not only with her presence but also with the more enduring influence of the harvested heart. Perhaps, without knowing it, Scoular had transplanted something more than a strong young muscle.

That evening they'd eaten at Midsummer House. Built, it seemed, by the architect who'd accommodated the Old Woman Who Lived in a Shoe, it was the middle slice of a terrace that had never been completed. Unsupported on either side, it had adopted a leaning position, for comfort. In its walled garden by the river, next to a paddock where undergraduates had once made bets on terriers catching rats, it was eccentric and inviting. Hugh had often read about it in magazines and had looked forward to eating there.

As he and Siobhan walked along the towpath from Magdalene Street, she thought she'd better warn him.

'I suppose you know it's an arm-and-a-leg job?' she'd said.

'No problem, I've got a few meetings lined up. Travel editors, glamorous commissions, oh dear me yes. They'll pack me off to foreign parts before you can say Aa.'

'Aah?'

'Big A, little a. It's a river in northern France.'

'Ah. But what's there left to say about these places you go to?'

'What's there left to say about anywhere? It's the way you tell 'em, isn't it?'

'Is it?'

'Certainly. There's nowhere new, let's face it. Not even cyberspace.'

'And do they fork out enormous heaps of pounds for this privilege?'

'Enormous might be pushing it a bit. We're talking more . . . well, we're talking more not enormous. Enough to pay for a good nosh, however.'

They sat in the conservatory, warm and glowing in the dark garden. Around them the diners were formal and subdued. Cambridge, Siobhan explained, took its pleasures with an air of academic reserve, even when it wasn't academic. Estate agents would affect the gravitas of ageing dons. But by contrast the service was friendly and attentive. They'd both chosen the lighter items on the menu, salad, fish, chicken and fruit, without any pangs of deprivation, and Hugh picked a New Zealand sauvignon blanc. While they waited for the first course, he wanted to tell her he'd missed her; missed sharing thoughts and small experiences, without having to preface them with explanations. But he found he couldn't. He was afraid it would come out sentimental and embarrassing. Instead, prompted by a casual question, he'd told her about Tilly and the love of her life. Siobhan had heard of Anthony Granger, had seen one of his plays, which had come to the Arts.

'He's brilliant,' she said. 'It was great. Gareth got tickets.'

'Good old Gareth,' Hugh said, before he could stop himself.

She didn't seem to notice the irony, or if she did she

thought it unimportant. When he told her about Sam and his collection of fire extinguishers, she laughed out loud and said she'd love to meet him. Hugh wondered what the other customers made of them: an old bloke – well, getting on – and a young woman. Dirty old man, most of them, he supposed. If only they knew what the old bloke and the young woman had in common. If only they realised part of her was part of him, the most important part. That would torpedo their academic reserve.

Siobhan talked about her work, and how it felt divorced from the real world. Slogging away at Roman stuff that had little apparent bearing on life at the modern Bar. She'd read a report that said 40 per cent of women barristers complained of sexual harassment in chambers. Hugh told her that was nothing: in newspapers the figure would be nearer 120 per cent.

At the end of the meal the handsome young chef, whose name was Pablo Gutierrez but whose accent was south London, asked them if they'd enjoyed themselves. Siobhan glowed as she enthused about the flavours. There was such a frankness in her, Hugh thought, such an appetite for the electric here and now, and such vulnerability in that livid scar on her pale skin.

As they walked back over the Common, in the direction of Downing, he felt a strong urge to tell her about the dreams. On average he was getting them a couple of times a week now, but hadn't felt able to discuss them with anyone, aware that they sounded spooky and peculiar. Tilly might have understood, but even she would wonder and worry about his state of mind.

People were unsettled by abnormalities. And the dreams were, without question, bizarre. Each one was more vivid than the last, though each was still composed of shifting moments, like looking at a series of moving tableaux on a continuous strip of film. One would fade to make way for the next, and each was arresting, often shocking. Wherever they originated seemed far away, both in time and place. Sometimes they left such a profound impression that he would catch veiled glimpses of them during the day. When this happened he would break into an instantaneous, momentary cold sweat, isolated from the real events around him. These brief lapses into unreality, or perhaps another reality, made him fearful. They were unpredictable and uncontrollable. They were involuntary exiles to an existence of which he had no conscious knowledge. And neither, it was safe to assume, had anyone else. In which case there was no point in burdening them with their strangeness. Least of all Siobhan, who had enough to contend with. Cystic fibrosis hadn't gone away with the domino transplant. It was something she would always have to fight. Always, as long as the fight lasted. By unspoken treaty, neither of them allowed themselves to think about their probable limits, let alone articulate such thoughts. No, there was nothing for it but to be as uncomplaining as she was, and to hope the dreams would somehow work their way out of him.

At the gates of Downing she'd thanked him and kissed his cheek. 'That was great,' she said. 'I couldn't have loved it more.'

'Good. Our inaugural meeting. I wouldn't be surprised if there's a piece about it in tomorrow's *Cambridge Evening News*.'

'Front page no doubt,' she said.

' "Beauty and the Beast!" ' Hugh began to invent. ' "In an unprecedented head-to-head, gorgeous, pouting infant legal genius Siobhan Herbert was last night seen dining with a brontosaurus at Cambridge's top eatery. Said Siobhan, thirty-something, twenty-something, thirty-something: 'I found him under a pile of papers on Jesus Green. The *Sporting Life* actually. He looked like he hadn't eaten since the Ice Age . . . ' " ' He'd wanted to ask her about tomorrow, but knew she was busier than him.

Once again, as though aware, she came to the rescue. 'Let me get you lunch tomorrow. I've got to work in the morning but we could have a drink outside at the Mill, if the weather's OK. If not we can always go inside.'

'You're on,' he said, smiling. 'See you then.' As he turned to go, she said, 'I'll bring Gareth.'

'Terrific,' he said, with as short a delay and as much enthusiasm as he could contrive.

In the event Gareth had turned out to be fine. He was reading medicine. Hugh knew at once he'd be very good at it. There was a feeling of great competence about him, worn with ease. Though he sounded impractical in small everyday things, his purpose had always been clear to him. Strange, he said, because there were no quacks in the family. He had no great ambition to be in Harley Street. As a matter of fact, he said, he had a great ambition not to be there. Nor was he driven by a burning desire to heal the sick. It was just that he loved it, all of it, and if what he did when he qualified made people feel stronger, then so much the better. He knew the money would be hopeless, and the hours gross, but nothing could shake his quiet certainty.

When he talked, with a wry and pleasing sense of irony, Hugh soon recognised what Siobhan saw in him. They seemed as good a match as could be imagined. For some reason it made him want to write about them, though it wasn't a story anyone would print, and it might well wreck their relationship. Maybe one day he'd be able to fictionalise them; disguise them as a couple he'd met elsewhere, on a journey. Meanwhile, as well as sensing the rightness of them, he felt to some extent excluded. Ridiculous, but he did.

When Gareth left them, saying he'd fixed a game of squash, Siobhan and Hugh took their drinks down the steps and sat in a moored punt.

'Next time we'll punt up to Grantchester,' she'd said.

He was glad she was thinking that far ahead. 'Bags be Rupert Brooke. I'll dust off my boater.'

Siobhan laughed. 'If you're in a boater, I'm out of here.'

'A pith helmet, then. We'll search for the source of the Cam. We didn't make the *Cambridge Evening News* by the way. I bought the early edition. The front page was covered in Clinton. Would you believe it? Big story right on their doorstep and they go for bloody Clinton!'

She'd smiled and moved her sleeve to look at her

watch. 'I'm going to have to go in a minute, Hugh. Exam.'

'Course. I'll get the next train.'

As he looked at her, he was aware of a pale, dark-haired, nondescript young man in a white shirt and black jeans heading away from the drinkers, in the direction of Trumpington Street. Something indefinable seemed to mark him out, as though he were the only monochrome figure amid colour and animation. For a sickening moment Hugh had the impression that he'd materialised from one of the dreams; that the frontier between real daylight and the unreal, surreal dark was becoming blurred. And wouldn't that be a reasonable definition of madness? Oh, for God's sake, this was absurd. He was a plain young bloke in black jeans. Probably worked in a bank. All this rubbish must be down to the trauma of the operation.

The shadow past, Hugh said, 'Are you on for the Smoke next time?'

'Sure,' she said.

'What do you want to do?'

'Theatre? Fish and chips? Anything you want. Anything of Anthony Granger's on?'

'Probably. There usually is, like Ayckbourn. I'll have a look. Maybe we could meet him.'

'That'd be brilliant.'

They walked down the passage to the corner of Silver Street. Siobhan pointed to the bridge and said she was going to Sidgwick Avenue. He'd find a taxi in the market place.

It was then that the dream caught him, unguarded,

with instantaneous nausea. Unable to speak, he could feel sweat on his forehead and in his palms. It was the suddenness that made him panic. And the fact that now, in this disconnection, he was no longer on this street, at this time, with this woman. He was ambushed by the past. But a past that was not his own.

There are eight wagons, each drawn by five powerful horses. Warhorses. Each horse is attended by a groom, wearing a new tunic. The grooms each have their own cart, with a horse and driver. Beside the wagons and carts, laden with iron-banded trunks and covered with sheets of leather, there are fierce hounds with silver-studded collars. Behind these, twelve packhorses with monkeys on their backs, and panniers bulging with gold and silver vessels, including chalices. Heading the procession, perhaps two hundred footmen, in groups of ten or a dozen, singing as they walk. The song is strange. The onlookers, wide-eyed, turn to each other and shrug. As the hunting dogs and greyhounds pass, they shrink back from the cries of the handlers. Grooms kneel on the rumps of packhorses; squires carry their masters' shields; falconers make fists for their hawks. The image fades . . .

    Sinuous, glistening shapes lie coiled on a wide gold platter. They are eels, stilled in their death-fight.

'Hugh?'

Silver Street was restored to the present. Hugh felt back in control, but drained. 'Sorry. It's just . . . I get this thing sometimes.'

'What thing?' Siobhan looked concerned. 'You've gone all white.'

'It's nothing, honestly. It's just . . . I think it's just, you know, reaction. I go a bit light-headed.'

'Are you sure that's all you go?'

'Yes, honestly. No worries. It's gone as soon as it comes. I feel fine now.'

She put her hand to his forehead. 'It feels cold. Sweaty but cold.'

'It's probably that Scotch egg.'

'Are you absolutely sure you're OK?'

'Promise.'

'You should tell Scoular, you know. Be on the safe side.'

'No. It's just my spavined old carcass is taking a bit longer to get over it than yours, that's all. A day or two and I'll be back in the ring.'

'I hate leaving you like this, poor old thing.'

'Less of the poor, if you don't mind. And less of the thing, come to that. Now buzz off to that exam. And good luck. I'll see you in a month.'

She hugged him. 'Look forward to it,' she said.

He stood and watched her as she hurried across the bridge. Would she turn back, he wondered. And wondered why he wondered. No. She was, like him, a creature of the next thing, not the last. Her mind would now be full of the exam, and the rest of the afternoon, and the evening . . . with Gareth. And then, just as he was about to head for the market place, she turned as she ran, dancing backwards for a moment, and blew him a kiss, followed by a wave. He raised his arm and smiled.

That had been a week ago. Now, as the twenty-four

bus neared Hugh's stop on Chalk Farm Road, his mind turned to Dacre's commission. Siobhan had been right, of course. There was nothing original to be done about Paris, or anywhere. But something told him he might now see these places in a fresh light. He might feel them in a way he'd never felt them before. At least that would make the sensations newish for him if not for the reader. Maybe he could describe them as though he were writing letters to Siobhan. Try and make them live for someone young, sceptical, intelligent. Try to sidestep the clichés for once. Except they were what Dacre wanted. The Paris Nobody Knows! The Paris nobody with a single surviving brain cell wants to know. Ah, well. See how it turned out.

Two mornings later Hugh had just finished packing a black-leather holdall when he heard an insistent car horn. How come you could tell an expensive one from the kind they put in family saloons? It sounded more mellifluous, somehow, more confident, richer, like a cello rather than a rock sax. His Range Rover parked on a double yellow line, Gary was already half out of the driver's door and waving in a comic mid-crouch. This was going to be all right, Hugh thought. Back in business, nothing too strenuous, and the sprightly Gary for company.

Courtesy of Dacre's deal with P. & O., they crossed the Channel in the club lounge. With a glass of champagne in one hand, and a Camel in the other, Gary was getting in the mood.

'Say what you like, if God had meant us to use

tunnels,' he said, 'he'd have made us bloody badgers.'

'How very true that is,' Hugh said. 'But by the same token, if he'd meant us to travel on water, wouldn't He arguably have made us ducks?'

'Good point. But since He didn't make us at all, it's not a major problem, *n'est-ce pas*?'

'Who did make us, d'you reckon?'

'Rupert Murdoch, wasn't it? That's what I heard.'

'Ah, well, that explains it then.'

'What?'

'Why we're all greedy sods with no style.'

'You speak for yourself, mate.' Gary put down his drink and, with the free hand, pulled back the collar of his shirt to reveal the label. 'What's that say then?'

'It says "Made by Starving Infants in a Bankok Sweatshop". Bangkok's spelt wrong, without the G.'

'Funny. It said Ralph Lauren three hours ago. Miss!' He held up his glass to the young stewardess, who got the message. 'So, what's the angle exactly, Huge?'

'In Paris? All will be revealed, Gaz.'

'I know, but when?'

'When it's revealed to me,' Hugh admitted. 'We will kneel in front of Notre Dame, you and I, and we will pray for guidance. And lo, a broad beam of blinding light will stream down from the heavens, illuminating our pious posture . . .'

'That'll be the Old Bill with a torch, nicking us for loitering.'

'I sometimes think, Gaz, that when they were handing out souls and sensibilities, and civilising things like that, you were fitted with a rusting piece of clockwork.'

'You're just saying that to wind me up,' Gaz said.

In the event they didn't kneel in front of Notre Dame. Instead they had a drink, that first evening, in the Place des Vosges, subdued by the ancient symmetry of its colonnades. A massive lens fitted to his new Canon, Gary caught young couples in tender attitudes; a bowed old woman pulling behind her a basket on wheels; a three-legged mongrel snouting a cocked white poodle. Still, discreet, and silent when he worked, he picked off moments that were not always apparent to Hugh, whose attention by then had sometimes been drawn elsewhere. It was as though Gary could read random patterns; could foresee outcomes, even though they could never have been rehearsed in just this way. When the defining image happened, he always seemed to be ready for it. Hugh was fascinated by this skill; this ability to distil in a way he'd never managed in words. And yet he knew it was something they couldn't discuss. Gary was sure in what he did, too sure to waste time on pompous analysis. Siobhan would like him, Hugh thought; would love the fact that he let his work speak for itself. Though when it spoke it was all too often muffled by poor printing. These pictures should be fine, though. They'd get posh treatment in the colour supplement. That's if Hugh could dredge up enough copy to go with them.

The following morning, refreshed after a good night at the Hôtel d'Angleterre in the Rue Jacob, Hugh's favourite when someone else was paying, he and Gary headed for the Welcome, a small, vertical hotel on the corner of the Boulevard St Germain and the Rue de

Seine. Hugh had telephoned the manager the previous evening, selling the piece as a landmark in British travel writing. Its influence, he said, would be incalculable. That at least had been true. The manager, bored but tolerant, had agreed to let them inspect and photograph the premises.

At the cramped desk in the narrow hall sat an elegant young woman with the gamine haircut of a groomed Parisienne. Hugh waited while she dealt with a booking on the telephone, patient and charming in spite of the caller's evident lack of fluency. When she'd finished, Hugh began his rehearsed speech: 'Bonjour, Ma'm'selle. Je m'appelle Severin, Hugh Severin . . .' He'd never mastered the problem of trying to render Hugh in a French accent. On the rare occasions he'd tried it, the sound produced was somewhere between a phlegmy cough, a vomit and plain *you*. Ever since, acknowledging defeat, he'd settled for the English version. 'Je suis journaliste Anglais. Hier soir j'ai téléphone Monsieur . . .' Damn. He'd forgotten the manager's name.

'Hervieu,' the young woman supplied, smiling. 'He told me about you.' Her English accent was more than impeccable. It was English, tinged with the north.

'You're . . .?' Hugh began.

'Blackpool,' she said. 'Helen Verrecchia. Pleased to meet you.'

'Good old northern name, Verrecchia.'

'We were in ice-cream. Wasn't there going to be a photographer?'

Hugh looked round. Now he could see that, instead of following him in, Gary had been seduced by the energy and colour of the Buci market. At that moment he was photographing a large woman whom he'd persuaded to balance a basket of cheeses on her head. When he'd finished, he took the basket off her and gave her four air-kisses, two beside each cheek. She laughed, while her husband, if that's who it was, brandished a baguette as though challenging Gary to a mock duel. Gary picked up his camera bag and retreated with exaggerated stealth.

Helen showed them two or three rooms, and Hugh chose a corner attic on the the sixth floor, with a commanding view of the Boulevard St Germain towards the Boulevard St Michel. The lift had only gone as far as the fifth, and the climb to the summit left Hugh breathless.

'Doesn't look a lot,' Gary said, when Helen had left them to it.

'Maybe not, Gaz. But just you wait till I tell the punters who's slept in it.'

'Go on then, amaze me.' Gary was framing the view through the window.

'Well, let's see. Charles Baudelaire, *Les Fleurs du Mal*. Manet spent a few nights here. Oscar, of course – he seems to have kipped in practically every hotel in Paris. Toulouse-Lautrec . . .'

'Suit a shortarse like him,' Gary said. 'It's giving me backache, bending double. Is that the lot then?'

'No. The list goes on and on. Unbelievable. Alfred de Musset, George Sand . . . you know, the one who was a woman . . . Madame de Staël, who was also a woman . . .'

'Must have got a bit crowded. Just sit on the bed and try and look poetic. Bit droopy. That's the one, lovely. So all those geezers actually stayed in this room, did they? No, go on, you're having me on.'

'Yes,' Hugh said.

'Yes, they stayed here or yes, you're having me on? Just lean on the end there. Head down a bit. Great. Now, to me. Think great thoughts. Like what's winning the first race at Kempton. Marvellous. Come on, which is it then, Huge, true or false?'

'Well, who's to say they didn't? Put it that way. The guy who runs the gaff's hardly going to blow the whistle is he? It's all good for business. And the punters couldn't care less. Mrs Whatserface from Croydon's hardly going to turn round to her old man and say, "Well, I'll be jiggered, Alfred. This lying bastard says Colette stayed here when any literary-type person, *comme moi*, knows perfectly well she had a charming maisonette in the Rue de Rivoli." I don't think so.'

'You little fibber, you. Now let's just get you talking nonchalantly on the dog. Like, asking this bird out to dinner at Whatsisname, Maxim's, or whatever. "Frankly, my dear, I don't give a monkey's." That's it. Lovely jubbly. You'll have 'em flocking here like leemings.'

'Bit of a mixed metaphor, Gaz. And, strictly speaking, it's lemmings.'

'Whatever. Right, that's me done. Let's go and get bevvied. Without more ado, as they say.'

Paying lip service to Dacre's suggested theme, Hugh guided Gary to La Frégate, on the Quai Voltaire, over-looking the Pont Neuf. Or at least it would have overlooked it, had the windows been clean enough. Inside, it had the displaced air of a tearoom run by Russian émigrés. The easy chairs were threadbare, the once cream paintwork bronzed with smoke. Madame presided at the till, with a large black cat to guard the takings. Hugh had always liked its shabby comfort, and its onion soup, the best he'd tasted in Paris. Gary felt at home there too. They ordered a bottle of champagne. Hugh would drink one glass, while Gary talked with knowledgeable admiration about French masters like Lartigue and Doisneau.

Encouraged by this almost lyrical appraisal, and remembering something Don McCullin had once told him, Hugh said, 'Do you ever wish you could snap the past? Like the Pont Neuf there, a few hundred years back? Just, maybe, one shot?'

'I think you sometimes do in a way. Not the gear and that, obviously, but now and again, just before you do the business, you get the feeling this frame's happened before. You know? Like this set-up, whatever, the people in it are different but the way they fit in the composition is like a repeat.'

'As though without knowing it they're going through actions that have been gone through before, maybe even in exactly the same place?'

'Maybe. Weird or what?' Gary refilled his glass. 'Not a bad drop of bubbly, Huge. Least I hope it's bubbly. Cats in bars make me nervous. Thing is, how do they get 'em to sit on the bottles?'

When they'd finished lunch, Hugh said a couple more days should wrap it up. He wanted to do this fabulous spice shop in the Marais, Le Monde des Epices, where every imaginable variety of glacé fruit, nut, oil, halva, spice, you name it, gleamed and lured and made you lust for it. Then there were a couple of little restaurants, which wouldn't break the bank, that he'd seen in the *Time Out* guide, and they should do a few shots at the Luxembourg, because it was free and time had stood still there.

As he outlined the rudimentary scheme, saying he could make up the rest, he wanted to show it all to Siobhan. Maybe she knew it already. Better than him, perhaps. Would they ever be able to take that sort of trip together? He doubted it. That was another sort of trip, one you shared with a lover, or a partner; or a contemporary, if love and partnership were off the menu. And yet this feeling he had for her, which he was afraid to magnify, seemed to want more than it was being fed. What the extra might be, he didn't know. It wasn't sex. He did respond to her in a way that was more than emotional, but it wasn't a physical desire. That, at least, was a relief. It would disgust her and therefore destroy him. No, it was more like he imagined the twin thing to be. The constant consciousness of something shared. Not a temporary binding, like a contract or agreement or mere mutual understanding, but something fundamental, substantial, ineradicable.

Two days later, while Gary went to a jazz club, Hugh opened his notebook and began writing the piece on his laptop. Below his window, which opened on to the courtyard, he could hear the murmur of guests making the most of the warm evening. He decided to use the form of a letter, which he'd thought about on the boat. But Dear who? And what relationship should the addressee bear to him? Niece, would be fine. No point in pretending he was younger than he was. His regular readers knew better. And call her, say, Millie. Rhymed with Tilly. Neither too posh nor too plebby. 'Dear Millie.' Sounded reasonable. Now he could write it in a more relaxed, colloquial style. Dacre should go for that. The paper wanted to attract a young, affluent readership as well as the reliable wrinklies. 'Dear Millie,' he typed. 'Papa Hemingway called Paris a moveable feast. What he really meant was a liquid lunch. There are more bars per square metre in this town than there are in Connemara. But here they're not just places to get legless in. They're a buzzy cocktail of club, pub, and fashion show. I've sussed out a few I think you'd like . . .'

It came with ease, like water. If you spilled it, it wouldn't even leave a stain. As good a way as any to share information, perhaps, but when he'd finished, an hour later, Hugh felt little satisfaction. The job was done, the fee earned. End of story. The only passage that had come from below the surface was the one where he talked about the church of his namesake, St Séverin, with its semi-circle of columns embracing the altar, and the deep blues and yellows of its stained glass. There he'd had the strangest sensation of being expected, hoped for, even; of an arrival welcomed with some reverence. A novel, not to say unique, experience for a journalist, he reflected, but there had been no mistaking it. He couldn't describe the moment in anything like those terms to his readers, of course. They'd think he was mad and turn to an interview with the star of a soap. Instead he tried to convey the strong sense of the past that penetrated the stones of certain buildings, and how that was not so surprising when you thought about it. It was like seeing a prehistoric insect preserved in amber. That was the past, right there in your hand. And he described the young American choir who'd been rehearsing when he'd popped in, a slight girl in black singing, 'Won't you buy my sweet blooming lavender?' watched over by the brass-eagle lectern caught in a beam of late sun.

For years, for Hugh's entire career, boiling down gathered facts until they fitted the allotted space had been enough for him. New stories, new people, new drinks, new expense claims, these had been, if not satisfying, then at least a living. No one could confuse it with real writing, but who cared? Journalism had its purpose, a valid one, and most so-called creative writing was tosh anyway. Of eight people standing at a Sainsbury's check-out in Camden Town, it was a safe bet that five would be writing novels. Mind you, three of them might be Beryl Bainbridge, Alice Thomas Ellis, and A. N. Wilson, so maybe that wasn't such a reliable test. But it still held true that good journalism was more worthwhile than second-rate fiction.

So what was he getting exercised about? Just that, for him, since Papworth, half digesting then regurgitating stale sensations had lost all its charm. He'd begun to hanker after a life, and not just a living. Something in him was urging him to work in more solid material. But what, and how, he had no idea. It was something

Anthony Granger would understand, he supposed, but not something he could ever discuss with him. That would be an acknowledgement of Granger's superiority, and Hugh was by no means ready for self-abasement. Maybe he could talk it over with Tilly. Or, one day, Siobhan. In Cambridge she'd made it plain that his kind of journalism seemed slight; slighter than he was capable of, had been the sub-text.

'I told you it was mad, bringing the car.' This from Hugh as, the following morning, he and Gary made their third circuit of the Arc de Triomphe.

'I heard about a bloke, truck driver, went round here for a week. They never let him out. Just went round and round. Finally, on the Sunday morning, the Old Bill cottoned on. Pulled up level with the cab, and bingo! He'd snuffed it. Stone dead at the wheel. Hands still clamped at ten o'clock and two o'clock. Just like the Ancient bleeding Mariner. Round and round and round. The Tomb of the Unknown Truck Driver.'

In the end they'd opted for the car because Dacre had come up with another idea the day before they left London. He'd got wind of a great human-interest story, he said. And for once he was right. Though he was an atheist, an electrician from Gravesend, whose eighteen-year-old son was suffering from a brain tumour, had decided to follow the pilgrims' route to the historic shrine at Santiago de Compostela, sponsored by friends. And he was doing it on foot. Dacre wanted Hugh and Gary to meet him at journey's end, if not before, and profile him. Hugh's initial reaction had been that it seemed an intrusion on private grief, but Dacre had persuaded him that the electrician was willing to co-operate, and that the paper was pledging ten thousand to the fighting fund.

The long haul across France didn't seem tiresome. Gary wasted no time; indeed, wasted so little that on one fast stretch two-thirds of the way there, he was fined six hundred francs by pouncing motorcycle police. They took the money in their colleagues' parked van with remarkable charm and efficiency, assuring him that now this unpleasantness was out of the way, nothing more would be said on the matter. It was as though an avuncular vicar had caught him scrumping apples.

When they reached Santiago de Compostela, the atheist pilgrim, Brian Glebe, wasn't hard to find. He'd arrived the day before and was already a local celebrity. Gary, to whom he responded at once, asked him if he'd mind retracing the last few hundred metres and, though he must have been footsore, Glebe agreed. That night they ate together in a small restaurant with half-tiled walls and fading photographs of celebrated visitors. They included the great Manolete, with his long, solemn, scarred face. The waiters made a big fuss of Glebe, indicating a space they were keeping for his picture. With a combination of sign language and rudimentary Spanish, Gary told them he'd be happy to send them one.

He and Hugh found Glebe impressive, in a way that was determined not to impress. If they'd told him so he would have been astonished and embarrassed. He'd taken on the walk, he said, as much for himself as his boy. Watching him there, in the hospital bed, the pressure and fear in his eyes, he'd felt useless. He'd needed to do something physical, to exhaust himself, even to cause himself pain. An ordinary man, he'd wanted to try something extraordinary, to use every last heartbeat of his energy. His wife had failed to see the point, and perhaps there wasn't one, but she had seen that anger and frustration were eating at him. Why Compostela, Hugh asked, if he didn't believe in a God? It was his wife's parish priest who suggested it, Glebe said, and it seemed as good as anywhere; a long walk with something at the end of it, a place with some sort of meaning for sponsors. And then, although part of the point of it had been not to have to think, to postpone thinking, it had proved impossible. Along the way he'd thought a great deal about what his son was going through, about the way he'd taken his wife so much for granted, about the little he'd done with his time. And he said there had been moments, often in the early morning or towards dusk, when he'd had this peculiar feeling that he wasn't alone; that there were other faint footsteps on the road besides his. Echoes, perhaps. But echoes of what? In any case, he said, he didn't want Hugh to print that because it sounded barmy.

Hugh and Gary talked a lot about Glebe on the long haul south to La Linea. Gary argued that he'd be better off at home, looking after the boy. What if he died while his father was away? How would Glebe handle that? Hugh, on the other hand, admired him. Perhaps what he'd done was in many ways selfish, but at least he'd refused to lie down. Maybe the boy would get something from that. Maybe the relationship with the wife would grow stronger. Maybe, even, the extraordinary experience would change everything, unsettle everything. In any event the money raised, and it looked like amounting to more than twenty-five thousand pounds, could only benefit the patient. And the encounter had given Hugh a story he wanted to think about, and tell in as simple and honest a way as he could. Honest was an adjective he hadn't used in a long time.

He wasn't sure he'd find much use for it in La Linea either. Frank McGuffog's hotel overlooked the litter-strewn beach facing the coast of Africa. The windows hadn't seen a wash-leather since the Civil War, and the plastic armchairs in Reception spoke of dentistry rather than creature comforts. Next door was Gibraltar, an unlovely outpost which the British had managed to turn into the Edgware Road. The customs area, guarded by scowling military, bore an air of complacent shabbiness reminiscent of a Lowestoft holiday camp.

As Hugh waited for the distracted receptionist to hand back his passport, up the steps of the Isla Hermosa bounded a tracksuited figure who could only be the great man himself. Hugh recognised him from a photograph. Sure enough it was El Franco, returned from a run along the beach. He was a slim, serious man, of medium height, no longer young, with a prominent nose and eloquent black eyebrows. Stopping in the middle of the sand-crunchy floor, he began to gyrate from the waist, hands on hips, with a slight groan as he stooped

'Frank?' Hugh adopted a gentle tone to break the

silence, not wanting to interrupt the routine. No reply. 'Frank!' Louder this time.

El Franco froze, in mid-gyration, and turned in Hugh's general direction. It was obvious that he only had partial hearing and, judging by his narrowed eyes, perhaps imperfect vision. These were not, Hugh reflected, the conventional attributes of a *matador de toros*. Deciding on a more direct approach, he stepped forward and held out his hand. 'Hugh Severin, Frank. I think the paper's been in touch with you.'

Frank straightened and took a careful look at the hand before shaking it. 'Hi. We've been expecting you.'

'Great. We've just got in. How's it going then?'

'Oh, you know, mustn't grumble.' Frank was still breathless. 'Get my wind back. We've had a little look at the bulls today.'

'And? Happy, are we?'

'I wouldn't say happy, like. You don't exactly get the *crème de la crème* in this neck of the woods, you know. But they'll do.'

'Do you get at all . . . you know, windy, the day before the fight?'

'I wouldn't call it windy exactly. A bit, you know, on edge, like. But we've been working out. Weights and that. We're pretty fit.' By now his panting had subsided.

Hugh wondered why most sportsmen, and he supposed Frank must be classed among them, used the royal *we*? Perhaps because it was a lonely business out there, and Frank's more so than most. Even an illusion of support must be a comfort. Hugh found himself liking this improbable athlete. He seemed unremarkable, unimaginative, but, then, imagination in a bull-fighter would be as helpful as a torn cartilage. Easy to turn him into a figure of fun. And yet, even if he was practising his skill, such as it was, in a town God hadn't had time to create, it must take mad courage to face an animal bred to kill him. And maybe there was unexpected grace in that well-kept frame. Hugh looked forward to finding out more. 'Can you spare me some time tonight? Me and Gary, my photographer? I don't suppose you want to be late.'

'No problem. There's a little caff,' he indicated the direction from which he'd run, 'La Casa Blanca. They know me there. Seven do you? I'll bring Jeff, my sword-handler.'

As Frank took his key from the receptionist, who appeared less than deferential, Hugh remembered what Gary had said about the sword-handler and the Leggy Lovely, his current companion. Curiouser and curiouser. Holding his anticipation in check, he started work on the piece which he knew the subs would headline 'A Pilgrim's Progress'. This one didn't come with ease. He found himself trying to think like Brian Glebe. Trying to come to terms with the imminent death of someone you loved, and carrying that terror with you as you ached through those relentless, jarring miles. Word had somehow got ahead of him, Brian had said, and even in small villages there had been welcoming committees. Generous people, recognising his urge to act, even if neither he nor they could define it.

When Hugh got to La Casa Blanca, Gary was already there, having a beer. He'd struck up a smiling relationship with the attractive girl behind the bar. She'd told him in sporadic English that the locals regarded El Franco as a bit of a freak, but a brave one. Whenever he fought here, two or three times a year, British supporters would troop over the border and cheer him on, though they didn't know what they were cheering. For herself, she preferred football: Manchester United. Was David Beckham happy with the Spice Girl? Gary said he didn't know but he thought so. The girl cried mock tears.

At ten past seven, Frank McGuffog led in his depleted *cuadrilla*. The sword-handler, Jeff, was a sallow youth with black hair slicked back like Antonio Ordonez, whose photograph had pride of place behind the bar. Behind him was a bronzed sapling of a woman wearing a short black skirt and a white T-shirt. Although she was part of the group, there was something about her that would never belong to any group. She had such apparent confidence in her own persona that, though she might choose to attach herself, she would never be attached. Not until the idea of attachment itself might become appealing, when she would take a partner who at least half understood, have two golden children, and run a small, stylish hotel in Cornwall. Hugh could see it now. Overlooking the harbour, Prussian blue and white, an eclectic collection of furniture and bric-à-brac, bright flowers in tall old vases, no locks on the bedroom doors. Her name was the Honourable Miranda Stokes. It was unwise for El Franco to be seen in her company since her presence, unlike his, was unforgettable. It even seemed probable that she'd have been happy to try her luck in the ring.

'*Olé*, babe,' Gary said, bounding up to give her a hug.

'*Amigo*,' she said, smiling at Hugh over Gary's shoulder.

'This is my mate Huge, the wordsmith,' Gary said. 'Miranda.'

'You sound like someone out of an Icelandic saga, Huge the Wordsmith,' Miranda said. 'Are you someone out of an Icelandic saga?'

'I am, as it happens,' Hugh said. 'I've just dropped in to warm up a bit.'

'Now, what'll it be?' Frank said, back in the real world. 'Miranda?'

'*Cerveza, por favor*, Frank.'

Drinks ordered, Hugh turned his attention to Frank. It took a conscious effort because the story with the real juice was Miranda's. How Dacre would love that one: 'Society Beauty Tames Swordsman'. But one look at her had persuaded Hugh that he wasn't going to do it. Another good reason why he'd remained a travel writer. Better for the digestion to be bitchy about places than people. On the other hand, the odd allusion to a mysterious and beautiful aficionada, no names, no pack drill, couldn't do any harm. Meanwhile, as he talked to Frank, he noticed that Miranda was animated with Gary while appearing to ignore Jeff, who concentrated on looking moody but something just short of magnificent.

'I know you've been asked this a million times before, Frank, but why?' Hugh said.

'Why the bulls, you mean? Well, it's canny, isn't it?'

'Canny? Is it?'

'We was hooked the minute we saw it. Fuengirola, 'ninety-two. Blew us away, man. We was still living in Gateshead then, like.' He took a ruminative sip of his Diet Coke. 'Then we found there was, like, this bull-fighting circle, club like, La Faena, in Middlesbrough. Watching videos and a bit of capework. Plenty of sangría. Well, we found we had a natural aptitude, didn't we? Then one thing led to another. We knew we'd never be happy until we'd had a go. Months of training, like, off and on. Some of them taking the piss, you know. But it's a hell of a buzz, I'm telling you. Hell of a buzz.'

'Do you make any money at it?'

'You're joking. Do you want to know what we're getting for tomorrow? For killing two bulls? Entertainment for the masses? Three hundred quid! Three hundred flaming quid! Out of that you've got your team, your *cuadrilla* to pay, your *traje de luces*, your suit of lights, to get cleaned . . .'

'That's the matador's fancy gear, yes? The gold braid and the satin and the pink stockings and stuff?'

'That's them. They cost an arm and a leg an' all, even to hire. Then there's your travel, your accommodation, and on top of that your flaming agent wants forty per cent. It's daylight robbery! Do I make money at it? It costs me a flaming fortune.' He took a moment to calm himself. 'But there. We can't help ourselves, can we? We'd rather spend a few bob any day than draw the flaming bus pass and moan we did sod all. When we face that bull, man, we're alive. Every nerve end.

Hundred per cent. Right on the edge. Most people can't say that ever in their lives, can they?'

Hugh conceded that they couldn't. And now wasn't the moment to talk about cruelty, or the real price the matador might have to pay. Those questions could wait until after Frank's fight. Hugh had heard, though, that bullfighters put on their suits of lights with some ceremony, and prayed before they went into the ring. Could Gary get pictures of that? Frank said no problem, and not long afterwards excused himself. As he said his goodnights, Miranda linked her arm in his and walked him to the door. It was a touching gesture, which somehow took Hugh by surprise. It seemed to recognise that, whatever the ethics of the enterprise and the shortcomings of the location, Frank was facing his Sunday-afternoon assignation with more than a little dignity.

At five o'clock the following day the sky was overcast, and the crowd in the small *plaza de toros* was truculent. A noisy group of English tourists, and off-duty military with their partners, were singing football chants. Hugh had enjoyed talking to Miranda while he waited for Gary to get back from the chapel. She told him she was leaving La Linea straight after the *corrida*, though she hadn't broken the news to Jeff or Frank. For her, the party was over. It had been great fun, had made her see some things in a new light, but it was time to move on. Did Hugh ever feel like that? He said it was funny she should say that because he was just beginning to. She reminded him of Siobhan, in her non-judgemental ability to take life as it was, rather than as it might be in a brochure, or a middle-class dream of pro-priety. In Miranda, though, the pleasure principle, the assumed right to do as she pleased, came higher on the agenda, with less regard for the consequences. But, to her credit, she had shown real concern for Frank, and it seemed unlikely that an abrupt departure would devas-tate the taciturn Jeff.

Gary joined them in time for the parade, which was accompanied by a homespun band. Out there in the front-line, Frank cut a solid, mature figure beside the two boyish matadors with whom he shared the bill. Adopting the traditional slow, macho walk across the sand, left arm tucked into the embroidered ceremonial cape, right unbending, he looked isolated and vulnera-ble. Watching him, while Gary caught him on the long lens, Hugh had a strong feeling that, however admirable Frank's determination to be part of all this, he didn't quite fit. There are some things, he felt, that are best left to those in whose blood they run.

The last of the three matadors to fight, Frank got an ironic, drunken cheer from the Gibraltar contingent. Ignoring them, white-faced, he concentrated on the bull, while his portly *cuadrilla* tested it with rudimentary passes. Before he'd left for the bullring, Frank had explained that this routine would tell him whether his adversary favoured a particular horn, whether he charged straight, and in which quarter of the ring he preferred to fight. When Frank was satisfied, he stepped out with the large cape, the *capote*, taking the leading edge between his teeth then spreading it until it was suspended just above the sand. A few more short, precise steps, back arched, and the bull began to take an interest. Closer still and the animal charged, hooking high with its right horn as it passed close to Frank's chest. The crowd roared, '*Olé.*' In Miranda's expression Hugh could see why she'd walked Frank to the door last night. At this moment, if at no other in his life, he was impressive. Jeff, trying to catch Miranda's eye from his station beside the swords and spare capes behind the *barrera*, no longer existed for her.

Frank moved closer, giving his cape an occasional twitch to incite the bull. Again it charged, several times. Though Frank was stiffer in his movements than the other matadors, more correct than graceful, he was not afraid to work tight to the animal. The sequence earned him a genuine, surprised, round of applause. As he performed a last, stopping pass, and turned towards the crowd, Miranda leaned back, relieved. Gary reloaded. Time now for the picadors. Never popular characters with any fans, least of all tourists, since more often than not they half crippled their disadvantaged enemy, they were greeted with booing and catcalls. Regardless, they proceeded to dig too long and too deep with the sharp *pics*. Together with the rest, Miranda shouted her anger, raising a white-knuckled fist. The *banderilleros* did little to restore any dignity to the proceedings. Two round, middle-aged has-beens, they launched the darts with minimal risk to themselves into every part of the bull except the target: the immense neck muscle. More boos. More catcalls. More outraged cries of '*Asesinos!*'

As Frank walked out for the last act, his short *muleta* stiffened with a stick along the top edge, the crowd went quiet again. He acknowledged them with his raised *montera*, the matador's black bonnet, then approached the *barrera* below where his small party were sitting. The only sound was Gary's motordrive, recording every significant moment. Frank was still now. Then, holding up his *montera* again, he threw it for Miranda to catch. A ripple of applause. From Miranda, a wide smile of pleasure and encouragement. At that moment it was possible to forget Frank's ridiculous ring-name and his unlikely ambition, his self-dramatisation in this theatre of cruelty. He was a man about to re-enact, as best he could, an ancient duel, and he was dedicating it to a beautiful woman. For even the most cynical, there was something elemental in that.

Striding back now with increased purpose towards the bull, Frank held the *muleta* behind his legs and used his body as a lure. The crowd liked this. If the animal made a sudden charge, Frank would have no means of diverting it. Bringing the *muleta* round to the front but still holding it low, he gave it a twitch and the bull, irritated by the *banderillas*, charged. Again the right horn hooked high as it passed within inches of Frank's chest. Jeff looked anxious and shouted something, inaudible even from the ringside seats. But the pass was good. And so was the next. And the next. The crowd began a rolling chant of '*olés*' and '*vales*', and Hugh found himself joining them.

Frank might never know an afternoon like this again. Hugh could see the sense of achievement in his face and his bearing. There was nothing comic about him as he came back to the *barrera*, took a mouthful of water from a small beaker, and drew the curved sword offered handle first by Jeff, who leaned over to say something that seemed urgent. Miranda was tense, eyes only for the final encounter. Even the Gibraltar contingent appeared to sense its significance. With slow steps, the sword in his right hand, Frank walked back across the small, overcast arena, to complete the ritual that had become his only passion. The bull was tired, its head lowered, its flanks vivid with blood. As Frank tempted it once more with the *muleta*, Hugh noticed the flag above the President's box animate with a sudden gust. Jeff saw it too and shouted again. If Frank heard, he made no acknowledgement. Coming closer and closer to the already defeated animal, he coaxed it into five more desultory charges, earning more respectful, though less enthusiastic '*olés*'.

And then, in the stillness, he decided the time had come. Miranda leaned forward, linking her arm through Hugh's. He could feel her tension. The bull's muzzle was no more than three inches from the ground. With calm precision, Frank profiled himself, holding the *muleta* low with the left hand and levelling the sword at chest height. The killing place, he'd explained, between the animal's shoulder blades, was no wider than two inches. Ready, in the breath-held silence, he raised the heel of his right foot, and pivoted, leaned, and drove in one movement, burying the sword up to its hilt. The crowd came to instant, raucous life. Cushions were thrown, water bottles, flowers, programmes. Hugh could see their catharsis reflected in Miranda's delight. Like them she was on her feet, cheering and shouting. 'Viva El Franco! Bravo! Bravo!'

But with a sickening feeling like the onset of the dream, Hugh could also see the elation switch to sudden horror. In the instant that Frank had killed, a sudden kick of wind had lifted the corner of the *muleta*. With a desperate, dying reflex, the bull had jerked up its head to follow the movement and, as it began its last fall to the sand, its right horn had sheathed itself deep in Frank's groin. There was shocked quiet again. Frank's *cuadrilla*, belying their age, sprinted to help him, together with the two younger matadors. Medics appeared from the gate where the opening procession had emerged. The mule team, in white, cracked their whips, undertakers to the dead animal. The crowd stood, in silence, but it was impossible to see Frank through the crush of would-be helpers. Miranda looked older with apprehension. Now the group in the ring parted to let out a stretcher, carrying the wounded Englishman. It was loaded with great care into a waiting ambulance. Before he disappeared from view, one of the *cuadrilla* stopped, picked up a red carnation thrown by an aficionado, and laid it on Frank's chest. The dark blue satin and silver braid of the matador's suit of lights was stained darker still with blood. He appeared to be unconscious.

At first, Hugh couldn't face the hotel. Instead he walked along the sea-front. The clouds had dispersed now, and there was a warm haze over the water. He'd called at the hospital with Miranda, Jeff and Gary, but they'd told him nothing would be known for some hours. An operation would be necessary but the outcome was unpredictable. It would be better if he left a contact number and came back in the morning. Jeff had decided to stay in any case, promising to pass on news as soon as he got it. Good for Jeff, Hugh thought. He might not be in the Noël Coward class as a conversationalist, but he'd shown great loyalty when it counted. Miranda had decided not to fly out that night after all, she told Hugh, though there was no need to mention it because no one but him had known of her plan. Gary, who was as shocked as the rest, had asked him to join them for a meal, but Hugh had said he wasn't hungry.

He sat on the prow of a fishing-boat, surrounded by the detritus of the beach, looking out towards Africa. The thought of it had always excited him, and the reality hadn't often disappointed. Had Frank ever gone across, he wondered. He supposed not. Frank's ambition had been too focused for that. He'd known what he wanted and pursued it, regardless of the mean surroundings. They hadn't mattered to him. What had mattered was being face to face with that maddened animal and, following an alien code of perhaps perverted chivalry, far from friends and family, risking his own life in killing it. Where was the sense in it? By any standards it was irrational; certifiable, almost. And yet, in that small, sunless ring, where few spectators could even guess at his motivation, he'd stood where he had always wanted to stand, and been someone he had always wanted to be. Frank McGuffog had heard a call, however insane or unsavoury it might sound to outsiders, and he'd responded with everything he had to give. In the end Hugh hadn't needed to ask him whether he was aware of the price he might have to pay, because that afternoon he'd seen the answer in his eyes. But how to convey this to a reader? As Dacre had said, the punters weren't too keen on poking things into dumb animals. How to tell them that, for twenty-five minutes, there had been more than a touch of nobility about the man from Gateshead?

Hugh thought he saw parallels too between Frank and Brian Glebe, the atheist pilgrim he'd met in Santiago de Compostela. Both men, for different reasons, had obeyed an unconventional urge, an urge with deep, old roots, and had been prepared to make great sacrifices for it. Both had achieved their life's finest moments by taking on a lonely, unfamiliar, uncompromising, demanding role. Though their motives might almost be seen as opposites, both had put on a suit of lights.

At ten past midnight, there was a knock on Hugh's door. Blinking, he opened it. Jeff was standing in the corridor with tears in his eyes.

'He's gone,' was all he said.

Hugh felt the urge to make a comforting gesture, put his hand on the young man's arm, but held back. 'That's terrible,' he said.

Jeff nodded and turned towards his own room.

'I'm very sorry. I'll tell the others.'

Jeff gave no sign that he'd heard. Hugh tried Gary's door, and then Miranda's. No reaction from either. Perhaps, like him, they'd wanted to get away from the place. Better leave a note. Hard to break the awful news this way. He agonised for a few moments about the form of words and then wrote, 'Poor Frank died before midnight. Hugh.'

At four o'clock he was still awake. For the first time in several weeks he felt frightened. His heartbeat seemed faster than usual. Taking deep breaths helped, but still, as the hours went by, panic seemed close to the surface. Perhaps he'd overdone it. He'd told Scoular about the trip and the surgeon had said it should be fine as long as he got plenty of exercise and avoided stress. Was this stress? Hugh supposed it was. He wished he was back at home. He wished he could ring Tilly, or Sam, or Siobhan. He wished Gary or Miranda would come in and talk. Above all, he wished Frank had pulled through. How quick it is when it comes, he thought. A cliché all right, but very shocking in its truth. One second Frank had touched his life's big moment, and the next it was all a red stain in the sand. Finished. Ended. Easy to say it's what Frank would have wanted, but who knew? Of course Frank didn't want to spill his guts in La Linea. It was all so bloody sad.

After Hugh had taken a couple of pills, grudging sleep came. And with it, the thing he'd seen approaching, and had been dreading.

The principal figure from the earlier dreams is now mounted on a black horse, in armour, a heavy broadsword, glistening red from tip to hilt, held high. The roars of his men and the screams of the dying. The gates of the walled city yield to thunderous battering rams. An old man defies him with a long stick of ash and the mounted warrior cuts off his hand at the wrist.

The pigs squeal and run blind. The city is taken. An example is made of six of the enemy. Their eviscerated carcasses are hauled on hurdles around the walls. When the warrior is helped off with his armour by two boys in crested surcoats, there is a deep, oozing wound in his lower belly. His strength retreating like the enemy, he falls.

The hospital has cots along both walls, with fresh linen and red coverlets. At one end is a large painted wooden statue of the Virgin. Women in black habits and starched white head-pieces lean over the wasted bodies of the sick. A supplicant wearing a mitre kneels at the bedside. The wounded warrior closes his eyes and, with a small, weary gesture, dismisses him.

The sky is greyer now. The building, gaunt and magnificent, reaches to heaven. The former warrior, now recovered, clothed in a white shift, lies prostrate on the stone floor, cruciform, illuminated by a single tall candle.

When he rises, he is transformed. His outer garment is of black silk. There are rubies in his silk slippers. Around him, his people bow in deference, though there are some whose eyes belie the tribute. Men of great power and influence watch for signs of weakness. A figure in purple gestures to a boy to open a bulky leatherbound volume at random. The boy walks to the lectern, laying bare two illustrated pages. The purple-clad figure intones: ' "Let no fruit grow on thee henceforth for ever." And presently the fig tree withered away.' The hundreds of onlookers, in their finery, cannot disguise their horror.

There follows a feast. The former warrior and his principal guests are served by youths. The crossbearer reads from a text. The table is splendid with decorations of fruit and flowers, and glazed heads of slaughtered beasts. Course after course is borne in: wild boar, venison, pheasants, chickens. The object of all eyes, the man of war become man of peace, who with his familiar stammer tells his neighbour, dressed in the utmost luxury, that his doctor has forbidden him to drink water, takes modest quantities of red wine. The others have no such inhibitions. The gathering appears to be joyous. There is laughter and loud, affable talk.

But even when the minstrels sing, unaccompanied, the cold words of the earlier text resound like an executioner's summons. 'And presently the fig tree withered away . . .'

Chapter Four

It was a wet Friday morning. Rain on water, Kate thought, was somehow sadder than rain on land; water meeting itself in a grey continuum. She'd telephoned the police minutes after she'd arrived at the gallery. The first sign of trouble had been the forced lock of the outer door. And then, in the small office, the filing cabinet open, the cash box gaping, though it had only contained stamps, and the desk drawer splintered. What could they have imagined they'd find? The Crick Gallery wasn't a cash business, neither did it have anything to hide. For a burglar it must rate as the least glittering prize in Cambridge. They hadn't even taken a picture, though at these prices that too would have been a bizarre motive. The only things missing, as far as Kate could see, were her personal address book, which she used for writing private letters when business was slow, and her spare set of house keys.

Her first thought was Taylor, or whatever his real name was. Now, since Hester's revelation, she didn't even know what to call him; this man who'd come into her life uninvited, unwanted, invasive. What the hell was he playing at? All that rubbish about Jesus, reading history, fencing . . . all lies. But why? What was the point? Had it been just a pathetic attempt to impress her? Surely he must have realised how easy it was to check his story – though in fact, if it hadn't been for Hester, Kate might never have found out; or at least not for a while. And if you wanted to change your name, why pick a dead man's? That was so sick. That was what frightened Kate more than anything. He could have adopted any pseudonym he wanted, but his choice meant he must somehow have known about the real Taylor's violent death. Could he have read about it in the local paper, maybe? Even if he did, it was still a disgusting idea.

Whatever his twisted reasons, he'd changed everything. Since Hester's call, Kate had become obsessive about her growing doubts and fears. She found herself putting out the lights in her sitting room two or three times a night while she drew back a curtain to check on the street below. Walking to work down Hertford Street, or coming back home in the evening, she'd look over her shoulder if there was the slightest suspicion of other footsteps. Most ridiculous of all, when she picked up her mail from the hall floor she did it with her back to the door for fear of her eyes meeting his through the letter-box. She'd tried the mobile number Hester had gleaned several times, without success, and had decided against leaving any message.

And now this: her sanctuary violated. Her small, tranquil, ordered world entered with insulting ease, as though it were no more private than a telephone box.

Furtive and silent, he'd made his way along the river at night, like a rat, and stood in this room, touching her things, trying to get close to her. That meant she wasn't safe anywhere, and neither were her belongings. He had the keys to her flat, for God's sake. She must contact her landlord and get the lock changed straight away. The thought of waking in her bed to find Taylor standing in the shadows, slight and menacing, gave her goose-pimples of apprehension. And the address book. That gave him access to the heart of her life. Friends, family, godchildren . . . he'd know where to find them all. There was nothing to stop him contacting them, threatening them, hurting them, even.

But why her? Even if, God forbid, he'd been attracted to her when they'd met in the bookshop, surely by now he'd got the message. She'd been cold to the point of downright rudeness, and Hester even more so. Maybe this was his way of punishing her then, in which case what could she do to make him stop? The frightening thing was that, for the moment, unless the police could deal with him, he held all the cards.

The call Kate dreaded most was the one to Roger Crick. She sometimes got the feeling that, given a respectable reason for closing the gallery, something other than outright failure, he would, with gratitude. He would make much in the press of the sacrifices he'd made for Art, and how it filled him with anguish to surrender the thing he loved, but he would sell it without a real qualm. If that happened, Kate had fantasised about buying it. What was it they called it? A workers' buy-out. Get together a few friends and go for it. But she knew that the promises of support made over the third glass of wine didn't count for much at the bank. Fat chance. No, for the time being anyway, until she won the lottery, she needed to keep Roger buoyant. The important thing was to stress that he'd lost nothing except a couple of locks and a cashbox. And, if they handled the publicity right, it couldn't do them any harm. Quite the reverse, in fact. It would be a free plug, would make them look plucky and wronged. Milk it for all it was worth. They'd announce a sale at the same time. 'Why steal it when we're giving it away?' she could hear herself telling the ads editor. She was pleased with that. Hester was always saying she needed to be more positive, and now was as good a time as any.

To Kate's relief, Roger saw it that way too. By the morning post he'd had a tax rebate, as it happened, and was feeling smug. He managed to make it sound as though he'd somehow beaten the system by his own brilliance. He liked her idea of the sale, saying what an extraordinary coincidence because he'd been thinking along the very same lines himself. He also said he'd tell the press because she knew what these boys were like, they were bound to want to hear it from the horse's mouth. But would Kate handle the insurance? She was so very good at that sort of thing. Within five minutes, therefore, Kate saw her boss steal all the fun and leave her with the washing-up. But that was fine. That was the perfect outcome. Roger had been distracted from the darker option. Her strategy had worked.

The younger of the two detectives who responded to her call, Spaull, the one with the volcanic boil on his neck, accepted her offer of a cup of coffee. The elder, Corcoran, declined. 'Caffeine gets me over-excited,' he explained.

The thought of a policeman getting over-excited, or even being ironic about it, made Kate rather warm to him.

'And you wouldn't want him getting over-excited,' Spaull said.

'No indeed,' confirmed Corcoran, his eyes taking in the pictures on the office walls, including the pair acquired from Gilbert. 'You keen on Chagall at all?'

Startled, Kate had to think for a moment. 'Erm . . . yes. Yes, I am.'

'Shag all,' Spaull said.

Corcoran raised an eyebrow. 'Only these put me in mind of him a bit.'

Kate was delighted. 'Just what I thought. They're lovely, aren't they? You must know Gilbert?'

'Oh, yes, we know Gilbert all right,' Corcoran said.

'Nutcase,' Spaull supplied.

Corcoran swivelled his eyes enough in his partner's direction to signify that his contribution was unhelpful. 'Same dreamy out-of-body type approach, isn't it? Very nice.'

'You're obviously a connoisseur,' Kate said.

Spaull froze an incipient smirk.

'You must come to our next private view,' Kate went on, and knew the moment she said it that Corcoran was made for higher things.

He took a cursory look through the office door at the pale watercolours lining the hessian-covered gallery walls. 'It's finding the time,' he said, with a kind smile.

Kate liked him even more.

'A plod's work is never done,' Spaull added.

Forbearance under considerable strain was still the keystone of Corcoran's expression. 'Now, then, exactly what have these villains privatised?' he said.

Kate told him about the address book and keys. Having warmed to Corcoran, she longed to go on and mention Martin Taylor, but thought it better to wait until the theft had been dealt with. While Corcoran took notes, another member of the team, sullen and sweaty, arrived to dust for fingerprints, but found nothing. Corcoran was pleased to hear Kate had already contacted the locksmith, and then, as if reading her earlier thought, he put her on the spot.

'Had anybody in lately that seemed out of the ordinary at all? Maybe get the feeling they weren't here just to look at the paintings?'

Deciding to risk Spaull's ridicule, Kate said, 'Well, yes, there is this man . . . Martin Taylor, he called himself . . .' She went on to give a brief account, including a description. 'The thing is,' she continued, 'it's completely shattered my peace of mind. I've just got no idea why he's picked on me, why he's using a dead man's name, why he's done this.'

'We don't know that yet,' Corcoran said.

'OK, we don't know it but it seems very likely, doesn't it? Why would anyone else take a risk like that for an address book?'

'Why would he, come to that?' Spaull said.

'Well, I know,' Kate said. 'That's what I've been wondering. Maybe it's a power thing; knowing he's got something that's important to me. It just worries me that he'll use it somehow . . .'

'Now, hold your horses a minute,' Corcoran said. 'I know you're upset but let's take this a step at a time. It could be kids, you know. They find there's no cash to speak of so they nick the keys and the address book for devilment. I'm not saying it was but we can't rule it out. So don't go getting yourself in a state. Leave it with us.' As he spoke Corcoran wrote down a number, tore it out of his notebook, and handed it to her. 'If you think of anything else, anything at all, give me a bell.' As if it were a casual afterthought, he added: 'Oh, and if chummy gets in touch at all, likewise.' He mimed holding a telephone to his ear.

As they left, Spaull said, 'Thanks for the coffee. Gold Blend, was it, by the way?'

'I honestly can't remember,' Kate said.

'I think you'll find it was,' Spaull said, with a small wink. 'I'm a bit of a connoisseur.'

Kate saw them to the door then went back to the office. The events of the morning had driven the weekend out of her mind. On a slim majority of two to nil, Hester's idea of an alternative break, recycling in Etruria, had been rejected in favour of taking the bikes and staying a night in Southwold. A friend of Kate's would look after the gallery on the Saturday. She and Hester had arranged to leave work at four thirty, and start for the coast at five. It meant plunging into the thick of the rush-hour, but neither could get away earlier. Now, if the plan was going to work, Kate would have to get moving. The locksmith had promised he'd have both premises done by three, and at lunchtime she'd buy a new cash box. By then there'd also be an early edition of the *Cambridge Evening News*, no doubt with Roger splashed all over the front page.

At twenty-five past five Kate and Hester were stuck in a sluggish shoal of escapees, their bikes perched on a frame clipped to the back of the car. Hester had bought it for seven pounds at a car-boot sale. The man had said you could fix it in two minutes flat. The man had lied. After the first fumbling attempt, both bikes had fallen backwards at the exact moment the car edged forward. Half an hour later, at the cost of two split fingernails and all composure, the machines had been persuaded to lodge.

Even in a jam, watching nosepickers and head-bangers and oglers and snogging couples, it felt great to be getting out of town, Kate thought. Though it was unenclosed, except by a virtual swamp, Cambridge could make you feel locked in. Unlike Oxford, which seemed to embrace outside influence, it was a sophisticated stockade. Perfect that it had been Cromwellian rather than Royalist, a stern face with warts rather than one rouged with indulgence. They still kept Cromwell's head buried at one of the colleges. Grisly household god. Typical too that the new industries, making the town prosperous, Silicon Fen, were mostly little companies in glass boxes staring at their own thought processes.

At last, released from the worst of the traffic, Kate and

Hester began to feel they were on their way. Hester started on a wild improvisation about her boss; a man, she said, with such a bad case of halitosis that one day he'd opened a window and a choking pigeon had plummeted to earth. There'd been nothing like him since Bertrand Russell, she said, who only had to exhale in London to asphyxiate a man in New York. Or woman come to that. Poor Ottoline Morrell. She must have worn a gas mask to kiss him. 'He's seriously brown,' she went on. 'Well, no, he's white, whiter than white, actually, but everything he's got on is brown. With leather patches. He's probably got little leather patches on his knickers. And he wears one of those milky-coffee type shortie coats. Apart from brown he is a man totally devoid of colour. Even the flowers in his garden are brown. Brown tulips, brown roses and, most remarkably of all, brown passion flowers.'

Kate laughed. 'Why don't you chuck it, then?'

'Because I love books. I am a slave to literature. I have devoted my life to the printed word. To me those little symbols covering a page are meat and drink. I devour them for nourishment.' She paused. 'Besides, what else can I do? Put on a micro-mini and serve at the Still and Sugarloaf? Hang on! What a great idea!'

Though Kate enjoyed Hester's distraction, it didn't postpone for long her preoccupation with Taylor and the events of the morning. 'It scares me, Hest,' she said. 'It just feels as though nowhere's safe.'

'This is,' Hester reassured her. 'There's no way anyone can follow you here, even if he wanted to. Which he doesn't. You're letting this thing get to you. He's just a lonely creep who wants – wanted – to get into your knickers. He probably had absolutely nothing to do with the robbery.'

'I don't know. Maybe.'

'No. Not maybe. Definitely. And if you mention him again this weekend I shall be forced to administer a very, very severe punishment. Do you hear me?'

Kate smiled and nodded.

At the turn-off from the A12, green and inviting, the country changed, and with it the pace. The anxieties of the week dispersed into the high hedgerows.

'I'm going to eat everything,' Hester said. 'Four courses, the menu, and then the waiter. Save the best till last.'

'What if he's old and bony?'

'We'll use him for stock and send for another.'

The lights of the ivy-covered Swan, standard-bearer of a vanished England, promised comfort and security. As they drove through the arch and into the car park, they felt alert with anticipation.

From the room they shared at the end of the corridor, they could see the lighthouse and the tantalising shine of the sea. Hester wanted to inspect everything, all at once; the bathroom, the wardrobe, the book about a French wine-growing village left on the table under the window. After supper, she said, they'd have their first walk, breathe in the ozone, get a feel of stringy old George Orwell loping along the front. When Kate asked her what he'd got to do with it, Hester explained that he'd come here for his holidays. And somehow he and the place went together. It wasn't a town for Evelyn

Waugh: it was lean, thoughtful, reserved. The excesses of Dickens' Yarmouth hadn't been allowed here. The upright white of the lighthouse, she said, was like a benign but admonitory finger.

The dining room, though full, was hushed. Diners turned to look at them as they walked in, smiling. Hester said a discreet but enthusiastic hello to a couple of tables before realising from their embarrassed response that, though not unfriendly, they weren't yet ready for the direct approach. Despite Tony Blair and the European Union, that would take several more generations. The waiter, it turned out, wasn't a bony old man but a delightful young woman whose warmth won over Kate and Hester at once. They chose a bottle of medium-priced Australian chardonnay and toasted each other while they waited.

By nine thirty, the tide was going out in the dining room. Only three other tables were left as they treated themselves to a last glass of Beaumes de Venise.

'I'm thirty-two,' Hester said, looking at a young couple holding hands in the corner.

'What's brought this on?' Kate said.

'I'm thirty-two and I haven't got a baby.'

'You're the one who keeps saying it's never too late.'

'I know. But I'm also the one who said I'd have three by the time I was thirty. I want one. Now.'

'She's taken the menu away.'

'What did you want to be when you were little?'

'The usual. Nurse, nun for a bit, rock singer.'

'I wanted to be an astronomer. I did honest. It was so much nicer looking up than down. Patrick Moore was my hero. I wanted him for my dad . . . Well, I'd have settled for anybody, really.'

'Do you think you'll ever . . . you know, feel like finding him?'

'My dad? You're joking. Who wants to find a rattle-snake?' She paused for a moment. 'Course I feel like finding him. Think about him every day. Until I was nine, when he buggered off, I thought he was the loveliest thing in the world. I'd have thrown myself in the Clyde if he'd asked me to. The day he didn't come back from work, and my mum said he wasn't going to, ever, I wanted to curl up and die. I hated him with all my heart. I went into my parents' bedroom. There was a cheap black comb of his on the dressing-table. You could still smell his hair on it. I took it back to my room and wrapped it in tissue paper. A bit of you still wants to believe he loved you really. Even though he obvi-ously bloody didn't.' She drained her glass. 'Let's have another.'

'Is that a good idea?'

'No. Let's get some air.' As they left the dining room, Hester linked her arm in Kate's. 'You're so wise, that's what I love about you,' she said. 'Just like a wizened old soothsayer.'

They walked past lively pubs to the rail overlooking the beach huts and the sea. For the first time since the journey, Kate thought again about the burglary. At this very moment Taylor – there was nothing else she could call him – might be turning the pages of her address book, with a voyeur's fantasies; maybe even dialling numbers then hanging up. Even if the book were recovered, it was knowledge she could never retrieve from him. Her intimacies were soiled. There were also addresses she couldn't remember. If those people didn't get in touch, she might lose contact for good.

Back in the room Hester, who'd done all the driving, fell asleep after a few minutes' drowsy conversation. An early start, they'd decided, and then down to the creek on the bikes and across the little bridge to Walberswick. Kate read for a while. Margaret Atwood's *Alias Grace*. At first she'd found it creepy but now she was settling in. After twenty minutes she closed the book and reached to switch off the bedside light. It was warm. Still unrelaxed, she got up to open the side window. It looked out over the car park and, beyond, a square compound of one-storey buildings which she supposed was some sort of annexe. Each unit had a small verandah. She was about to turn back into the room when a slight movement caught her eye. In the far right-hand corner a figure wearing a white shirt and dark trousers had detached itself from the shadows, and was now looking in the direction of the hotel. As she watched, breath held, the figure raised right hand to mouth. Was he smoking, maybe? Taylor didn't, as far as she knew. And then the telephone rang. Could that be him? Was that what he was holding to his mouth? She let go of the curtain and rushed to the bedside table. By now Hester, groaning, was feeling for the light switch. Kate picked up the receiver, and sat on her bed.

'Hello? Hello?'

Silence, not even breathing.

'Hello? Look, whatever your name—'

Click. A different silence.

'Hello? Hello?' Kate slammed down the receiver.

'Kate?' Hester sounded fuddled.

'What?'

'What's going on?'

'Good question.' Kate got up and went back to the window.

'What are you doing?' At last Hester made contact with the switch.

'Put it off!'

'Why?'

'Just put it off, will you?'

Darkness again.

'What the hell's going on?' Hester said.

Kate eased back the curtain. 'He's out there.'

'Who's bloody out there?'

'Who do you think?'

Hester groaned. 'Oh, Christ, not that again. What makes you think . . .?'

'I saw him. Over by the annexe, beyond the car park. And that was him on the phone.'

'What did he say?'

'Nothing. But it was him. He had his mobile.'

Hester sat up. 'Now, look, this is getting beyond a joke. You see something half a mile away in the pitch dark and you hear nothing on the phone and you reckon it's him? That's what we call paranoia. What are you looking at now?'

'The annexe. It's not pitch dark, there's a moon.'

'And?'

'He's obviously realised I'm watching him. That's why he rang.'

'So what's he doing? Cartwheels, is he, stark bollock naked on the grass?'

'He's gone.' Kate let the curtain drop.

'Surprise, surprise.' Hester switched on the light again, picked up the receiver, and tapped four digits.

'Who are you ringing?'

'One-four-seven-one.' Hester paused. 'Can't do it on this one.' She tapped again, this time a single number. Another pause. 'Night porter must have gone for a pee. Did you bring Taylor's mobile number with you?'

'Left it in Cambridge. Stupidly. I didn't want anything of his near me.'

'Terrific. Well, that's it, then. Come back to bed, take two paracetamol, and for God's sake get a grip, woman. You're getting yourself into a ridiculous state over nothing.'

When she'd taken the pills and put out the light, Kate tried hard to think of other things but her mind refused to be sidetracked. She hadn't noticed a red car when they arrived, but that could mean Taylor had come some other way. Anyway, if you were following someone, you'd make sure you weren't easy to spot. In any case, the car would only be here if he was staying at the hotel. He might have got himself a room at a guest-house, and just come over to prowl. And there was nothing she could do about it. The sympathetic detective, Corcoran, had said ring him if Taylor turned up. She'd try him in the morning, though she supposed he had Saturdays off. She imagined him getting an early start for the Tate and, released from his tiresome side-kick, Spaull, spending the day in quiet reverence.

Meanwhile maybe, just maybe, Hester had been right. Perhaps it was paranoia. After all, there had been nothing to stop Taylor getting right into the hotel itself if that was what he wanted. If he'd really been up to no good there were any number of places where he could have hidden until everyone was asleep. Was the door of the room locked? Kate got up to check. Hester stirred and turned over. Yes, it was firm, but the security chain was hanging loose. Kate placed its head in the slot. She was tempted to take another look through the side window, but couldn't decide for a moment whether she was better off not knowing. Unable to restrain her curiosity, she took the edge of the curtain between index finger and thumb again and moved it just enough to expose a sliver of window. The moon was brighter now. Starting at the edge of the car park, she forced herself to make a steady 180-degree sweep. Nothing. The verandahs were clear. The shadows were straight-edged. The lighthouse looked both solid and ethereal. She found it reassuring. A guardian. She let the curtain rejoin its other half.

When she woke up, at quarter to eight, Hester's bed was empty. Kate's first reaction was alarm. Funny Hester hadn't woken her or left a note. Suppose something had happened to her? Suppose she'd gone looking for Taylor, in spite of her reassurances, and been pounced on as she was coming round a corner, gagged and . . .? No, hang on. Get a grip, she'd said, and she was right. Do the normal things, think positive, assume the best.

The sun was bright behind the curtains overlooking the sea. Almost without thinking, as though it was part of a daily ritual, Kate went to the side window again. First, and above all, she needed confirmation. A woman and her small daughter were walking hand in hand towards the hotel. The curtains in the annexe were still drawn and there were no other signs of activity. Preferring to leave these curtains closed too, Kate went to the bathroom. By the time she'd had a shower Hester would be back from wherever she'd been and they would go down together for breakfast. It was a perfect day for the ride along the coast.

Kate looked at herself in the mirror as she brushed her teeth. She saw a face to which she had become reconciled. The years of pining for prettiness were past. She'd seen too many pretty lives fall apart. Neither did she feel plain. There was an openness about her, a frankness, that wasn't unpleasing. Her top lip wasn't as full as she'd like, and freckles weren't the magazine ideal, but her auburn hair and her eyes were good. Brown, understanding eyes. Hester called them 'trust me, I'm not pushy' eyes. And her body was in decent shape. She'd always wanted larger breasts. Maybe after a baby. A baby!

Like Hester she was beginning to wonder if that would ever happen. Down at the sea last night Hester had said that if the worst came to the worst she'd pay a bloke to do it and then get lost. The ideal candidate would be a good-looking tourist on his last day in England, before he went back to . . . she couldn't think of anywhere far enough. Anchorage, say. Kate smiled at the memory.

The shower was hot. She stood aside and readjusted the control. Better. She resettled under the flow, reaching out for the shampoo. As her hands were raised above her head there was a sudden sharp rapping on the bathroom door. Paralysed in her improbable pose, Kate held her breath. God, what if that lunatic had somehow got into her room? Dressed up as a waiter and pretended to be Room Service. No, nonsense. Even if he had a spare key he couldn't have undone the chain. Unless he'd reached round and somehow eased it out of the slot. And then she remembered that the chain wasn't on. Hester would have disconnected it when she went out. Best to stay still. Best to do nothing and wait. For no good reason, Kate lowered her arms and covered herself. She felt her heartbeat must be audible in the car park. There was another rapping. A tentative foot first, she started to ease her body past the shower curtain. If she could reach the door without a sound, she might be able to look through the keyhole. With elaborate caution she took a bath towel from the rail and wrapped it round herself. Braving the last few steps, she withdrew the key and bent to look.

'Yoo hoo!' a familiar voice said. 'Get a move on. It's practically midday.'

Kate felt the panic subside like a cured migraine. 'You stupid woman,' she said, as she opened the door.

'Oh, thanks.'

'You frightened me, hammering like that.'

'Aaaah! Diddums!'

'Go away. I'll be down in a minute.'

In the dining room, the couple who had held hands

the night before came in late, looking sheepish. They negotiated the short route to their corner table heads down, as though it were a minefield, requiring undeviating concentration.

'Disgusting I call it,' Hester said. 'Sex, sex, sex. What's wrong with trainspotting, for heaven's sake? Or – or making swiss rolls?'

'Swiss rolls probably are sex in Switzerland.'

'True!' Hester was delighted by the idea. 'And probably Eccles cakes are sex in Eccles. Currant affairs.'

She went on to tell Kate that she'd woken at six and couldn't bear not to be up. She'd walked in the opposite direction to the one they were taking later, so she wouldn't spoil it. That way, she said, you come to the other Southwold, which was like part of a different, more downmarket resort. A sort of Deep Southwold, where deprived people had to make do with simpler pleasures. There was an ice-cream parlour and a car park, then a scrubby bit of hinterland behind the beach. She'd sat there for a long time watching fishermen, who'd been up all night. Each had a little arched green tent behind him, and a kettle on a Primus. They didn't seem to catch anything. They were just playing housey, with no bills to pay and no one else's needs to satisfy. These were probably the happiest moments of their lives, because they couldn't be shared. So why, she wondered, did men even pretend they wanted to share, when it was quite clear they didn't have the talent for it?

She warmed to the theme. 'You mark my words, young lady,' she said. 'One day soon men and women will abandon all pretence. They'll just couple, like re-fuelling aircraft, and go their separate ways. Pick each other on the Internet – "Colour of eyes, favourite film, annual income, do you like archery?" and book into one of these coupling-type places, like Centre Point – that's nice and phallic. And they'll go there and do the business, twenty quid for half an hour, and then they'll catch the four fifteen to Exeter and the Pullman to Aberdeen. Maybe an e-mail at Christmas, and bingo! Sorted. That way you can have several interesting kids by different blokes. Like that old shagger in Byron's day, Lady Oxford. Lady Oxford's Miscellany, they called her lot.'

'Can't wait,' Kate said.

As Hester poured the coffee, Kate leafed through the colour supplement she'd picked up at Reception. Five pages in the middle were gory with pictures of some English bullfighter who hadn't got out of the way in time. One horrific sequence, taken with a motor-drive, showed him leaning forward with a slim, curved sword in his right hand. Held low in his left was a piece of red cloth. It was like following an animated strip. As her eyes travelled across, the sword sank deeper and the bull's head rose until its right horn seemed to be half-buried in the bullfighter's body. The two must have fallen more or less together, because in the last grim tableau they were almost indistinguishable from each other. The piece was headed 'Death in the Afternoon'.

For much of the meal, Kate's fears about Taylor hovered unspoken. To her surprise, it was Hester who raised them.

'What can we do to make you happy?' she said, as she munched her toast. 'As long as it doesn't take more than five minutes of this fantastic morning. We can't exactly do a house-to-house search.'

'I know, Hest, I know I'm a pain. But at least I think I should try and contact the policeman who came to the gallery. And see if anybody remembers whoever it was who called last night. Then I'll shut up, promise.'

'He'll be off duty now, the night porter. Be well choked if you wake him up.'

Nevertheless, after breakfast, Kate asked for his number at the desk and was allowed to use the telephone. Whether Hester was right, or the night porter had gone elsewhere before crashing out, there was no reply. Kate also drew a blank when she rang Parkside police station in Cambridge. No, Corcoran was not on duty, and no, they couldn't give her his home number. Try again Monday morning.

'It's God telling you to get on your bike,' Hester said.

Bowling along the quiet road to the creek, they felt released and exhilarated. At the far end there were wooden beach houses that reminded Kate of Derek Jarman's cottage near a power station in Essex. In that barren landscape he had made a garden without frills, of stones and driftwood and no-nonsense plants. She admired that. It had said more about him than a book or a film. Beyond the houses, a little blue yacht was tacking its way to the sea.

At the bridge over the creek they stopped and looked back towards the town. In the foreground the tall grasses bent to the breeze with lazy grace. The lighthouse, sturdy and angelic, dominated the gentle skyline. Standing here it was hard to imagine ugliness. The view seemed a confirmation of the opposite. Tranquil and unchanging, it soothed and reassured. Kate forced herself not to blink, letting the harmony sink in deep so that she would never lose sight of it. As perfect in its way as the Grand Canal, it would become a greener, more absorbed memory than a photograph. But after a few moments her mind superimposed on the scene an image of the bullfighter she'd read about, locked with the dead animal on the sand. A group in what looked like fancy dress had watched without helping. The grasses became the waving arms of the crowd, though whether it was a cruel celebration or an obscure gesture of mourning she couldn't decide. Whatever it was, the instant had been darkened by it.

By the time they got back to the Swan that afternoon, after lunch in an Aldeburgh pub, their legs were aching and their arms and faces felt gorged with sun. Strapping the bikes back on to the car was easier than it had been at home, though still not the work of a moment. They left the doors open and sat for a few minutes, hoarding the warmth, remembering the uncomplicated pleasure of the ride, reluctant to break the spell. With its indistinct summer sounds, this seemed a place where childhood could be revisited. Or, in Kate's case, reinvented. Holidays with her ailing father and anxious mother had been restrained affairs. Alderney, where it rained for five days and a man had a fit in a pub doorway. Morecambe, where, instead of being on the limitless beach, they had sat on deckchairs and listened to an orchestra, led by a man called Tony. The tunes were so old her sister Jo said they must have been dug up with the Dead Sea Scrolls. Kate had been impressed that Jo, who was four years older, had even heard of the Dead Sea Scrolls.

'What are you thinking about? Not that creep again?' Hester said.

Kate shook her head. 'Holidays when we were kids . . . Oh, bum. I forgot to hand the key in.'

She crossed the car park and went through the back door to Reception. The two young women behind the counter were looking anxious as they listened to the manager and another man. At once Kate could see something was wrong. As she drew nearer, the group became more uneasy, as though they wanted to hide something. But they were looking in her direction, so she felt the silence needed breaking.

'Forgot my key,' she said, smiling.

The young woman who'd dealt with her bill tried to smile back but was less than convincing.

'Is something the matter?' Kate said, putting her key on the counter.

Realising that a denial would sound lame, the manager said, 'Bit of bad news, I'm afraid.'

The others looked down, leaving it to him.

'A local boy, Danny Ryan . . . they've found his body, up by the water tower.'

Kate didn't know what to say. A body, on that beautiful day, in that beautiful place. It didn't seem real. 'Oh, God,' she said, feeling nauseous and inadequate. 'Was he . . .?'

'They don't know,' the manager said. 'They don't know anything yet.'

Should she leave or should she stay? How did you end such a devastating conversation without seeming abrupt and insensitive?

The manager must have sensed her dilemma. 'Heading back home?'

'Er, yes. Yes, we were.'

'Hope you've enjoyed your stay.'

'Very much. It's been brilliant.'

'Good. We'll look forward to seeing you again. I'm only sorry you had to . . .' Even he had run out of platitudes.

'Thank you. Goodbye.' Grateful for the chance to leave, Kate went back the way she'd come. As she reached the car park and saw the annexe ahead, the night before was sharp again. The watcher on the edge of the shadows. Damn! She'd meant to check the register. See if there was a name that rang a bell. But she couldn't go back now, not after what she'd been told. In any case, she supposed killers didn't advertise themselves. If he was a killer. If he was *the* killer. If, if, if, . . . Oh, God. In any case they hadn't said it was murder, not in so many words. But that was what had been written on their faces. That poor boy. On a warm night, maybe only a few hundred yards from where he lived. Moments ago she'd felt more carefree than she had for weeks. Now it was as though a happy child on the beach had been swept out to sea.

'I thought you'd eloped,' Hester said, when she got back to the car.

Kate tried to concentrate on doing up her seat-belt but there was no strength in her arms. On the edge of tears, she put her hands in her lap and lowered her head. 'Something horrible's happened,' she said.

Chapter Five

A summer night. Thirteen men, filthy, undernourished, are ushered into a bare room. They stand, unsure. After some while the door opens to admit the principal figure in the dreams, escorted by two monks. Though not poor, he wears a tunic made of coarse goats' hair, which leaves his skin reddened around the neck. With a small gesture he dismisses his attendants, one of whom leaves a wooden bowl full of water on the floor. He kneels and, without words, bids the thirteen step forward, one by one. As they do so with much hesitation, the dark, kneeling man washes their feet.

Time has passed. A terrified woman watches as her father is stabbed by a priest. She sees the knife in the priest's hand. Its blade, broad at the hilt, narrows to a perfect point. Her father's mouth is flecked with foam. His blood finds the hollows in the flagstones. The priest turns to her. She cannot move. Slipping the knife under his belt, next to the rosary with the large wooden beads, he comes towards her. There is no expression in his eyes, but she knows he means her harm. He seems to grow taller as he advances, until he looms like a tower. His soft white hand is on the neck of her woollen dress. It is too well woven to tear. She wakes from her trance and tries to reach his eyes, but he pushes her hard and she falls, hitting her head on the floor. As she looks up, she sees another figure beside the first. This is the kneeling man transformed; the goats' hair tunic no longer visible, he now appears in rich robes. The frightened woman wants to cry out, but her voice will not obey. She wants to cry out her horror at what she now under- stands. For the dark figure in rich robes does not seek to restrain the priest, but to aid and protect him.

Now there are skylarks. The two horses are restless. Their hoofs trample the yellow flowers in the long grass. Their riders, one of whom is the erstwhile protector of the violent priest, tug at their reins to control them. This distracts the men from what is a clear disagreement. The horses will not stand. They shy away from each other and threaten to rear up. The angrier and more powerful rider, confronting his stammering adversary, beckons to a henchman. The men dismount while new, more docile horses are led forward. This does nothing, however, to make the meeting more amicable. The one is vengeful, the dark man unbending. At length the vengeful one, his patience exhausted, dismisses the obdurate party who, inclining his head, turns his horse and rides away.

'You've caught the sun.' Hugh's former wife, Tilly, leaned back a little to assess the full effect. 'Suits you.'

Hugh was about to make the appropriate noises when a loud woman's voice at the next table said, 'He's so bloody boring. Sooooo boring. Keeps grinding on about "grammar" for God's sake. "But have we got the grammar right?" Do me a favour. It's only a bloody quiz show. "Grammar!" Most of our punters think that's who's shagging your grandad. Assuming they think at all. It's pathetic. They ponce around in these crap clothes, bursting out of their bloody blazers, seven-hour lunches at the Ivy, buggering off to MIP. MIP! Sounds like something out of a French cartoon. Farting around on yachts all day. Pissed every night. And then fly back club, caning the old G and T, lash together another crap quiz, where the hardest question is "What colour's an orange?" or some balls, and they talk about "grammar"!'

Hugh smiled. 'Thank you,' he said. He'd suggested a coffee at Pâtisserie Valerie in Old Compton Street because he'd wanted to tell Tilly about the dreams, but the minute he'd come in he knew that wouldn't be possible. This was a place better suited to public statements than intimate conversations. They didn't have to be as obvious as the one they'd just overheard. Often they were subtler, even silent, projections. The body language of a man in black, his arm draped along the back of his unshaven partner's chair, was eloquent. It seemed to Hugh that most tables were tableaux, presentations, semi-conscious, semi-not. It wasn't so much that they wanted to be judged, but they sure as hell didn't want to be ignored, though some went to elaborate lengths to camouflage the fact. In this almost competitive atmosphere, trading real concerns seemed inappropriate.

'I read your piece about the bullfighter chap. Funny name,' Tilly said.

'Frank.'

'Other name.'

'McGuffog. Frank McGuffog.'

'Mmmm. I thought it was rather good.'

'I'm rather glad.'

'No, you know . . . I hate it, needless to say, bull-fighting, but you made him seem . . .'

'Dead?'

'The opposite, in a funny sort of way. Sort of . . . I don't know . . . sympathetic. Mad and misguided, of course, but oddly sympathetic.'

'He was. I liked him.'

'It was a bit different from, you know, your usual stuff.'

'No spellos you mean?'

'No, you know, more thoughtful. About something. It was good. Are you going more that way?'

'Don't know. Maybe. Feel like a change, certainly.'

'Is that to do with the operation, do you think? Feeling a new man and all that?' Tilly's smile was warm and encouraging.

'Think it might be. Bound to make a difference, I suppose.'

'How's your other half?'

'Isn't that supposed to be my line?'

'Your donor.'

'She's . . . remarkable. Very, you know, strong. Good fun. She wants to meet you and your old man.'

'Does she now? Is she gorgeous?'

'Not gorgeous, no.'

'Well, that's all right, then. Come round for supper.'

'She wants to see a play. How many's he got on at the moment?'

'Just the one. Give me a date and we'll eat after.' Tilly took his hand between hers. 'I worry about you.'

'I'm OK. I'm fine.' At moments like this Hugh realised how much he missed her. Missed the warmth of her skin and the entire generosity of her; her certainty about what mattered. To be truthful he wasn't OK. Both in his life and his work he was floundering. It was as though, with the operation, he had shed some aspects of his old self, but was far from sure about his new one. Added to that, Frank's death in the ring had made him feel vulnerable all over again. For a few days afterwards he'd had the feeling that he was identifying with the half-ridiculous, half-sad figure. It was as though, in some way, he too was about to confront a looming threat. It made him feel uneasy, insecure. And the dreams, which were growing more intense and involving, compounded the effect. Hugh had woken from the last one, the frightened woman, the washing of the feet, still so immersed in the images that it had taken half an hour to control his sense of helpless witness to impending savagery. Tilly was perhaps the one human being alive capable of hearing all this without backing away. And yet, for the moment at any rate, he couldn't ask her for help.

'Sure?' she said.

'Sure,' he lied. 'How's Sam?'

Tilly let go of his hand. 'The boy done great. Assistant editor of the school rag no less.'

'It's in the genes. Whatsisname's. That husband of yours.'

'However, the bossy-boots mother of the editor has denied him a single mention, even though he wrote half the wretched paper.'

'I'll alert the NUJ. Picket the joint. It's an outrage.'

'No need. Sam's completely cool about it. And that is decidedly not in the genes.'

'He's my hero.'

'Well, as it happens you're a little bit his.'

This caught Hugh unprepared. 'Good Lord . . .' The words came out half swallowed.

Tilly rose to leave. 'Must go, Hugh.'

'Oh, right.'

Outside, on the busy pavement, Hugh felt a strong urge to kiss her lips. It was a need, almost. He didn't want her to go. He didn't want to be alone.

Tilly held out her arms and put her head on his chest as she hugged him. 'Take care of yourself,' she said.

Hugh held her tight. 'And you,' he said.

Before they parted, he looked in his diary and gave her a date for their evening with Siobhan. When Tilly left, making for Charing Cross Road, Hugh stood watching her for a moment. She must have known because, without turning, she raised her left hand in a small flutter of goodbye. He was about to wave back when he realised how futile it would be. When you lost a partner like that, he thought, nothing you won afterwards could make up for it.

Not that he was winning. He was treading water. More or less the same water he'd been treading for years. Before Papworth, in fact, he'd almost drowned in it. But the piece about Frank McGuffog had given him the sort of satisfaction he hadn't known since he started in journalism; since his first few bylines in the *Northwich Chronicle*. Waking up in the morning, feverish turning of the pages, and there it was, *Hugh Severin*, quite small, but bold black type. If someone had kept it, which they wouldn't, that bit of paper, with his name on it, might be around as long as Caxton's books. It was imperishable social history. The feeling didn't last long, however. By the time he'd reached the sports page the wet duvet of cynicism had reminded him that the entire publication was also an adequate substitute for lavatory paper. The writing on the wall.

As he walked towards Wardour Street he felt an unfamiliar surge of resolution. He'd go and see Dacre; tell him he wanted a crack at more in-depth features, with a travel connection. That seemed a sensible way to start. Maybe do interviews with explorers, or charity workers in the field, or Brits who'd settled in strange places. Like the man who'd tried to recruit a group of loonies for a commune God knows where. South America somewhere. Or see how Europeans were surviving the change-over in Hong Kong. Something with a bit of balls to it. He'd emphasise colour, of course. Fatal to frighten Dacre off by making it all sound pompous and worthy. Even if you were the first reporter to unearth Lord Lucan, living in a maisonette near Stoke, you'd still have to emphasise colour. Bite the bullet, Hugh decided. Find a telephone. Ring the man, get a taxi, and to hell with the expense.

'Bit worthy, isn't it?' Dacre said, when Hugh had outlined the scheme. 'Bit broadsheet.'

'Well, that's the challenge, isn't it? Give it loads of colour and make it not broadsheet. I mean the McGuffog piece, that wasn't broadsheet, was it? That was bullseye tabloid. Pardon the pun.'

'I like that, Huge. Bullseye tabloid. Wicked. No, fair dos, mate, that was quite tasty.' Dacre put both hands behind his head, revealing two new Rorschach puzzles, this time offset by pink. 'Quite tasty,' he repeated. 'Oh dear, oh dear.'

'What?' Hugh swivelled to see what he was looking at. The young secretary, or whoever she was, whom Dacre had found so distracting on his last visit, was once again passing his desk, this time wearing tight jeans and a T-shirt with the word SCALLYWAG in bold upper case on the chest.

'Scallywag,' Dacre muttered. 'Oh dear, oh dear.'

Hugh waited for more but none was forthcoming. 'So what do you think, Daks?'

Dacre began to scrabble among the unruly heap of papers on his desk. At last he came up with a glossy photograph that Hugh half recognised. It was the lean, weathered, unsmiling face of a man in his . . . what? Forties? A man whose eyes seemed to look beyond the camera to some far horizon. Hugh took the photograph with a slight questioning frown.

'Rupert Kent-Doodah,' Dacre said.

'Kent-Imison. I thought he looked familiar.'

'They still call them Rupert,' Dacre said, with a head-shake of wonder.

'Who?'

'Toffs. Kids. You'd have thought it would have gone out with the trenches.'

'Walked to the Pole in his slippers, didn't he, Kent-Imison? Something like that. Up the Nile in a tin bath.'

'Type thing. Dying breed. If they hadn't got him out with a chopper he'd have been a dead breed. Extinct.'

'So what's the scam then? Is he planning another trip?'

'No. We are.'

'Papua New Guinea? Lost City of Atlantis?'

'Birmingham.'

'Birmingham?'

'Birmingham.'

'That's what I thought you said.'

Dacre rooted among the debris on his desk again, pulling out a letter in red Biro. 'Punter saying it's harder finding your way to the middle of Brum than it is to get to the North Pole. Bingo. Rupert Kent-Doodah. We blindfold him, drop him at some Godawful spot on a B road, and he's got to find his way to the Bull Ring, or whatever they call it, without a map. Or a compass. Or a polar bear for R and R, on Saturday nights. Yeah?'

Hugh hoped his hesitation wouldn't prove fatal. 'Er . . . yes. Could be a laugh.'

'Take Gary. Get a few shots of old Roopie baby with his goggles on. Bivouac by the side of the strasse. Talking to a friendly native in sign language. Do Linguaphone do Brummie? Maybe a few huskies. 'S a natural. *Heart of Darkness*!' Dacre laughed, delighted with his own daring concept. 'If you can't get huskies, get a few corgis. Least HM'll read it.' Dacre chortled again.

At once Hugh regretted his misplaced bid for freedom. He wondered for a moment whether he should be true to his earlier resolution and turn the idea down. 'He'd never go for it, would he?' he said, playing for time.

'Dunno. Ask him.' Dacre took back the photograph and turned it over.

' "Northampton-based explorer Rupert Kent-Imison . . ." Don't say you don't get all the best gigs, Huge. And if Gary's taking that poncy Range Rover, tell him I'm clocking the mileage.'

To Hugh's surprise and disappointment, Kent-Imison accepted the challenge. Any slight initial hesitation had evaporated at the mention of a thousand pounds. Later, Hugh elaborated on the theme in the large sitting room of the explorer's Victorian semi-detached. The furniture consisted of three upright chairs on a bare wooden floor, and the handsome French windows looked out on a wilderness. Hugh reflected that the prospect must have made him feel at home in the same way that roses and York stone did for less adventurous souls. Kent-Imison offered Hugh and Gary beer, served in plastic beakers. Since the invitation had been so eager, both accepted. Eagerness was the keynote of Kent-Imison's driving force. Though he had no discernible sense of humour, he smiled a great deal, often using language that was still in short trousers. The more they talked about the Birmingham mission, the more he warmed to the idea, stressing that there must be no question of cheating.

And the more he warmed to the idea, the more Hugh wondered about him. He supposed Northampton was as good a place as any for a nomad to lay his head, but Kent-Imison never referred to any human being closer to him than former members of expeditions, some of whom, entombed in ice, were now beyond communication; even cold-calling. It was as though his whole life was a lonely trek towards some unachievable goal. His true pleasures appeared to be in the planning and the suffering. Hugh realised how different he must seem when he set out on one of these unthinkable journeys: fit and determined, eel-lean under layers of insulation, his version of Frank's suit of lights. Here, in this Spartan house, which was not a home, he was more like someone in a waiting room. There, in his element, he must be tough, decisive, resilient, obsessed. His target might seem pointless to outsiders, but he was prepared to risk his precious life for it. That, at least, was something you had to admire. But how to tell the story of his most fatuous adventure, the search for Dacre's *Heart of Darkness*, without seeming to send him up?

When they'd been talking for half an hour, while Gary lit the room and started taking pictures, there was a firm knock at the door and a good-looking young man in a black polo-neck came in, followed by a girl who must be his twin sister. They greeted Kent-Imison, whom they called Pa, with great affection, quite at ease in the company of strangers. It emerged, in the course of his conversation with them, that the house was only bare because a buyer had been found and they would soon all move to an old rectory in rural Somerset. Not long afterwards the explorer's delightful blonde wife joined the party, and Hugh's perceptions were turned on their head. This was no sad loner, but a loving family man with more than his life to lose. That made his profession, if you could call it that, all the more remarkable. Heading into a blizzard, your fingers dropping off with frostbite, with that beautiful image in your head wouldn't do much for your resolve. Or maybe Kent–Imison had found a way of using it to spur him on.

Before they left Northampton, Hugh and Gary took the family down to the pub. They played up with great good humour for Gary, pretending they were seeing brave Pa off on a hazardous expedition. Gary was much taken with Belinda, Kent–Imison's daughter, who handled him with patient tact and charm. Mock farewells said, Hugh, the explorer, and Gary headed for Birmingham.

'Why do you do it, Rupert?' Gary showed remarkable restraint in not asking the question until they were well on their way. 'This exploring game? Why freeze your balls off for weeks on end when you could be down the pub with your lovely lady and the sprogs? Can't see the point, myself.'

'I know it seems a bit potty,' Rupert said. 'Totally potty, probably. The only thing I can say is I feel it's what I'm meant to be doing. Have to be doing, really. Don't know why. Those are just the cards I drew.'

'I think you got lumbered with the joker, mate.'

Rupert smiled. 'Maybe that's it, Gary.'

Hugh found himself thinking about Rupert's honest explanation. If asked, he couldn't have described his own *raison d'être* in the same straightforward terms. He might have when he started out, but not now. Rupert's certainty reminded him of a writer who'd said in a recent interview that you had to follow your dream, whatever the cost. That was what marked out the achievers from the rest. But what if the dream meant losing that marvellous family in Northampton? And would Charles Manson have used the same rationale? Whatever the answers to those questions, which he supposed achievers wouldn't even ask, Hugh felt an increasing need to move on. If only the road would make itself clear to him, even if it turned out to be as eccentric as Rupert's. Even if it meant making less money.

That didn't seem to bother the hero of the dreams. Charismatic, iron-willed, though, with his stammer, touching in his vulnerability, he seemed to pursue his lonely, obscure destiny regardless of his trappings. Ageing as the picaresque story unfolded, he seemed to possess the same sureness as Rupert, and Frank McGuffog, and the pilgrim on his way to Santiago de Compostela. But where was he heading, and to what purpose? What was the meaning of his stubborn determination? His growing isolation, and the sense of impending crisis, made Hugh half afraid to find the answers.

In the evening Gary got a shot of Rupert gazing towards the concrete towers of Birmingham city centre from a minor road as though they were Trebizond. Hugh had briefed Gary on the feel of the piece. No bivouacs or huskies, let alone corgis. On no account were the pictures to make the explorer look foolish. They must reflect his willing co-operation in the joke. If it was a joke, and Hugh was beginning to feel that, if he worked it right, it just might be. The thing was to keep it light, make the most of incidents along the way, and bring in a parallel strand about Rupert's great journeys and his reasons for doing them. That, plus a fair deal for Birmingham which, by all accounts, had undergone an enlightened transformation. This was confirmed at once as they drove to the Hyatt, arranging to start the phoney trek the following morning. The new piazza spoke of civic confidence and flair. As they looked up, lights on the ground illuminated the white undersides of a passing flock of birds, lending fragile beauty to the scene. Gary captured the unforgettable moment, forced to rethink the unfavourable opinions he'd been offering about the city.

By lunchtime the following day the mission was complete. With his boyish appetite for the job in hand, and an impressive though unsurprising sense of direction, Rupert set a businesslike pace. From time to time Gary would stop the Range Rover and set up a shot, while Hugh got out to make notes of conversations with the occasional passer-by. One, a woman emerging from a newsagent's, mistook Rupert for an actor in a washing-powder commercial. Later three children, apeing the explorer's loping stride, followed him for a couple of hundred yards like Lilliputian versions of Titus Oates. When Hugh asked the eldest whether she'd like to walk to the South Pole she said she'd rather go to Alton Towers. They liked Rupert, who talked their language, and would have gone much further. However, they were soon called back by their panic-stricken mother who, seeing them with three men and a car, assumed the worst. Hugh tried to reassure her by explaining the story, but even as he spoke he realised it sounded absurd.

Back on the M6, heading for London, having had an enjoyable lunch with Rupert and dropped him off at the station, Hugh was feeling better about the assignment. Rupert had turned out to be so engaging, with his quiet, unworldly dignity and his sense of purpose, that the piece was beginning to write itself. Far from being Dacre's search for the *Heart of Darkness*, the trip had turned out to be a journey into light.

'I reckon I've got it sussed,' Gary said, as they hugged the fast lane at a comfortable ninety. 'Why he does it.'

'Why's that then?'

'It's like golf, isn't it?'

'Last time I saw the Ryder Cup . . .'

'It's not beating the other geezer, it's beating yourself.'

'There's a name for that.'

'It's pushing yourself to the limit, isn't it? It's what you're capable of, not the other geezer. That's the trip he's really on, isn't it?'

'Yes,' Hugh said. 'I think it is.'

When he settled down to his laptop, Hugh put Gary's words into the mouth of a man they'd met in Broad Street. It seemed to work. He hoped Rupert would see it, would see that he hadn't taken advantage. Hugh had described him as, among other things, a total stranger to cynicism. Though he hoped they wouldn't lose touch, he feared that very quality might make an ongoing relationship difficult. Just as saints must be impossible neighbours, so it was hard to imagine a close friendship with a man who reserved his only criticism for enemies of the environment and paedophiles. But then again, he was a man who was at his most content when he was furthest removed from humanity of any sort. Perhaps he disliked more than he was prepared to admit. Hugh hoped he would do great things, and not feel the need to do them for ever.

Three days later, on a Friday evening, Hugh was at King's Cross to meet the fast train from Cambridge. Siobhan had said she'd get a cab, but he'd wanted to be there; had been looking forward to it. For the first time since his visit to the fens, he felt a little nervous, reminding himself that he must never assume anything. There might come a time when she wanted to put the operation, and all its associations, behind her for good. It could well be sooner rather than later. It could be today.

She smiled and waved as she came towards him. Even from here the thin snake of livid scar tissue was visible above the V of her black sweater. He started to move then checked the impulse, self-conscious as his imagination replayed a scene from a hundred films and commercials. Uninhibited, Siobhan hugged him with her free arm.

'Great to see you,' she said.

'And you.' Hugh gestured to her red canvas holdall. 'Do you want me to take it?'

'No, it's fine.'

She linked her arm in his as they headed for the tube. 'You've been busy,' she said. 'Someone showed me that bit about the bullfighter. Very classy.'

'Thanks. What've you been up to?'

'Winding up. Winding down. I got a two one.'

'Come again?'

'Law degree. Two one.'

'Sounds good.'

'Good enough. So, what's the plan?'

'Tonight I thought we'd have a couple of drinks and a nice nosh. Then tomorrow we're going to see Anthony's new play and, be still my heart, actually break bread with the great man and his charming lady wife. Who, as you may recall, was formerly my charming lady wife.'

'Amazing,' Siobhan said. 'How fantastic.'

Supper that first night, at a small Vietnamese restaurant in Chalk Farm Road, Thanh Binh, had been easy and fun. Binh herself, a vivacious former boat-person, had taken a great liking to Siobhan and had insisted on giving them two free courses. She made them laugh by telling them Mick Jagger had been in for lunch and she'd failed to recognise him. Only when she saw dozens of young noses pressed against the front window had she realised he must be someone special, and her chef had been brought up to identify him.

When they'd talked on the telephone, Hugh had offered to sleep on his sofa, leaving his bed for Siobhan, but she'd said she had a friend in Hampstead, a girl she hadn't seen for months, and staying with her was no problem. After the meal they waited at the twenty-four bus-stop opposite the restaurant. The strip was alive with young people heading for pubs and clubs. Hugh felt conscious that, given the options, Siobhan might have preferred a quite different evening. While her contemporaries were having a great time, which wouldn't end till early morning, she'd been stuck with a middle-aged man who couldn't name a single stand-up or fashionable band. Maybe she and the Hampstead friend would go out again when she got in; make up for the earlier restraint.

'What do you fancy tomorrow?' Hugh said, expecting Siobhan to suggest they met at the theatre.

'Have you got stuff to do?'

'Nothing that won't wait.'

'How about the zoo?'

'God. Haven't been there for yonks. Not since some poor guy jumped in with the lions. There's a little boat goes up from Camden Lock.'

'Perfect. Eleven?'

'At the Lock? It's a deal.'

The bus was clearing the iron bridge. Siobhan put the carrying straps of the red holdall over her shoulder.

'This is me,' she said. 'Night night. And thank you, Hugh.' She kissed his cheek. 'You look anxious.'

'No,' Hugh said, as the bus drew up with a soft exhalation of doors. 'Bit knackered, that's all. Sleep well.'

'And you. See you in the morning.'

He watched as the bus pulled away, feeling much as he had when he and Tilly had parted in Old Compton Street. Only more so. In some way he couldn't begin to understand, there was an even closer connection between him and Siobhan. So much was unspoken in their relationship that he was almost afraid to examine it. Best to let it ride. Unless it turned into a Lolita thing, of course. Could that, after all, be at the root of it? Could it be that he'd wanted her from the start, but had so far managed to deceive both of them? No, this was all getting out of hand, Hugh thought, as he walked down Hartland Road. Tonight had been good. Enjoy tomorrow. Don't ask for more than you've got. A few months ago he'd been dying. They both had. Now they had so much to live for. Settle for that.

Back at the flat, still replaying the evening, he picked up Jim Crace's *Quarantine*, a brilliant alternative account of the Christ-story. Spare and imaginative, it called to mind aspects of all three men who had impressed Hugh in the past few weeks: the agnostic pilgrim, the unlikely bullfighter, and the explorer driven on by a passion he couldn't express. Were they all, including Christ, deluded? Or were they all pursuing the only rightness that mattered: the conviction that what they were doing was not an option but a necessity? Too tired to reason, Hugh put down the novel. Now, for the first time since Cambridge, the dream was preceded by a physical sensation: a hollowness like hunger, but with an edge of apprehension as he surrendered to an alien world where there was no comfort or protection. In his headlong fall into sleep, the terrifying thought surfaced that it might be a world which could, if it chose, refuse to release him.

Four men, riding hard, at night. Other than the moon, and the occasional glimmer of a candle in the villages through which they pass, there is no light. Caught in a sudden rain-

storm before they can find shelter, the riders are wet and cold. Unsure whom they can trust, if anyone, they cannot know where it is safe to sleep. Their leader, the charismatic figure at the forefront of all the dreams, his fine robes replaced by a drab woollen cloak, urges the others on with a reminder of the consequences if they are caught.

Before dawn, huddled close in a small boat, regretful as they look back at the land, they embark on the hurling sea. The followers share stale bread and cold meat, given them by a well-wisher, but the leader eats nothing. Instead he kneels in the stern, pale and intense. At first the wind is powerful, but by mid-morning it relents. The white, flat beach is visible for miles before they reach it; alien, blank-faced. It might be the gateway to a desert.

The boat furrows the sand at the edge of the surf. The men disembark. The leader stoops and rearranges two long, narrow shells in the shape of a cross. The next wave washes over it, disturbing the pattern, leaving the shells separated. Further back, towards the coarse green fringe that marks the junction of sea and land, a figure stands watching, then turns his back on the small party.

The leader looks about him. Exhausted, he hitches his robe so that the wet hem hangs clear of the beach. Instead of following him, his three companions, with expressions impossible to read, get back into the boat. The leader is alone, small in the vast expanse. With firm steps, he sets himself at the unknown.

The little steamer on the Regent Canal was full of excited children, among them Hugh and Siobhan. Siobhan had given her camera to an American tourist and asked her to get a picture of the two of them. The boat in the dream still vivid and disturbing in his mind, Hugh felt his smile wasn't as spontaneous as it might have been. Nevertheless he was delighted to have a record of the moment. Even since he'd woken that morning, sweating and unrested, finding it difficult to shake off the images of the night, he'd wondered if he could risk mentioning them. He needed so much to share these strange experiences, even if they were beyond interpretation. He'd missed his chance with Tilly, but here was another. As long as he didn't alarm or frighten her, he was sure Siobhan wouldn't laugh or think him mad.

'Are you getting any funny dreams at all? You know, since . . .' He made the question sound as casual as he could.

'Not particularly, why?'

'Just wondered.'

'Sounds as though you are.'

'I am, yes.'

'Ooh, good. Bags I be Freud.'

Hugh began to tell her about his frequent journeys into what appeared to be the past. 'Thing is,' he said, 'they're not like most dreams. They're not, you know, ragbags of assorted bits and pieces, like you usually get. They seem to be more or less a sequence, like a story. And the thing goes forward every time I'm back in it. Seems to move on a chapter, with this same bloke playing the lead all the time.'

'What's he like?'

'Dark, striking-looking, big nose. Speaks with a stammer. There's a tremendous strength about him. I don't mean physical. It's an inner thing. This iron will. It started off with his christening. Mum and Dad there in the dark church. At least, I assume it was them. Very well-to-do. Dressed in furs and silks. Then later on the man himself is wearing all this rich gear too, and he's got this powerful friend who's even richer, but you get the feeling there's some sort of tension between them. In one dream they wrestled in the mud, arguing about a red cloak. The very powerful one wanted the dark man to give it to a beggar. He did, after they'd tussled for a bit, but reluctantly. You could tell he resented it. Then you get these amazing processions. Monkeys riding horses, wolves on leads, gold and silver plates and goblets and chalices . . . The details are so vivid. A huge plate of eels, quite sinister-looking. And all the while there's something almost fanatical about the dark man, like he's got some bee in his bonnet. You don't exactly like him but you kind of admire him.'

'He obviously speaks English, does he?'

'Good question. All the dialogue's in a sort of archaic English but I get the feeling it's a translation for my benefit. Almost as though it's dubbed. But all the background chat and singing and so on isn't recognisable as English. This is all God knows how long ago so I suppose anything's going to sound strange.' Hugh paused, thoughtful. 'He's a soldier a bit later. Big hero. And then all of a sudden the posh gear's gone and he's wearing this hair shirt under a plain habit-type-thing. After a bit he meets the powerful man again, the one he wrestled in the mud with. They're both mounted in this beautiful meadow. Thousands of wild flowers.

Idyllic. But you can tell they're having a row. The dark man turns and rides away. Then he's in a boat. You get the feeling he's on the run from someone or something. Some danger. They get to this beach. Long white beach, with shells in the shape of a cross on it. It's weird, the whole thing. There's this terrible sense all the time that the whole thing's going to go pear-shaped for him.'

'Fantastic story. I hope you're making notes?'

'I started to this morning, funnily enough.'

'Make an amazing article.'

'Don't think my illustrious employers are into dreams. Not unless they reveal the lottery numbers. Anyway, I couldn't write about this thing in a sketchy way. It goes too deep. There's something really intense, insistent about it, as though it's got something to say. Tell you the truth it's getting to me a bit. Sometimes it seems almost more real than reality.'

'I shouldn't worry. It's probably all down to the operation. The trauma and that. Maybe you just had one dream and your mind latched on to it, got hooked and decided to make up some more. Probably one day soon it'll just not happen again; end as suddenly as it started.'

'Probably. You must think I'm a head case.'

'So what? I like head cases. My friend Hester's a head case. You haven't met Hest, have you?'

Hugh shook his head.

'She's this amazing Scot. We met when she was working at Heffers, which she thought was crap. I went in to get a Dick Francis for Gareth but she talked me out of it. Made me get a thing about some detective in

Venice instead. Now she's at the CUP, which she also thinks is crap.'

'Has she ever considered working somewhere she doesn't think is crap?'

'She says the only thing that isn't is literature, and she can't write. So she has to be around books instead.'

At the zoo they bought ice-lollies and ambled in the sun. In a small amphitheatre, a young keeper was giving a talk about conservation with the help of cooperative residents. An owl skimmed the heads of the audience on cue, landing on the keeper's outstretched arm, and an otter darted round the stage, squeaking with a performer's sense of theatre. In the gorilla enclosure, the magnificent leading male was poking a delicate black finger through the wire netting in an attempt to curl it round a green shoot. Making a shape like the scroll of a cello with their trunks, the elephants blew dust over their backs. At the elegant penguin pool, with its twin white walkways as graceful as billowing chiffon scarves frozen by the camera, the awkward birds shuffled in single file towards the water, devout as Dominicans gathering to bury their prior.

Siobhan didn't want to leave. And because she didn't, neither did Hugh. Watching her uncomplicated delight had made him feel as close to absolute contentment as he'd been since he last saw her in Cambridge. As he got older, moments like this were rarer. He supposed that was the case with everyone. You laughed a lot and made the best of every situation, but it wasn't often you were touched by that deep sense of well-being. It went beyond mere circumstances to a feeling of shared wholeness and affirmation; a small but significant mark on the landscape that no storm could wash away.

They'd arranged to meet Tilly and Anthony at the Aldwych. The polyglot audience, in cottons and linens, were cluttering the pavement, some loud and attention-seeking as though the performance were here. Anthony's play was called *Marking Time*. According to the selective quotes on the marquee and posters, it was '. . . achingly poignant . . .', '. . . painfully relevant . . .' and 'bitterly funny . . .'

'Thank God for adverbs,' Hugh said, seeing that Siobhan was absorbing them.

'Quite,' she said. ' "Achingly", "painfully", "bitterly"; sounds like an unwanted pregnancy.'

'They're all on the old laptop, you know. When critics are knocking off these pieces they just press the button marked Adverb and it bungs them in at random.' Hugh caught sight of Tilly and Anthony approaching the mêlée from the direction of the Waldorf. 'Ah, I spy the author, walking briskly, triumphantly, bowleggedly.'

Anthony Granger, unrecognised by anyone else, was no taller than his wife, with a comfortable paunch, a preoccupied expression, and a crumpled linen suit. His beard was threaded with grey and the flesh revealed by his open-neck shirt was very white.

Hugh did the introductions. 'Tilly, Anthony, Siobhan.'

'Hello,' Siobhan said.

'Hi,' Tilly said.

Anthony seemed uncomfortable. Not rude or standoffish but unpolished at coping with strangers. He gave

Siobhan an uncertain smile and, shifting his focus, said, 'Hugh.'

'I see it's achingly poignant then,' Hugh said.

Tilly's slight incline of the head and a small cloud of a frown told him she found this a touch disappointing.

'Apparently,' Anthony said. 'Though I lean more towards the bitterly funny myself.'

Siobhan laughed. 'It's doing awfully well, isn't it?'

Anthony softened. 'Bit early to say,' he said. 'Not a bad start. How about a drink?'

As they followed him with some difficulty through the crowd, Tilly gave Hugh a sharp nudge. 'Less of the sarkiness, Mr Sharp,' she said. 'He's better at it than you.'

'True,' Hugh conceded. 'And he gets paid for it.'

Marking Time, Hugh had to admit, was a good play. The central character was a young British soldier on compassionate leave from Northern Ireland. His father, a lapsed Catholic, full of fear and guilt, was dying. His mother, a Protestant from Portrush, full of rage and resentment, was torn between pity and a sense of having been double-crossed by life. The soldier's feckless younger brother got his kicks by stirring the already volatile emotional mix. His older sister, married to a black Everton footballer, proud of her BMW and her Japanese runabout and her detached four-bedroomed house next door to a company director, was contemptuous of all of them. Granger's skill lay in weaving these elements into a piece that was as funny as it was truthful. The audience, for many of whom English was a second language, recognised in it universal prejudices and dilemmas.

When they gave the cast five curtain calls, Hugh felt an acute pang of envy, mixed with a smug sense of privilege at being in the company of the author. The generous part of him wanted Anthony to stand up and take a bow for a genuine achievement, but a meaner voice called for the play to be unmasked as blatant plagiarism. What he coveted was this instant, unfeigned expression of public pleasure and gratitude. For two and a half hours, Anthony had transported these people into a world that for them, until tonight, had never existed, and had made it both real and, for once a critic had been right, relevant. Maybe some would never forget it. And tomorrow night, in the same seats, another audience would come fresh to the experience, and also leave a little enriched. This was not the writing on the wall. It was something more than that. In spite of himself, Hugh admired it.

'Good stuff, Anthony,' he said, as they were borne along in the scrum leaving the theatre.

'Thanks, Hugh.'

If only Anthony had been insufferable, Hugh thought. If only he'd been arrogant and conceited, how much easier it would be to hate him. But he wasn't. He was like a master cabinet-maker who had just been complimented on a fine chair. He knew it was good, and he knew how to make the next one better. However much one hoped to find it, complacency was not in his nature.

Siobhan had been thrilled by the play. On the way to the restaurant in Covent Garden, she walked ahead with Anthony, her enthusiasm evident in her animation.

'She seems really nice,' Tilly said.

'She is,' Hugh said. 'I feel very lucky. Not just, you know, for what we in the transplant business call the organ, but for her too. She's a good mate. I suppose we look a bit funny together . . .'

'If we bothered about that we'd all be in trouble, wouldn't we? Look at my tubby little chap.'

'Clever bastard.'

'Thank you, Hugh. That's the nicest thing you've ever said about him. Shouldn't be surprised if they add it to the quotes outside the theatre.'

Supper was a great success. Drawn out by Siobhan, Anthony told funny stories about actors and other writers. He even had a stab at answering the unanswerable: how the business of writing a play worked. Hugh told him about the trip to Birmingham with Rupert Kent-Imison, and how nothing the man was asked to do seemed to diminish him. He noticed that, while he was describing the exercise, which seemed even more ridiculous in hindsight, Anthony was as attentive as though he were listening to a declaration of war, absorbing every small detail. Later, Hugh wondered whether Kent-Imison might one day find himself transformed into a character on the West End stage.

As they said their goodnights on the pavement, they all arranged to meet again when Siobhan next visited Hugh. Boarding the 168 in Kingsway, Siobhan was still high on the evening.

'What's the plan tomorrow then?' Hugh said.

'Have to get back first thing, Hugh, sadly. I've got this job waitressing. Just to make some loot before I move up here.' She put her arm through his. 'This has been one of the best weekends ever,' she said. 'Thank you.'

'Good,' Hugh said.

'Not for you too? Not one of the best weekends ever?'

'Oh, me, no question. I've had a lovely time.'

'Anthony's smashing, isn't he?'

Hugh considered an ironic put-down, but abandoned the idea. 'He's not bad, is he? Bit of a moody old sod at times apparently.'

'Oh, Lord, sorry. Bit of a sore point? Now you know why I didn't go in for the diplomatic.'

Hugh laughed. 'No, honestly. Was once. Not now. You've got to hand it to him. And Tilly's very happy. Next time you'll have to meet Sam. He's got the best of both of them.'

'Must be quite a boy.'

They talked a little about their next meeting, and punting up to Grantchester. Ten minutes later it was over. Hugh looked back as he went down to the bottom deck. Siobhan was smiling but there were dark crescents under her eyes. He'd told her not to work too hard, meaning it, though it was just something people said. She'd assured him she wouldn't, though that was just something people said too. As he watched the bus begin its gentle climb towards the Roundhouse, he realised how much she'd come to represent in his life. If she drove herself too hard, overtaxed that borrowed heart, he would be unable to bear her suffering, or his own.

Tonight, he thought, as he walked down Prince of

Wales Road, please don't let the dream come back. Not tonight. Just let me fall into the black hole. But as he listened to his own footsteps on the dark pavement, he sensed the shadows at the periphery of his vision. He sensed the mysterious figure, weary but resolute, ready to resume his journey; this figure so unlike himself in every way, and yet with whom he felt more and more associated, shoulder to shoulder with this fierce spirit, though separated by hundreds of years, and by the barrier of consciousness. The dream had developed an impetus; had begun to suggest that the story might end in violent confrontation. If that were the outcome, and Hugh drew even closer to the lonely traveller, could he remain a witness or might he, in some strange, inexorable way, be drawn into the vortex? His tired mind allowed itself to wonder whether the dream might turn to nightmare.

Chapter Six

All the way back from the coast, the events at Southwold had troubled Kate; the night prowler in the annexe, the telephone call, the death of the young man by the water tower. Hester was right, of course, when she insisted there was no proof that the man Kate had seen was Taylor; that it might just as well have been an insomniac having a quiet smoke; that people got killed all over the place. But suspicion, which had settled in Kate's mind like a squatter, had now become something more substantial. It had become closer to sureness, irrational but no longer susceptible to comforting theories. If Taylor had wanted to get to know her because he fancied her, he must have got the message long ago. If he was still hanging around, therefore, his motives were unlikely to be friendly. And wherever he was, there seemed to be sad victims. The frustration lay in making these intuitions plausible to anyone else. The art-loving detective, Corcoran, might think her hysterical. Nevertheless she would call him first thing Monday morning. Even if it did make her sound flaky, she hadn't the right to keep information like this to herself.

In the event Corcoran listened to the broad outline of Kate's brief narrative without interrupting. When she'd finished, her voice unrelaxed, he said he'd get down to the gallery as soon as he could, but that Mondays were busy with the weekend backlog. He asked her for a description of the man she thought she'd seen in the annexe, and she regretted she had so little to offer by way of detail. She did add, however, that Taylor himself had brown eyes, claimed he was in his last year at Cambridge, reading history, fenced, and took size seven shoes, or said he did, facts that had lodged from her lunch with him at the Eagle. The act of unburdening herself even of this trivial information made her feel better.

Now, until Corcoran arrived in person, she must put it all aside and concentrate on the new exhibition. This was to consist of a number of vibrant collages by Tom Pinsent, an artist she'd first spotted at a small show in Fen Ditton. She'd liked his sense of colour and the fact that, though his work was abstract, it didn't threaten conservative tastes. It would, she hoped, give timid buyers a small sense of daring, a sense that they were moving on, maturing. As she was about to call him, she was startled by a familiar voice.

'Morning, lovey.'

Kate turned. It was Roger Crick, his face reddened by the weekend sun; a mild clash with his pink bowtie.

'Roger! Nice to see you.'

'Thought I'd say hello to the workers. No intelligence from the fuzz?' He began to look through the mail.

'Not yet, no. You'd hardly expect it yet, though, would you?'

'Speaking for myself I expect very little of the boys in blue.'

'Actually he was very nice, Corcoran. Knew a bit about art. Quite a lot, probably. His sidekick was a bit of a dope.'

'An art-loving copper. Whatever next? Screaming popes, probably. Piles of bricks in the Tate. The insurance in hand?' Roger went on.

'Done that. Not much to claim, of course. Just the cash box and the damage to the lock. They fitted the new one on Friday.'

'Excellent.'

'How was your weekend?' Kate asked.

'Curate's egg,' Roger said. 'Fabulous meal on Saturday, courtesy of Tim and Susan Berger . . . Lucretia to her friends.'

'Why?'

'The naughty Signora Borgia did it with horses, so they say, and Susan is awfully attached to Newmarket.'

'Ah. And Sunday?'

'Sunday, parents in-law. Roast beef of old England, much talk of Glaxo shares, the wondrous properties of Gro-bags, isn't Tony Blair a hypocrite, and why do people want to go to Thailand when Torquay's so lovely? I made my excuses. Said I had a lot of paperwork to do. Thence to my study and an in-depth analysis of the *News of the World*.' He paused. 'Yours?'

Kate had to edit as she answered. One hint of her concern and Roger would be in there like a butcher with a carcass. 'Hester and I went to Southwold. It was great.'

'Didn't I see something in the *Telegraph* about some dastardly deed in that neck of the woods? Somebody bumped off, was it?'

'They did find a body apparently.' Kate tried to hold her voice in neutral.

'Probably died of boredom,' Roger said. 'The east coast can have that effect on people. Seem to remember it said he was a novice or something.'

'A novice at what?'

'A monk with an L-plate, darling. A monklet. Walsingham was mentioned. What was he doing out on his own at night, one asks oneself. Maybe he wasn't such a novice, after all.'

Kate was shaken out of her neutrality but did her best not to show it. According to Hester, the porter at Jesus had said the real Martin Taylor, the victim of a hit-and-run, had wanted to be a vicar. They'd assumed that meant he was reading theology. Was this an insane pattern emerging? If so, how did Kate fit into it? She went to church three or four times a year, when she visited her mother, but that would hardly qualify her. Or was the religious link mere coincidence? At any rate, it wasn't something Corcoran could ignore.

After a cursory look at the previous week's figures, revealing six sales yielding five hundred and eighty pounds, Roger left to open the antique shop.

Kate spent the rest of the morning making calls, paying bills, and writing letters, anything to keep her mind occupied. Hester had said she'd call round about one and they'd have lunch together at the Old Spring. By midday, when there was still no sign of Corcoran, Kate was tempted to ring him again, but managed to restrain herself. That really would make her look over-anxious. She was sure the poor man was doing his best. As she watched a precarious punt-load of tourists, and pondered what to do next, she thought she heard a small cough from the gallery. A customer? She got up and went to the door of the office. The figure she saw, with his back to her, shocked her into going no further. Slight, wearing a white shirt and black jeans, he looked as though he'd just stepped out of the hotel shadows. At once the warm night came back to her, with the awful sensation of being stalked, of having no private place to hide. Sensing her, he turned and smiled.

'Hi. Seems like a long time. These aren't bad, are they?'

Kate felt stupid with fear. He sounded so calm, so normal. Yet this calm, normal man had stolen the name of a dead undergraduate, had lied about the college, might have broken into the gallery and taken her address book, had, she now felt sure, spied on her in Southwold, and might have killed the novice by the water tower. The tumult of thoughts was overwhelming. Full of mights and maybes, but also underpinned with a stubborn conviction. Always alone, pale and unreadable, always in black and white, he seemed to signal himself and yet, for much of the time, submerge himself in the background. His very ordinariness had become unnerving. Had he been watching the gallery this morning? Had he driven behind them from

Southwold? Did he follow her all day long?

Though the more or less simultaneous worries flooded her mind within seconds, it felt to Kate like a minute. She considered confronting him straight away; telling him she knew about the college and the real Taylor; accusing him of the robbery, the Southwold murder, and of stalking her; telling him she hated him and was frightened of him and that the police would be here any minute. Give it to him straight. Get rid of him for good. What was stopping her, then? What diluted that inner resolution, turning it into meek reluctance to offend? Reluctance which, the longer it was allowed to restrain her instincts, might dig her deeper into unhappiness and even danger. Hester wouldn't feel constrained, but Hester hadn't been born into the English middle class.

Aware that she had to say something, in the end Kate managed a dry-mouthed 'No.'

'I'd like that one,' he said, pointing to a small rectangular homage to Mary Fedden. 'Is that OK? It hasn't got a red dot or anything.'

The question had Kate pinned. Ridiculous to say no, he couldn't have it. At the same time she was reluctant to say yes, because that would draw her into a momentary bond; even call for a little gratitude. Clever move, she thought.

'Yes,' she said. 'It's OK.' In this situation the normal thing to do would be to join the buyer, exchange pleasantries, tell him something about the artist. But Kate was immobilised. 'How would you like to pay?'

'Big hurry, is there?' he said, looking round the

empty space. 'Doesn't look, you know, completely packed out at the moment.'

Kate clasped her hands in front of her, aware that the gesture stressed her unease. 'No,' she said, longing for Corcoran to arrive. She wished she had a panic button, like they had in banks.

'Good.' He took three steps towards her. 'You do recognise me?' he said. 'We have met, you know.'

'Of course.'

'It's just that, as welcomes go, this isn't absolutely right up there with the great ones.'

Damn, Kate thought. Now he was even managing to make her feel guilty. The one thing she was determined not to do was apologise. 'Sorry,' she heard herself say, out of craven habit. 'It's been a bit . . . Monday morning . . .'

'Ah, Monday morning,' he said, somehow emphasising its meaninglessness. 'How've you been anyway?'

This was surreal, Kate thought. He knew how she'd been, more than likely. Even knew where she'd been; and yet this ludicrous inhibition, injected in the cradle, was forcing her to perform a ritual dance with a man she was beginning to loathe.

'Fine.' With an effort she unclasped her hands and tried to strike a casual pose against the door-frame.

'Good weekend?'

'Yes.' Kate realised the dance was leading her towards a large, smoking hole in the floor.

'You look as though you've caught the sun, as they say.'

'It was . . . sunny.' Fatuous reply.

'Anywhere nice?'

'Why do you assume I wasn't here?' Kate felt encouraged by her own first trace of assertiveness.

'Just that it wasn't specially hot here. It rained a bit on Saturday.'

Kate made a mental note to check later. Meanwhile he'd handled that well. 'Southwold,' she said. 'Do you know it at all?'

Taylor frowned and pursed his lips. 'Somewhere near Aldeburgh? Out that way?'

Kate nodded. To hell with it; time to call his bluff. What was there to lose? He couldn't very well do anything here, in broad daylight, with the possibility of a customer coming in at any minute. 'As a matter of fact I could have sworn I saw you there.'

Not a flicker, as Taylor shook his head in slow, elaborate denial. 'Not me.'

'Where were you last Friday night? As a matter of interest?'

Taylor's eyes had turned cold again, as they had at the Eagle; eyes that had abandoned any pretence of sympathy. 'I'm not absolutely sure that's any of your business, is it?'

It was one thing to challenge him, another to antagonise him. Perhaps that was what his victims had done. The change in his manner, when it happened, was disturbing. 'You asked me a question, I asked you one. Fair's fair.'

Taylor shrugged, seeming to lower his guard a little.

Despite the risk, now that she'd started, broken the ice of her own caution, Kate couldn't stop herself. 'You aren't at Jesus, are you, like you said?'

He waited for her to say more.

'You're not an undergraduate there. That wasn't true, was it? And your name isn't Martin Taylor.' Now she'd gone further than she'd meant to; further than was safe. Would he go mad and fly at her throat; trash the place and hurl her lifeless corpse into the river? Would he give her that pitiless look again and take out a horrible knife? Come in, someone, quick. For God's sake – please –!

To her amazement, Taylor appeared to soften. 'It's a fair cop,' he said.

Though it went nowhere near explaining anything, Kate allowed herself a tiny release of tension. 'Why then? What was the point of making it up?'

'I thought you'd find it more impressive.'

'Than what, for heaven's sake? Who are you really?'

'My name's Richard Bright. I work for an estate agent. Not very exciting, is it? I was going to tell you anyway. When we'd got to know each other a bit . . .'

Kate knew she had to tread with particular care. This might just be a new lie. If it was the truth, and she could never know for sure, she mustn't give the impression that it made everything all right. There remained a dozen unanswered questions, which his apparent frankness had now made it more difficult to ask. Another smart move. 'What's wrong with working for an estate agent?'

'Not exactly a caring profession, is it?'

Kate conceded the point. 'But why choose a dead man's name?'

'Pretty well any name you chose would be a dead man's, wouldn't it, if you think about it? It was just something I read in a paper. Could have been Groucho Marx.'

So plausible; a hint of self-deprecating charm, even. Now he seemed more relaxed, maybe Kate could push him a little further after all. 'Are you quite sure you don't know Southwold?'

'Quite.'

'How do I know that's the truth?'

'You don't.'

'What about my address book? The robbery?'

'What robbery?'

This was hopeless. Bright was too good a chess-player. Kate thought of trying to catch him out, but nothing came to mind. A straight question instead; one he'd have to answer. 'Why do you . . .? What is it you want from me?'

For the first time he seemed to hesitate before he answered. 'I . . . Not much, really. I like your company. Being with you. You're not a point-scorer.'

Kate frowned. 'Meaning?'

'With most people it's like a competition. They tell you what they do before you ask them. They want to win. They don't listen.'

The compliment sounded genuine enough. Kate wished she hadn't asked. But she was determined not to weaken. This was it. Now or never. 'Look, the thing is, I don't particularly . . . I don't really want this to go on. You make me . . . I don't know . . . nervous. I'd just rather you didn't come again. That we didn't meet again.'

Bright let out a small breath, as though he'd been holding it. In that moment he was without arrogance or pretence. Kate fought off second thoughts. What if she'd misjudged him all along? What if he wasn't guilty of any of these things, except the borrowed name? And he'd owned up to that. But no. Her instinct was still strong. Something about him – the way his mood could change in an instant, his evasiveness when she'd asked him about Friday night, the fact that there was no warmth in him, that she imagined his flesh would be cool to the touch – confirmed her fear and distrust.

'That's a shame,' he said at last. 'I'm really sorry about that. If it's something I said . . . I know I can come on a bit strong sometimes.'

'It's not that,' Kate said, her confidence growing, though her inclination was still to be considerate. 'I'd just rather we didn't.' Practical now that the moment had passed without anything fearful happening, she realised that if Bright disappeared Corcoran might never trace him. 'Do you still want the picture?'

For a second he seemed to have no recollection of it. 'Yes. I do, yes. A souvenir.'

'We could get it over to your house for you, when the exhibition's over. Or work, if you like.'

He wasn't falling for that one. 'It's OK. Maybe we could meet for one last drink. Just a final quickie. You bring it with you and I'll pay cash.'

Though Kate would have much preferred a clean break, at least this way Corcoran would know where Bright would be at a given time, and she could get

Hester along for added protection. 'OK. Friday night, say. Sevenish?'

'The Blue Ball in Grantchester?' he suggested.

'All right.'

To Kate's alarm, he moved a step closer.

'I think you're being very unjust,' he said.

Justice. That was what he'd banged on about at the Eagle. Not the law, justice. Did he punish people who were unjust? Was that what he got off on? Had she made a fatal mistake; gone too far and antagonised him? The thought shook her flimsy, new-found assurance. She didn't know what to say. Whatever happened, she mustn't apologise again.

'I think you're being unkind,' he went on. 'I never meant to . . . I only wanted to . . .'

Oh, God, please let this end, Kate thought. Now he was in a different key altogether. He seemed hurt and unsure; talking more to himself than to her, as he might in the presence of a psychiatrist. But just as he was about to reveal far more than she wanted to know, her prayer was answered. Through the gallery door she could see Gilbert, the tramp-artist, his not unhandsome, sunburned head a startling contrast to Bright's pallor, even at that distance. Bright noticed her distraction and turned.

Now Gilbert stood framed in the doorway, biblical in his vigour and brightness, a man who, like John the Baptist, knew how to survive the rigours of Nature. He wore a long, belted garment in faded orange, with an Indian scarf draped over one shoulder and knotted at the waist. Though the costume had seen much wear, and been bleached by many summers, the effect was of a man whose appearance was not unimportant to him. He seemed dressed to sit for a painter, or perhaps to inhabit one of his own works. Best of all, as far as Kate was concerned, his eyes blazed with a quality not acquired from living a mundane life. They were like a fox's eyes, she thought, feral, unfathomable. They had seen everything, might even see beyond everything, but how much had they understood? They could seem fierce and fearful at the same time; eyes that had learned as much from the night as the day.

'Gilbert!' Kate said. 'How lovely to see you!'

With one last, uninterpretable look at her, Bright took his cue and left. Gilbert stood aside to let him pass and watched him go, monochrome against the paintings and, outside, the trees and grass.

'God, Gilbert, am I glad to see you,' Kate said again.

Unaware of what he'd done to deserve such an elaborate greeting, Gilbert looked both pleased and embarrassed.

'Would you like a cup of coffee?'

'Ta,' Gilbert said, advancing a couple of steps. His voice was light, with an unplaceable accent; a patchwork of gathered sounds and intonations.

'That man gives me the creeps,' Kate said. 'Have you ever seen him before? You know, around town?'

Gilbert turned this over in his mind. 'I have,' he said.

'Where?'

Again Gilbert paused before giving his deliberate answer. 'Best not say,' he said.

Something about his dignity, his quiet but adamant

tone, made it impossible to challenge him. Maybe he'd be more forthcoming about the weather. 'Gilbert, Saturday: can you remember if it rained here at all?' After a moment's silence Kate realised that, to Gilbert, the naming of days might be a redundant concept. 'Day before yesterday?'

Gilbert cocked his head at a slight angle, remembering. 'Rain, yes,' he said at last. 'Gardens were glad of it.'

As Kate and Hester walked along Chesterton Lane to the Old Spring, having left a note on the gallery door for Corcoran, Kate could talk of nothing but Bright's extraordinary visit, Gilbert's timely appearance, and his strange reluctance to tell her more.

'Did Bright, or whatever his name is, say which estate agent's?' Hester said,

'No. I was afraid to push him. He has these mood swings. One minute he can be quite, you know, charming almost, and the next he's all hurt. You have to keep telling yourself he might be a murderer.'

'Well, there can't be that many estate agents. Between us we'll check. Did he say it was in Cambridge?'

'Didn't say where it was.'

'Could be out of town. Could be Ely, Newmarket, God knows . . . Haverhill. Could be another porky. So could his new name, of course.'

'Could well be.'

'Strange he was so cagey about Friday night. He could have made up any old thing. He was washing his hair, he went to a movie . . . Why get all defensive?'

'You tell me.' Kate drew some small encouragement

from the fact that Hester was no longer as sceptical as she had been.

'Bright's a slightly funny name to invent, isn't it? Assuming he did . . . again. I mean, Taylor's ordinary but Bright's a bit unusual. Unless that's another dead bloke.'

'Or the truth, for once.'

'Possibility.' Hester paused. 'I'm not sure the Blue Ball was such a good idea.'

'Maybe it wasn't. I just thought the minute he left the gallery he might disappear for good. Absolutely no way of tracing him. And then it seemed a way of ending it. What do the Americans call it, when you put a full stop to something?'

'Closure?'

'Closure. I know it sounds ridiculous but I still didn't completely want to hurt his feelings.'

'You're right. It does sound ridiculous. I don't give a toss about hurting his feelings.'

'I'm sorry, Hest. This thing's doing my head in.'

'Don't you worry, babe. We're cleverer than this bastard, you and me. Friday night we'll flush him out for good.'

When Kate got back to the gallery, somewhat reassured by Hester's rallying cry, the policeman she least wanted to see was already there, facing the river as though thinking about torpedoing ducks. Spaull had his hands in his pockets. His careful hair shone with bottled brilliance and his deep shirt collar was a startling white. For an irresponsible moment, Kate thought about holding her breath and retracing her silent steps. She could go and do some shopping; pretend she'd forgotten the note said she'd be back at two. Too late. Spaull was turning and looking at his watch.

'Afternoon,' he said.

'I'm sorry,' Kate said. 'I make it five to. Been here long?' The thought of having to make conversation with this preening half-wit depressed her.

'Couple of minutes. My distinguished colleague's a bit delayed. Zimmer frame's not run-in yet.' The intended joke lay on the path like a stone.

'Shall we go inside?'

'Why not?'

For a second Kate thought about heading not for the office but straight for the river. Diving in and not surfacing until she reached the lock. She imagined the fish for yards around floating belly-up, stunned by the tediousness of the man.

While she excused herself to make a telephone call, taking as long about it as she could, Spaull toured the paintings, calling out perceptive comments from time to time. 'Do they just, like, doodle these? . . . big lady. Looks like she's swallowed a couple of airships.' These and other aspects of the work that had not hitherto been spotted by the local critics. With an effort akin to a pearl-diver's breathing discipline, Kate endured the commentary without taking issue. When it felt impossible to hide any longer, she emerged.

'Get plenty of time off, do you? Doesn't exactly look all go,' Spaull said.

'It's not a supermarket, it's an art gallery.' Little Ms

Prim. Why hadn't she come up with something witty and urbane?

'Really?' Spaull said, looking towards the door. 'Hello, here's the boss now.'

Corcoran joined them. 'Sorry I'm a bit late,' he said. 'Medieval cities weren't made for the internal combustion engine.'

Kate smiled, glad to see him.

'You're better walking,' Corcoran went on. 'Better for you. I'm starting to feel like that bloke Lucian Freud used to paint a lot. Bloke who died. Bowery, wasn't it? Leigh Bowery?'

'Was that it?' Kate said. 'He was enormous.'

'Mmmm,' Spaull said.

Corcoran ignored the innuendo. 'Now then, what's on your mind?'

Kate made the account as plain as she could, trying not to offer fears and theories but just the sequence of events. At first she was hesitant, expecting Spaull to interrupt with unhelpful remarks, but when she saw him listening and taking notes, she grew braver. Starting with her lunch at the Eagle, she told the whole story, emphasising the points she thought important, such as Bright's reluctance to say where he was on Friday night and Gilbert's refusal to reveal where he'd seen him. The trickiest part was trying to convince two cynical detectives of her strong intuition. She did this in the simplest of terms, calm and reasonable, assuring them that she wasn't an hysteric, and stressing that even if she was, it would be hard to overlook the apparent religious connection between the two deaths.

'Interesting,' Corcoran said, when she'd finished. 'We'll get on to the Suffolk boys.'

'Meanwhile he's out there,' Kate said. 'If he's out of control . . .'

'Evidence,' Spaull said.

'This is it, unfortunately,' Corcoran said. 'You've been very helpful, very helpful indeed, but it wouldn't get very far in front of a jury, would it? I'm sure you understand that. I don't disbelieve you thought you saw this man in Southwold but the mind can play tricks, can't it?' He indicated the paintings. 'At the end of the day that's what these are all about, isn't it? If van Gogh's mind hadn't played tricks he'd probably have stayed a Sunday-school teacher.'

'But can't you get him for using a false name? For – I don't know . . . impersonation? Isn't that like fraud?'

'If we arrested everybody in this town who isn't what they say they are, we'd need a nick the size of Parker's Piece,' Corcoran said.

'I've got his mobile number. At least, we think it's his but he's never on it.' Kate was aware that this sounded desperate.

'If you can dig it out . . .' Spaull said, sounding weary.

Corcoran, however, was more positive. He asked her a number of questions, some of which had already been raised by Hester. Did she remember Bright touching anything while he was in the gallery? Had he any distinguishing marks or features? Did he have an accent of any sort? Had he given any clue as to where his workplace was? Though she wanted her answers to be useful,

Kate could add little to her earlier account.

When he'd finished, Corcoran said, 'We'd like you to go ahead with this meet at Grantchester. Take your friend, of course. Just act perfectly naturally. Meanwhile we'll get on the blower, make a few enquiries.'

'Will you be there?' Kate said.

'There or thereabouts,' Corcoran said. 'This matter wants clearing up, doesn't it? One way or another. Meanwhile don't hesitate to get in touch.'

Kate imagined he couldn't have any idea how good that sounded. She wanted to prolong the conversation with him for a while; perhaps get him back on to art, as a sort of thank-you; a recognition that under the crumpled double-breasted suit, there beat the heart of an intelligent, sensitive human being. But art would have to wait. Corcoran and Spaull were already making their way to the door.

Just as he was about to leave, and Spaull had already gone out into the sunshine, Corcoran turned. 'What you have to understand is there's a lot of people in this town living on the fringe,' he said. 'Been here for years, some of them. They're not part of the university, but they're drawn to it. It's what you might call the glamour of learning. And the place is young. Every year of every century, it's young. Tide goes out, fresh one comes in. You can live on the edge and you can kid yourself you belong. You're in Cambridge. Student life's all round you. Pretty soon you can start to believe you're at Cambridge. Nothing to stop you going to lectures, even. There's folks in their fifties here behave as though they're students. But they're not. Never have been. It's fantasy time for lonely people. Doesn't make them mad. Doesn't make them criminals. But it can make them very annoying. It's just a shame you've got on the wrong end of one.'

'But if that's what he is, why hang around someone who isn't a student?'

'He might think he had a better chance of conning a non-student into believing he was one. Impress you. Then again when he's with you he's not on his own, is he? Folks see you together, they see a bloke with a girl-friend.' At that moment Corcoran's bleeper went off. He read the message. 'Stone me,' he said. 'Dozy old Cambridge. You'd hardly credit what goes on. Anyway, 'bye for now . . . Oh, and if I could just trouble you for that mobile number.'

On Wednesday night Kate went for supper at Hester's house in Eden Street. Built for railway workers, the small terrace houses were now, for the most part, smartened and colour-supplemented by young wannabes. Abstract prints, muted shades from esoteric charts, plants in pro-fusion, kitchens spilling into tiny conservatories, back-yards with passion flowers and Cretan pots. Hester's, however, was untypical. Her kitchen was in Monet's yellow and blue, while the sitting room was fifties bright, with the maddening gobbets of wax in the table lamp, and every detail loving. The rugs were orange, the parody ducks were going up the wall, and a wooden cut-out of a short-skirted cigarette girl held out a small tray, handy for glasses.

When Kate arrived Hester was panicking over the pastry base for a lemon tart.

'That bloody Delia, I'll kill her next time I see her,' Hester said.

'What's up?'

'This rotten pastry. When she does it on the telly it folds round the rolling pin like it's on a magnet. In real life, of course, it all falls totally to pieces. They ought to do her under the Trade Descriptions thingy.'

'Here,' Kate said. 'Let me have a go. Bit more icing sugar's the secret.'

'Oooooh! Hark at her! I tried some more estate agents by the way.' While she talked Hester filled two glasses with white wine. 'Here, get some of this down your neck. Cheers.'

'Cheers. Any luck?'

'Big zero. Must have rung twenty now. No one's heard of a Bright. One had a Wright and one had an Allbright, but no Brights. You?'

'Same. I thought I'd got lucky in Cottenham. They knew the surname but it turned out he'd moved out of the area years ago.'

'Was he a Richard?'

'Chester, would you believe! Apparently he was an American.'

'Chester Bright. Poor bugger.'

'I can't stop thinking about old Gilbert,' Kate said, as she transferred the now coherent pastry to the baking tin. 'Why on earth would he want to stay shtum about where he saw Bright? Unless he saw something he shouldn't.'

'Probably sees a lot he shouldn't.'

'What could it be, though? He obviously wasn't in Southwold.'

'Some nameless act of horribleness. Maybe he saw him breaking into the boat.'

'If he did.'

'Oh, here we go. If, if, if. Look, let's have a truce. Tonight, no Bright. Tonight Brightless, *capisce*?' She raised her glass. 'Here's to his final, ultimate, definitive disappearance from our lives.'

Twenty minutes later, Hester's other two guests arrived, Gareth and Siobhan, whom Kate liked at once. Though much younger than her, Siobhan seemed in some ways older. There was about her a sense of will and direction, combined with an easy, uncombative manner. At first glance she looked what Kate's mother would have called 'delicate'. Large eyes which, though engaging and alert, seemed also to harbour concern; skin that had a faint luminous quality, like light shining through parchment; a vein prominent in her temple; her heartbeat visible in the hollow of her throat; no makeup; a generous mouth, often smiling. And almost shocking against her white chest, the beginning of a red, snaking scar. Kate wondered about this. Perhaps a routine operation. Perhaps the result of an accident.

Gareth seemed the ideal complement to her. Straightforward, sensible, amusing, he showed no sign of the competitive urge that made so many men tiresome. He also had the gift of listening. Most new people Kate met paid superficial attention but gave the impression that they had half an eye on more exciting or more useful possibilities. They only listened in order to time their next line which, with rare exceptions, wasn't worth the effort. But Gareth was different. He seemed to want to understand, asked questions, had to be encouraged to talk about himself. If it was true that bedside manners mattered, or even existed in the age of battery medicine, he would make an ideal doctor.

As the lively conversation moved from the sitting room back to the kitchen, where the table was set, there were small signs that Siobhan and Gareth had grown just a little too used to each other; no longer surprised each other. At one level it was mutual comfort, the shorthand of familiarity. At another it was a sense that they'd begun to exhaust what they had in common. Kate had no idea what, in any case, that might be, since they didn't seem to share the same interests. Siobhan talked of the theatre, and of travel, the novels of Brian Moore, and extraordinary things she'd come across. Gareth spoke of science fiction, and vintage Aston Martins, and classic westerns. He took Hester's teasing in good part. But though Siobhan's fondness for him was plain, Kate had the feeling that she'd heard all this before, and that its fascination had almost run its course.

Hester's meal was a triumph. This was clear to her guests before they tasted it, since as she brought the first course, bruschetta, to the table, she said, 'I have to say, this meal is a triumph.' After the seared peppers, shining with olive oil, on a piquant tapenade, came slow-cooked pork with a herb crust, marinated in stout, and the sunny lemon tart with a dusting of icing sugar.

Over the pudding, the talk turned to dreams.

'I fly,' Hester said. ' 'S great. 'Bout once a week. Arms out, wind in your hair. You can see your shadow on the ground. Magic. Very happy-making. Sometimes I fly over Glasgow. Even that looks good. Sun on the Clyde, the Burrell sitting in its green park, all the messy bits tidied up. I'm thinking about taking passengers. I'm Hester, fly me!'

'Certainly not Virgin,' Kate said.

'That's a very common one,' Gareth said.

'Here, who are you calling common?' Hester said.

'Wishful thinking,' Kate said. 'Weightlessness.'

Hester laughed. 'Probably. Pass me the cheese. I don't think I'll be taking off tonight.'

'I fail my university entrance on a regular basis,' Gareth said. 'It's grim. Panic, cold sweats, prospect of telling your parents . . . the awful feeling that it's all your own fault. You didn't do the work and you thought you'd get away with it. Then you wake up and just for a second you wonder whether it's true. Then you know it isn't and it's great.'

'Fear of failure,' Siobhan said. 'Weird for you 'cause you've never failed at anything.'

'Come on, Kate,' Hester said. 'Time to own up about the bloke with the huge pecs.'

'If only,' Kate said. 'I get this one where I'm a kid again. There's this clump of bamboo in the middle of this bit of marshy ground. I know the others are in there somewhere, but I'm frightened of sinking in the bog and they won't tell me how they got there, or where the way in is. So I just sit there for hours . . . feels like hours.'

'Aaaaah, the puir wee bairn,' Hester said. 'What it is is they're smoking pot and they think you'll tell their mums.'

'Quite right too, disgraceful behaviour,' Kate said, laughing.

And then it was Siobhan's turn. 'This isn't mine, it's somebody else's. Friend of mine, good bit older than me. He has the weirdest dreams I've ever come across. They're like a life-story, told in instalments. But it's obviously not his life. This is all a long time ago. Centuries. There's always this man, dark, with a long nose and a bad stammer. When they started he was just a baby. My friend saw the christening. Well, you know, dreamed he saw it. Saw the man's mother and father. He can describe the clothes they were wearing, silks and furs, obviously well-off. Later, when this dark man grows up, he's dressed in incredibly rich gear, and he has an even richer friend, but you get the feeling there's a big power thing going on between the two of them. There's this amazing scene where they wrestle in the mud over a cloak, a red cloak. The more powerful one wants the dark man to give it to a beggar, which in the end he does. And there are these extraordinary processions . . . monkeys on horseback, wolves on leads, unbelievable treasure . . . Strange images like a huge plate of eels, all twisted and sinister . . .'

The listeners were rapt, silenced by Siobhan's complete immersion in her account.

'Later the dark man goes into battle, where he's a big hero. But then it all changes. Suddenly all the fine clothes have gone and he's in a very simple sort of habit thing. Underneath that he wears a hair shirt. He's obviously got on the wrong side of somebody because he's in a boat and my friend says he seems to be getting away from something dangerous. He lands on a white beach and there are these shells in the shape of a cross on it. But before that he meets the man he wrestled for the red cloak again. This time they're both on horses in a meadow full of flowers. There's some kind of terrible falling out and the dark man rides away. Hanging over it all there's always the feeling that something awful is going to happen to him.'

'Makes flying over Glasgow seem a bit tame, doesn't it?' Hester said.

'But the weirdest thing is my friend's beginning to identify with this character. He's beginning to feel what he feels, as though there's some strange connection, some kind of bond between them. And it's all getting more vivid and more threatening all the time.'

When Siobhan had finished there was silence for a moment, broken again by Hester with characteristic directness. 'So who is this mystery guy, the one who's getting these amazing trips?'

'You know who he is,' Siobhan said.

'I do?' Hester frowned, and then her brow cleared. 'Not the guy who . . . ?'

Siobhan nodded.

'Oh, right. God, weird or what?'

Seeing Kate's bafflement, Gareth explained, 'It's someone Siobhan met in hospital. Hugh Severin. He's a journalist. Travel writer. Writes for the *Mail* and various people.'

'He's not into Ecstasy by any chance?' Hester said.

Siobhan shook her head, smiling.

It wasn't until Gareth and Siobhan had left that

Hester told Kate the full story of the operation.

'So that's the scar,' Kate said.

'She doesn't like talking about it, you know, the transplant. She thinks people'll think she's a bit of a freak.'

'She's about the unfreakiest person I've ever met.'

'Thanks a lot. Here, have another bevvy and chuck us a fag.'

Kate didn't see Hester again until Friday after work, by which time she'd still had no luck with estate agents and Gilbert hadn't reappeared. It was such a mild evening she decided to walk to the Blue Ball. When she'd bedded the painting in bubble-wrap, she'd resented the time it took; going to all that trouble for someone she couldn't stand. In the end she'd told herself she was doing it for the artist. And now, in this soft light, with a timeless sense of well-being in the air, it was possible to forget the man she was walking to meet.

As she turned into Grantchester Road, she thought for a moment of the ghosts who had come this way over the centuries: scholars and saints, poets, scientists, explorers, innovators; men and women who had changed the world. Well, men. For most of the university's history women hadn't been allowed a look-in. What a blazing injustice that seemed now. Erasmus and Christopher Marlowe, remote figures she knew little about; Isaac Newton, who was supposed to have built that bridge at Queen's; Byron, limping. Kate thought of him as a sort of nineteenth-century Mick Jagger, so loud and flamboyant the curtains must have twitched as he passed – except that, judging by the age of the houses, there couldn't have been any curtains there then. Perhaps the rabbits had pricked up their ears. Charles Darwin, head down, intense, not many laughs with Charles as he broke off from his friends to pluck a wild flower from a ditch; Rutherford, atoms chasing each other round his brain like a spin-drier; Rupert Brooke, all floppy grace, heading for crumpets at the Old Vicarage, or maybe just crumpet; Augustus John, in a swirl of cape, his olive-brown lover on heat in the wooden caravan; Bertrand Russell, Wittgenstein, E. M. Forster, and on, and on, and on . . . Kate could see what Corcoran had meant by the glamour of learning. On evenings like this she felt it a little herself.

Hester, sitting on a bench outside the Blue Ball, waved as Kate passed the terrace of cottages with their random, reckless summer flowers. Bright hadn't arrived yet then. Nevertheless the greeting brought Kate back to the present with a slight sick feeling of apprehension.

'What do you fancy?' Hester said. 'I'm on the Guinness.'

Kate put the picture on the table. 'Do they do wine?'

'Don't know. Ask.' Hester put a five-pound note on the table.

'No sign?' Kate said, as she went through to the bar.

'Maybe he's cruised past and seen me here,' Hester said. 'Thought he'd be better off with a good book.'

'What about Corcoran?'

'Well, I've never met the gentleman so I don't know. Certainly nobody's been by with a truncheon.'

Ten minutes later, the familiar figure in white shirt

178

and black jeans appeared, not from the direction of the town but from the village end. Alone, as usual, he seemed smaller than either of them had remembered. 'Hello,' he said, recognising Kate first and then, with evident disappointment, Hester. 'Sorry I'm late.'

'We've been practically inconsolable,' Hester said.

Since neither of them offered to buy him a drink, Bright said, 'Anyone ready for another?'

Both women shook their heads. He went through to get his own.

'Doesn't look very frightening, does he, in Grantchester, in the evening? Where the corn is as high as an elephant's eye?' Hester said. 'Looks like one of those nerdy film buffs you used to see blinking outside the Arts.'

'Maybe he isn't frightening,' Kate said. 'Maybe it's just me.' She stood up to see if there was any sign of Corcoran.

'Where blokes are concerned, assume the worst. And sit down. You're making me nervous.'

'That's what life's taught you, is it?'

'That's what life's taught me.'

Bright emerged with a half of lager. 'You brought it, then,' he said, seeing the bubble-wrap.

'Yes,' Kate said.

'Like art, do you?' Hester said, as Bright sat opposite them.

'Some,' he said.

'Who's your favourite, then?'

'That's a bit like saying who's your favourite – I don't know – cyclist.' He'd taken his cue from an ancient black bicycle ridden by a Pre-Raphaelite young woman, which was squeaking by as he spoke.

'That's a bit like playing for time.' Hester was unrelenting.

'I don't know. Blake?'

'William or Sexton?'

'Who's Sexton?'

'Before your time.'

'So was William, marginally.' Bright took a sip of his lager. 'Are you always this aggressive?' he said.

'Only when somebody makes me feel aggressive.' Hester gave him a level look.

'Meaning me?'

'You said it.'

Kate was starting to feel uncomfortable. While part of her welcomed the confrontation, one she should perhaps have contrived herself, another part feared the consequences. And where was Corcoran, with his promises of being there or thereabouts?

Instead of reacting to Hester's provocation, Bright put his hand in his back pocket and drew out some twenty-pound notes. 'You'd better count it,' he said to Kate, his tone natural; friendly, even.

'I'm sure it's OK,' she said, cool, unencouraging.

'Do you get a buzz out of frightening people? Is that what you get off on? Fear?'

Hester's question seemed to catch Bright off-guard. He frowned before he spoke. 'What exactly are you talking about?'

Kate grew tense. Hester had been right. This had been a bad idea, now made worse by Hester herself.

'Is this a God thing of some kind?' Hester said. 'Are your victims your little crusade?'

Sensing the building unease, the young couple at the next table picked up their drinks and retreated indoors. It was then that Kate noticed, at the edge of her vision, an unmarked black car making very slow progress from the direction of Grantchester. At first she assumed it was more customers looking for a parking space, but as she turned to take it in, she recognised the face in the passenger seat. It was Spaull. Whether the driver was Corcoran she couldn't tell. She turned back to Hester, trying to alert her without making it obvious to Bright. Somehow they had to keep him talking, but the more Hester insulted him, the less likely he was to stay.

His fingertips joined on the table, something in him had changed: some resolution, some abandonment of a position. Now there was an abrupt, hard-faced disregard for the way they perceived him. Once again he was set apart in the warm summer light by his unsmiling intensity. 'Who do you think you are?' he said to Hester. 'What gives you the right to say these things?'

'Hest . . .' Kate wanted to warn her, to draw her attention to Spaull.

Hester ignored the signals. 'The fact that I'm her friend,' Hester said. 'I'm not afraid of you.'

The black car had stopped. Spaull was opening his door.

'You don't know what it is, fear. You use the word but you don't know what you're talking about.'

Spaull got out of the car and closed the door. With gentle acceleration, the driver moved on, perhaps to park.

'Hester . . .' Despite herself, Kate's tone had become more urgent.

'Which means you do, presumably?'

'Yes,' Bright said. 'I know what fear is.'

Neither of the women was in any doubt that he meant it. At that moment he caught sight of Spaull, and the tail of the black car disappearing behind the other parked vehicles. Hester, too, realised what was happening.

Bright got up, decisive but unhurried, and reached across for the packet.

'Where are you going? You can't just leave us in suspense. You can't just say a thing like . . . What are you afraid of?' Hester blustered, trying to hold him up.

Ignoring her, Bright said, 'Thank you,' to Kate.

'Oh . . .' Kate couldn't think of anything to keep him there. 'You haven't finished your—'

'I will see you again,' he said, as he turned and headed for the unmetalled lane separating the pub from the terrace.

'Not if we see you first,' Hester called, as she made a frantic gesture to Spaull, who was still at the foot of the path.

'No, no,' Bright said, just before he disappeared from view. 'You won't see me first.'

Chapter Seven

Hugh, Tilly, and Anthony sat at the back, with some of the staff. In front of them the residents of the old people's home in Clapham craned forward to hear the children's performance, several with hands cupped to ears. One old man wearing an Ivor Novello silk cravat disconcerted the rest by laughing in unexpected places. Anthony watched his reactions with particular interest. Sam, meanwhile, oblivious of his audience, inhabited the part of the Mad Hatter with robust conviction. Without a trace of self-consciousness he commanded his anarchic tea-party as though it were an unremarkable daily event, underpinned by a logic only fools could fail to understand. Because he didn't try to be funny, he was, and Hugh felt proud of his nine-year-old godson.

'Oh, God, please don't let him be an actor,' Tilly murmured.

'There's worse things,' Hugh whispered.

'Name one.'

'PR?'

'QPR?' Anthony added.

Chris Kelly

'What's that?' Tilly said.

'It's like acting, only in shorts,' Anthony said.

As the Dormouse fell into the teapot, made out of a cardboard box, the audience were invited to sing 'Food, Glorious Food'. Everyone joined in with varying appetite, except the man in the cravat who took it upon himself to conduct. After this the cast bowed to the applause and mingled with the residents. Sam shook hands with most of them and answered their questions, before working his way over to his parents and Hugh.

'Can I have your autograph?' Hugh said.

'Felix says when he's famous he's going to invent a machine to do them automatically,' Sam said.

'Tell me you wouldn't like to do this for a living, love. Make an old woman very happy.' Tilly made a mock-beseeching face.

'Trouble is, you just have made an old woman very happy,' Anthony said. 'To say nothing of two relatively old blokes.'

'Get your slap off, love. We'll treat you to a Huge Mac,' Tilly said.

Hugh would have liked to join them at McDonald's but Dacre had asked to see him. Since the piece about Rupert Kent-Imison, which had been well received all round, Hugh had written for three other editors. One had sent him to Seville, a city he'd always loved, for a long weekend. Charlesworth, of the *Telegraph*, had commissioned three thousand words on Romania, which Hugh had described as a country lit by a single forty-watt bulb. (In the translated fish section of a menu in Bucharest, due to an unfortunate typo, he'd come across one of the world's least appetising dishes: Steamed Crap.) And Rutter of the *Guardian* had asked him for a piece about Bruce Chatwin, whom Hugh had met on several occasions. In it he touched for the first time on a not altogether flattering insight. Having read and admired *Songlines*, with its extraordinary passages about aboriginal intuition, he had once found himself sitting next to a distinguished Australian anthropologist at a supper party in Melbourne. Eager to hear what he assumed would be an admiring endorsement of Chatwin's mystical revelations, he had asked the Professor for his opinion of the book. 'Total bollocks,' the academic had said, with startling economy. According to him, Chatwin's engaging theories about complex inherited song-maps were elaborate embroidery.

Hugh had felt that this piece, in particular, was a step in the direction he wanted, though the ultimate goal was still unclear. At least it was an advance on descriptions of featureless resorts and the most obvious cultural characteristics. But best of all had been an enquiry from a publisher. An editor at HarperCollins, Amy Casarotto, had written asking if he'd be interested in doing a travel-based book for them. Something fresh. Something that reflected changing, more demanding, more affluent tastes. They hadn't any strong preconceived ideas and would welcome his. But the trouble with that sort of book was that it tended to date so fast. Trends were trendy. They didn't last. Added to which, the scant demand for his first attempt in that genre was less than encouraging. That's where Chatwin had been so clever. Invented or not, his well-written observations had seemed to touch deeper, longer-lasting issues. Keep the flattering Ms Casarotto on the back burner then, until he had a better idea.

Meanwhile, as the bus headed for Kensington, he found himself thinking about Anthony and Tilly and Sam. They were still the nearest he had to family. Always would be, he supposed. Shame that he'd arrived at nearly fifty without one of his own. Hard not to think of it as a failure, even though his rational self knew it wasn't. Thank God Tilly was a generous friend; in many ways his closest and best. But the real bonus was Sam. He was getting to know Hugh for the first time, without prejudices of any sort. Hugh was determined never to let him feel like a surrogate, but always to make the most of his growing up; to spend as much time with him as Tilly and Anthony allowed; help broaden his already broad horizons. No doubt there were plenty of things Sam could teach him too.

The funny thing was that Hugh was also beginning to think of Siobhan as family, though in conventional terms they knew little of each other. He thought about her often, as though they were near-contemporaries with an atticful of shared experiences. That was so strange. He was sure he wouldn't have felt that way if the transplanted organ had been a liver or a kidney. They were mere offal. Then again, what else was the heart? It was a thing with a function, like the stomach or the bowel. But a feeling as profound as this couldn't just be put down to a piece of meat. It was written through him, Brighton rock-like in the bone. It had changed him. Given him an insistent awareness that he wasn't the only important person in his life. To some extent the divorce had forced that realisation on him about Tilly, and the birth of Sam had underlined it. But this thing with Siobhan was stronger even than that. And yet, at the same time, it was more vulnerable because he couldn't assume it was shared. More reasonable, perhaps, to assume it wasn't.

How, he wondered, did she link with these dreams? What possible connection could there be between a modern young woman and obscure events hundreds of years ago? But there must be a connection, he was clear about that. The fact that they'd started with the operation couldn't be accidental. Could there have been some form of weird transmission from her to him? If that were the case you'd expect the dreams to strike a chord with her too. Even if they'd lain dormant in her subconscious, they should have rung a bell when he described them. But it was clear that they hadn't. They had been quite alien to Siobhan.

Maybe he should talk to somebody about them, a shrink. Lie back on the old couch and chat his way through them. Thank you very much, that'll be two hundred quid. Next! No, what was the point? What could a shrink know about them that he couldn't find out himself? Because he knew he would find out. A sequential story was unfolding in his head. It was travelling a route, and its impetus was leading him to expect an eventual end, an end that seemed bound to be tragic. As events accumulated, the mood was growing darker, and his identification with the struggles of the principal figure was becoming stronger. Anticipation and apprehension had combined in him to form what he supposed a shrink would call an obsession, but one with a stubborn claim on reality. Whatever reality was. Some Spanish writer had reckoned life is a dream, and dreams are dreams. Meanwhile Hugh's notes on his night-world were beginning to look impressive. Even the bizarre, uninterpretable details seemed part of an overall logic which, when revealed, might, at a stroke, become coherent.

'I'm feeling generous.' Dacre was pacing, a sign that his travel editor's brain was working overtime.

'What's brought this on?' Hugh said.

'Dunno, but don't knock it. Remember old Jimmy Cameron?'

'The by-line, of course. I never met him. Wish I had.'

'I wish you had. He was a prince, Jimmy. Piss-artist and a prince. Best foreign correspondent I ever knew. He could sober up for half an hour and write what you'd been trying to say about a place for a week.' Dacre chuckled. 'Gibraltar. The first border bust-up. I had breakfast with him one morning. He looked like shit. I said, "Where were you last night, Jimmy? We looked all over." He said, "I went to see the Governor." "Oh, yes," I said. "And?" He said, "I was met by the aide-de-camp, charming chap, and by way of conversation I asked him how long he'd been with His Excellency. Two years, he said. Two years next Tuesday, as a matter of fact." "Good," Jimmy said, "because despite hours of research there's one thing I'm still not absolutely clear about. What actually is the Governor's name?" Whereupon the young man furrowed his brow and said, "There you have me!" ' The laughter took years off Dacre. He sat down, shaking his head at the fond memory. 'And what have you got now? Children in designer flak jackets. Jimmy had more talent in his earwax. Anyway, point is, Jimmy's editor once had him in and said, "Look, you've been everywhere, twice mostly. Here's your chance to go to the one place you've never been and've always desperately wanted to. Where'll it be?" Jim thought for a second and said, "Blackpool!" ' Dacre smiled at the illogical logic of the choice. 'And for you, Hugh my boy, in a similar sort of a way, opportunity knocks. The world, my son, is your pork pie. Pick a card, any card, where'll it be?'

Hugh wished he had an answer as unexpected as James Cameron's, but he didn't have an answer at all. There wasn't anywhere he longed to see. Nevertheless he heard himself saying, 'Boulogne.' Where on earth had that come from? True he hadn't been there for years, but then it had seemed just a plain little place with a nice old bit at the top of the hill. If he wanted to go there, he was the last to know.

'Boulogne?' Dacre said. 'Sure you don't mean Bologna? Bolivia? Bali?'

'No, Boulogne,' Hugh confirmed. 'I seem to want to go to Boulogne.' As well as being a surprise to him as a location, it wasn't consistent with his new ambition to move on. It was as though the part of him that took over at night had made a brief, unannounced break-through in daylight; had spoken with its own voice, rather than his.

'Well, Boulogne it is, then,' Dacre said. 'Good news is, it's cheap. Bad news, remind me again what's the story exactly?'

'Er, there isn't one. But there will be.' Hugh did a swift, imaginary recce. 'Did the beef-ban make the Channel wider, despite the Tunnel? Deep down, are we kidding ourselves with this Europe lark? Will it one day come to another Waterloo?'

'So crap, basically?'

'Basically,' Hugh conceded. 'No, honestly. Something tells me it's a Promised Land.'

The encounter made Hugh smile on the top deck of the bus as he made his way home. He liked Dacre, despite his contradictions. On the one hand he would come on strong in the pub about the inequities of the class system, but he'd sent his son to Westminster, and his daughter was doing a doctorate at Warwick. His muscle-flexing was all camouflage; the rather futile rearguard action of a man surrounded by colleagues who, though they'd had a better formal education, knew next to nothing. Hugh had seen them patronise him, as though youth were a talent. That made Dacre behave more like a brontosaurus than ever, and so the cycle repeated itself

Boulogne, though. What the hell was he going to find to say about Boulogne? It had been like the opposite of a brainwave. No point in consulting the cuttings library. Maybe he could dig up a wartime anniversary. Take a veteran back to the military cemetery high above the town, off the road to Wimereux. He remembered the terrible silence of the place. The rows and rows and rows of white, precise, well-drilled head-stones. The obsessive need to impose order on the bloody, panic-stricken chaos that had slaughtered them all. An attempt to give it spurious rationalisation. They'd have been better served by a great thicket of old roses, Hugh thought. Something disordered, un-neat, that came to life again every spring. The graves gave them dignity, it was argued, but it was the cold, soulless dignity of a corpse on a mortuary slab.

Anyway, that wasn't what the readers wanted to hear. Maybe he could save it for the book. Get together a collection of contentious, travel-based essays. How tourism in the Caribbean had replaced one kind of slave economy with another; chefs sweating their guts out in airless kitchens for a pittance. The shrinking world as a paedophile's oyster. Great title for a chapter, that, 'The Paedophile's Oyster'. Horrible but great. The fatal erosion of one culture by another. The Philippines was the ideal spot, Hugh thought. In Manila everyone spoke with a phoney American accent. Even the gaudy taxi-buses were called Jeepneys. And that terrible restaurant . . . what was it? The Hobbit House! Built two-thirds scale, with a staff of dwarfs, front of house and kitchen. And a blind band; all five of them wearing dark glasses. Oh, God. The saddest city he'd ever seen.

Back at the flat, Hugh listened to his messages on the answerphone. Sam was on, saying he'd worked out a way of reproducing his autograph with a potato-cut and he was going to fax one. He also ran through a quick recipe he'd invented for savoury pancakes, which he said were lovely. Some PR woman asked if Hugh wanted to come to a P. & O. lunch at the Lanesborough. Martha said she'd like to talk about a piece on the great writer and traveller Wilfred Thesiger. She said he had the sexiest face since Thomas More. Hugh smiled. Martha's unfashionable Catholic certainty was made user-friendly by a quick and often racy wit. Built like a tugboat, she hurtled round town on a motor scooter, often sticking Fisherman's Friends to the dome of her crash helmet. This aromatic decoy, she insisted, would divert attention from the smell of whisky if she was stopped by the police. She'd once told Hugh that she'd had an audience with the late Pope John XXIII. When she'd knelt to kiss the papal ring, she'd been all but overcome by a sudden urge to bite his plump knuckle. She'd only managed to quell the impulse by concentrating hard on thoughts of Enoch Powell. Hugh made a note to call her and Sam.

And Siobhan was on the tape. 'Hi, Hugh. Greetings from St Ives. This friend of mine, Stella, runs a wine bar down here and I'm helping her out for a couple of weeks. And looking at paintings. Lovely paintings. The Tate's great. Little Alfred Wallis. Amazing. When they discovered him all these big names started doing pictures like uneducated fishermen. Quite funny, really. Anyway, thing is my dad's going to be in London on Saturday and he wants us to have dinner. At the River Café. Typical. Remember what I told you? This weird thing about public places? I've never been, have you? Sounds yummy. So I hope you don't mind but I've said to make it three. Think you might like him. Please come. See you there, eightish? Only ring if you can't.

But please can. Dying to see you . . .'

Hugh switched off the machine. He was surprised by the invitation. And excited. Surprised because when Siobhan had first told him about her father it had seemed such a closed, private relationship, not for sharing. The fact that she was now prepared to open it up to Hugh was generous and trusting. At the hospital they'd only just been introduced, but what if the elegant antiquarian bookseller didn't like him? Any father was bound to be a bit thrown when his daughter turned up with a bloke thirty years older. And this bloke had her heart inside him. If the positions had been reversed, and he were the father, Hugh wasn't sure he could have handled it. But the great thing was that Siobhan wanted it to happen. Nothing else mattered. 'Dying to see you . . .' she'd said. Hugh had planned to take the ferry on Friday, but now he'd delay the trip to Boulogne until Monday. The later the better. He still hadn't come up with an angle and had begun to think the whole thing had been a whimsy too far.

Had it been a racehorse, the River Café would have been the winner of a prestigious race at Goodwood. Its breeding was impeccable. Out of two stylish chefs by a world-famous architect, it combined glamour with a passion for real food. Not designer minimalism, showy and insincere, but big flavours carrying the colours of owners with something intelligent and consistent to say. Hugh had only been once before, when he was being wooed by a television producer trying to impress. Not impress Hugh, but his fellow diners. It was soon clear, however, that they hadn't the slightest idea who he was. And if they had recognised him, they still wouldn't have given him a second look. This large room fronting the river had seen more celebs than a name-dropper's wet dream. In fact that very time there had been an electrifying frisson when Imran Khan had arrived to find himself a couple of tables away from Salman Rushdie. The former cricketer appealed to the umpire in a loud rage, and the then fatwah-stricken writer had to be moved to the outfield.

Not wanting to be the first, Hugh had timed his entrance for eight fifteen. Sure enough the room was full of faces he recognised from television and the papers. But his eye was soon drawn to the most distinguished-looking figure among them. With his back to the window, Siobhan's father projected lean, handsome charm like an antique bronze of a young athlete. That was it. He didn't look his age. He didn't look any age. Even from this distance he seemed easy, animated, alert. But what was missing? Hugh wondered. Why hadn't he taken more care of that marvellous girl?

As the waiter showed Hugh across, Siobhan got up to meet him and held out both hands in greeting. 'Hello,' she said.

Hugh kissed her on both cheeks. 'Hello.'

'This is my dad. Alexander Herbert, Hugh Severin.'

Alexander stood. Creased black linen jacket; cream linen trousers; pale blue shirt; brown skin much creased by a smile. A man who would have looked good dressed in Sainsbury's shopping bags, Hugh thought, a little daunted. They shook hands.

'Good to meet you,' Hugh said. 'I've heard . . . You

know, Siobhan's told me . . .' It was rare to find himself tongue-tied.

Sensing this, Alexander said, 'If it was good, discount half of it. If it was bad, don't believe a word.'

Feeling easier, Hugh sat down.

'It's very good of you to join us,' Alexander went on. 'I'm afraid I'm very dull company for my daughter.'

'That's not what I've heard,' Hugh said.

'He's just looking for compliments,' Siobhan said. 'But he isn't getting one because he gets far too many.'

Over a glass of champagne, Hugh asked Alexander about living in the Caribbean.

'It's the sounds,' Alexander said. 'Sweet sounds. And there's a wonderful spoiled innocence about it, like Paradise after the Fall. I love it, really. I can't take noise any more. And all the grubbiness. So I decided to postpone it. Indefinitely.'

'Is Paradise utterly Paradise? Nothing you miss?' Hugh said.

'Not a thing. Not a single thing. I think people are always a little disappointed when I say that, but it's true. If I were a thrusting young man it might be different, but I fear that even when I was young I wasn't particularly thrusting. Such a charmless lexicon, isn't it? Thrusting, motivated, upwardly mobile . . . They're all about machines, aren't they, not people?'

'You've opted out, haven't you, Daddy?' Siobhan's question was one Hugh wouldn't have dared ask.

'Have I? Perhaps I have. Or might I have opted in, do you think? Is that a possibility?' Either way, it was clear that Alexander wasn't very concerned. As the first course arrived he went on, 'Mind you, service isn't frightfully rapid in Paradise. On one occasion I was lunching with a friend at the Hilton in Port of Spain. We could see that the pace was leisurely so we ordered something terribly simple. Ham and eggs, something of that sort. After half an hour still no ham and eggs so my friend finally said to the perfectly charming waitress, "Do you think you might see your way to feeding us relatively soon?" Whereupon she said, "Sorry about the delay, folks, but the chef has lost the frying pan!" After that we didn't much mind if lunch never appeared at all.'

To Hugh's relief, Alexander didn't ask about the state of their health. But then, of course, he wouldn't. That would have been far too obvious. It was also in the past which, although he made a living as an antiquarian bookseller, didn't appear to interest him. And it concerned other people. Even though one of them was his only daughter, it seemed to Hugh that he was more concerned with ideas and sensations than the messy business of relationships. Perhaps it was the noise of the latter he was escaping rather than the literal din of the traffic. Hugh remembered a pompous old political pundit he'd once met who'd uttered the sad and tiresome line, 'My books are my children.' On the other hand, Alexander was neither sad nor tiresome. Nor did he seem self-obsessed. But maybe Siobhan was right. Maybe he had pulled into harbour, like one of Alfred Wallis's fishing-boats. Except that he'd be a sleek yacht, its grace enhanced by age.

Hugh and he got on well, and that pleased Siobhan.

Unlike his notable absence on her degree day.

'Everybody had parents and brothers and sisters and everything, and there was me with nobody to show off to,' she said.

'Poor darling,' Alexander said, without a trace of remorse.

Despite their apparent ease, Hugh thought, he and his class had an inner toughness which, though in some ways admirable, was also callous. It outlawed self-pity, but it also short-circuited sensitivity to human emotional needs. Implanted behind the granite walls of public schools, it had built an empire but at fantastic personal cost.

At the end of the evening, Hugh assumed that father and daughter would leave together, but as they walked to the door Siobhan said, 'Daddy's going west, young man. There's a book fair in Bath. Share a cab? I'm up in Hampstead again.'

Hugh was delighted. They watched Alexander get into his hired family saloon, waving as he drove away towards Hammersmith. Then they walked between rows of modest, expensive terrace houses to the main road.

'Well?' Siobhan said.

'Well what?'

'What did you think?'

'Truth?'

'Of course.'

'Mixed feelings, a bit. I mean, I liked him very much. You can't help but, can you? But it's this strange non-involvement thing. Semi-detached. I suppose my father was the same. Not breeding-wise obviously, but emotionally. What is it with these people?'

'Maybe they don't need attachment.'

'But can't they see that other people might?' Hugh paused. 'I mean, how couldn't he be attached to you, for God's sake?' What he'd said took him by surprise. It expressed something about his feelings that he hadn't been ready to reveal. It was protective, the enquiry of a friend, but it was also something else. It was hurt and angry on her behalf, on their behalf, almost.

Siobhan didn't reply, but looked at him. And held his look for a moment.

In the taxi, Hugh told her about Boulogne. He said he'd been hasty and hadn't the foggiest idea what to write about.

'Can I come?' she said.

'What – Boulogne?' Hugh felt stupid even as he said it.

'I mean, if I wouldn't be a nuisance.'

'Course you can. I'd love you to. What about your chum in St Ives?'

'Oh, Stella's fine. I'll ring her. Sure?'

'Oh, yes,' Hugh said. 'Absolutely sure.'

The Monday-morning ferry was only a quarter full. Hugh had arranged to meet Gary on the other side, in mid-week, when he'd settled on a story, so he and Siobhan felt like holidaymakers. They went up on deck to look at the dingy white cliffs.

'I still get excited,' Siobhan said, 'even though it's only twenty miles away.'

In itself, the act of travelling no longer stirred Hugh.

Hours of listlessness at ghastly airports, like Tunis, endless discomforts, international petty officialdom, cramped seats and offhand service had long since inoculated him against excitement. But here, now, on the least adventurous journey in tourism, he felt, for the first time in years, the unmistakable fission of anticipation. He also had the underlying sensation that he'd been here before. No, it wasn't that. Of course he'd been here before, countless times; stood at an identical rail, filling his lungs with the freer air and looked at the unchanging, clichéd view. No, this was more like something deeper in him responding to the crossing; some unidentified piece of music that found its answering harmonies on this busy, unremarkable gusset of water.

Women could travel so light, Hugh thought, as they sat in the bar with a glass of chardonnay. Siobhan's slender red holdall looked hardly bigger than a wallet, and yet it had everything she needed for a stay of several days. His packing had taken half an hour. This shirt or that? Those trousers or the chinos? A tie in case of a formal meeting, or to hell with it? But here she was, spotless and creaseless in white jeans and black T-shirt, while already he looked as though he'd been playing the Eton wall game. This was the central mystery. Why did the world's creases target men? And not just their clothes but their faces too? A man of forty looked like a ploughed field, but Meryl Streep was lineless.

'It's a shocking conspiracy,' he said, drawing Siobhan's attention to the issue. 'And, quite frankly, men have put up with it far too long.'

'Well, at least to realise it's a conspiracy is a start,'

Siobhan said. 'Now you can do something about it. All you've got to do is suss out Mister Big and just tell him it's not good enough. Just say, "Look matey, it's high time women had some of the wrinkles".'

'Half.'

'Exactly. Half the wrinkles.'

'He's probably got a lot Himself, hasn't He? You know, running things.'

'For zillions of years. Probably. So He'd probably think it was a great idea.'

'Do you think matey is, you know, the proper form of address? He wouldn't think it was a touch . . . *lèse-majesté*ish?'

'Perhaps a touch. Obe Wan Kenobe?'

'Gary thinks He's called Rupert.'

'That's nice. Rupert.'

They both giggled. The sun was on the Channel. The lounge was half empty. As far as Hugh was concerned the crossing could take a month.

'What am I going to write about?' he said.

'Something amazing. We'll find something amazing that's never been written about before. Ever. It'll be the scoop of all time.'

They took a taxi from Calais to Boulogne and checked in at the Metropole, a quiet hotel in the refurbished shopping district. Hugh then suggested they hire another taxi and drive back along the coast, towards Wimereux. He hadn't anticipated this before they landed, but the moment they were ashore, he knew it was what he wanted to do. It was as though another layer of consciousness was taking over. Not a sinister manipulator but an unseen navigator sure of his way.

At Terlincthun they turned off the main road so that Hugh could show Siobhan the war cemetery. Nearest the entrance, the countless graves of the Germans: *Martin Schurer, Willy Schroder, Wilhelm Burkhardt*, all killed in November 1918. Further on, in the polite uniform of the immaculate grass, the battalions of the British dead, many of them nameless: *A Soldier of the Great War, known unto God* . . . More victims of the slaughter's last November: *Second Lieutenant Walter Hall, Private Bertie Mallows, Signaller James Sidney Smith* . . . *Our Darling Son – Thy will be done* . . . *We cannot forget our Bobby* . . . And high on the hill, in ironic command of these last, silent trenches, Napoleon on his column, looking towards England.

Neither Hugh nor Siobhan said anything. Not in the cemetery and not in the taxi afterwards, driving through the undulating country with few trees, until they reached Wissant. Hugh had never been here before but the sureness he couldn't identify told him to direct the driver down the hill into the village. They parked in the square, facing the Hôtel Normandy. Outside the restaurant, Le Vivier, stood a fishing-boat on wheels, bellied like a pregnant mare, filled with geraniums. They went first to the church, cold inside even on a warm evening. More memorials. Grey marble plaques. *Priez Dieu pour le repos de l'âme de Joseph Altazin – disparu en mer* . . . *A mon fils, Henri Malfoy – perdu en mer, le 18 Octobre 1939, âgé de 16 ans ½* . . . *Jean Ledet. Marin mort pour la France à Saigon* . . .

'I feel shivery,' Siobhan said.

They walked down to the beach and sat on the terrace of a long low bar facing the sea, Les Sirènes. To the west, the tapered headland with its slender lighthouse. The pale shy waiter brought a small saucer of fresh shrimps with the drinks. They watched the bright sails of the sand yachts, the dogs chasing driftwood thrown by children, the sleek windsurfers carrying their boards, the colours of the sea: glossy, light grey in the foreground; the brown underbelly of the curling waves; a dozen shades of blue, patched and banded with shadow. More than ever Hugh had the feeling that some part of him knew this place. But he also had the extraordinary sensation that it wasn't somewhere he'd arrived at. It was a leaving point. A point of embarkation. A place left with some regret, and not without apprehension. As he traced the patterns of the children's kites, there was a hollowness in him like hunger. But he knew it wasn't the lack of food. It was a sudden fear. He felt isolated, alone, as though some inexorable, ancient potency was drawing him towards a hostile confrontation. Like Private Bertie Mallows, and Signaller James Sidney Smith . . . Like Frank McGuffog.

'Fancy pushing on a bit?' Hugh said.

Siobhan nodded, and finished her drink. They drove on towards Calais, quiet in the calm mood of the afternoon. In half an hour they reached Oye, where high dunes with a sparse covering of long coarse grass hid the sea. The taxi pulled into the car park. A sign said it was a nature reserve. The wide, white beach stretched as far as they could see. A few children were playing on the sand, while parents lay, leaning on one elbow, or smoking while they talked. Hugh walked down towards the Channel. He had a strong feeling that this place too held a special significance for him, though he was certain it was the first time he'd been here. And if he'd felt that the beach at Wissant was a point of departure, this one had the strangeness of arrival. As he walked back up the sand towards where Siobhan was standing, watching him, his unidentified guide told him he was retracing footsteps. And the footsteps were not his own. For a moment, as he drew level, the dream broke through. He stopped where he stood. His forehead felt clammy. He had no consciousness of his immediate surroundings.

His legs feel heavy. His feet are wet from his landing at the edge of the water. He glances to his right and left. Empty. Inhospitable. Is this a warning of the treatment he can expect? Used to the company of men, he feels friendless, abandoned, though the abandonment has been of his choosing. As he makes his uncertain, reluctant way to the beginning of the land, darkening now as the day nears its end, he says a prayer . . .

'Hugh?'

Hugh felt a hand holding his.

'Hugh, are you OK?'

He was back now. Back from wherever he'd been. Back from where he was standing at this moment, that was the unsettling thing. And Siobhan was holding his hand. He wanted her to go on holding it. But spontaneous gestures couldn't be prolonged, otherwise they were turned into something else. Their meaning was meant only to be momentary, unburdened with deep intention. If he squeezed her hand now, held it tight, walked away holding it, the thing was spoiled. 'I'm fine,' he said. 'Just a bit of a dizzy spell.' He let go of her with a gentle disengagement.

'You didn't look fine. You went all white.'

'No, I'm OK, honestly.'

'Tell me,' she said. 'Don't bottle it up. We don't have to do that.'

Hugh looked at her. 'It's just I got one of those flash-backs again. It's like . . . it's like – not that I've been here before exactly, but that the bloke in the dream was here and . . .'

'Go on.'

'Well, up to now it's like I've been watching his story, if you like. Like watching a film in bits . . . But more and more it seems like I'm becoming him. I can feel what he's feeling. It's like I'm the story too. And part of it happens here, but God knows when.'

'Well, I think that's great. You've got your very own private soap, with an audience of one. And no need for a telly. Only you'll know how it ends.'

'That's what worries me.'

'Why? It's only a dream, Hugh. It's not real.'

'All these people have left him now,' Hugh went on, 'and he's . . . he seems quite apprehensive. And when I'm in the dream, I feel apprehensive too.'

'Look,' she put her hand on his shoulder, 'we all get recurring dreams. It's nothing to get het up about. Honestly. One day it'll go just like it came. You've been through some pretty traumatic stuff. But you're fine.

You're not mad. You're not somebody else. You're you, and you're fine. Mmmm?'

Whether or not she really believed what she was saying, Hugh knew this wasn't the moment to pursue the matter. In any case, she might well be right. This thing was getting out of proportion. Who knew what the mind was capable of? There was the story of that Russian. They'd sat him ten feet away from a tank full of saline solution, broken an egg into it, and sealed it up with lead. Half an hour later he'd separated the white from the yolk, just by concentrating. It was alleged. Maybe Hugh's mind, in a bit of a confused state after the operation, had picked on an image at random from the bran tub of his memory, decided it quite liked it, and spun it out to make, as Siobhan said, a sort of serial. But why was he starting to identify with the leading actor? Because dreams didn't follow any conscious logic, he told himself. Because the invisible director in his head had decided it was an amusing way to go. 'I'll shut up,' he said. 'Come on, let's go and have a stupendous meal. Apparently the French are quite good at it.'

They ate on the first floor of a small restaurant opposite the aquarium. Perhaps assuming they were lovers, the *maître d'* had shown them to a table by the window, overlooking the lights of the yacht marina. The atmosphere was relaxed, the service attentive without being either officious or obsequious. And the food, well judged, without pretensions, cooked to its strengths without a mask of rich sauces, was perfect. Mindful of Scoular's little lecture about alcohol, they settled for a glass of red wine each, though Hugh felt in the mood for a couple of bottles.

'Do you know something?' he said.

'What?'

'I'm happy. I feel . . . happy.'

'That's funny. So do I.' She lifted her glass in a toast. 'To you being happy, and also to me being happy.' She drank. 'It's been a lovely day. A day of unusual loveliness. Thank you.'

Later, alone in his room, Hugh opened his notebook. He felt that writing about the moment on the beach might help him interpret it. As with the rest of the growing narrative, he would try not to put down more than he knew. Where he couldn't remember details he would resist the temptation to invent them. Tell it like it was. No tarting up. As he was poised to begin, the telephone rang.

'Hello.'

'Hugh?'

'Yes.'

'Daks.'

Hugh looked at his watch. Five minutes past eleven. Had the French President been assassinated? Had British football hooligans sunk a ferry with the combined weight of their beer bellies? What had these things to do with a travel writer? Furthermore, a travel writer on a sabbatical.

Anticipating his reaction, Dacre went on, 'Sorry about the time, matey, but I wanted to be sure I caught you.'

'You've caught me.'

'What it is is Kaiser Bill's brother-in-law, Ronnie

Something-or-other, is in the property game . . .'

Kaiser Bill was the office name for Dacre's boss, William Cautley, a born-again Canadian bully. Hugh began to fear the very worst.

'Hello?'

'I'm all ears, Daks, well, mostly ears but also quite a lot of apprehension.'

'. . . is in the property game. In France. I'll fax you all this stuff in the morning. Buys and sells type thing. Holiday homes for the man who has everything. Bent as buggery by all accounts. Anyway, old Bill's obviously had a bell from Ronnie Bent-as-Buggery, who's gone, "Do us a favour, Bill old chap. Property game's a bit on the slow side. How's about you get one of your lackeys to do a piece on how it's a great time to buy in France? Pound's strong. Sun's shining. Brits with homes here already are as happy as *cochons* in *merde* type thing. And by way of a sweetener, Bill old bean, I promise I'll stop asking your dear sister to wear a bridle and bit every time we do the business . . . Oh, and you know that little place you took a fancy to in Clochemerle? It's yours, squire. Little pressie from *moi*. Forty acres of olive trees, its own vineyard, Olympic-size pool . . . My pleasure." Hello?'

'Still here, Daks.'

'Get the picture, Huge?'

'I get the picture, Daks. It's not a Rembrandt, is it?'

'Look, I'm not saying it's the story of a lifetime . . .'

'Good. I'm glad you're not saying that.'

'. . . and I know I promised you a nice little skive in Boulogne, but what can I say, Huge? This is the man who pays the bills. Anyways, not all bad news, mate. Schlep down to Burgundy, take your time, chat up a few Brits, including Monsewer Bent-as-Buggery – that's hyphenated by the way – guzzle your way through great steaming piles of top tucker, sample the local plonk and there you go. Plus, you've earned the undying gratitude of Kaiser Bill. I know blokes who'd kill for the job.'

'Where does he hang out, this Monsieur Bent-as-Buggery? Hyphenated.'

'Er, place called . . . Hold on . . . Pontigny. That's where his office is. Near Auxerre, apparently. And Chablis, Huge. How about that? Sounds like paradise to me, mate. Beats bloody Boulogne any day of the week . . . Hello?'

'Yes, hello.'

'Are we on, then?'

'I suppose so.'

Dacre again promised to send the details in the morning, reassured Hugh that this act of co-operation would never be forgotten as long as newspapers were printed, and rang off. Hugh felt deflated. This was what he'd always hated about the job: the cynical, routine manipulation of trivial facts. The you-rub-my-back-and-I'll-rub-yoursism. The arse-licking. It wasn't like lying because of genuine misinterpretation, or lying with a purpose, as you might have to in wartime. It was a complete abandonment of even notional principles. As a young man he'd gone along with it. Found it funny, even. He still did find it funny, come to that. Quite ridiculous, in fact. But time was getting shorter.

In his mind he'd set his alarm clock at ten years, not daring to hope for longer. Ten years. Three thousand six hundred and fifty days. Didn't sound many when you put it like that. Minus the months since the operation. No. Don't count them. Start the clock again tomorrow, but that must be the last cheat. And two or three of these precious days he was going to have to spend with some creep who sold houses. Or, rather, who wasn't selling houses so was about to be handed thousands of pounds-worth of free publicity.

Hugh wondered how Siobhan would react to news of the assignment. He couldn't quite imagine how he'd put it to her. It sounded so pathetic and humiliating, as though he were a small boy made to nick fags by the leader of the gang. She'd think he was gutless. And she'd be right. Maybe he should have just told Dacre where to shove the story. Nothing personal, of course, but this is a lumber too far. I'm out of here. If only. But with ten years left you didn't want to be struggling. You wanted to be able to enjoy it. Squeeze the very last drop out of it. On the other hand, you wanted to make it count. Produce something worth leaving behind . . . Oh, bollocks. Do this last one, then think again. And if he could persuade Siobhan to come, with an honest, straightforward please, the three days could be a glorious bonus.

Hugh picked up his notebook again, determined to get something down. At least it was a way of putting the conversation with Dacre out of his mind. As he paused at the end of a paragraph, he felt a sudden tide of utter weariness. It was as though all of him had let go at once. The mechanism had worked just as long as it was needed and now, with fine timing, had sighed the last of its energy. He lay on the bed, too tired even to take off his shoes.

The dark man lies on the straw-filled mattress, too exhausted to undress. He remembers every yard of the ride on the rough, unlit road, with only the sound of the horse's hoofs for company. He remembers other rides, accompanied by many men in rich clothes who lean forward with eagerness to please when he turns to address them. He remembers, too, the quiet of the early-morning hours, and homage given rather than received.

With the coming of the light, the first conversations of birds, he leaves the poor place where he slept and walks as far as the river. The boatman agrees to take him on board and, flanked by tall bulrushes, they glide into a tableau of sky and water so untarnished that they might have been the first men ever to see it. Hope returns with the warming of the sun, and a certainty that this lonely course is the one destiny requires of him.

Now, once again, he is among friends, who show him deference. His refuge is a large settlement of solemn buildings surrounded by trees. He can smell the sweet pines the moment he dismounts, separating their fragrance from the pungent scent of the horses.

His heart is emptied of bitterness. As he stands in a small bare stone room, he removes his drab outer layers of clothing. Beneath, next to his poor skin, unseen by anyone but him, is a garment made of goats' hair, covering him from neck to knee. With care he pulls it over his head. His bare back is scored with long, thin, lateral cuts. Some have not yet healed. Others are covered in yellow scabs. Where the blood still oozes from wounds reopened by the exertion, there is also the corruption of pus. And scavenging in these shallow, obscene trenches, there are maggots.

There is a discreet knock at the oak door. Head bowed, a figure enters. In his hand is an object with a short handle, bound with horsehair. From this hang stiff leather thongs. The newcomer seems to ask the dark man's forgiveness, which is granted. He then proceeds to flay the already raw back until the flesh is obscured by blood. The dark man utters no sound, though the tightness of his jaw betrays his suffering. The beater retires. The dark man lies, face down, on the floor. Blood runs down his flanks and darkens the stones. After a while, with a painful effort of will, he raises himself. Once again he takes up the shirt of goats' hair, which he had obscured with his other garments. When he raises his arms, lice are visible in the dark nests of his armpits.

Eyes closed against the agony, he pulls on the shirt . . .

Chapter Eight

As Kate and Hester had walked back through Grantchester Meadows from the Blue Ball, Kate's anxiety and frustration had turned to anger.

'That was unbelievably stupid and selfish. You didn't give a damn about me. You just – you just ploughed on being confrontational. You could see he was getting pissed off.'

'So what? Let him,' Hester said. 'I'm not going to apologise for antagonising a little creep like him. What did you want me to do? Be all charming? Yes, Mr Bright, no, Mr Bright, or whatever his bloody name is. He's a murdering little bastard and the sooner you get that into your head the better.'

'Exactly. So what's the point in provoking him? It's all right for you. It's not you he's been stalking, is it? And what's the point in driving him away just when Spaull turns up?'

'Oh, yes, and what was he going to do? Mmmm? Charge him with having a half of lager?'

'We don't know what they know. We don't know what they've heard from Southwold. Maybe he could have put him on the spot.'

'He'd have to have caught him first, wouldn't he? He couldn't even manage that.'

'He only wanted him for questioning. He wasn't going to arrest him.'

'He was still amazingly slow off the mark. Mind you, chummy must have made himself scarce very fast after he left us. Obviously knows the place.' Hester stopped. 'Let's walk down by the river.' They abandoned the path and headed for the elbow in the Cam where the water was at its deepest. 'Look, I know how you feel, and I'm sorry if I went over the top.'

'I'm frightened, Hest. I told him at the gallery I never wanted to see him again and he seemed OK with that. Then you get him all worked up and he says that's not the end of it. I feel like a crab without a shell. There's nowhere I feel safe any more.'

Hester took her arm. 'Listen, honey. You can't go round never saying boo to a goose for the rest of your life. Most people are like that. Every day they take the easy option. They compromise, they fudge, they tell people what they want to hear. What they pay them to hear. They chip away at their own self-respect until it's non-existent. Then they give a few quid to charity to make up for it. Make them feel good about them-selves. Run the London Marathon. I do it too. But I'm fed up with it. I despise it. I'm not going to do it any more, and I'm not going to let you do it. I love you too much for that. No more bullshit. We're going to face this thing together and we're going to see him off. Right?'

For the moment, Kate was comforted. 'Easier said than done,' she said.

'Do you want me to move in for a bit?'

'I feel such a wimp.'

'Is that a yes?'

'Yes.'

'No problem.'

'But what can we do? This estate-agent thing was obviously just more lies.'

'We can assume the police'll make some progress, I suppose. Maybe they'll get prints off the money.'

'There'll be thousands on it presumably.'

'And I think we ought to have another go at Gilbert. He knows something. We've probably got a better chance of getting it out of him than PC Plod.'

By Monday, Gilbert still hadn't put in an appearance at Professor Bukovsky's. The Professor had explained to Hester that his lodger sometimes took off for weeks at a time, without announcing his departure. Hester said Bukovsky had sounded a touch envious. She'd left her number with him and asked him to ring her when the wandering artist turned up.

Despite her friend's support night and day, since Hester was now sleeping on her sofa, Kate couldn't get Bright's warning out of her mind. It still seemed to her that he'd decided to see her again, despite her ultimatum, because he wanted to punish her for his humiliation at the pub. Now that he'd seen Spaull she assumed he wouldn't try anything at the gallery, where there was always a danger of being interrupted by a potential witness, but she couldn't spend her whole life on the boat. All she could do was make sure that when she wasn't there, she surrounded herself with people, as far as possible. Meanwhile, whatever the wretched man intended, her peace of mind was in rags. Once, in the bathroom, she caught herself looking over her shoulder to make sure Bright hadn't somehow materialised through the locked door. And in the town, she found herself glancing in shop windows for his reflection, pale and isolated from the passers-by.

She sometimes thought about Peter. The only thing she missed about him was his presence. And his sense of humour. Not his agile mind, or his considerateness. They hadn't been his strong points. But he had been kind, in his way, and he had made her laugh, with his self-deprecating drollness; attractive because it was honest, but maddening because it acknowledged, even accepted, under-achieving as Peter's lot in life. And there had been times when the love-making was good; tender and wholehearted. Mostly, though, he came too soon and then rolled over, like a man relieved to have paid his road-fund tax. Hester had called them his shortcomings.

Kate realised now she'd hardly known him. Sometimes he'd cried in his sleep. That had been the only sign of real emotion. He'd been into archery, often travelling to Leighton Buzzard for lessons; dead impressed because his teacher, Bob, sometimes did film work, and had told him how the tacky tricks were done. Hollow arrows shot down nylon threads so they hit the target every time. He'd bought an ancient Morgan, which he'd been doing up. He loved that more than her; more than himself, come to that. But despite his many faults, his shortcomings, at least he'd been there; a warm body next to hers in the mornings; an arm to hold her when she snuggled close; a reassurance that she wouldn't always have to arrive alone at parties, or other dos where she knew no one. Rotten reasons, but real reasons. And she sensed that Peter hadn't lacked a sort of dumb courage. He wouldn't have run away from a fight. The last time she'd heard from him, he'd just got a rather good job in Manchester, working as a researcher for Granada. Typical! With perfect synchronisation, she'd dumped him just before he got interesting.

Since then, little sign of life on the man front, apart from the alleged actor. A third of the blokes she met ruled themselves out in any case because they were gay. And then she hadn't the sort of looks that fanned instant lust. She had what people called a neat figure. Ordinary, in other words. In jeans she might get a whistle or two. She had a good bottom, though she said it herself. It was coming to something when men took more notice of your bum than your face. Why was it, she wondered, that men only went for pretty women, while women rated lots of things above looks in men? The whole thing was a shambles. Of all the animals, men and women were the least adapted to living with each other. And it seemed to be getting worse. Perhaps Hester's bleak prediction in Southwold had been right. Perhaps one day they'd be segregated altogether: the men in England, the women in Scotland. Or maybe the other way round. England was warmer and softer. So much for higher intelligence.

Business at the gallery was sluggish. There had been a flurry of activity last week when a local hotelier, provincial camp and partial to wearing absurd opera cloaks at the Arts Theatre, had bought eight water-colours for his new restaurant-with-rooms. He'd brought his partner with him, Klaus. Klaus looked like a refugee from a touring company of *Springtime for Hitler*: blond hair with dark roots and an expression of sulky disdain, as though the entire history of western art was exhibited in his head. From the few words he'd uttered, it seemed more probable that the entire history of western fatuousness was nearer the mark. At one point he announced in a loud voice that bourgeois art was fit only for brothels, whereupon his partner warned him that if he went on misbehaving he'd be sent back to Wolverhampton. This awful threat had shut Klaus up for good.

On the Thursday morning, after a bowl of cornflakes with semi-skimmed milk and a black coffee, Kate locked the flat and went down to the hall. Half a dozen letters on the mat. She picked them up. Four for the other flats and two for her. One was a bill from British Telecom. She'd open that later. The other, in a scuffed white envelope, which looked as though it had been dropped and stepped on, was addressed in shaky Biro. The uneven handwriting wasn't familiar to her. Stranger still, although there was a stamp, it hadn't been franked. Either the machine at the sorting office had somehow missed the target, or, overnight, this letter had been delivered by hand. Should she open the thing now, or take it down to the gallery? Nothing could be so important that it wouldn't wait a few minutes. On the other hand curiosity would make those minutes anxious. Do it now and get it over with. But not here. Instinct told her to read it in the flat, on her own territory. She climbed back up the stairs and unlocked the door.

Taking the Swiss army knife she'd found at last year's Strawberry Fair from the oak office table she used as a desk, she slit the envelope. Force of habit. Ripping them open seemed like a violation somehow; a harsh way of treating something that had taken time and trouble to write. It struck her now that there was a sadness about this pale object in her hand, as though a child had written about a loss in the family. The name and address seemed unsure of themselves; new to the writer.

Inside was a single white sheet, typed on a word-processor, single-spaced; no address, no date. A new artist introducing herself? A crank? A long-lost friend getting in touch? She began to read:

> Kate,
> In the end we have to act. We can't just go on saying things as though they're nothing more than noises. Nobody means anything any more. They make faces and the noises come out of them but they have no meaning. The only thing with meaning is a deed. Once it's done it can't be called back. In its absolute-ness it can't be mistaken. It's clear and clean and final. Truthful. Time to stop crying wolf like Ted Hughes says.

You might say well if words have no meaning why write them? Fair point. It's because you're decent. You deserve an explanation.

I have things to do. A destiny. I will never hurt you. You are important to me. One day soon you'll understand why.

The painting isn't great. It isn't even good. But it reminds me.

R.

Kate found herself staring at the page even after she'd finished reading. It was him. No doubt about that. The mention of the picture, of Ted Hughes, the sense of apartness from people. He'd sat at his laptop, in some lonely room, and written her this . . . this what? All this stuff about action, and destiny, and not crying wolf, determined intention of some sort, but no way of knowing where it was headed, despite the promise of understanding soon. It was part mad, part injured . . . part affectionate: that was the bewildering thing. There seemed a sort of weary, disillusioned caring about parts of it. Could it be that Bright had never been a threat, after all – not to her, at least? But why the drama of the scruffy envelope? The handwriting on that seemed at odds with the sentiments in the letter.

Kate put it on the desk, feeling she didn't want to touch it again. Overall, there was something eerie, disturbing about it; the sour smell of solitary disillusion and revenge. Its apparent rationality, sensitivity even, couldn't mask its cold, hard resolve. She'd have to tell Corcoran, of course. She'd take it down to the gallery with her and meet him there, so as not to be late opening up. That would mean handling it, and apart from the fact that she found it distasteful, like a curse, she supposed she'd have to be careful about finger-prints. Best to pick it up with tweezers and put it in a tear-off plastic bag from the kitchen drawer.

It was Spaull who answered the telephone. Corcoran was tied up on another case, he said, but he would get to the boat as soon as he could.

Ten minutes later, the protected evidence further shrouded in a Tesco's bag, Kate headed down towards Chesterton Lane. Maybe it was time to leave this town altogether, she thought. She'd been happy enough here but now it felt tainted. This whole thing with Bright had left her feeling she needed a fresh start. Where, though? She couldn't afford London. She didn't want to go north, and the thought of starting over in another smallish town was unappealing. Besides, there was Hester. And there was her work. And there was an incipient determination not to be chased out by a freak; a freak who, in any case, said he wished her no harm. Unless that was the way he anaesthetised all his victims.

Beside the gallery the ducks patrolled the river, oblivious. What a great life, Kate thought, watching them. Untroubled by anything except sex and hunger. A bit like Klaus. The thought cheered her up. While she was waiting for the police she opened the mail. A letter of appreciation from Tom Pocock for the success of his recent exhibition; a bill from the framer; another from Eastern Electric; an invitation to a private view at the Old Fire Engine House in Ely. As she read this, she heard someone in the gallery. Couldn't be Corcoran yet. For perhaps five seconds she stayed where she was, paralysed by the possibility that the visitor was Bright. She debated whether to pick up the telephone and whisper a nine-nine-nine call, but if it was Bright, and he caught her in the act, it was impossible to predict what he'd do. And if it wasn't him she'd feel a fool. She steeled herself and walked to the door, with as much front as she could manage. No sound now. Maybe whoever it was had thought better of it. Good. And then she heard the voice:

'Hi! Morning.'

She looked towards the gallery entrance. 'Oh, morning!' Surprise and relief. It was the man she'd met at Hester's house; the one who'd come with the girl who'd had the transplant, Siobhan. He'd been reading medicine, Kate remembered, but she drew a blank on the name.

'Gareth,' he said. 'Gareth Vaisey. We met at Hester's.'

'Yes.' There was pleasure in her voice. Not very flattering for him. It was only because he wasn't someone rather than because he was. 'Of course. Kate Mellanby.'

'Yes.'

There was a hiatus. He seemed shy, she was slow to react. 'Haven't seen you here before,' she said, realising she'd given him an unanswerable cue, poor man.

'No,' he said, and aware of the need to move things along, he put on a spurt. 'No, I've often seen the place when I've been, you know, passing. Just . . . sitting there, on the water. Rather inviting. So I thought, have a shufti, why not?'

'Absolutely.' Shufti! What a funny word. Like mufti and . . . she couldn't think of another. Ticketyboo. Old-fashioned. Bit military. Maybe his father had been in the army. Major Vaisey. Sounded about right. Major Reginald Vaisey.

'My father's a painter,' he said. 'Strictly what do you call it . . . figurative? Ducks on marshes type thing.'

Kate wanted to laugh at her own assumption, but at least it sounded as though Vaisey Senior favoured the sort of work a major might paint. 'Really?' she said. 'Well, you ought to bring him in. We're infested with ducks.'

'Oh, he's been many a time. Not here specifically, but Cambridge. Can't keep him away. He's painted practically every brick. He was up here himself. In the Middle Ages.' He laughed.

'You didn't feel like having a go yourself? They're sometimes in the genes these things, aren't they?'

'Not in mine. I once drew a car as a kid and Dad said it looked like one of those containers. Those big rectangular metal things? I tried to argue a car is a container but he wasn't having any. I think I knew then that Constable had nothing to fear from me.'

Constable; a conservative choice. And he'd called his father Dad. How sweet. Kate didn't think men did that. Peter had called his Father. Macho. No nonsense. 'I expect he encouraged you in other ways, though, didn't he? Medicine, wasn't it?'

'No, and yes. No, he wasn't big on encouragement. Still isn't. Too wrapped up in his work. He just let us get on with it, really.' He paused. 'Don't know why I'm telling you all this. Must be dead boring.'

'Us', he'd said. There must be more where he came from. Hunky brothers, or a lovely sister you could make a friend of. For a dust-speck of time Kate wanted to say, 'No, actually, it's one of the least boring things I've ever heard. Please go on talking and don't stop for about an hour and a half.' Instead she said, 'Fancy a coffee?'

'You sure it's not . . . ?'

'I was just going to make one.'

He followed her into the small office. 'Do you get many in?' he said.

'No, not very many.' She plugged in the kettle and switched it on. 'That's why I like it in a way. Gives you time to think. I couldn't cope with an office again.'

'I know what you mean. That's one good thing about medicine. At least no two patients are alike. There's no routine, in that sense. Unless they're both dead, of course.' He laughed again.

She wanted to ask him about Siobhan, but realised it mightn't be a good move. Leave Siobhan out of it. He was here, and she was enjoying his company. No point in complicating things. 'Do you live this side of town, then?' she said.

He shook his head. 'I'm in digs out at Great Shelford. I like a bit of green round me. You know when you wake up in the morning? Take your first look at the day? I like it to be green. I think maybe I'm stocking up the memories for all those years when I'll be stuck in big, ugly hospitals. Nothing to look at but boring brick walls. Half the time too knackered to look at anything.'

'Sounds grim. What is it makes you want to do it?'

'Be a quack? It's hard to say, really. I've never wanted to do anything else. God knows how the idea got planted but it's always been there. I think it's trying to solve problems, but flesh-and-blood problems, that make a difference you can actually see. If you're lucky. I don't know.'

The kettle came to the boil. Kate handed him the coffee, which he drank black. 'I thought that wasn't supposed to be very good for you,' she said.

'Doctors talk a lot about what's good for you but they hardly ever do it themselves. They drink a lot, smoke a lot, commit suicide a lot. They're hypocrites a lot. The hypocritic oath!'

Kate found herself at ease with him. There was a real purpose in his life, and yet he didn't make a thing of it. Didn't much want to talk about it. And he didn't seem in any hurry to look at the pictures. Could it be that he hadn't come for them but for her? Come all the way from Great Shelford just for a chat? No, hang on. Not very likely. Not likely at all. He'd just popped in on impulse and she might never see him again. But she very much didn't want that to happen. Already he'd made her forget the shock of the letter, the apprehension that had never been far away since the Blue Ball. He was a solid reminder that Bright was an outsider, a blip on the graph, not to be got out of proportion. 'Would you like a little tour?' she said. 'Or maybe you'd rather go round on your own.'

'Great.'

'Great what? Great you'd like a tour, or great . . .?'

'Tour, every time.'

She showed him round, telling him about the artist and what he was trying to achieve. Apart from the occasional question Gareth didn't say much, content, it seemed, to listen and absorb. When they'd done the full circuit, he still showed no signs of wanting to leave, but Kate couldn't summon up a strategy for making him stay. Perhaps she could invent a sudden pain in her stomach, or better still display symptoms of a rare tropical disease that would take him several weeks to diagnose and at least a year to treat.

' 'Allo, 'allo.' Kate's lightning review of the options was interrupted by Spaull, who had somehow come in unheard. His left arm in a sling, he had a foolish grin on his face. The spell was broken. Now Gareth looked awkward.

'Morning.' Kate made it sound as cold as she could. 'Gareth, this is Mr Spaull. He's a policeman.'

'Detective Constable.'

'Morning,' Gareth said.

'We can do this later if you like.' Kate prayed for Spaull to say all right, he'd come back in an hour, but knew that in fact he'd say, 'No time like the present.'

'There's a thousand stories in the Naked City,' he said.

This silenced both of them. Spaull was lapsing into gibberish. Perhaps the job was getting to him. Perhaps dealing with the underworld had dismantled his already bruised brain.

'The boss is down the common,' Spaull went on.

'Problem?' Gareth said.

'You could say that,' Spaull said. 'Bloke found dead in the toilet.'

'What, natural causes?' Gareth said.

'Not unless you call murder natural. I'm not supposed to tell you that but it'll be all over the telly anyway tonight.'

Kate's confidence evaporated. She resented Spaull's intrusion. She resented the insensitivity of his announcement. She feared this escalation of violence. 'How do you know it was murder?' she said. 'Aren't you supposed to do a thorough investigation of these things before you go sounding off?'

'Trust me,' Spaull said.

Kate thought she wouldn't do that if he was her last chance of survival; standing alone on the deck of a sinking ship and him the man on the wire dangling from the helicopter. 'What have you done to your arm, then?' She was about to add something terrible; something suggesting he was a thief or a pervert. But she managed to gag herself in time.

'I was nicking a villain, if you want to know, so you could sleep safe in your bed. Belted me with a crowbar. You should have been there. You'd have had a good laugh.'

Now Kate felt mortified. Perhaps the man couldn't help being an annoyance. When they made him they'd thrown him on the annoyance pile. And now she'd upset him. Turned a natural ally into the opposite. 'I'm sorry, I didn't mean . . .'

'I think you did,' Spaull said.

'I think you'll find she didn't, as a matter of fact.' As

he drew closer to Spaull, Gareth's bedside manner was irresistible. 'It's just that when you tell someone something deeply shocking, like you just did, it can do funny things to them. I'm sure you know that better than I do. How it can traumatise them, to a certain extent. In extreme cases it can send them into shock. You know? And then they can behave in profoundly uncharacteristic ways. Like Kate just did. That's all it is. Nothing sinister at all.'

Spaull wasn't going to be pacified without a display of manly scepticism. 'Who are you then? Mystic Meg?'

'He's a doctor,' Kate said.

'Oh, is he now?' Spaull was coming round.

'Not quite. On the way. How about a coffee?' Gareth turned to Kate. 'Could you rustle up another?'

Kate nodded with a smile, and went to make it. Gareth followed her. When they reached the office he said, 'Got to go, I'm afraid.'

'Oh.' How could she feel so much disappointment, she wondered, after just a few minutes? 'OK.' Brave face. Stiff upper lip. But something drastic was called for. Something bold. 'Can I buy you a drink?' she said.

'What, now?'

She laughed. 'No. Not now. Sometime. Soon.' This was where he made an excuse and backed out. She'd misread the vibes. He was still besotted with Siobhan. She'd made a complete fool of herself. There'd be nothing for it but to go back and be horrible to Spaull. Tell him she wasn't in shock at all, she just hated him. Simple as that.

'Love one,' Gareth said.

Had Kate heard him right? This wasn't the trauma talking? 'Well, that's . . . Good! How do we . . .? You know . . .?' Her vocabulary had shrunk to a hazelnut.

Gareth was writing a number on a pad. Then he took a business card from a neat pile next to it. 'This OK?'

'Course,' she said.

'Great. Give you a buzz, then.' Gareth was turning to go.

'Fine,' she said. Fine! Imagine an Italian woman saying fine. The pride and the passion. It was the sort of thing you said when the meal had been crappy and the waiter asked you whether you'd enjoyed it.

'Will you be OK with . . . ?' Gareth gestured towards the gallery.

Kate nodded. 'Fine. Thank you.' For God's sake, woman. This was the language of Shakespeare, rich in metaphor, capable of infinite shades of meaning.

'Right.' Gareth half raised his right hand. 'See you soon then.'

He'd gone, and Kate realised she hadn't said goodbye, hadn't even given him her home number. She felt a little dazed as she made Spaull's coffee. What a morning. First the bad news, and then the sun comes out. Hot, hot sun that you didn't even guess had been hiding behind the coal-dust clouds. Sun that just made you want to lie on the grass; safe, content, every sense sharp. Hearing the bee in the trombone-head of the yellow flower; the children in the playground; the car horn at the lights; the laughter from the pub; the punt pole scrunching on the gravel-bed of the Cam. Alert. Every sound stored on the mind's CD, so that for ever you could replay the soundtrack of that moment, on that morning.

And now she had to face Spaull again. Spaull, who'd had a different morning. No bees, or children, or laughter for him. Instead, a body slumped in a public lavatory. The smell of urine and screaming loneliness. Sex as a bodily function. Joyless, heartless, pitiless. And Spaull, for all his irritating manner, had to witness the ugliness of it. Had to note every shabby detail; every loveless stain and wound. How could he be anything other than insensitive? How could he cope with stuff like that without becoming brutalised himself?

Because she felt confident again in her sudden happiness, she decided to ask him. 'Here,' she said, handing him the coffee. 'Can I ask you something?'

Spaull was on his guard. 'Thanks,' he said, with a suspicious enquiry in his eyes.

'How do you cope with all that – that horrible stuff? Finding bodies and stuff. Can you switch off when you get home?'

Spaull thought for a moment. 'I think of my kid,' he said. 'I think of her playing by the sea at Cromer.'

'How old is she?'

'Six. Seven in December. Natalie.'

This was a side Kate hadn't seen. The marrow of him. 'Do you take her there a lot?'

'Did. Used to. Her mother's got her now.'

'But you still . . . ?'

Spaull didn't seem to hear the question. 'Canada,' he said. 'Vancouver.'

Kate felt ashamed of her earlier outburst; of her

readiness to assume and judge. The man looked burst. The only memory that kept him sane was one of loss. She wanted to reach out, but knew he'd be embarrassed.

'Now then,' he said. 'What about this fan letter of yours?'

Kate led him through to the office and gave him the Tesco's bag. 'I thought I'd better not touch it,' she said. 'You know, after I'd opened it, obviously.'

'Quite right.' Spaull put down his mug and held up the tear-off bag with his good hand. The letter and envelope slid out. With practised concentration, he read both. 'Envelope's knocked about a bit,' he said, after a few moments. 'Biro. Doesn't seem like the same person that wrote the letter, does it? Must have meant to post it and then had second thoughts. See what Forensics make of it.' One-handed, Spaull tried to pinch the letter and envelope between index and second finger and slip them back into the transparent bag.

'Here,' Kate said, and did it for him.

'There's one thing,' Spaull said. 'If it is Bright wrote it, he's obviously got nothing against you, has he?'

'I don't know what to think,' Kate said. 'It seems like it, but then why does he go on, you know, bothering me? I thought he'd got the message but now he's sounding as though he hasn't. He can change so fast. You haven't seen him. It's such a shame you missed him in Grantchester.'

'I came quick as I could. Strangely enough there's a few other things going down in this town.'

'I know, I didn't mean . . .' Another thought struck

Kate. 'You don't think this thing on the common . . .?'

Spaull looked her in the eye. 'Look, I don't think anything about this thing on the common. Could take weeks. Years, even. Sometimes you never find out. Just forget it. I should never have mentioned it.'

Kate hesitated before asking one last question. 'No luck with the mobile, I suppose?'

Spaull shook his head. 'We reckon he's dumped it. Probably paid cash, gave false particulars, then got rid after a few calls. Not without money, obviously. Either that or he helped himself to it. Spotted somebody else's PIN number.'

When he'd gone, Kate sat at her desk and tried to separate the impressions of the past hour. Gareth's surprise appearance; Gareth Vaisey. The names of people you liked had a harmony. Gareth Vaisey did. Martin Taylor and Richard Bright didn't. Gareth had been thoughtful, unpushy, charming. He'd even bounded to the rescue when Spaull got stroppy. No one was perfect, of course. There must be all sorts of things about him that might infuriate her. But the perfect things were perfect, and that was more than you had a right to expect. And then Spaull; all the stupid cockiness stripped away. A man doing a horrible job, thou sands of miles from his only consolation. he deserved the bust-up; driven his partner grating out-of-tuneness. But he didn't dese see his child. No one deserved that.

And Bright. Despite Spaull's attempt at blu ance, was it possible that Bright had gone ing the letter in Hertford Street to

Perhaps that was what he'd meant when he said he must act. The slight figure making his furtive way down the street like a rat, crossing the river just a little way down from the gallery; feeling freer under the arching trees in the dark. Over the road, unseen. Making for the long, low building by the gate where a man waits . . . doesn't even hear the footsteps that'll be the last he'll ever hear.

Kate started to cry. All the uncertainty, the apprehension, the sense of invasion of the past few weeks overpowered her fragile self-control. Maybe she'd been going through a breakdown, she thought. All these weird thoughts, eddies of suspicion. Maybe Gareth had just been humouring her. Just said he'd have a drink to keep her quiet. Maybe Bright, or whoever had written the letter, was right. Maybe words weren't to be trusted. But even the solitary writer had admitted there were times when you could believe them. Ironic that he should expect her to believe his, of all people's. What had he meant by this destiny business? People hadn't talked about destiny since those Victorians, made of solid mahogany. And for them it had meant robbing other people of theirs. Of course! Bright, she remembered, was a historian. Or so he'd said. Maybe that was his idea of destiny too.

During the afternoon Kate tried four times to get hold of Hester. First she was out at lunch, and then she was either in a meeting or engaged. Hester had said the University Press didn't like her being rung at work in case it made her laugh, and laughter hadn't been heard in the office since somebody had put a farting cushion on the boss's chair and been fired on the spot. Even then, she'd said, the laughter was more at the firing than the cushion. Nevertheless, at five to five, Kate tried again. What could they do? Throw books at her? This time she was told Hester had just left. Nothing for it but to tell her about the day's events when she got back to the flat. Meanwhile she might as well close early and catch up on some paperwork. Her plan was disrupted, however, by the arrival of two enthusiastic American customers from upstate New York, and their less enthusiastic daughter. No sooner had they left, half an hour later, carrying four paintings in Sainsbury's bags, than Roger Crick turned up in expansive mood, with a bottle of champagne. He had just sold a wardrobe to an Arab racehorse owner for two thousand pounds, and the additional excitement of Kate's most recent success propelled him into entrepreneurial heaven.

At ten to five, just as she was starting to fantasise about the cold dew on a glass of chardonnay, Hester had taken a call at her CUP desk from Professor Bukovsky.

'Ms Edmond?'

'Hello? Who's this?'

'Bukovsky. You asked me to ring when the wanderer returned. Gilbert.'

'Oh, yes, hi, Professor. He's back then is he?'

'He is.'

'Great. I'll be right over. If that's OK?'

'By all means.' Bukovsky gave her directions.

Hester thought about calling Kate first, but decided instead to see what she could get out of Gilbert, in the hope of surprising her friend. Cycling against the rush-hour traffic in the crisp winter twilight, she reached De Freville Avenue twenty-five minutes later. The Professor's house was substantial and grave-looking, with a curved gravel drive, now smattered with leaves, and a garage at the side, which Hester took to be Gilbert's home. Judging by the number of bell-buttons by the front door, the building had been divided into lodgings; the traditional Cambridge means of bolstering meagre academic income and cheating the taxman. Before she had time to press the one marked Bukovsky, the professor himself had opened the door. White hair stranded with care over balding dome, deep-set, friendly eyes, thick lips; baggy grey cardigan over open-necked Viyella shirt, green corduroys, blunt brown shoes that looked like canal barges.

'Hello,' he said. 'I saw you from my study.' He indicated the garage with a gracious gesture. 'Allow me to introduce you.'

He led the way, advising Hester not to put Gilbert under too much pressure. The artist responded best, he said, when he himself was allowed to set the pace. Despite the cold the door of the garage was ajar. Bukovsky knocked.

'Gilbert, you have a visitor. A young lady.'

There was no reply. With a reassuring smile, Bukovsky said in a half-whisper, 'Just because he doesn't answer doesn't mean he doesn't hear.'

He opened the door further. The garage was lit by a bare hanging bulb, and by an ornate standard lamp with a torn, tilted shade at the far end. This shabby beacon lit a workbench cluttered with jam jars, tins of domestic paint, their sides thick with drips, cardboard boxes, paintbrushes, stones, and pieces of what looked like driftwood. Gilbert himself, seeming unaware of his visitors, was standing at a makeshift easel, made of nailed off-cuts he must have found on his travels. His canvas was a rectangular piece of cardboard. Beside the concrete wall to his left was a blanketed mattress set on a carpet of newspapers, and on the other side of his studio was a sagging armchair. On the wall behind this was tacked a collage of photographs from magazines and newspapers; many smiling studies of the Royal Family, prominent among them Princess Diana; some of animals in the wild; and a surprising number of imposing-looking men with full beards. Beside these were perhaps twenty of Gilbert's own paintings: variations on a theme; joyous celebrations of the way he wanted the world to look, or perhaps of the way it had once looked when he was a child.

Bukovsky ushered Hester into the presence. 'I'm sorry to disturb you, my dear Gilbert. This is Ms Hester Edmond. She's a close friend of the lady on the boat. Your gallery friend? I'm going to leave her with you for a little while.'

For perhaps half a minute after he'd gone, there was silence. Hester couldn't think of an appropriate opening gambit that wouldn't sound too intrusive. 'I hear you've been away,' she said at last, aware of her inadequacy.

No reply. Gilbert had eyes only for his dream landscape, with what looked like an outsize peacock in the foreground.

This could be a disaster, Hester thought. Unless she could find a way in, she might very soon have to find a way out. 'Are there any peacocks in this part of the world . . . at all?' she said, clutching at anything.

The desperate enquiry proved to be inspired. Gilbert nodded. 'Out Shelford,' he said, animated by the vision. 'Big garden out Shelford.'

Hester felt elated. 'They're lovely, aren't they? My friend Kate loves them too. You know, Kate, at the gallery?' She had no idea whether this was true or not, but she mustn't lose this unexpected opportunity. 'She loves the feathers. They look like they've got big eyes in them, don't they?'

Gilbert stood back for a moment to view his work. 'Yes,' he said. 'Eyes.'

This was tremendous, Hester thought. But how to turn it to Bright? 'Gilbert, when you saw Kate the other day, you said you knew the young man she had with her. You said you'd seen him before. He was a young man wearing a white shirt and black trousers. D'you remember that? D'you remember where you might have seen him? You know, before? Only it's rather important.'

Gilbert looked at her, his alert, animal eyes not unlike the ones on the wall. They seemed to be focusing not so much on her as on the implications of her: as though at the same time Gilbert was scenting her; weighing up her species and the threat of her. Perhaps she'd gone too far, encroached on forbidden territory. Perhaps now he would clam up again; make it plain she should leave.

Instead he put down his brush and, with slow, deliberate steps, crossed to the workbench, where he opened a drawer. A few moments later he rejoined her at the easel. One hand was closed into a loose fist, and in the other he held a piece of cardboard. Hester had no idea what to expect. Nothing about him was predictable. Society's norms were alien to him. There was about him the mystery of the magician; but a magician whose effects might derive from something deeper than magic.

Without taking his eyes off her, he held out the closed hand. Hester felt apprehensive. What if it was something frightening or vile? What if it was more than she wanted to know? She watched the fingers. Weather-browned, smudged with paint and grime, strong. As she watched they opened. And what they revealed when they opened, lying in the nest of the palm, was a brown plastic crucifix.

Hester was baffled. Had he understood her question? Was this some trophy he wanted to show off, as a cat might present a dead bird? Before she could frame a question, Gilbert held up the other hand. He seemed to be inviting her to look at the piece of cardboard, though the side facing her was blank. She took it and turned it over. To her astonishment, on the other side was a crude but unmistakable image, quite unlike any on Gilbert's walls. Instead of his customary scenes of flowers and birds, it was harsh and violent. On the left was a huge, straining, menacing black shape, recognisable as a car. In the beam of its yellow, asymmetrical headlights was a broken body, smaller than life-size, lying in the road, its head surrounded by a blotch of red. Visible behind the car's windscreen was a white face. But what made Hester catch her breath was the third figure in the picture: the misshapen figure dressed in a white shirt and black trousers, standing over the body. The startling thing was that his face matched the Munch-like mask behind the wheel of the car. It seemed that, like an aboriginal artist, Gilbert was telling a sequential story in the picture. The driver and the onlooker were the same man, separated only by time. And when Hester looked closer, she could make out a small cross on the victim's chest.

Good God. Gilbert must have witnessed a hit-and-run; Bright's hit-and-run, the death of the real Martin Taylor on that sad night. It had traumatised him so much that he'd made a record of it, even though it was the sort of picture he didn't like painting. This dingy piece of cardboard was evidence. Proof, of a sort, though Hester could foresee problems in making that acceptable to a jury. But what was the cross all about? Was that an imaginative touch Gilbert had invented? Was that his childlike blessing on the broken man in the road?

'Gilbert, you saw this happen? You were there that night?'

Gilbert pointed to the trees beside the road, writhing shapes in the darkness. Beside his blackened fingernail Hester could now just make out an outline; a bulky shape, orange in colour, facing the road. Was this a shadowy self-portrait?

'That's you?' Hester said.

Gilbert nodded. 'Me,' he confirmed.

'And the little cross, was it yours? Was it you who put it there?'

'No,' Gilbert said.

'Did you find it on the body? This poor man in the road?'

Gilbert gave a vigorous nod.

'So it was his, do you think?'

'No,' Gilbert said. 'Not his.'

'Whose, then?'

Gilbert took the picture from her hand and pointed at the figure standing over the body. 'Him,' he said.

'So the man who knocked this poor man down, the one in black and white, he put the cross on the body? Is that what happened?'

Gilbert nodded. 'Him,' he said, still pointing.

The possibilities swarmed in Hester's brain. Bright had put the cross on the victim. His victim. But as far as she knew he hadn't reported the accident. It hadn't been an accident. It had been deliberate. The crucifix hadn't been a blessing at all. It had been a mark of his first kill, if this was his first; a confirmation of his mission. Could such a symbol link the real Martin Taylor with the murdered novice in Southwold? Had she been right at the Blue Ball when her intuition had led her to use the word crusade? A lunatic crusade? She must warn the police. But first she must tell Kate; Kate who, even if the targets so far had both been men, must now be more at risk than either of them had realised. Since the gallery was on her way back to the flat, she would call there first. It might be best if Kate left town for a while; just until this vicious psychopath was caught.

'Gilbert, you've been great. Thank you,' Hester said.

Gilbert made no acknowledgement. Crossing to the workbench again, he replaced the picture, face down, and the crucifix in the drawer. Like a man who has transacted his business and sees no point in further engagement, he then took up his brush and resumed work at the easel, oblivious of his departing guest.

Roger Crick had insisted that Kate join him in a couple of glasses of champagne. Euphoric, he had been full of plans for expansion. This was just the beginning, he'd said, twice. More antique shops, more Crick galleries; today Cambridge, tomorrow the Internet and world domination. It had all been madness, but Kate had been happy to humour him. Better Roger optimistic, even if half drunk, than Roger in whingeing mode.

When he left, Kate switched on the answerphone, made sure all the lights were off, and locked the office door and the outer door of the gallery. For a moment she stood watching the lights on the river; the home-bound traffic crossing Magdalen Bridge, the passers-by on the riverside footpath opposite. Then, clutching her coat tighter round her neck, she set off up the sloping path. After a few steps she thought she heard a rustle among the trees and shrubs to her left. She stopped, listening. Must have been a dog or something; or a cat, perhaps, hunting a bird. She walked on. Only a few paces from the road now. Soon be home for a glass of wine. Hester's turn to cook. Good news and bad news, that: good because Kate didn't have to do it herself, bad because Hester's technique could best be described as erratic. Kate smiled at the thought.

And then there was another sound: an unmistakable sound. This was no animal: this was a weightier movement; a chilling sense of something or someone breaking cover; someone who had hidden and waited and whose wait was over. This was harm coming; sudden and violent. Now it was behind her, wrenching back her head with a cold hand. The shock forced the breath out of her. She could feel something over her mouth. Though it was soft, it was stifling, terrifying; not a mere restraint but a sensation of losing control, of being outside the attack and watching it happen, of fear and panic. She tried to scream but the muffled sound was only loud in her own head. She tried to wrench her body free but it wouldn't respond. The hair-fine lines of communication between her brain and her muscles had gone slack, or been cut. She kicked out behind her but was aware that her heels had no force.

Before she lost consciousness she was aware of one last, blurred image. It was a red car parked at the point where the path met Chesterton Lane.

Chapter Nine

Hampstead
Tuesday

Dearest Hugh,

    Thank you again for Pontigny. And Boulogne. And Wissant. And all the places in between. Kaiser Bill's brother-in-law was every bit as horrible as you said he'd be. Quel dommage we have to inflict him on the French. We get croissants and Gerard Depardieu and all they get in return is hooligans and tacky estate agents. As ententes go it's not very cordiale, is it? I read your piece. Very clever, I thought. If you read between the lines you could tell exactly what you were thinking, but on the surface it seemed straightforward. I think you're a really good writer. I don't believe everyone has a book in them. Or if they have, it'd mostly be a telephone directory. But I know you have and I'm dying to read it. So, vas-y, mon brave!

    The prospect of Bar exams fills me with . . . well, not gloom exactly, because that's pointless, but no sooner have you got the degree out of the way than here's another lot. I'll be fine once I'm in the groove a bit. The thing is I'm not sure they're teaching us the right things. I know we have to know the basics of law, but there are other basics a female barrister – especially a female – needs to know just as badly. Like how to fend off lecherous silks and suck up to the Senior Clerk. At the chambers I'm hoping to get into, in Devereux Court, he's called Barry and they say he used to be a mate of Ronnie Biggs. From what I've heard, clerking is great train robbery, without any of the concomitant risks, as Oscar might have put it.

I think I've found a flat in Archway, not a million miles from you. God knows how I'm going to pay for it. I've got a part-time job at a caff in Primrose Hill. All sorts of celebs come in. Alan Bennett was in the other day with his bicycle clips still on. Anyway, that's great, isn't it? Now I can pester you on a regular basis. If you'll let me.

The reason I'm writing instead of ringing is I haven't heard from you for a couple of weeks, apart from a card or two. I know you had that Greek thing and seeing your mum. But I miss you, and I think I'd still find that hard to say. Must be my peculiar upbringing. No, mustn't blame the parents. It's probably just me. Anyway, I do. I like it when we're together. There! Said it.

Drink at the weekend? Lansdown maybe?

Love, Siobhan xxxxxx

Hugh had got the letter when he came back from a

visit to his mother in Northwich. Before that he'd had a week's trip to Skopelos and another to Cyprus. He'd reread it several times. It was hard to see it as anything other than a declaration; not of love, nothing as committed as that, but some sort of step forward none the less. 'I like it when we're together' was pretty unambiguous. You might say it to a friend, or a cousin, or even a dog, Hugh supposed, if you were in the mood, but he hadn't ever used it except in an emotional sense. It wasn't something she'd just said on the spur of the moment, after a really good evening, say, or a sunny walk on the Embankment. She'd sat down at a table, and chosen the words, and made a deliberate record of them.

Hugh was excited and confused. All this time he'd kept the door closed on his feelings, not daring to over-analyse them, or to encourage any ridiculous hope of anything other than special . . . no, unique, friendship. And it had been because it was unique that he'd held back. The word incest kept hovering in his head. Nonsense, of course. There wasn't even the remotest family link. In fact no two families had ever been less linked. But it was a very substantial wooden warning sign, planted in a minefield. Siobhan was already part of him. He contained her. The thought that making love to her might be the most complete fusion two human beings could ever know had never been allowed to flower. And how weird to think there'd be a third party represented: Siobhan's young donor. Troilism by proxy. The more Hugh pursued the idea, the more its complex associations disturbed him.

Even if he could overcome the taboo of the physical thing, there were so many other factors. Age, for a start. They were separated by almost thirty years, for God's sake. Ten years longer than she'd been alive. He was . . . well, not a semi-invalid, but someone who had to take care not to over-exert himself, not to forget his pills; someone who, in many ways, was forbidden to be spontaneous. What use was that to a woman who'd only been out of school a few short years? And what use was a relationship that had the stopwatch on it before it even began? If the best he could hope for was a decade, give or take, all sorts of pressures came into play. Children for a start. 'Hello, Dad, goodbye, Dad.' What kind of legacy was that? By the time he went to the great cuttings library in the sky, they wouldn't remember a thing about him. And yet . . . How wonderful it would be to have a child like Sam. Hugh had never forgotten a single day with him. Perhaps time didn't matter that much, after all. If you set out thinking you had for ever, you wouldn't get much done anyway. But where did Gareth come into all this? Or had leaving Cambridge meant leaving him? And to what extent was Siobhan inhibited by the age thing and the physical kinship?

In many ways things had been simpler before the letter. The worst possible outcome now would be to misinterpret it and, the next time he saw Siobhan, make a complete prat of himself. Before, he'd known where he stood. Now he assumed he wasn't standing in the same spot, but quite where he was remained uncertain.

And there were other decisions to be made. The

French trip had confirmed his growing misgivings about his job. As Siobhan had said in the letter, Kaiser Bill's brother-in-law, Ronnie Tremlett, had turned out to be every bit as slimy as he'd feared. Slick black hair like one of those polo-playing South American play-boys from the fifties; drawers full of white linen shirts with baggy sleeves, turned back at the wrist, black trousers; Jermyn Street shoes. A man whose insincerity, if plugged into the mains, could light Las Vegas. A man whose every manoeuvre was motivated by a compul-sion to ignore fair play and win by professional fouls. A man who, the one night he and Hugh had played chess together on the terrace of his stunning eighteenth-century château, had managed to cheat at that most honourable of games. Hugh had looked away for a moment when Ronnie's wife, Olivia, had asked him what he'd like to drink, and when he turned back there had been a strategic alteration in the position of his opponent's queen, leading to mate in three moves. There was no question of accusing your host of cheat-ing in his own imposing home, the evening vibrant with crickets, and the chill veil on the glass of *premier cru* chablis. So Hugh had bitten the bullet and congrat-ulated him on his remarkable win, investing the adjec-tive with as much ambiguity as he dared.

He'd written the piece about him with jaw clenched, though he had, without effort, found nice things to say about Olivia. In fact, in what he hoped was not too transparent a shift of emphasis, he'd tended to make her the focus of the article. Here was a striking woman, beautiful, capable, charming, educated. What a mystery it was, this coupling business. Had her husband been different when she married him? It didn't seem possible. The sort of man he was must have been obvious when he was in his pram, stealing his sister's rattle while she was concentrating on her rusk. Had Olivia thought she could change him? Was money that sexy? Did a touch of low-down, mean-minded skulduggery appeal to the cool beauty from the shires? Who knew? Ever.

Gary had soon got Ronnie's number. He'd photographed him with unflattering lenses, including a fisheye, which made him look like Keith Moon. Miranda had come down too. Tremlett had made no secret of fancying her, but she'd treated him with stylish cool, making him sound like the oaf he was. Olivia had liked her, and so had Siobhan. One evening, when the oaf was out of town, Hugh and Gary had taken the three of them out to supper. It was the happiest time of the trip. As they left the restaurant, Gary, playing the paparazzo, had snatched an impromptu shot of Hugh and Siobhan, side by side, with Miranda and Olivia behind them. For their sake he'd had a set of prints made the next day. This old man with this glorious girl. And in the background, plain to see above the ancient stone lintel, was a cross chiselled by a medieval mason. Hugh hadn't seen a photograph of himself since the operation. It shocked him. He felt like cutting himself off it and just keeping the others. Siobhan said if he did she'd never speak to him again.

Hugh had come back from France with his mind made up. Never again, in his work, would he allow himself to be put in such a compromising position. He

didn't blame Dacre. He didn't even blame Kaiser Bill.
He blamed himself. And from now on he was determined that blame wouldn't be allowed to enter the
equation. He'd drifted, acquiesced, lain on his back with
his feet in the air long enough. Skopelos and Cyprus
had both been straight reporting jobs, and now the
decks were clear. Even if it meant selling the flat and
finding something smaller. Even if things were a bit thin
for a few months. No more garbage. Or if there was
more garbage, at least let it be his own.

He hadn't told his mother. There didn't seem any
point. She hadn't even mentioned the operation to her
friends. She'd just said he'd been poorly for a while.
Something he'd picked up abroad. Even in the age of
convenient, far-flung travel, that had been quite enough
to satisfy them. Abroad might be easy to get to, but it
would never be easy to trust. It remained alien, unsym-
pathetic, unhygienic. Nameless diseases lay in ambush
there, poised to strike like scorpions. And there had
been a deliberate, worldwide plot to make foreign lan-
guages more unpronounceable than was necessary, in
this day and age. That phrase cropped up a lot. Hugh
had even heard a friend of his mother's express the view
that there was little point in Mexicans speaking a different language from Americans . . . in this day and
age. They lived next door, for heaven's sake. It was plain
bone-headed of them to go on jabbering away in
Mexican. Didn't Hugh think so? Hugh had found this
perhaps the most challenging question he'd ever been
asked. In the event he suggested she write to the
Mexican embassy, urging a plan more revolutionary

than any even that civil-war-prone nation had ever known. The woman said she had far too much to do for that sort of nonsense and, anyway, if they couldn't see it themselves, let them get on with it.

The town had grown prosperous. Powerful Japanese cars and posh vegetables. Most of Hugh's childhood friends had moved away. Two contemporaries were dead, one of a heart-attack, the other drowned on the *Herald of Free Enterprise*. Among the survivors, Paul was a red-faced solicitor, his bare-faced irreverence now quite untraceable. They had a pint together. Within five minutes Hugh knew it would be their last. Paul said he must come round for dinner before he left. Hugh plucked an important appointment out of the smoky atmosphere, like a conjuror producing an egg from an empty palm. It was perfect in its spontaneity, and even he marvelled at it. He could tell the excuse was as much a relief to his former friend – former hero, even – as it was to him. Paul told a crude joke about a footballer and his new wife, as though unable to depart from a well-worn script, whatever the circumstances.

And yet all those years ago, when they'd gone together to watch Northwich Vics, the oldest league team in the country, with Eric, and Taffy, and Mel, Paul had seemed a wild man. Quick and inventive, the sort who went his own way, led the rest by his independence, the sort you wanted to be with, but who didn't need to be with you. And now here he was, a fat old bore the colour of a Tudor brick, pining for a retirement fenced in by the masonic lodge, the odd soft-porn video, and golfing holidays in Portugal. He talked of things he remembered being 'in old money', and called a lay acquaintance across the bar 'vicar'. The saddest thing was, Hugh thought, that Paul himself wouldn't now like the boy he'd once been; the boy who'd shown signs of talent and individuality. That boy wouldn't have fitted in at the Rotary Club.

When he'd slammed the carriage door, at the start of his journey back to London, Hugh had felt the tension lift. It was the tension of being someone he wasn't, because the tension of being the someone he was would have been explosive, unbearable. If, at any stage, in any encounter, he'd expressed his true feelings, the game would have been up for good. Hurt, incredulity, disappointment, rupture. So instead, as always, he'd strapped in his emotions, his ideas, his preferences. Just as he had, for far too long, in his work. He hadn't demurred when his mother gave her friends inaccurate descriptions of what he was up to. There had been no point. Contradicting her would have made her look silly and him petulant. So he'd smiled and made noises that seemed appropriate. He'd watched the soaps with her, and talked of the past, and walked with her to the shops. Once or twice she'd put her arm in his. It was the truest contact they'd had.

Still, the visit had helped steel his resolve, a resolve fostered not just by the undernourishment of his work, but also by the dreams. More and more, as the strange story developed, he felt himself identifying with the leading figure. Maturing with him. Growing stronger. It was strength deriving from adversity, rather than success. Like Hugh, the lonely, dark man in the dream had been transplanted. He was set apart, living in an alien landscape. Even in a gathering, and there was no shortage of people around him, he seemed isolated.

Sometimes, when he woke from the dreams, Hugh could still sense the man's pain: the constant, teeth-clenching torture of his back, raw from the cut of the whip, irritated beyond endurance by the coarse hair of his undershirt; the anguish of his separateness; the certainty that his greatest test had yet to be faced. More extraordinary still, Hugh had developed peculiar cravings. He'd never much liked the taste of ginger, but in Inverness Street market he'd found himself buying it, from a hollow-chested stallholder in a baseball cap who said it was the poor man's Viagra. He also longed for the smell of cloves. He'd bought a large bag from Holland & Barrett in Camden High Street, which he kept beside his bed, having studded two oranges with them. These new enthusiasms didn't alarm him. They seemed not unnatural. He didn't recall seeing them in the dreams, but he was certain that was their derivation. And something told him they did him good; that his desire for them had more to do with their medicinal properties than with pleasure. He must look them up sometime. See what they used them for . . . When? When had the dark man lived, if he'd lived at all? And if he hadn't, how had such a complete image of him, and his journey, formed itself in the mind of a twenty-first-century journalist?

There was a faint smell of cloves when he opened the door of the flat. And read Siobhan's letter. And sat on the red sofa, reading it again. Like the man in the dream, he began to feel that the many strands of his life were gathering, plaiting together, and starting to tug. Impossible at this stage to see the road ahead, but the prospect had begun to excite him. At a time when most men were planning for the end of things, he seemed to be lining up at some sort of start.

He made himself a camomile tea, since Scoular had warned them off coffee, and played back the answer-phone. Martha again, about the veteran traveller, Wilfred Thesiger. She called Hugh a very wicked boy and said unless he responded within the hour she'd report him to the Vatican. Since he had no way of knowing how old the message was, he must assume that by now he'd incurred the Pope's displeasure; a Pope with knuckles no one would want to bite. He wrote Martha's name on a pad. Next Tilly was on, asking him to a small family party to celebrate Sam's birthday. Hugh looked at the wall calendar. That was in two days' time. Perfect. (He'd sent Sam a card from Skopelos, telling him it wasn't an island but an anagram, and that there was an international prize for the first person to unlock it.) Then Amy Casarotto from HarperCollins. Had he had any ideas yet? No urgency, but they were still very keen to work with him. Meaning there was great urgency and they were growing less keen to work with him. A couple of bleeps with no message. Gary, saying he had something colossal to tell him, but he didn't want to do it on the phone. And a mysterious salsa band. Mysterious for a few moments, until a voice said, 'Only me. Welcome home,' followed by a number. The tone was warm and bright. Siobhan.

Hugh had got Gary to blow up the photograph he'd taken outside the restaurant in Pontigny. It was on the wall above the sofa. There he was, his expression a little uncertain, smiling, but with his mouth closed. A face that had been through it a bit. Drawn. Not letting its feelings show. The thickening at the waist camouflaged by a baggy, black linen jacket. And beside him, that fantastic exuberance, eyes shining, vivid, alive to the bone. Just the tail of the scar in the V of her shirt. Her arm through his. Behind them Olivia, like a bridesmaid, with Miranda, laughing at Gary. And that old stone cross over the door. Must once have been a religious building of some sort.

Hugh rang the number Siobhan had left. No reply. Damn. He wanted to talk to her. And never stop talking. He hadn't felt this happy since Tilly; the early days. The novelty of being loved. The realisation that another human being meant this word love that he'd never heard in all his growing up. Well, heard on the radio, but never from a living mouth. He should leave Siobhan a message, but the right formula wouldn't come straight away. If he said what he was feeling now she might get scared. He put down the receiver. Keep it simple. Warm and smily. The rest, whatever it was, could ease out when they were face to face. He dialled again.

'Hi. I'm back. Well, that's fairly obvious, really, isn't it? Well, actually, not that obvious because theoretically I could be in Kurdistan and just saying I'm back. But not only am I not in Kurdistan, I don't completely know where it is. I'll have to ask Sam. Anyway, thank you for your brilliant letter. The Lansdown would be great. Or here. Or the Carpathian mountains. I also don't completely know where they are. What I'm saying is – this tape's going to run out, isn't it? – what I'm saying is I'd love to see you as soon as possible and anywhere you like. Please ring me. I've got a few people to see, so I'll be in and out. But ring, is the thing. Because . . .' Careful. Don't get heavy. Don't assume anything. '. . . Because . . .' Before he could say something he still hadn't quite formed, the tape ran out. Blast. How stupid. Should he ring back and add a bit? No, the moment was gone. It wouldn't sound spontaneous any more. But even if the ending hadn't been articulate, at least it had been intriguing. He hoped.

She'd mentioned a café in Primrose Hill. Must be the one with the good cakes and the snotty staff. Maybe he'd walk over and surprise her. Just take a seat on the pavement, with his back to the place, and turn when she asked him what he wanted. Daft idea, but he'd spent too much of his life surrendering to other people's whims. In future he'd encourage his own. Prince of Wales Road; Harmood Street, sounding like something out of an Indian bazaar but named, or so he'd been told, after a very English couple who'd leased a house there, among watercress meadows, two hundred years ago; up into Chalk Farm Road and past the Roundhouse, over the Painted Bridge and swing into Regent's Park Road. Although he'd walked at an easy pace he began to feel breathless. Stop for a moment, opposite where Kingsley Amis used to face his unforgiving typewriter. He could feel his heart, her heart, bumping with anxiety. Her heart going to meet its rightful owner. That was something he'd never get used to. Being young at heart but not anywhere else. Don't say he was going to break down. Please, not here, among strangers. Please. Be calm. Take deep breaths. Doesn't matter what you look like. Fill your lungs. And le-e-e-e-t it out. And again. Fill. Relee-e-e-ase. Fill. Let go-o-o-o-o. Fill . . . That was better. The regular rhythm was coming back. Nothing to do with exertion, maybe. Just a panic attack brought on by anticipation. Nerves. He felt a touch on his elbow. A passer-by, a black man with dreadlocks, was asking if he felt OK. Hugh said yes, thank you, he was fine.

The pavement tables were full, in spite of the crisp cold. Mobile phones; new acquisitions from the bookshop, the more arcane the title, the more likelihood of it being encouraged to reveal a tantalising glimpse of itself above the edge of the bag; demonstrative conversation; eloquent gesture; loud greetings; sheeny limbs still brown from Umbria. But no Siobhan.

Among these relaxed people, Hugh felt bunched and sweaty. This hadn't been a good move. Even if she had been here they wouldn't have been able to talk. Still, better go in. She might be working inside. Might even have spotted him. A tall woman at the counter was complaining about being overcharged. She said she expected to be robbed in Turkey but not in Primrose Hill. Nearby customers looked scornful. The patient young woman serving her said as a matter of fact she was Turkish. And yesterday her bicycle had been stolen. In Gospel Oak. There was a small but supportive ripple of applause. The lean woman said Gospel Oak practically was Turkey. She thought the customers were laughing with her. But they weren't.

When the woman had gone, Hugh approached the Turkish girl. 'Well done,' he said.

She smiled. 'Thank you.'

'I'm looking for Siobhan Herbert.'

'She's not here on Thursdays.'

'Oh, right.' Hugh tried to look nonchalant. After a pause he added, 'Sorry to hear about your bike.' And left. If he'd thought for a moment before he'd come out . . . Or rung the place. Ah, well, Scoular encouraged them to exercise. The last time Hugh had been for a check-up, the surgeon had given him a mild telling off. The human machine, he'd said, had not been designed to travel in a sedan chair. Hugh had said that seemed an oversight because sedan chairs were a great way of two other human machines getting plenty of exercise.

When he got back he rested for an hour, reading background on Wilfred Thesiger. Somehow the exploits of the leathery traveller, eyes fixed on the horizon, failed to spark his imagination. What you wanted was Evelyn Waugh trekking the wilderness. But perverse Nature had seen to it that the dazzling writers were too tubby and puffed to go on punishing, fascinating journeys. There were exceptions, of course, but for Hugh, Thesiger wasn't one of them. Better ring Martha and tell her.

'You're mad,' she said, in a voice loud enough to fill Westminster Cathedral. 'The man's a lay saint. An ikon. Besides, he's got marvellous legs.'

'You couldn't see much of those in this book. His shorts were too long.'

'Well, he has. Those alone qualify him for your veneration.'

' "In olden days a glimpse of stocking was looked on as something shocking, now heaven knows . . ." '

' "Anything goes," ' Martha supplied in a tuneful bellow. ' "Good authors too, who once knew better words, now only use four letter words writing pro-o-o-se. Anything goes . . ." Well, in that case you'd better buy me dinner.'

'Done. How about tomorrow night?'

'Perfect. Let's go somewhere lovely.'

'Novelli? The Notting Hill one?'

'See you at eight.'

'I might have somebody with me.' Hugh hadn't known he was going to say this.

'Course you will. You'll have me.'

'Somebody else.'

'Good. I'm dying to meet them. Goodbye.'

Try the Hampstead number again. Still no one home. 'And another thing,' he said when the beeps had stopped, 'how about tomorrow night? I'm meeting Martha Kimmeridge. She's an outrage. We went strawberry-picking together once, in Kent. She picked pounds and pounds. Fingers stained like a surgeon in the Crimea. We christened her the Dark Lady of the Punnets. Not good, is it? Anyway, I said I'd have somebody with me. You, I hope. Bit of a liberty I know. You'd enjoy her. Say you'll come. And remember: Nina Baden Semper.'

Before he could call anyone else on the list, there was a ring at the door.

'Hello, mate. How's it going?'

It was Gary, brisk and beaming. If Hugh had been writing a piece about him for Dacre, he might well have been tempted to say the only negatives he recognised were the ones in his darkroom. Gary was all that was best about popular journalism: talented, professional, inexhaustible, able to make people feel easy, aware of universal flaws without being palsied with cynicism.

'Just passing, as they say,' Gary went on. 'Apparently there's a chihuahua in Crouch End that shares his basket with a squirrel. Wonder where he keeps his nuts?'

'Now there's a funny thing.'

'What's that, Huge?' Gary settled himself on the sofa.

'The minute you mentioned the squirrel, a little voice told me you'd wonder where he kept his nuts.'

'Public's got a right to know, mate.'

'Coffee?'

'Ta.'

Hugh filled the kettle. 'So? What's this colossal news, then?'

'I'm only getting married, aren't I?'

Hugh turned. 'D'you want to just give me that again?'

' 'Strue. December the fifth.'

'Gary!'

'Yeah. Grown-up or what?'

'Anybody we know?'

'Have a guess.'

'Germaine Greer?'

'Close. Miranda.'

'Good God. Well, that's absolutely great, Gaz. She's
. . . amazing. Wonderful girl. What the hell does she
see in you?'

'Well, this is it. I think seeing that creep in Pontigny
did the trick. She must have thought if Olivia could put
up with him, anything's possible.' Gary laughed.

'In that case, sod the coffee.' Hugh opened the fridge
and took out a bottle of champagne. 'I'm really glad for
you.'

'Thanks, mate. Look, you wouldn't do us a favour,
would you?'

Hugh eased out the cork. 'Probably. Almost certainly.
Yes.'

'You wouldn't be best man, would you? Only we
talked it over and yours was the only name that came
up.'

Hugh poured out two glasses. 'Bit short of friends,
are we?'

'Exactly.'

'Well, in that case how can I refuse? I'd be glad to,
Gaz. Here we go. Cheers.' He handed Gary his champagne. 'Here's to you and the lovely Miranda.' He took
a sip, conscious, as always, of the ghost of Scoular.
'D'you know, what's so particularly attractive about it is
the speech. Saying all those things about you that have
been festering all these years.'

'What's it worth to keep shtum?'

'Unimaginable amounts of dosh. Mountains of
moolah the size of coal tips. Where are you going to

live? I can't quite see her in that hovel in Battersea.'

'Bury St Edmunds.'

'Bury St Edmunds! You're a town rat, Gaz. The country's for potatoes, not people. Besides, you'll spend half your life on the road.'

'I know. I don't care. If she wants to live in another galaxy it's absolutely fine by me.'

'You have got it bad, haven't you?'

'Terminal, mate. Love her to death.'

'Well, that's it, then. Seriously good news. I'll order the carnation. Are we honeymooning somewhere smart? The Maldives? Kerala? Little houseboat made for two?'

'No chance. Too much on.' Gary finished his glass in one. 'She wants kids. Loads of them.'

'And you?'

'I want what she wants. I've always wanted to have a crack at a garden. Get an old vicarage, say, and plant hundreds of trees. Big beds of irises, like old whatsisface – Monet. Few ponds with waterlilies. I fancy it, Hugh. She's made me feel I can do all sorts of things. You can't always see it yourself, can you?'

'That's a fact.'

'Got to go, else we'll have the chihuahua eating the squirrel and then we're in the shit.' He got up. 'Thanks, mate. Appreciate it. I'll be in touch with the venue and that.'

'Give her my love.'

Gary married! Hugh looked again at the photograph. Pretty soon the only unmarried pair in it would be him and Siobhan. He'd be standing on the edge of yet another family. Well, that was fine. That was a part he could play. One he enjoyed. But it didn't have destiny written on it. It called for him to witness other destinies. And now that he was identifying more and more with the figure in the dreams, that wasn't enough somehow.

Pontigny. It struck him now with force that this was a place the dream figure had known. Something about the old building that housed the restaurant. That cross over the door! That's what had triggered the connection. It had appeared in his dream last night. At one point the dark man had emerged from that very doorway and there had been the self-same cross, a recurring symbol, above his head. And also there was something in the spirit, the pulse, the light of the place. Something in the memory of the landscape. Those things that didn't change from generation to generation. Hugh had the strange feeling that if he concentrated hard enough, and long enough, the man's face, too, would reveal itself in the photograph, as it had in the dream. Perhaps if he fasted, or meditated, wished it with enough passion, this mysterious but palpable presence would manifest itself. Like one of those puzzle pictures that concealed a design not at first apparent. As he tried to look through the image to the deeper truth, he felt the familiar half-dreaded, half-welcome cold sweat on his brow and the sick apprehension in his stomach. He turned and sat on the arm of the sofa. Now the smell of cloves was almost overpowering.

The dark man rides at the head of a short procession up a

steep, cobbled street. The neck of his horse glistens with sweat. He sits poplar-straight, forcing back his shoulders to hold in check the sapping pain. On either side, at every window, men and women and children, who have been expecting him, watch his arrival in silent awe. This is a day they will never forget; that will never be forgotten. The man does not see them. Or, if he does, he does not acknowledge them. He looks ahead to the white building on top of the hill. The agony and determination in his eyes are so intense, he looks like someone possessed. Every step of the horse on the echoing cobbles is a Calvary.

Inside the white building the man and his small group of followers pass under a great arch. The arch tells a story in stone. There are jubilant, adoring figures and, beneath them, figures in torment. Men and women with gross deformities — stinking holes in their faces through which teeth and bone are visible; goitres the size of gourds; contorted limbs screaming for comfort; weeping sores so foul that no one can bear to look — press forward for pity. There is none. The man looks beyond them to some far horizon only he can see.

Alone now, he walks through a great plantation of people, parting them as he advances. His face is dull, grey, chiselled with suffering. His mouth is open. The onlookers are silenced by his agony. They are in the presence of something they have only seen in kings and princes. But this man has no trappings of power. His power is in his fierce sense of purpose.

He climbs steps and rises above them. All eyes are turned to him. If they were expecting solace, they are to be disappointed. What the righteous man has to say is harsh. He himself has made such sacrifices that he will not condone anything less in others. He makes no gestures. His voice is calm,

sure, uncompromising. In his forthright delivery there is no sign
of his stammer. The listeners are shocked by what they hear.
They turn to each other to confirm that their ears do not
deceive them. They know, this day, the world has changed, and
they fear change. They fear also for the man who speaks like
no other they have ever heard.

Afterwards the man seems drained; exhausted but exultant,
as though relieved of a burden. He sits at a plain table, with a
goblet of fine wine diluted with water. No one dares speak to
him. His words have set him apart.

As he rides back down the hill, parents crowd their children
at the windows again, urging them to memorise the sorrowful
lines of his face. The children draw back. To them, his pale
fervour is as frightening as evil . . .

Hugh could still hear the hoofs on the cobbles. He
could feel the sun, much hotter now than it was on the
way up. He could sense the terrible isolation, riding on
a road with a certain end, though he couldn't imagine
what that end might be. He knew the man had taken an
irrevocable step. And he knew something had ordained
that, in an almost mystical way, he must accompany him
on his journey. Call it destiny, pre-ordination, chance,
fancy, paranoia – something had set him on a parallel
horse.

It was clear the white building had been a church.
Now he looked back, Hugh could see the consistent
clues to the man's religious connection: the crosses on
the beach and on the stone lintel; the hideous penance;
the Christ-like climb to the top of the hill; the depic-
tion in stone of Heaven and Hell. But this made the

dream more impenetrable than ever. There couldn't be a less appropriate match than one between him and an ardent Christian. There had been a brief period, in his late teens, when Hugh had thought he might be getting the bug. He'd picked up a book by C. S. Lewis that seemed to talk sense about why, if God was so good, there was still appalling suffering in the world. But a few weeks later he'd been in a girlfriend's house when the Catholic parish priest called to see her mother. The priest had spotted a copy of Somerset Maugham's *The Moon and Sixpence* on a bookshelf and had gone into a big number about it being on the banned list – the 'Index', he'd called it – and not suitable at all for a Catholic household. Hugh had thought it the stupidest thing he'd ever heard. He reverted, on the instant, to what he liked to think of then as tolerant agnosticism. Soon after his collapse, however, he'd begun to wonder again. It was disappointing in a way; such a predictable, cowardly reaction to fear. Signing on under duress couldn't count for much. But still there was an urge at least to reopen the debate. To give the faint, wispy possibility of deliverance another chance. After all, if you went along with it, what was there to lose? The answer, he'd decided in the end, was what little self-respect remained, after a lifetime in journalism. Even then, when he needed it most, he couldn't bring himself to ask for help from a source he'd never believed in.

So what on earth was it all about, this twinning with a figure so unlike him in every conceivable way? This man whose dogged single-mindedness was so reminiscent of the charity walker, the bullfighter, and the explorer. One of them had paid for his determination with his life. All of them had shown Hugh how flabby his own sense of purpose had become; in their suits of lights; their lonely, singular, utter conviction. These meetings, these dreams, didn't feel random. They seemed part of a consistent pattern. In some obscure way the men seemed to be taking him by the arm, encouraging him to follow their example.

He made notes while the details of the dream were still vivid. More and more, lately, he'd begun, after all, to embroider a little on these spare narratives; to fill in the gaps with invention. He'd been to so many places like the ones he dreamed about that calling to mind appropriate colours, and smells, and faces came with surprising ease. He enjoyed the exercise. Instead of settling for the first words that came into his head, he would try to find truer ways of painting the picture. Sometimes it meant spending two hours on a paragraph; a work rate that would have got him fired as a journalist. Sometimes, in spite of his best intentions, the clichés, allies of a lifetime, reached critical mass and he had to junk the lot. Sometimes there was satisfaction, in a thought whose expression he felt he couldn't improve on.

That evening he made sure he was in between five and seven, in case Siobhan rang. She didn't. Hugh was disappointed. The desire to see her was making it hard to concentrate on anything else. He decided to go to the Camden Odeon. Built to last ten years, out of a plastic kit, it housed a number of screens, some in rooms no larger than preview theatres, and all smelling of hamsters. The thoughtful designer had placed holes in the armrests at the exact point where the average elbow rested, for maximum discomfort. The film, a re-release, was about a fat man who did nothing except smoke, drink, and go ten-pin bowling. Had his script been shorn of the word fuck, his entire dialogue would have fitted on a bus ticket. The critics had raved. It was, they said, the quintessential expression of nineties *zeitgeist*. A man on the aisle, two rows ahead, belched. In silent agreement, Hugh got up and left. Fuck nineties *zeitgeist*.

'Hi. I was out. But now I'm in.' It was the only message on the answerphone.

Hugh dialled Siobhan's number. 'Finally!' he said, when he heard her voice.

'You OK?'

'Fine. You?'

'Yes.'

'I couldn't get you so I went and saw a film.'

'Any good?'

'No.'

'You went to the caff. That was nice of you. Irina rang me.'

'That must be the one who was having a hard time with a punter.'

'It's not unusual.'

'That's what Tom Jones reckoned. Long before your time.'

She hummed some of the tune. 'Good old Tom.'

Hugh wanted to ask her if it was too late to meet tonight, but funked it. 'This thing tomorrow night, are you on for it?'

'The Dark Lady of the Punnets? Absolutely. I've seen her on telly. She's great, isn't she? Shall I come to you?'

'Yes. Come about seven.' Or six. Or five. Or nine o'clock in the morning. Or, better still, now, Hugh thought. 'Gary's getting married,' he said, on safer ground.

'God! That's great! Miranda?'

'How did you guess?'

'It was obvious. She's mad about him.'

Hugh was beginning to feel he understood nothing of human relationships. Maybe journalism had blunted his perception. Maybe it had been blunt in the first place. But he understood something about this one, at least from his own perspective. He knew he wanted to keep Siobhan talking, about anything, as long as he couldn't hear boredom in her voice. He hadn't this sense of ease with anyone, except Tilly, and with her the possibilities had been defined; ring-fenced by his own inadequacy. The journey with Siobhan had only just begun. 'Better buy a hat,' he said.

'You bet. How was Greece?'

'Little churches. Cold food, except for the best chicken ever. The stuffing was out of this world. Poor people in black. A few rich yachties in white, most of them missing the point. I sometimes think that's why they all wear dark glasses. Not to keep the sun out but because they're blind.'

'Very profound.'

'Well, it's writing for the papers, isn't it? You've got to be very profound to squeeze all the world's wisdom into five hundred words. In short sentences. Some without verbs.' He paused. 'I'm not going to much longer, I've decided.'

'What? Be profound?'

'Yes. Not in the papers anyway. I've decided to take your advice.'

'Ooh-er. No one's ever done that before. The book, is it, then?'

'Seems to be.'

'Brilliant. I couldn't be gladder.'

'Do you know what's remarkable about you?'

'No.'

'You can be really, genuinely happy about someone else's news. Very rare, that.'

'Oh. Right then.'

'I could talk to you for hours.'

'Me too.'

'We'd better not. Else I might bore you tomorrow.'

'Theoretically it's a possibility, I suppose, but you never have yet.'

'Seven o'clock then?'

' 'S a date.'

'Night.'

'Night.'

The following afternoon, Hugh went to see Amy Casarotto in her Hammersmith office. At once he doubted whether she was capable of rejoicing at someone else's good news. The jaw was set beneath the ready smile. The sunburned fingers played with an expensive ballpoint pen, tapping first its head and then the other end on a notepad. Tension in check, and competence, were written through her demeanour. She would never be nicer to an author than at this initial meeting. She talked a little about other stuff they were about to publish; famous names, inhibiting rather than encouraging. And then her mental chronometer, precise to the second, told her it was time to get to the point.

'So. Any thoughts?'

'Er, yes.'

'Good. That's great.'

'I want to do a novel.'

'Ah.' Such warmth as there had been left her smile like a slammed door. 'The thing is we were hoping for travel. Seems crazy to waste your big name. That's after all what the great British public knows and loves you for.' Even allowing for the irony, this sounded perfunctory.

'Do you not think it's just conceivable that someone might be able to write both? Like, say, Bruce Chatwin?'

'Ah, well, he was a one-off.' In her tone Hugh could hear the unspoken half of the reply: 'Besides, he had talent.'

'Paul Theroux . . .?' Something made him want to throw in a non-existent writer. So he did. 'Waldo Reutermann?'

It was a tricky one because if she picked him up on it, she stood a one per cent chance of seeming ignorant. And Ms Casarotto was not a gambler. 'Point taken. But the thing is, at this stage in your career, the book we want from you, the book the public wants from you, is basically travel. Travel's hot. Everyone can afford it. Nowhere's too exotic for them. You've been everywhere and you write so brilliantly about it. We think it'd do really, really well.'

There was nothing wrong with what she was saying. Some of it might even be true. The trouble was it sounded so much like Kaiser Bill's brother-in-law. It was the 'really, really' that did it: the marketing mind on automatic; the mind that had sent him on so many pointless stories.

'And to be honest, Hugh, I can put you on to our fiction people with pleasure, but at the end of the day don't you think if you were going to write a novel you'd have done it by now?'

Looking back, Hugh recognised this as the exact moment when he realised a novel wasn't out of his reach; indeed must be started the minute he got home. Yes, there were thousands of them every year. Yes, most of them finished up in the shredder. And yes, chances were his would join them. But it had become imperative that he did it. He might even dedicate it to Ms Casarotto . . . at the end of the day.

There was a smile on his face as he said, 'Thank you. But I'm a stubborn old bastard and you've just inspired me.'

Amy Casarotto tapped her pen faster. This meeting, however brief, was no longer showing a return on her investment. 'All part of the service.' Her smile was stretched like a gloved fist. Moments later she'd have a more pliable author sitting in the same seat, moist with pride and gratitude. The metronome of her daily routine would have resumed its accustomed rhythm.

When Siobhan came round at ten past seven, Hugh told her about the meeting.

'Are you sure?' she said.

'Very.'

'She wants a book from you and you say no thanks?'

'That's approximately the top and bottom of it, yes.'

'Isn't that a bit . . .?'

'Stupid?'

'Thank you. Stupid?'

'I'd have to give that one a yes.'

'I keep reading it's very hard to find a publisher.'

'It is.'

'Look, can we be just a touch more co-operative here? Not, you know, a completely comprehensive reply or anything, but something just a fraction more enlightening than, say, yes? Please? At all?'

Hugh smiled. 'I hoped I was being enigmatic.'

'No. No, I'm sorry, what you were being was infuriating.'

'Ah, right. Well, what it is is this. I'm going to write a novel, and if no one publishes it I won't be all that bothered. It's what I'm going to do.'

'Well, that's . . . great. If you can afford to.'

'I can't. But I also can't afford not to.'

'There's no point asking you what it's about, I suppose?'

'Yes. There's very much a point. But telling you that means telling you a whole lot more. And I will, but . . .'

The bell rang. The taxi was early. As they cut through to Notting Hill the back way, Siobhan told him about the Inns of Court School of Law. She said thank God it wasn't the seventeenth century when it had taken some people ten years to qualify. The worst thing was watching ambitious students cosying up to barristers in bars, buying them drinks they couldn't afford, trying to shine in their company. And if the barrister happened to be a head of chambers the ingratiation factor could be embarrassing. Anything to be offered a tenancy when they passed the Bar exams. The old school tie still counted for a lot, she said, as did a pretty face, if its owner was prepared to use it. And a depressing number were. She'd wondered if she was cut out for all this competitive stuff, and had reconciled herself to the fact that she was. It was unusual for her to mention time passing, but in this context she did say she had none to waste on dithering. Meanwhile, she said, working in the café helped a lot. It kept her in touch with people, the staff, not the customers, who had a more user-friendly sense of values.

At Novelli Martha Kimmeridge's arrival, with a crash helmet in one hand and a Sainsbury's bag in the other, excited some attention, even in a neighbourhood where there were more famous faces than dogs. This wasn't because she invited it, but because nature and conviction had made her singular. All spaces she entered were alike to her, except Brompton Oratory, and all were charged by her energy. She was an event; a force who made those around her seem supine and timid. This was not achieved by bullying or bombast, but by the rare and simple means of knowing who she was and being prepared to share all of it, indeed, unable not to. Her shape, more or less that of an orange, removed any sense of threat, though her wit, not always charitable, was more than capable of cutting liberty-takers down to size.

Hugh got up to greet her and at once she looked small. She kissed him on the mouth. He introduced Siobhan by her full name.

'Oh, but how distinguished, my dear,' Martha said, as she sat. 'One of the great arterial dynasties. Part of the body proper, the Herberts. England was built on families like yours.'

'Was it?' Siobhan said.

'Of course. Soldiers, statesmen, poets, patrons. None greater. Most of us are mere Johnny-come-latelies by comparison.'

'Very large vodka and tonic,' Hugh said to the attentive waiter, pre-empting Martha's request. 'With an avalanche of ice.'

'You know of George, of course. Forsook the Court for the Church in the seventeenth century. Pious poems of great wisdom. An ornament, my dear.'

'I've heard my father talk about him, but I'm ashamed to say—'

'No matter. Time is on your side.'

Siobhan smiled as though this were true. 'Is that your passion? History?' she said.

'That and Holy Mother Church, the only passions permitted to a barrel-shaped spinster centuries beyond the menopause.'

Martha's enormous vodka arrived. They ordered. It was clear that she had taken a great liking to Siobhan. From time to time, as she talked of recent triumphs and disasters, she would lay her hand, with its elegant red nails, on Siobhan's arm for emphasis. The affection was reciprocal. Siobhan was delighted by her, warming at once to her honesty and her ability to advance on life without subterfuge or deviation. It was impossible to imagine her daunted by even the most testing circumstance. She could have worked alongside Florence Nightingale at Scutari, treating the injured with firm love; or crossed the Empty Quarter, complaining that a surfeit of anything was vulgar, including sand; or somehow survived the terrors of a concentration camp. Even the ultimate black hole, death, didn't scare her. She would stare it in the face, unblinking, turn once with a toodle-pip to those she cared for, and take it by the arm.

Hugh was forgiven for not doing the Thesiger project. She hadn't informed the Pope, Martha said, because the poor man had enough on his plate. And the mention of plates reminded her that the waiter had taken an unconscionable time bringing her second drink. The remedy was to hand. Siobhan watched, fascinated, as she fished in her Sainsbury's bag and pulled out a plastic tonic-water bottle filled with a pinkish liquid. Pouring it into her glass, Martha explained, 'Private stock, dear. Never leave home without it. Cheap vodka with a few bitter tears of Angostura.' Next, from a small tartan Thermos she took six ice cubes, making the drink a bumper. She took a thirsty draught. 'Rather lovely name, don't you think, Angostura? Should have been a saint if it hadn't been a place. St Angostura of Siena, the patron saint of something rather wonderful . . . people who press flowers, perhaps.'

As they ate their main course, a pig's trotter in a dark sauce with creamy mashed potato for Martha, sea bass for the other two, she said to Siobhan, 'Well, what are we going to do with him if he won't write for me?'

'You'd better ask him.'

Hugh wanted to take his cue from her openness and tell her everything; about the operation, the dreams, the way he felt about Siobhan, the book. Well, she knew about the operation, of course, but he hadn't told her Siobhan was the donor. And if she thought there was anything odd about their being together, she was far too worldly to mention it. As for the dreams and his feelings for Siobhan, they couldn't be expressed yet, now, here. Better settle for the book, then, though before he spoke he could hear her withering reaction.

'Dame Fiction has clasped me to her bosom,' he said.

'Not another.' She hadn't disappointed him.

' 'Fraid so.'

'Poor boy. Well, in that case you'd better meet my friend Tom Massingberd.'

'What, *the* Tom Massingberd?'

'Are there more?' She put down her knife and fork, not enough left on her plate to feed a humming-bird. 'He's a great one for lost causes. In a lifetime of publishing he's been responsible for the death of more trees than Waring and Gillow.'

Siobhan was baffled by the allusion.

'Furniture purveyors to the bourgeoisie,' Martha supplied.

'Well, that'd be terrific,' Hugh said. 'What do you have to do, send a few sample chapters?'

'In Tom's case a pair of tight trousers might suffice, and an expression of potential compliance. I fear he buggers for England.'

The evening ended with much laughter. Hugh taxed Martha with the fact that her political incorrectness made an awkward bedfellow with her advocacy of Christian virtues. She replied that God had made her that way to be a scourge of fence-sitters, and that she was content to be judged by Him. As she sat there smoking a last Woodbine, Hugh couldn't help imagining the scene. How would she cope if, without the consolation of her travelling bar, she discovered that Heaven was as dull as Thurrock? Dauntless, she would no doubt seek out some of the more entertaining inmates, Marilyn Monroe, say, and Noël Coward, and inject a little more life into the afterlife for the likes of Martin Luther and Oliver Cromwell. Just when they thought they could be grave beyond the grave.

Before they parted, Martha wrote her address and number on the back of a napkin for Siobhan, making her promise to get in touch. Siobhan needed no urging. Together she and Hugh watched and waved as Martha put on her crash helmet, hooked the plastic bag on to her handlebar, started her scooter, which she described as claret-coloured, and pulled into the traffic with the eccentric progress of a small, tacking yacht.

'Anyone who doesn't believe in miracles should see that,' Hugh said. 'Interesting how confident toffs never get killed, whatever risks they take. If she was a lager-lout she'd be mown down in a minute. Fancy a stroll?'

Siobhan took his arm. 'We can always get a cab if we flag.'

After a hundred yards in contented silence, somehow encouraged by the city's gift of anonymity, Hugh began to talk once more about the dreams, telling her how they were developing and how he was identifying more and more with the central character. He found he could recall them in great detail: the damp flanks of the horses, the flecks of foam where the reins touched the neck; the agonising irritation of the hair shirt on the dark man's raw back; the slow, momentous ride, up the steep, cobbled street; even the faces of the onlookers; strong, characterful faces, their features somehow coarser, more exaggerated than those of passers-by in the Bayswater Road, crooked, bulbous noses, gap-toothed mouths, eyes cloudy with cataracts. As he spoke, above all he could see the dark man's face, the colour of soiled linen, sweating with the effort of keeping pain in check. He could sense him riding at his side, determined, revealing as little of what he was feeling as a tree or a stone cross, while the poor, parting crowd bowed their heads in reverence, told by their instinct that this was greatness passing. And then, as he approached the huge, cream-coloured building that dominated the small town, Hugh felt he was becoming the man himself. Talking of the last few steps, and the certainty of a mission about to be accomplished, he could sense again the indescribable pain and irritation of his open wounds. Every slight chafe of the hair shirt on the flayed flesh made him want to howl for relief.

He was aware of the obscene creatures living off his suffering: the blind, bloated, pus-coloured parasites, sucking life from his slow dying. If it were possible to get close to them, their sounds would sicken. And yet in their host there was a sense of great goodness; of an indestructible desire for justice. It burned with such contained ferocity that, despite the fearsome demands it made, it must transmit itself to others, and never be forgotten.

For a while, when Hugh had come to the end of his account, neither of them spoke. The traffic always seemed less aggressive at night, as though competition were reserved for office hours. The stream of lights was beautiful. If you half closed your eyes it looked like one of those photographs where the exposure made the headlamps trace irregular phosphorescent lines in the dark. Photographs that froze time, like the dreams. Hugh hoped he hadn't frightened Siobhan with them.

'Where do you think the story's going?' she said at last.

'I don't know. Somewhere. He'll either do whatever it is he's trying to do or . . .'

'Not.'

'Or not. Die in the attempt.' For the first time it occurred to Hugh that if the man in the dreams did fail, and die, the same might happen to him. Perhaps this was all some elaborate premonition. Had the two been linked in his imagination to warn him that, despite Scoular's optimism, he didn't have long after all? Was it Nature's way of letting him prepare for that? His heart had begun to race. 'Hang on a minute,' he said. 'I just need a breather.'

Concerned, Siobhan stood in front of him. 'What is it?' she said.

'Nothing. Just a bit puffed.'

'Let me feel.' She put her hand inside his overcoat and under his jacket. 'It's going berserk, you poor old thing. Put your arms above your head.'

'What?'

'Do it. Now take deep breaths. In. Out. In. Out. In . . .' After half a dozen attempts Siobhan could feel his heart's rhythm get back to normal. She withdrew her hand. 'There,' she said.

Hugh wanted to prolong physical contact with her; to hold her hand, hug her, kiss her, out of gratitude, affection, relief, a need for comfort. But in this situation he felt like the patient, and patients didn't kiss their doctors. It happened the other way round of course, which was what kept the *News of the World* in business. As he lowered his arms she said, 'Shall we give in and get a cab?'

Hugh waved one down. 'Archway then Kentish Town,' he said, not wanting to make any presumptions.

As they drove through Sussex Gardens, heading for the Marylebone Road, Siobhan asked numerous questions about the dreams. She wanted to know whether there were colours, and Hugh said there were. She wanted him to try and describe the clothes in detail, and he could, though he said that wouldn't be an automatic key to the period. Since he himself hadn't been around at the time, or even read about it as far as he knew, he must have invented them. Siobhan told of cases where people had recalled what appeared to be past lives with fantastic accuracy, only for it to emerge later that once, perhaps even in childhood, they'd had a glimpse of an old, illustrated manuscript. Their hidden memory, and their imaginations, had done the rest. Hugh said he supposed this was possible. But when Siobhan asked him if it might help to see an expert, a counsellor, or a shrink or someone, just to get the thing unlocked, he said that would somehow seem like a betrayal. The more he identified with the man, the more he felt he was meant to experience the story himself, not share it with voyeurs offering trite explanations. He was convinced the man wanted him to know the truth of it, and he'd see it through to the end.

As they turned into Regent's Park, at the mosque, Siobhan said, 'Still, it frightens me a bit. You can't kid yourself it's, you know, usual.'

'Normal, you mean?'

'Well, yes, I suppose that is what I mean.'

'No, it's absolutely not normal. And that's the whole thing in a way. I feel like it's the greatest story that's ever been given me. It is a bit spooky at times, specially when it happens in the day. But I just feel I've got to go with it. I feel I kind of owe it to the man, whoever he is. I know it sounds daft but it's as though I'm all he's got. No one else is listening. And yet you get this tremendous sense that it's him who's right all along. He's wrecking himself because he's right, and they're not listening because he's not saying what they want to hear.' Hugh checked himself. 'Anyway,' he went on, smiling, 'the other thing is, that's what I want to write about.'

'The man?'

Hugh nodded.

'Well, that's great! How fantastic! That's the Booker in the bag, right there!'

Hugh laughed. 'Oh, sure. I haven't even got a publisher. And I also haven't got a story. And I may also, also, not have any talent. These do not necessarily add up to a cheque for twenty grand and the vinegary patronisation of smartarse critics.'

'Get it down, then we'll see. I think you're going to surprise yourself. And everyone else.'

'Oh, well, haven't done that for a bit. You coming back for a chat?' The casual invitation had slipped out unconsidered.

'Look – what was it, twenty-five minutes ago? – you were standing in the Bayswater Road with your heart, that heart of ours, pounding like mad. You need to take it easy. You need to go home, make a boring hot drink, and go to bed. You do too much still. We can chat tomorrow. I'm counting on it, in fact.'

'Come to Sam's birthday party, then.'

'Will there be jellies?'

'You bet.'

'You're on.'

The following evening they went by tube to the Oval and walked the rest of the way to the Grangers'. Sixteen years ago Anthony had done the clever thing and found a beautiful house in an unlovely area, a move made possible, as Anthony told it, by a rich uncle who had celebrated his return from Kenya by dying over his kippers. It sat, open-faced and handsome, in a crescent of lookalikes, conveying style and comfort without smugness or ostentation. The birthday balloons in the now darkened front garden lent it an air of pleasing frivolity. It was a house that knew how to enjoy itself

The light from the open front door, and the warm colour of the hall, with its drawings and small paintings and collected objects of little value but great significance to the family, confirmed this impression. Even while Hugh's finger was still on the bell, Sam came running to meet them.

'Pessookl!' he said.

'And pessookl to you too,' Hugh said. 'Sounds like Happy Birthday in Eskimo.'

'It's an anagram of that place you sent me a card from – Slopalop.'

'Skopelos.'

'You can get spooks as well but there's a few letters left over.'

'Well, that's it, then. The international prize has finally been won. Congratulations. The committee asked me to give the winner this.' Hugh produced a carrier-bag from behind his back. 'And this is Siobhan by the way.'

'Hi,' Sam said.

'Hi, Sam.'

As Siobhan and Hugh moved into the house, preceded by Sam already tearing open the package in the bag, Tilly appeared from the kitchen wearing a red apron. 'Hello, Siobhan,' she said.

'I hope you don't mind me gatecrashing.'

'What are gates for? You're very welcome, my dear.

Come and have a drink. Anthony's just finishing something off.'

They sat in the kitchen surrounded by colour and clutter. Siobhan had to dislodge a large cat the shades of a herring from a dilapidated wicker chair with fancy curlicues. On the table were glass and earthenware bowls, some with smears of blue and acid green in them, cookery books with the stains of constant use, spilled flour enlivened with hundreds and thousands, three bottles of food colouring, six egg shells, packets of sugar and baking powder, wooden and metal spoons, the spiralled rinds of oranges and lemons, and a bottle of Vladivar vodka. In the background, frying sausages tantalised in sound and smell.

'What can I get you?' Tilly said.

Siobhan asked for anything soft, water would be fine, and Hugh settled for a red wine. While Tilly was getting them, Sam rushed in carrying an open box full of numbered plastic pieces.

'Mum! This is incredible!'

'Give me a clue,' Tilly said.

'It's a kit for a railway station with a watermill next to it.'

'Coo-er.'

'It's wicked. Thank you, Hugh.'

'Glad you like it.'

'It's even got lights that work.'

'Well, that's one up on Clapham North, then.' Tilly gave Siobhan her fizzy water. 'Are you sure?' she said.

'Yes, thanks.' Siobhan smiled.

'The train now arriving at platforms eleven, twelve

and thirteen is coming in sideways,' Hugh said.

Sam giggled and left to start work on the kit.

Tilly, Hugh, and Siobhan had been talking around the table for ten minutes when Anthony joined them.

'You look tousled,' Tilly said.

'Good,' Anthony said. 'I cultivate it. They all looked tousled, all of them. Tolstoy, Coleridge, Baudelaire . . . Name me a writer who didn't look tousled and I'll give you . . .' he looked round the kitchen for inspiration '. . . a bottle of cochineal.'

'Proust?' Hugh offered.

'God, yes, Proust,' Anthony said, helping himself to a large vodka. As he poured he said, 'Siobhan, how's it going?'

'Great,' Siobhan said. 'I'm learning to be a baby barrister.'

'Now, they're hardly ever tousled. Cheers.' He took a deep gulp. 'Best moment of the day. Eliot, too, wasn't there, in the untousled brigade, come to think of it? Coward, Rattigan, Somerset Maugham . . . I may have to rethink this.'

'Sam didn't want any of his friends,' Tilly said. 'Today he just wanted it to be us grown-ups. He's been cooking for hours. As you can see.'

'That way he gets more cake,' Anthony said, sitting next to Siobhan. 'Do you know, I still hardly recognise myself in the term grown-up? Just a bit of me's still surprised to be included. And actually not flattered. Not all that pleased.'

'Because it's them instead of us, isn't it?' Hugh agreed. 'It's all up-and-over garage doors, and blazers with regimental buttons, and PEPs and ISAs and TESSAs.'

'What are Tessas?' Siobhan said.

'Débutantes, used to be,' Hugh said.

'They're mostly Traceys and Taras now.' Anthony looked rueful. 'The rot's well and truly set in. Not even noble rot.'

Hugh laughed. 'Are you a republican, Anthony?'

Tilly got up and went over to the stove. 'Bangers,' she explained.

'Yes,' Anthony said. 'Trouble is the next question's always who would you have for president and I still haven't worked that one out. Julian Clary, possibly?'

Tilly said, 'Wouldn't it be a bit tricky, constitutionally, having a queen as president?'

'Well, there is that,' Anthony said.

When the sausages and mash were served, Sam rejoined the party. He made Anthony move and sat next to Siobhan himself. Within a minute they were easy with each other. He told her about his train layout, laughing at the fact that some of the buildings were German and some English, so the passengers must be very confused. They'd get on at a small station in Sussex and the next stop was Hamburg. Of course, he said, with the Channel Tunnel that wasn't so silly, and he told her how the actual journey would work. Later, seeing her scar, he asked her about the operation, in the matter-of-fact way of an enquiry about the dentist. Tilly frowned, but Siobhan was unembarrassed. In simple terms she explained the problem and the solution. She told him her heart was now in Hugh, and Sam thought that this, the ultimate in sharing, was great: an unremarkable, sensible way of doing things.

'So do you feel a bit like her?' he asked Hugh.

Hugh looked at him, unable to say anything. It was a question he'd never confronted before. Was this it, after all? The dreams, which had started with the operation, had they come with the heart? Were they her dreams? No, they couldn't be, or she'd have mentioned it. But might they have been born in her subconscious, rather than his? Impossible. How could a pump absorb ideas? Aware that his delay might have begun to seem odd, he said, 'Good question. But I don't know how she feels so I can't really say.'

Siobhan smiled at him.

After the sausages came Sam's cakes: small round ones with a variety of icing patterns; some decorated by School of Jackson Pollock, others by less identifiable artists. Two larger cakes as well, spilling cream and chocolate and strawberry jam. Then Tilly got up and brought from the kitchen a third, with lit candles on it. Anthony switched off the light. As Sam inhaled to blow them out, Siobhan looked at Hugh, the flames reflected in her eyes, and took his hand. The contact only lasted a moment. One long puff quenched the candles, the light went back on, and everyone clapped and whistled. Tilly cut into the smooth, white surface, decorated with a red steam train, the curly smoke from its stack forming Happy Birthday, Darling.

'This is the first I've heard of a European cake mountain,' Anthony said.

'He's giving the big one he made to your mum,' Tilly

said. 'He promised her when she came.'

The party over, Tilly insisted on driving them home. Siobhan said it was easy on the tube but Tilly wouldn't hear of it. She said she'd only had one drink – well, two, but vodka didn't count because you couldn't smell it. And, anyway, she liked driving in the city when it got dark. It was only then, she said, that she felt it was hers, and that she belonged to it. In the day it was full of trippers and workers who raided it, taking something and putting nothing back. At night it was a vast community again, and the air was calmer.

Crossing Waterloo Bridge, with the river and the lit buildings glamorous to either side, Hugh wanted to take Siobhan's hand again; just for the togetherness of it; the warmth and reassurance; the pledge of something; the commitment, if only brief; the two bloodstreams close, within two skins' depth of mingling; her feeling in his wrist the pulse of her own heart. But reaching over to her from the front seat was too clumsy a manoeuvre. In any case, Tilly asked Siobhan a question and the moment had gone.

Ten minutes later Hugh was dropped at his door. Bending, he kissed Tilly. Siobhan wound down her window and he kissed her too, on both cheeks. 'Give you a ring tomorrow,' he said.

'Great,' she said.

For a few seconds Hugh watched the car as it turned left towards Kentish Town Road. How much of his world was in that tiny, wheeled box. Viewed from the top of the Post Office Tower it would be just one among tens of thousands; insignificant, inching round a haphazard layout, with no apparent destination. For him its fragile shell contained perhaps three-quarters of everything that mattered. If anything should happen to it . . . if a split second's inattention, or a drunk, or some other malign hazard should cause it to . . . He didn't even want to think the word.

It was still only ten fifteen but he felt exhausted. Maybe Siobhan was right. Maybe he was trying to do too much, little as it was. Depressing thought. Not yet fifty and showing all the signs of senility. Well, some of them. Rage against the dying of the light. That was it, even if for Dylan lights-out had been pretty premature. No self-pity. No surrender. An early night, though. Maybe read for a bit. Maybe a chapter of Cormac McCarthy, mining spare, lean poetry from a barren landscape.

But behind all this, in his head, was Sam's question, like an underground river only potholers could find: 'So do you feel a bit like her?' A nearby explosion on a battlefield. The one that wakes you up to the real and present danger. How come he'd never thought of it before? Since heredity explained so much, why shouldn't he, to some extent at least, be Siobhan's inheritor? There seemed to be evidence that people could transmit their thoughts to each other. Maybe body parts played something of the same game. Organ music.

Moments after picking up *The Crossing*, Hugh put it back on the bedside table. Already he sensed the indistinct outline of a darker figure on McCarthy's prairie, dwarfed by the mountains of Mexico. In some ways this anachronistic stranger seemed not inappropriate there.

He, too, knew almost indescribable hardship; to a degree almost welcomed it. He knew the companionship of the horse; servant and ally, yet independent spirit. And he knew too well the mission that might cost him everything.

The meadow, flanked by woods, lies beside the river. The many horses have made tracks among the wild flowers. The dark man, mounted, with six attendants, waits. Since movement causes him pain, he remains still, except when the horse lowers its head to crop the fragrant grass. A party approaches. The colour and richness of their costume make them look like swallowtail butterflies, flaunting themselves at a gathering of moths.

His agony apparent in the dullness of his eyes, his hair matted with sweat, the dark man dismounts and, in a plain and public display of obedience, prostrates himself, face down, among the white and yellow flowers. His host, the same companion with whom he once rode in pomp, also dismounts. He bends to raise the dark man and, holding his stirrup, urges him to remount.

Together they ride towards the rich pavilions, pitched at the edge of the wood. The dark man is offered wine in a gold goblet, but declines. There is a sudden expectancy. The followers, in their drab and their splendour, are intent and silent. His steps slow and considered, the dark man approaches his host, unsmiling, his pallor shocking against the deep green. Two paces away, he raises his forearms so that the palms of his hands are cupped to the sky. It is a gesture of profound humility and forgiveness. It is as if, naked, he is laying bare his heart, in utter acceptance of his fate; be it the embrace, or the cruel, raping steel. The silence is inhabited only by the crickets and birds.

As though in slow motion, the host looks to his side, seeming to ask counsel. For a moment it appears that he will put an arm round the dark man's neck, halting his gradual crucifixion. The onlookers are alert to the smallest movement. There is none. With an agonising, inexorable rhythm, and not without regret, the host shakes his head three times. It is clear to all present that, for the dark man, this is a sentence of death. He looks at his former friend, his expression stripped of any emotion.

'Then we shall never see each other again in this life,' he says, his language, in this moment, understandable.

Once more the dark man rides to the sea, his retinue now shrunk to two. On a cold winter's night, after waiting for a favourable wind, nauseous with pain and fatigue, he boards a small ship. From a respectful distance fishermen, woken by the sound of horses in the square by the church, watch what they realise is no ordinary departure. Soon the ship is devoured by the darkness.

In the ashen morning, on a calm sea, the vessel approaches white cliffs. A cross is raised in the prow. As he makes landfall, the dark man is recognised by watchers on the shore, who prostrate themselves. His entry into the small town becomes a progress. There is hubbub, and cheering, and wild hope fired by an exiled champion returning. But the champion's face tells a different story. Though he raises his hand in weary blessing, he seems to see beyond the crowd to a future they cannot envisage; one that he must enter alone. As he passes a creature in a ragged cloak she shouts, 'Beware of the knife!'

She is hushed, and jostled to the ground by the shocked townsfolk.

But to the traveller, her words are a confirmation . . .

Chapter Ten

The small room, and everything in it, was white. The bed, bedspread, bedside table and lamp, the woollen throw on the bare, spotless floorboards, the walls, ceiling, and woodwork, the armchair in the corner by the barred window, the curtains, the three-legged table, the chest of drawers and wardrobe; even the dressing-gown that hung on the door leading to the bathroom. And because they were all white, Kate had soon been able to distinguish one white from another: the creamier shade of the curtains, maybe Indian; the light oatmeal of the throw; the doctor-white of the walls.

She'd been here three weeks. She knew that because every morning she'd made a tiny mark with the handle of the white toothbrush he'd provided. This secret calendar was just above the skirting-board, behind the bed-head. Three weeks without a radio, a colour, other than the flat, bleak landscape, a voice, except his, or a book of her choice. (The ones he'd provided: Ted Hughes's *Birthday Letters*, a life of Thomas Becket, *The Rise and Fall of the Third Reich*, the biography of Lewis Carroll, Koudelka's photographs, a manual of Catholic ritual, and a children's set of history books, though no doubt fascinating in their own right, were not, with the exception of the Hughes, what she wanted to read. In the end, however, boredom also forced her to plough through the Carroll and much of the history.)

Even the winter birds seemed mute in this desolate spot. The occasional jet would break the silence, fast and low, or trailing high white plumes on the way to who knew where? Other than these, nothing. No sound of farm machinery, or dogs barking, or boats on the waterway she could see in the middle distance. (Was it a river or a dyke? She couldn't tell.) Just the baleful stare of the black earth. Kate knew the fens well enough to realise that was where she must be. She'd never seen anywhere quite like them. Though this land, reclaimed from the sea, was the ultimate in fertility, it would even bear its crops as though in mourning.

In the house itself, the occasional noise at least re-assured her that the entire planet wasn't dead. Bright must be there most of the time because he served her meals; had done ever since the night he'd ambushed her near the gallery and brought her here. Simple, good meals, in which he seemed to take a certain pride. There was a hint of anticipation in his face when he asked if she'd enjoyed them. And as he prepared them she would sometimes catch the bang of an oven door, the clack of plates, or the whine of an electric mixer. Several times she had heard music: a keening, un-accompanied voice; beautiful but eerie. The sound would hang in the air like smoke. And then, every second night or so, she would hear a car start up and accelerate away from the house, though she couldn't see where it went. She assumed it was the red one; her last visual memory before blacking out.

What a dreadful night that had been; what a sudden and terrifying change in her life in the space of perhaps fifteen seconds. One moment she'd been locking up the boat, a bit light-headed after Roger's champagne, and the next she was oblivious. Something fumey and nauseating, gauze soaked in chloroform, she now supposed, pressed over her mouth and nose, a rising scream that wouldn't come out, a sensation of malevolence having caught up with her at last; long-felt dread materialised. No escape. No one to turn to. Like a heart-stopping fall from a high place. And then, who knew how much later? unsteady, misty-headed, being urged out of the red car in the cold darkness; into a small, isolated house; up a narrow, uncarpeted staircase, Bright behind her, to the white room she had never left since.

At first exhaustion had blanketed confusion and terror. She'd slept until six in the morning. When she woke, she found she was wearing her underwear but that all her other clothes were missing. Instead, folded at the foot of the single bed, lay a new white tracksuit in a transparent plastic bag. In the bathroom, as well as the toothbrush, she found all the other basics she might need, all in white, including cotton-buds, tampons, hand cream, and Johnson's baby powder. A jailer who knew at least something of women. Kate had made a mental note that a man buying such intimate female items might have seemed unusual to whoever served him, assuming that Bright had bought them himself.

She noted too that there were no nail-scissors or anything else sharp. Later he'd told her to ask for those
when she needed them. After a more methodical search
in the bedroom she also found half a dozen pairs of
modest white knickers, white T-shirts and white cotton
socks from Marks and Sparks.

Surgery or religion were her first thoughts, neither of
them reassuring. What else did white stand for? A virgin
bride? That was a laugh. Death, of course, but that was
something she'd tried not to think about. In any case,
why go to all this trouble? If he'd wanted to kill her,
why not do it straight away, down by the gallery, instead
of all this poncy white stuff? She'd asked him the question right off, that first morning, when he'd unlocked
her door and come in looking quite sheepish, with a
breakfast tray: cornflakes, toast, honey, tea.

'Why have you done this?' she'd said, sitting on the
bed in the dressing-gown. 'What's the point?'

He hadn't answered. He'd left the tray on the round
table and locked the door again after him. Black jeans,
white shirt. Face almost as pale as the room. In these surroundings he seemed smaller than she'd remembered;
insignificant, unsmiling, unthreatening. She'd eaten the
food and then tried the door, just in case. After this she'd
crossed to the window. There must be no more unre-
warding landscape on earth. Siberia couldn't look flatter,
or more inhospitable, or less accessible. She couldn't
even see a road. She supposed that meant she was at the
back of the house. Below, in what must be the garden, a
collapsing, blackened wooden shed was the only ghost
of habitation. The rest was dank neglect.

Soon people would miss her, Kate had thought: Hester, her mother, Roger, her sister, even Gareth with a bit of luck, despite the fact that he was so much younger than her. That age gap hadn't seemed to matter when they met but now, with separation and his opportunities to meet new, younger women, it seemed to stretch and darken. Nevertheless, after a while those who did miss her would raise the alarm and pretty soon the fens would be swarming with police. Corcoran and Spaull hadn't been very impressive up to now but this might be the positive development they'd been waiting for. Perhaps all along they'd known more than they were prepared to tell her. If only Spaull had got a good look at Bright in Grantchester they could have done one of those photofit things. Plastered his face all over the county. Maybe, with Hester's help, they had.

When the initial fatigue had worn off, anger and uncertainty had taken its place. It was outrageous that this could happen in a so-called civilised society. This was anarchy. Lunatics left to roam the streets, killing and raping. CCTV cameras everywhere, politicians spouting pious rubbish about the fight against crime, and yet there was nothing to stop people like Bright running amok. This was a psychopath, she was sure of that now. Hard to reconcile that with his behaviour so far, the almost timid creature with the breakfast tray, but that must be the nature of the condition. Meek and mild one minute and a pitiless killer the next. He'd revealed that side of himself when he attacked her. The man who had written the not-insensitive note had carried out a cold, clinical act of violence. He had stolen her liberty. But not her life. Why was that? It was a question that haunted her. He could have killed her at any time during their acquaintanceship, and with the greatest of ease down by the river, or now, in this house. And yet he hadn't. That was the mystery. If it wasn't about sex and it wasn't about murder, what then? Going to these fantastic lengths just for her company was even more mad than a lust for violence.

It must be that he wanted to draw it out. That was what turned him on. Lead her to think there was nothing to be afraid of, lull her, enjoy the control, the power, and then . . . How would he do it? Something in the food? Somehow get behind her again with one of those gag things and do it while she was unconscious? Creep in while she was asleep and . . .? Oh, God, how lonely she felt. Alone, vulnerable, confused, frightened. How desirable the gallery seemed from here. Her own little world, familiar, secure, controllable. Nothing prepared you for being stripped of all the things you knew. There was nothing to draw on for comfort or support. There was only hope, and a little bit of that leaked away every day.

She'd tried to work out a daily routine. Get up when she woke, often about seven, fifteen minutes of as many Canadian Air Force exercises as she could remember, have a bath, eat the breakfast he brought, try and draw him out, so far without success, then force herself to write something in the notebook he'd provided. At first her efforts were pathetic: the bare, boring details of the day before; times of meals, a depressing record of moods, wondering what her friends were doing at certain times. Would Roger have replaced her at the gallery? Would Gareth think she'd had second thoughts? Self-pity brought tears to her eyes. Instead of trying to fight them off, she surrendered to them. And then she would write a resolution; an injunction to herself to keep bright; to focus on survival.

After a few days, the notes became more discursive. She began to unravel ideas in more detail. She tried to find ways of describing the landscape, concentrating hard on every nuance. Because it was so bleak and featureless, it tended to draw her thoughts beyond it. She attempted to sketch clouds, with the spare, loose line of artists she admired, but the marks she made were unrecognisable. Soon she gave up in frustration. She started a children's story about Hester, a deprived child from a housing estate abducted by her vile stepfather. It was only when she was imprisoned in a house not unlike Bright's that she discovered a magic bobbin of unbreakable gossamer thread. With its help she would, in the end, abseil from the window, then use it as a sure but invisible guide-line to the kidnapper's lair. Often Kate found herself making the narrative too dark. She realised that she was project-ing her own fear and uncertainty on to her characters. Though this might have therapeutic value for her, it was liable to give a young reader nightmares. In the writing she tried to imagine the stepfather's motives. Most of the options were cruel and ugly, but in one passage she sur-prised herself by speculating that he himself might be driven by sheer loneliness, and a longing for protective love. At the start of the new, uncaring millennium, that one would take some believing.

In spite of her unexpected absorption in this project, every day the enemy had to be fought off many times. Boredom and despair would come bullying over the low horizon like accelerating storm clouds. Combined with the silence, that bloody silence, they would threaten to engulf her, multiply and intensify and suck her into their tumultuous waves. When she felt this happening she would whistle and gibber and sing snatches of half-remembered songs. She longed to open the window and yell with all her energy, until she was on the verge of hyperventilating and her throat was sore, but even with only herself for company she felt an absurd inhibition. Instead, wound tight with unreleased, unspecific rage, she would fling herself on the bed in tears. Often, afterwards, she would sleep, waking to find the storm had passed and the early dark had come down to join the black fen.

Sometimes, when Bright brought in the tray, Kate would goad him, or just be plain offensive; desperate to draw something, anything out of him. To hear another human voice, no matter what it was saying, might almost be enough. Twice, on the edge of hysteria, she'd tried to hit him, but both times, shrinking from contact, he'd been much too quick for her. In answer to direct questions he would be polite but evasive; the more aggressive the enquiry, the more guarded the reply. It was as though all he wanted from her was her presence, like the stepfather in her story. Perhaps around that basic reassurance he was able to embroider the fantasies that sustained him. When she asked him how long he meant to keep her there, he said she only had to be patient for a little while. Though that might be either good news or bad, depending on his intentions, she chose to be encouraged by it.

After three weeks, however, reckoning that Christmas was now only a week away, Kate had become obsessed with the idea of escaping. Day and night she thought of little else. Even while she was writing the story, she had a horror that her mind was playing tricks, that she was in fact repeating the word 'escape' thousands and thousands of times, like Jack Nicholson's mad mantra in *The Shining*. But how? Since the window in the bathroom was too small and the one in the bedroom barred, the only way out was through the door. Though Bright was slender, he was much the stronger of the two, as he'd already demonstrated.

And then it occurred to her that there was more than one form of escape. Though meals were the highlights of her wretched day, she would somehow find the mental strength to go on hunger strike. If Bright needed nothing more than her existence to satisfy him, the sight of her fading away might make him think twice. If, on the other hand, he was fattening her up like a turkey for a Christmas kill, she would be depriving him of his pleasure. After so long without company it was hard to be sure her thought processes were rational, but at least the scheme would provide the illusion of action. At least it would give her the upper hand, empower her, give purpose to her endless days. Was she tough enough, she wondered. What an easy life she'd led, never knowing hunger, cold, excessive pain.

The soft generation. Could she find the determination to do this thing, when her stomach began to crave? At least she could try.

On day twenty-two, 19 December according to her reckoning, Bright was prompt with the breakfast. Eight o'clock, on the dot. As usual he put the tray on the table and, without looking at her, turned to leave.

'You might as well take it with you,' she said. 'I'm not eating. Not now, not ever. Not till you let me go.'

Bright frowned. 'That's not very intelligent,' he said.

'Oh, and I suppose keeping me locked up here is, is it? Just take it away.'

He left the tray where it was, and locked the door behind him. Kate eyed the food, already longing for it. This was going to be impossible. This temptation, sitting there, taunting her; that crispy toast, the lovely creamy butter . . . Nothing for it but direct action. She opened the window, picked up the tray and, slotting it between the bars, tipped the entire contents, china and all, into the garden.

After that, every day the routine was the same, except that now Bright substituted plastic for china. He replaced the rejected trays with fresh ones, each one looking more appetising than the last. And every day Kate hurled them out of her sight. At least she was doing the birds a favour, she thought. The regular bonanza broke their silence, filling the garden with a frenzy of disbelieving gluttony.

In the long hours between Bright's appearances, however, she'd begun to pay a high price for her strategy. Hunger was making her even more fearful and haunted. She often thought of the police, and her friends and colleagues, as betrayers, and of their failure to find her as deliberate. It was possible that she was no more than twenty miles from Cambridge, and maybe even closer to Ely, so how could they miss her? Didn't these people have dogs and helicopters? Couldn't they check every red car in the region? Of course they could, if they wanted to. They just preferred her out of the way. And if she was still alive she'd spend Christmas in this horrible place. Alone, except for the lunatic downstairs, and who was to say his mood wouldn't change, as it must have changed that night by the water tower in Southwold? He was unstable; she was starving and defenceless. Time was so slow to pass that she had to take her watch off and steel herself not to look at it. And even on crisp, sunny days, the black fen yielded no hint of relief. Oh, God . . . Please, God . . .

Then, on the fourth day of her hunger strike, 22 December, Kate woke to find Bright sitting on the side of the bed, nearest the window. He had a tablespoonful of cereal in his right hand. She turned her head away, frightened. After a few moments he spoke. His voice was flat and calm. 'I'd like to tell you something,' he said.

After her visit to Gilbert, Hester had called at the gallery on her way back to the flat. The lights were out, the door locked. Kate must have gone home. Full of her discovery, Hester was bursting to tell her. Here at last was real evidence that Bright was as evil as they'd thought in their worst imaginings. He had killed poor

Martin Taylor: followed him in his car on a dark night, slowed behind him on an empty stretch of road, watching his laborious pedalling in the stare of the headlights, accelerated into him, seeing his head snap back and his body lurch and fall, lifeless. Then he'd pulled in, stood over the spot, and placed that obscene cross. His mark. Moments later he'd gone, congratulating himself on getting away with it. Smiling, perhaps, in the light from the dashboard. But unknown to him, silent in the bushes, had been an all-seeing shadow: a witness. Gilbert had, in his own childlike way, recorded everything. And Kate still knew none of this.

'Kate! Kate!' Hester shut the door of the Hertford Street flat behind her and flung her coat on a chair. Maybe Kate was in her room. Maybe she'd had a heavy lunch and crashed out. Hester knocked on her friend's bedroom door, calling again, 'Wakey, wakey!'

The room was empty, the bed made. Kate must have gone out for a drink, Hester thought. Maybe with her boss, Roger, or one of her artists. Unusual for her not to leave a message of some sort but not unprecedented. Hester checked the answerphone. The dial showed zero. Damn! All this hot news and no one to share it with. Should she ring the police now, or wait until Kate got back? Wait, on balance, and then they could see them together. With a conscious effort to keep her excitement in check, Hester went into the tiny kitchen and started to make pesto in the old marble mortar Kate had bought in Ely.

After supper she switched on the television: Channel Four news. All the usual suspects. A scandal in the

Health Service – body parts plucked from cadavers without the relatives' knowledge; a politician caught with his hands down someone else's trousers; a report on a sink housing estate where families were living in unrelieved squalor. Too depressing. Hester opted instead for a comedy, repeated from twenty years ago. Even more depressing. She switched off and tried to concentrate on a magazine.

By eight thirty she was starting to get anxious. Kate had known she was doing pasta for supper. Maybe she'd met Gareth and was too starry-eyed to notice the time. No point in ringing Roger or anyone: they'd think she was behaving like a neurotic old hen. Kate had her own life, after all. Why should she account for her every move? Hester thought how much she was missing her own little house in Eden Street. She'd been more than happy to help her friend through a bad patch but now she had withdrawal symptoms.

At eleven o'clock there was still no sign. Hester felt both sleepy and on edge. Again she told herself there needn't be anything sinister about Kate's non-appearance, but some other nagging little voice kept interrupting. It insisted there was something wrong. It whispered Bright's name and nudged Hester to ring the police after all. No point this late, she thought. The two detectives would have gone home. There was nothing they could do in any case, and if Kate turned up in half an hour, flushed with lust, Hester would look an idiot. No, first thing in the morning. Meanwhile there was nothing for it but to try to sleep. Hang on to the thought that if Kate didn't come back, it meant Gareth was making her a happy woman.

The following morning Hester was still alone in the flat. By now she was alarmed. The small voice had become strident, discounting any comforting theories. Leave it till nine, she thought, then ring the office, tell them she had flu, and call – what was his name? Corcoran.

At nine thirty-five he was in the flat, standing with his back to her, looking out of the window.

'What did it look like, this cross Gilbert found?' he was saying.

'Just a little plastic thing. Brownish. Like they have on rosaries.'

Corcoran turned. 'You a Catholic?' he said.

'Used to be.'

Corcoran walked over to the mantelpiece. Hester got the feeling that he knew more than he was saying.

'I'll get round and see Gilbert's artwork as soon as we're done here,' he said. 'And you're sure Ms Mellanby wouldn't be staying with friends?'

'I'm not sure, no, but it's very unlike her. She's very . . . you know, competent. Methodical. She'd have rung, I'm sure.'

'Has she family in the area?'

'No.'

'Does she ride a bike?'

'What, are you thinking she might be in hospital?'

'Possibility.'

'No, she walks everywhere. Her work's only five minutes away.'

'And this . . . Bright. When you saw him at the Blue

Ball you got the impression he'd be back? That's what you told DC Spaull.'

Hester nodded. 'He said we wouldn't see him coming. Looks as though he was right.'

Corcoran looked at the sofa. 'May I?' he said.

'Course.'

He seemed to prepare for a moment before he spoke. 'Ms Edmond, I have to say I'm concerned.'

Hester sat down, too, on the arm of an easy chair. She felt winded, apprehensive. Corcoran's tone could only mean news she didn't want to hear.

'I don't want you to alarm yourself unduly,' he went on, 'but there's one or two things you should know. The note your man left for Ms Mellanby, the one with the handwritten envelope . . . She'll have told you about that?'

'Yes,' Hester said. It came out as little more than a whisper, so she repeated it in a firmer voice: 'Yes.'

'Well, the handwriting wasn't Bright's. We assume he typed the note on a laptop or whatever but he didn't address the envelope.'

'How do you know?'

'Because it matched some other writing we found.'

Hester frowned. 'Do we know whose?'

'The murder on Midsummer Common? The body in the toilet? The writing was the victim's. We found a little diary-type notebook in his jacket pocket.'

'I don't quite see . . .'

'Bear with me a minute,' Corcoran said. 'I know this is a bit hard to take in. The victim's name was Betts, Timothy Betts. He worked at Addenbrooke's hospital as a porter. You'll have seen that in the papers. Whoever killed him got him to address the envelope sometime before he—'

'But why would anyone do that?'

Corcoran shrugged. 'Cover his tracks?' Corcoran paused while Hester absorbed this. 'Betts was also in the Salvation Army. That's why what you've just told me – about what Gilbert found – that's why it's very interesting.'

'I'm afraid you've lost me.'

'We found a little plastic cross on Betts's body, just like the one you say Gilbert's got. And they also found one on the lad in Southwold.'

'He was something to do with the Church, wasn't he?'

'Correct.'

'A novice or something?' All at once Hester saw the pattern. 'So that's a novice, someone in the Salvation Army, and Martin Taylor. He was reading theology.'

Corcoran's expression confirmed the link.

'All marked with a cross,' Hester went on. 'So what are we dealing with here? Are you saying Bright's a religious fanatic?'

'I'm not saying anything yet. You'll appreciate there's very little by way of evidence. We don't even know for sure if Bright was in Southwold at the time of that murder.'

'What about Gilbert's sketch?'

Hester could tell that, though sceptical, Corcoran didn't want to discourage her.

'Let's have a look first.'

'But if they *were* all Bright, and he's got Kate . . .?'

'We don't know that either.'

'No, we don't know it but, let's face it, it's highly likely, isn't it?'

'He's certainly a man we want to find as soon as possible, put it that way.'

'But why?' Hester said. 'If it's religion he gets off on, where does Kate come into it?'

'Like I say, as yet there's nothing conclusive to say he's involved in her – in the fact that she appears to be missing. If it turns out that he is, then I haven't got an answer for you. I wish I had.' Corcoran got up from the sofa. 'I'll get over and see our artist friend. Get our people down to the gallery. They'll need to have a nose round here too.'

Despite her growing confusion, Hester sympathised with him. The job was grim and sordid. He was a good man doing his best. The last thing he needed was a barrage of premature, uninformed questions.

As he left, Corcoran said, 'We'll be in touch. If there's anything, anything at all . . .' He ripped a page out of his notebook and scribbled two numbers. 'Anytime. I know nothing I can say'll stop you fretting but, rest assured, we'll find them. Both of them. We'll not rest till we do.'

From the window, Hester watched him get into his car. He was right. Nothing he'd said had made her feel any better. The likelihood remained that somewhere, beyond those rooftops, or even, perhaps, in a building visible from here, Kate was the prisoner of a killer. All those walls hiding all those secrets. It was the most terrifying thought she had ever known.

Within an hour she'd rung everyone she could think of who had any connection with Kate. With no address book to help her this didn't amount to more than a dozen, and even for some of those she had to rely on directory enquiries. Roger Crick was concerned but optimistic. Perhaps a member of Kate's family was ill, he suggested, and she'd had to leave in a hurry to be with them. Meanwhile did Hester know of anyone who could take over at the gallery? Hester's negative reply was vehement. Typical of that slick bastard to put profit before his employee's well-being. But he had made Hester wonder whether she ought to try and get in touch with Kate's mother or sister. She knew the sister lived in Leamington Spa but had no idea of her married name. And she remembered Kate saying her mother had gone to Tenerife with a friend for Christmas. Maybe Kate had kept letters from them? Feeling a little guilty, Hester rummaged through drawers but came up with nothing. If she stayed on in the flat, much as she longed to get home, it was likely that the family would soon ring to find out why they hadn't heard from Kate. Last of all she tried Siobhan in London to get Gareth Vaisey's number, but the answerphone was on.

Forty-eight hours later Hester's assumption was borne out. Both Kate's mother and sister did ring. Though she'd rehearsed what she would say to them, to spare them undue concern, she found the conversations awkward. She'd tried to appear neither light-hearted nor gloomy, but on both occasions she knew she'd sounded less than convincing. So implausible, in fact, that Kate's mother had said she was catching the next flight back. Meanwhile Siobhan had called Hester with Gareth's number, and at least with her Hester was able to be frank. Gareth himself had been shocked. He said he'd rung the gallery several times and wondered what was going on. He quizzed her on details, wondered what he could do to help, and arranged to meet her after work so that they could review every possibility.

As the weeks passed Hester became more and more frustrated at her own impotence. She rang Corcoran so often that she was afraid even his remarkable patience would implode, creating a mushroom cloud over Parkside police station. Right at the start he said he'd found his visit to Gilbert very useful, and he kept assuring her that the biggest manhunt since the Cambridge rapist was under way. He hadn't needed to tell her that because the nationals and the *Cambridge Evening News* had been covering the story for some time. Hester had been nagged by reporters both at work and at home, since she'd now moved back to Eden Street. Her instinct was to tell them to get lost, but she realised that would be unhelpful to Kate.

At first leaving Hertford Street had felt like a small abandonment, as though she were somehow turning her back on her friend. She told herself this was absurd, and that it made no difference where she made calls from, but the unease lingered. What if Kate, or someone on her behalf, managed to contact the flat and got no answer? To solve that problem Hester left her own numbers, both work and Eden Street, on Kate's answer-phone, and made regular checks on the incoming calls.

Meanwhile she and Gareth had met twice a week. She'd been impressed with his seriousness, his obvious commitment to doing whatever he could for Kate. Like Hester, he hated the gnawing frustration of being a bystander; the practical impossibility of succeeding where even the police were failing. Three times, at weekends, using Ordnance Survey maps provided by Gareth, they drove round remote areas, hoping for a chance sighting of something suspicious. As they did it they knew it was hopeless, but at least pooling their impotence felt like a form of support.

At first Kate hadn't been sure whether this was part of her dream; Bright sitting on the bed, talking in a quiet, mesmeric voice. If it wasn't, why had he made the sudden decision to speak after all this time? And why in such a confessional way? He must know that the more he revealed about himself, the more she was a potential danger to him. Unless when he'd finished he planned to . . . No. Don't even think about it. Let him talk. To interrupt him in such a strange mood might be dangerous, like waking a sleep-walker.

Bright had put the tray down now. His hands, back to back, rested between his legs. He seemed to be looking at the corner of the room, where the ceiling sloped. It was as though he could see his past there; a past that possessed and directed him. Beside him on the white coverlet was a yellow plastic carrier-bag with something firm-edged inside it. Better not to ask, Kate thought. If it was to do with her, he would find his own way of introducing it.

'. . . he'd make us sit in the back row, my mother and me. It always seemed cold, even in summer,' he was saying. 'He'd be there on the altar, with his hands held up, cupped slightly . . .' Bright imitated the gesture he was describing, like a man surrendering to an armed opponent '. . . head slightly to one side, reading from the book. The gorgeous embroidery on his vestments. The women's faces, adoring him. Not God, him. That voice saying the sacred words. Sacred!' He repeated this as though it were poison. ' "*Ecce agnus Dei, ecce qui tollit peccata mundi . . .*" He knew all about those, *peccata mundi . . .* the sins of the world. Not just listening to them . . . Not just confessions in the dark church with maybe a candle burning . . . The real thing. The real filthy thing. The sly, slimy, filthy thing. The thing in the corner, where you can't see it at first, and then you can, and you know you shouldn't but it gets a hold and it's on you . . . it's in you . . . it's making your blood hot . . .'

Though he was beside her, he was not. His hurt mind was back somewhere in his childhood. Some terrible suffering that had scalded its memory in him; changed him; maimed him. Perhaps this was the first time he'd ever shared his pain. But the sharing meant a burden for the listener; an unwanted responsibility that might carry a fatal price. Once again Kate wondered how he could let her go when she possessed his secret. She wanted to restrain him; in a gentle, coaxing way to guide him elsewhere, away from this nightmare. But who was this monster he was talking about? What part did he play in Bright's tortured imaginings?

'This was a vicar, then?' Kate said, her voice tentative, anxious not to upset him further. At this moment, despite what he might have done, it was impossible not to feel a little pity.

'A priest,' Bright said. 'My father was a priest.'

'I – I don't understand,' Kate said.

'My mother was young. Nineteen she was. She'd come over from Newport, in Mayo. She knew nothing. Nothing about life. The nuns had taught her. They'd taught her nothing. Guilt. Superstition. Honour the priest. Honour the priest! Over there they were ignoramuses the lot of them. Seamus ignoramus.' Bright's tone was bitter. 'Anyway, she's here, alone, in Hounslow. Doesn't know a soul. Goes to Mass, like a good Irish girl. Meets the priest after. "Hello, my dear," he says, "welcome to the congregation. What a delightful new addition. What a pearl. Have you work at all?" She says no, she hasn't. She's modest, shy. He's a good-looking man in his thirties. Father Thomas. "I have a little put by," she says, "but I need something badly." "What an extraordinary coincidence," he says. "God does indeed work in mysterious ways. It just so happens I'm in sore need of a housekeeper. Now, what do you say to that? So many pounds a week and all found? Bed, board, and the blessed sacrament never far away. A ready-made family. A holy family. A home from home. What about it?" She thinks for a moment. He can see what she's thinking. "You're a bit young to be sharing a house with a man? People might talk? Is that it?" he says. "Not at all," he says. "This isn't Mayo you know. We'll not have any of that nonsense. Anyway, evil is in the eye of the beholder. We're both God's servants, it's as simple as that." '

Bright paused. As he spoke for the priest, he became him. He entered into his manipulative mind with growing confidence, never looking at Kate, becoming more and more remote from her even as he communicated. 'She looks up and smiles,' he went on. 'Nods. "Good," he says. "Well, that's settled, then." She carries her small brown suitcase from the boarding-house to the big, draughty, gloomy presbytery. Cold, inhospitable, footsteps down empty corridors, the smell of polish and disinfectant. She cooks, she cleans, she collects the spent candles. In the half-dark she sees the figure bleeding on the altar. There's blood everywhere. Martyr's wounds. The stigmata. The crown of thorns slicing into His head like razor wire. She's homesick and frightened. She starts to cry. All of a sudden he's there behind her. She hasn't heard him coming. But now he's there behind her. His voice is soft and soothing. He's telling her not to be afraid. He's telling her God is watching over her. "He's got you in the palm of his hand," he's saying . . .'

Now Bright was agitated. As he spoke he began to rock from the waist. He was getting to the core of his madness, entering the place he feared most. Kate didn't want to hear any more. She didn't want to hear the scream that was building in him; that might tip him over the edge into violence. Perhaps this was the process that brought him to the rage he needed: the rage that made him an executioner.

' "He's got you in the palm of his hand," ' he

repeated. 'And he has. He's put his arms under her arms and he's. . . he's touching her.' For a moment Bright fought the memory. 'This — this priest, Thomas, he's touching her. And he leads her away from there. Talking all the time. Words. Soft words. And he leads her to her small bare room with the metal bed in the attic. And he starts. She's frightened. "This is wrong," she says. "I don't want this." And he reassures her in that soft voice. "It's not a sin if you love someone," he's saying, "and I love you, my child." "But I don't love you, Father," she says. "Not in that way. I'm frightened. Let me go." And she starts to cry. And he says, "Trust me, my child. It's God's will. It's God's way of bringing joy to the world. It's His blessing on us." ' The pain of it made Bright lower his voice. The shame made the words indistinct. 'And he takes her. He forces her. He uses her.'

For a moment he was silent. Kate's instinct was to offer him sympathy, but if she did he might come to hate her for seeing him out of control. In any case she mustn't allow herself to be drawn in. Not for a moment. She must never forget what this sick creature had done, and might be prepared to do again.

'He uses my mother,' Bright went on. 'And there's no one to hear her crying. Just the long, dark corridors, and the bleeding statues.'

For the first time in several minutes Bright seemed to remember where he was. He gave himself a moment to readjust to reality, picked up the yellow plastic carrier-bag, stood up, and left the room, locking the door behind him.

There was no way to be sure, but what he'd said had

sounded like the truth, or at least the truth as he saw it. The raped mother, the rapist priest, the motives for revenge on the Church. The hate that had taken hold. And it seemed there was more to come. Kate wondered how far he'd go. Either deluding himself that she could be trusted, or not caring because he planned to silence her anyway, he'd already perhaps told her more than he'd ever told anyone. Now, whether she wanted it or not, she had become his confessor, without the power of absolution. She was condemned to listen.

Meanwhile the hunger pains had become unbearable. No longer able to resist, she took two of the three dry pieces of toast from the tray, hoping he wouldn't notice, and ate them like a starving refugee. December 22. Lights in the streets, carols in King's College Chapel, Christmas trees in the windows, excited children, a shopping stampede. Her mother, abroad, would worry herself sick. She'd have rung the flat and got no answer. Then she'd have called the police. And then, day and night, she'd have imagined the worst. Poor Mum. But never, in her most elaborate imaginings, could she come near the truth of it: her daughter the prisoner of a paranoid schizophrenic who killed people – a theology student and a novice – because of what he said the Church had done to *his* mother. More to the point, what did this shipwrecked mind have in store for Kate?

For the next two days, despite her questions, Bright was as silent as he'd been before the sudden outburst. If he noticed that Kate was now eating bits and pieces from the trays, he didn't mention that either. And then, on Christmas Eve, when night was already closing in at twenty past four in the afternoon, he came into the room and sat in the corner chair, once again resting the yellow carrier-bag beside him. He looked at her. She could either return his look or turn away, but she couldn't ignore him. It seemed like the moment to say something.

'Why did you tell me those things?'

Instead of answering he got up and switched the light off. Then he sat down again. Alarmed, Kate put on the bedside lamp.

'Put it off,' he said.

'I'm scared of the dark.'

'Put it off,' he repeated.

Afraid of what he might do, she reached out. After a silence of perhaps half a minute, he started to speak in the quiet, unemphatic tone of almost three days ago.

'Time passed. When he realised my mother was pregnant the priest made her leave the presbytery. Threw her out, didn't care where. A child was born. A girl, Catherine. He said if my mother told a living soul what had happened, he'd get in touch with her parents in Ireland, tell them she'd had the child by another man, a bad man. He said he'd have her put in a mental home, and the child fostered. He could do these things, he said. He knew people. Anyway, he said, who'd believe her? Who'd believe the word of an ignorant Irish girl against the priest they loved and respected? The good shepherd. But even though he'd thrown her on to the streets, he still made her come to Mass every Sunday. Sit at the back. Watch her tormentor, and the people thinking he was a saint, and she was mothering a stranger's bastard. Eventually she plucked up the courage to go to another church. She didn't dare go to confession, of course. She knew she wouldn't be believed. She felt cursed. But she managed to find herself a part-time job in a tobacconist's, and after a time in a squat she got a council flat. She met a man. A good man. An electrician. . . Michael. They made a home together. She couldn't forget the past, she could never do that, but she was happy enough. Until one night . . .'

Bright paused. Kate sensed that it took all his strength to keep himself from breaking down. It was now so dark in the room that she could only make out his shape, hunched forward in the chair.

'Four years have passed. One night she's in the flat, alone. Michael's working late. There's a knock on the door. It's the priest, Thomas. She's frightened. At first she won't let him in, but just then someone passes by and rather than make a fuss she stands aside. She asks him how he's found her and he says there are no secrets from a priest. He sits down. "So how are you?" he says. "And the little girl?" He hasn't even remembered Catherine's name. "I often think about you both," he says. "Say a prayer for you." She says nothing. "I miss you," he says. "I miss that blessed closeness, the sacrament we shared. Because that's what it was you know," he says. "A sacrament." Still she says nothing. Catherine's asleep in the next room. "Come and sit by me," he says. "Just for old times' sake." My mother stays where she is. "Oh, come on," he says. "I'm not a monster you know. Far from it. I'm full of love. God's love." He gets up then and gets hold of her arm. She's very frightened, but she doesn't want to wake Catherine. "Michael will be back any minute," she says. "He just went out for . . ." He puts his hand over her mouth. "Hush," he says. "No need to talk. Just let me hold you again, like we did. Where's the harm? Just a moment's comfort in a hard old world. God's love made flesh. There, that's it." His voice is soothing. He starts. She backs away. She wants to scream but she can't. She wants to hurt him but she can't. There's something holding her back. There's generations of fear and superstition pinning her arms, telling her to hold her tongue. "God's will," the Irish voices are saying, "God's will . . . Thy will be done . . ." The priest is strong. She struggles but at the same time her mind goes blank. If it wasn't for Catherine she'd want to die. He's on her. He's stealing her body. My mother. He's breaking her . . .'

Bright started to rock again. 'Me and hate were conceived at the same moment,' he went on, calmer now that he'd reached the point of his story. 'The drug of it was in my blood. My mother was slim. She didn't show till very late. When she did she told Michael the truth. He couldn't take it. He was a kind man but he couldn't take it. He said he didn't want to go, but he abandoned them, just like everybody else. I was born a month later.'

After another pause his voice changed. It had become harder, allowing itself no emotion. 'Seven months after that my mother and Catherine were found in the canal. She'd left me in an office at the hospital. She felt she had no choice.' He put his hand in the carrier-bag and drew something pale out. 'There were several sheets of paper with writing on them tucked under the shawl she'd wrapped me in. Those and two photographs. They went with me to the children's home. They've been with me ever since. Every moment of every day and night. I don't know why my mother and Catherine didn't take me with them. I wish they had. I've always wished they had.'

He put what Kate now realised must be his mother's last note, her tragic account and fateful legacy, back in the bag, got up, and began to come towards her. She could sense the sudden tension in herself, her body making ready without any conscious act of will. Now, at last, he must be about to reveal her connection to this dreadful story; a story she would have given anything never to have heard. Now he was beside her. Was it some sort of perverted revenge he wanted from her? Were there women among his victims as well as men? As he leaned forward she shrank back. But instead of threatening her he switched on the lamp and sat at the end of the bed.

'Don't be afraid,' he said. 'I wouldn't ever hurt you.'

'What do you want me for, then?'

'Just to be here.'

'But what about what I want? You've kept me here for . . . God knows, weeks. Scared to death, bored out of my head, a prisoner, for Christ's sake. You can't do that to people.'

'The priest was the first,' he said, ignoring her outburst. 'Thomas. As soon as I was able I looked for him. I was sixteen. Small but strong. I made myself strong. To be ready. I found him in Liverpool. A winter's evening. He was sitting in the confessional. Just him and me in the big, dark church. I thought of my mother. Alone with him. His hands. This pitiless hypocrite. This disgusting animal. I knelt down. His voice was very soothing. Oh, yes. He knew how to use it all right. I could smell his breath. Like my mother must have done. My father's breath. He called me "my child". Ironic, isn't it? Little did he know. He never knew. While he was talking about how we must always be on our guard against temptation, this man who killed my mother and my sister, Catherine, I got up very quietly, and pulled back the curtain across his cubicle. He looked up. I put my hands round his throat. At first he was too surprised even to struggle. When he did it was too late. I saw the panic in his eyes. I always need to see that. See them pay the price. When the breath had gone out of him I laid his head back, against the wall. "Bless me, Father, for I have sinned," I said. It was the happiest moment of my life.'

Bright's tone was colourless now, as though he were recounting the dry details of an inventory. 'I made it my life's work. To rid the world of these dangerous people. There were four more before I came to Cambridge. One was an assistant to a bishop. Then, when I moved here, there was Taylor, on the road. Then a young man I'd got talking to in Southwold. It was his mobile I used. He wanted to be a monk. I'd nothing against him personally. I quite liked him. It was what he represented. I couldn't let that go unpunished—'

Kate interrupted him. 'Why were you in Southwold?'

'To be near you, of course. That's why I wanted the address book too. Your keys. Just to be in your life.' Bright made it sound natural and obvious. 'To share something with you.'

'But why? Why me? How did you know I was going to be there?'

'I watched.' Bright didn't allow himself to be distracted. 'And then there was the creature in the Salvation Army. I got him to address the envelope I sent my note to you in. He'd got me some chloroform from Addenbrooke's. He looked peaceful. He was better off out of it. I marked them all with a cross. It was my . . . signature. The irony appealed to me. I'd been around a lot by then. Lived all over the place; few months here, few months there. Weeks sometimes. All kinds of jobs, temping, bookshops, kitchens, computers, colleges, hospitals, didn't matter to me where I was. All the time educating myself. Making my mind strong as well as my body. Poetry and art, but history mainly. That's for the last one. There'll only be one more. One magnificent final act of justice that will end it once and for all. Take it out by the root. Kill it in the present and the past. I'll know it when it comes along. It's all I'm living for. It'll be what I'm remembered by.'

There was a short silence. Now she was in this deep, Kate found the courage to speak again: 'Is that important, being remembered?' she said.

'Of course. What's the point if we aren't remembered? If we haven't used our talents to the absolute limit, whatever sacrifice it takes? Those are the people who are remembered. I've always known I was one of them. I've always dreamed of it.' Though what he was saying was as mad as before, there had been another subtle change in his tone. For the first time it sounded as though he was talking to her, rather than himself. 'What do you dream of?' he said.

This development was so sudden that Kate felt blank. 'Er . . . well, you know, the usual . . . Anxiety things, flying sometimes . . .' This was pathetic. She wanted to hold his interest. Now he seemed to have come down for a moment from whatever rarified state he'd been in, she was desperate to keep him talking. That way at least she had a chance of appealing to the remains of normality in him. He might even relent and let her go. But what to tell him? She still couldn't think of anything special about her dreams. Unlike other people's, they were never Dali-esque. Or if they were, she could never recall them. Better make something up, quick, or he'd be off, and the next time she saw him he'd be raving again.

And then she remembered an evening in Eden Street: an evening when she had heard something so extraordinary that it had stuck in her mind in vivid detail. 'There was this weird one, though . . .' Claiming it as her own, she repeated Siobhan's account of her friend's amazing sequence of dreams. There was no need to embroider. The more she talked, the more the strange narrative came back to her: the christening in the dark church; the handsome young man with the aquiline nose, even the stammer; the gaudy procession with the wolves and monkeys; the struggle in the mud over the scarlet cloak; the huge plate of eels; the central figure fighting like a hero; the change from gorgeous clothes to a hair shirt and a plain habit; the boat landing on the white beach, and the shells in the shape of a cross; the argument on horseback in the meadow with the man he wrestled for the cloak; and the overwhelming sense that the story would end in tragedy.

Bright's stillness told her he was fascinated. She wished there was more, but the dreams were so far outside her own experience that she didn't know where to go with them. A false note of her own inventing might make him think she'd made the whole thing up and then there was no knowing how he'd react.

'And these are your dreams, you say?' he said.

'Mmmm.'

'When did you have the last one?'

'Er . . . when would it be? Day before yesterday?' Damn. Not very convincing.

'When did they start?'

'Er . . . ooh, fair bit ago. Few months, maybe?'

'How often do you get them?'

'How often? Well, sort of . . . two or three times a week.'

'This man, is he dark or fair?'

'Dark.'

'What does he wear on his hand, in the boat?'

'His hand?' Kate was growing more and more uncomfortable. Now he sounded more reasonable, maybe he wouldn't mind if she told him the truth. What difference did it make whose dreams they were? 'Look,' she said, 'the thing is they are actual dreams but a friend of a friend told me about them. And they're not her dreams either. They're somebody else's. A friend of hers. Well, apparently he's a bit more than a friend . . .'

'In what way?' Now Bright sounded more urgent.

'Look, it's none of your . . .' Steady. Don't wreck it all now.

'In what way, more than a friend?'

'They both had transplants. He got her heart and she got somebody else's. Apparently it's called a domino transplant.'

'Do you know his name, this friend?'

'Why are you so—?'

'Do you?'

'If I tell you, will you let me go?'

Bright pondered this for a second. When he answered he sounded reconciled but regretful. 'Yes,' he said. 'If it's the truth I'll let you go.'

Kate was so shocked she almost asked him to repeat it. All this time, all this misery, all this fear and boredom and it all came down to a name. The name of a complete stranger. Which she couldn't remember. Make one up. How was he to know? Play for time, anyway, while she saw whether it materialised. 'When?'

'December the twenty-ninth.'

'God, that's another five days. Why the twenty-ninth specifically? Is that the date you've had in mind all along?'

Bright shook his head. 'No. But now I can see it was meant. It's illuminated everything. This is extremely important to me. Now, please, think very carefully.'

'What's so important about it?'

The impatient look in Bright's eyes told Kate she was entering forbidden territory.

'Tell me his name,' he said, his voice edged with threat.

Half of it had come back. She'd have to bluff the rest. 'Hugh . . . Hugh S-something.'

'Think! And don't lie to me. If you lie to me you'll never get out.'

'The Hugh bit's right. I can't remember his other name. It was unusual, French-sounding. Apparently he's a freelance journalist. *Mail on Sunday*, I think Siobhan said, things like that. Travel mostly. Apparently he gets the feeling these dreams are leading him to some dark . . . I don't know . . . Like I said, he thinks they're heading for an ending.' Please let that be enough. Please. Please. Kate found herself remembering the hazy outline of a prayer. 'Can I still go?' she said. 'Please let me go.'

Instead of replying at once, Bright reached for the yellow carrier-bag. Out of it he took a picture frame. From where she sat, hunched against the bed-head, Kate could only see the back. What was this? His mother? A victim? A mutilated corpse, violated in his mission of revenge? Now, when he turned the frame, all she could make out was that it held a black and white photograph. As he angled it so that it confronted her, she felt a sudden, intense shock of recognition. It was her! The face in the frame was hers! It was a child's face, perhaps four or five years old, but there was no mistaking the likeness. Kate was seeing herself at that age, with all the hope and innocence that life had eroded. She felt moved to tears by the freckled image of her lost self.

'Catherine, my sister,' Bright said. 'This was one of

the photographs my mother left me. They're all I've got.'

Now, at last, Kate understood, and was overwhelmed by her understanding. Catherine . . . Kate. The white room, a shrine to a small, forlorn ghost. A pale face in a canal, drowned beside her mother.

'That's why you mean so much to me,' Bright said. 'That's why I'm letting you go.'

Chapter Eleven

Gary and Miranda's wedding had been a luminous day. The mustiness of centuries in the little village church was sweetened by the fragrance of extravagant flowers. Well-known faces from London were at ease among local friends of the bride's family. Her impoverished aristocratic parents, benevolent muddlers, beamed with genuine pleasure to see their wayward daughter content. The emphysematous organ, played by a Mrs Popham, panted to keep up with the lusty hymn-singing like an old labrador.

Hugh did the honours for a dry-mouthed Gary, while Siobhan watched, smiling, from the second row. The vicar made the customary noises about binding and cherishing, words which until now had not been prominent in Gary's daily lexicon. With a last rasping bellow the organ gave its all to the recessional, and a hundred happy guests enlivened the crisp, pale blue December afternoon.

The reception, in the ballroom of Miranda's parents' stately but shabby home, was a great success. In his speech Hugh managed to combine wit and affection without being untrue to the groom's unruly spirit. He told selective stories about his travels with Gary, judicious in his editing, and ended with a brief, unembarrassing but heartfelt tribute to a good friend. When he sat down Siobhan put her arm through his and nestled her head against his shoulder for a moment.

'Clever old thing,' she said.

'Why does "old" always have to undermine that otherwise charming compliment?'

'Probably because you don't get that good in five minutes.'

'Fair enough.'

Later there was dancing to a band whose lead singer, Julian, was an enduring rocker friend of Gary's. Though he must only have been in his late thirties, the impressive furrows in his lean face testified to harmonies more demanding than those of Mrs Popham. Lost in the ecstasy of his lyrics, he perhaps more than anyone present personified the recklessness of the true aristocrat. Byron, who, according to legend, had once visited the house, would have adopted him. The wedding guests also loved him, none more so than Miranda's parents. Without coercion, they danced a figure of such startling unpredictability that at the end everyone stood back and applauded.

'Come on, if they can do it you can,' Siobhan said.

'They can't do it. They just magnificently don't care that they can't do it.' Nevertheless Hugh got up, glad the next dance was a slower, smoochy number. He ambled round the floor, feeling Siobhan's warmth. 'Do you know something?' he said. 'I feel very, very happy.'

'Me too,' she said.

When they sat down Gary came and joined them. 'Do you know something?' he said.

'Yes,' Hugh and Siobhan chorused. 'You're very, very happy.'

'I am, as it happens. Very, very happy. Who'd have thought it, eh?'

'Parents-in-law seem very jolly,' Hugh said.

Gary laughed. 'They're priceless. Guess what they've given us for a wedding present.'

'Blenheim? A box at Ascot?' Hugh said

'Leave it out. They can't afford a box at Tesco's, bless their hearts. Give up?'

Hugh and Siobhan nodded.

'A wheelbarrow! I'm not kidding. It's an antique wheelbarrow. Miranda's old man, George, says it was designed by Joseph Paxton, whoever he was. I thought he stuffed turkeys.'

'That was Joseph Paxo,' Hugh said. 'This one built the Crystal Palace.'

'Oh, right. Well, anyway, they're totally skint and I love 'em to death.'

When all but a few diehards had gone, Hugh and Siobhan walked back to the Crown.

'Well wrapped up?' he said.

She smiled. 'Seems such an awfully long time ago, doesn't it? I feel like a different person.'

'Different how?'

'Calmer. Surer. Happier. Less puffed.' She stopped. 'Come here,' she said, taking hold of the lapels of his overcoat and drawing him to her. 'You need to relax.'

She kissed him on the mouth.

Hugh felt like saying thank you. Instead he said, 'Your face is cold.'

'I never feel cold when I'm with you,' she said, taking his arm again.

Over the next three weeks they saw each other almost every day. Some nights they'd see a film, or have a cheap meal. Once they went to the Festival Hall for a Ladysmith Black Mambazo concert. Anthony and Tilly took them to the National for the first night of Anthony's new play, *The Top Pocket*, about a provincial fan club devoted to great snooker players, past and present. Afterwards they all had supper in the glass-fronted Mezzanine restaurant, where the young wait-ress, an aspiring actress, pronounced claret 'claray'. At the end of the meal Tilly asked them round for Christmas lunch. Since they'd decided to spend the day together in any case, they accepted at once.

They were becoming, had perhaps become, a couple. Hugh often wondered about the nature of their coupledom, which couldn't be called conventional. He didn't know whether what he felt for her was love. It was love of a sort, that was clear enough; but whether it was the sort Siobhan wanted or welcomed, he couldn't be sure. For that reason he tried not to think too much about where it was leading. All he knew was that if fate withdrew it, or Siobhan tired of it, there'd be a dreadful emptiness in his life; one he'd never be able to fill.

Meanwhile the dreams had become darker, more fre-quent, and more intense. Hugh sensed that they were reaching their climax. Having returned to whatever it was he'd been escaping in the first place, the dark man gave an overwhelming impression that he was about to confront his fate. In his demeanour, foreboding was mingled with acceptance and resolution. More and more Hugh felt a shared identity with him, though in daylight his reason told him such a relationship was impossible. He longed to know how the story ended, though he was apprehensive that it might imply some sort of ending for him too. However, with that catharsis at least he might hope for an understanding of why the dreams had chosen him. Already his notes on them, which had become more detailed with every sequential episode, filled three black books. Feeling the writer's instinct for ritual and continuity, he'd bought a stock of these from a stationer's on the corner of Broadwick Street.

At five fifteen on Christmas Eve, as he was making notes in one of them, the telephone rang.

'Hello.'

'Mr Severin?' It was a young woman's voice, speaking up against a raucous background.

'Yes.'

'Hi. My name's Carrie. I'm Mr Dacre's new secretary?'

'Oh, hi.'

'Look, I didn't know whether to bother you at the festive season and all that, but I've just had this bloke on. Says he wants to get in touch with you urgently. Asked if you were the one who'd had the whatsisname – transplant. I hope you don't mind but it had been in the papers anyway so I couldn't see any harm. Says it's about – hang on, I can't read my own shorthand . . . er, oh, that's it. It's about this dark man who scarpers in a boat, with a big ring on his finger. He said to mention a red cloak, a plate of eels, and monkeys on horseback. Sounds dead weird, doesn't it? But he said you'd know what he meant. He sounded quite normal, apart from that. Not your average nutter, which is why I thought I'd better pass it on. Didn't get funny or anything. Honestly, this time of year, talk about goodwill to all men. Abuse to all men, more like. He was about the first caller I've had today who wasn't legless . . . Mr Severin? You still there?'

Hugh was silent. For a second he wondered whether he could be dreaming this too, but Carrie persevered. 'Hello? Mr Severin?'

'Sorry, I just . . . Sorry, go on.'

'I wasn't going to call you at first but then I thought, well, you never know, do you? Might be a code. Just my luck if I didn't pass it on and it turned out to be the story of a lifetime. And, like I say, he sounded quite sensible. Quite nice, actually. Soft-spoken. Polite. Anyway, he left a number. Said his name was Richard and he'd be there for another twenty minutes. Then again same time tomorrow. Got a pen?' She read out the number.

Hugh wrote it on the pad. 'Thanks a lot. You did absolutely the right thing,'

'Phew! Thank goodness for that.'

'Have a great Christmas.'

'And yourself. See you in the New Year. Take care. 'Bye.'

Hugh stood and looked at the number as though willing it to reveal something. This development was shocking. His heart-rate accelerated. He must sit down, try to think it through. He hadn't made any great secret of the dreams. The people he'd told might in turn have told other people. Fine. No problem. But there'd be no reason for any of those people to contact him. Not unless they felt they could help in some way. Either that or by some unimaginable means the dreams had broken through into reality. No. Rubbish. Science fiction. Take a few deep breaths and call the bloke. What was there to lose? He got up again and tapped out the number. Four rings and a man's voice answered: 'Hello.'

'Hello, is that . . . Are you Richard?'

'Mr Severin?'

'How do you know my name?'

'The woman at the paper confirmed it.'

'How do you mean, "confirmed"?'

'I thought I had it right and she confirmed it. I've read your stuff. It's good.'

'What is it you want?'

'I think it's you who wants something, isn't it?'

'Is it?'

'I think I can help you.'

Hugh didn't know how to play this. Might be best just to hang up; forget the whole thing. Take the phone off the hook. But his curiosity wouldn't let him. He'd travelled a long way with the dreams and he couldn't let it drop. Besides, by now, if he was on a private line, the man might be able to find out his number. 'How?' he said.

'With the dreams.'

'How the hell do you know about—?'

'I can't explain on the phone. We need to meet.'

'Can you get to London?'

' 'Fraid not. I'm a bit tied up at the moment.'

'Where are you?'

'In a call-box.'

'No, I mean where are you suggesting—?'

'Oh, Kent.'

'You expect me to go all the way to Kent just to chat to some total stranger? You must be mad.'

'Do I sound mad?'

'I don't know how mad sounds.'

'How are you on the twenty-ninth, say? It's a Tuesday.'

Enough was enough. 'No,' Hugh said.

'Shame. You see, I know how it ends.'

'What?'

'The story. The one that's been . . . that you've been dreaming.'

'How do you know?'

'I told you, I can't do it on the phone. Apart from anything else it'd take too long. I'm freezing.'

Hugh paused for a few seconds before he considered capitulation. 'Where, exactly?'

'Let's make it, er . . . Let's think. Do you know Canterbury at all?'

'No.'

'Oh, OK. Well, let's make it easy for you then. The railway station? Three thirty, say?'

'Can't you make it any earlier?'

'Can't, I'm afraid. Don't get away till three.'

Away from what? Hugh wondered.

'Probably best to come on your own, if that's OK,' Richard said. 'I can't really explain if we're mob-handed.'

'How do I know you're not some wild-eyed fanatic armed with a Kalashnikov?'

'You don't. But if I was, I think I'd tend not to meet you at a crowded station, wouldn't I? Then again, I'm not on intimate terms with all that many fanatics.'

Hugh found the irony almost pleasing. 'How will I know you?' he said.

'Oh, you'll know me.'

After a slight pause, the stranger's phone went dead.

Funny thing to say, unless they'd met before somewhere. Perhaps, after all, this was some gigantic wind-up: some devious friend with an elaborate hoax, planning to pop out of a photo-booth wearing a red nose. But a friend wouldn't have needed to ring the paper, or confirm his name.

Remembering that he hadn't got a present for Anthony or Tilly, Hugh made a quick note of the conversation and set off through the Christmas Eve shoppers to Primrose Hill. The caller had seemed sensible enough; calm, not pushy, not over-familiar. Perhaps he'd heard Hugh's story at second hand, perhaps it had rung a bell. What other motives could there be? No one in their right mind would tap a journalist for money, and in any case there were no grounds for blackmail. At worst it would make another few paragraphs in the notebook; maybe a twist Hugh couldn't have foreseen.

Though he knew Siobhan would be on her way back from her mother's, he still peered through the window of the café where she worked part-time, out of habit and faint hope. In the bookshop he bought Tilly Claire Tomalin's life of Jane Austen. But what writing would a writer enjoy? Work better or worse than his own? Three of Anthony's plays were there, in a Penguin collection. In the end, staying in the arts but away from literature, Hugh opted for Christopher Frayling's life of Sergio Leone.

The following day, when he handed it to Anthony, in its clumsy wrapping, the idea seemed to have paid off.

'That's kind and clever,' Anthony said. 'I'm a big fan and I know nothing.'

To save repeating himself, though he'd been bursting to tell Siobhan about the telephone call in the taxi on the way over, Hugh had decided to hold it back until lunch. Before that, new CDs were played, prominent among them a gutsy band of Afro-Cuban All Stars; Sam tried out magic tricks on everyone in turn, some more successful than others; Tilly fixed Bloody Marys; relatives rang to wish them a happy day; the floor was strewn with wrapping paper and ribbons; neighbours dropped in for hugs and champagne; the curtains were drawn to show off Anthony's bow-tie with built-in flashing lights; and, in a moment quieter than the rest, Hugh and Siobhan exchanged presents. He gave her a framed cartoon, in the style of Donald McGill. It featured a buxom woman barrister behind a counter, handing a cup of railway tea to a bewigged silk in boxer shorts. The caption read: 'Brief Encounter'.

'It's brilliant,' Siobhan said. 'Thank you.'

'He did it specially,' Hugh said, unwrapping her present to him.

It was a leather album, full of small mementoes of their time together: a photograph Gary had taken at Papworth, and the one from Pontigny; a menu from Midsummer House in Cambridge, theatre programmes, one signed by Anthony – 'To Hugh, the only journalist I've never wanted to hit. Happy Christmas. Love, Anthony'; cinema tickets; a collage of stuff Hugh had written, cut together to make hilarious nonsense; a limerick by Sam, and many more items calculated to please. Hugh was touched. 'Must have taken you weeks,' he said. 'It's great.'

'Good,' Siobhan said.

It wasn't until Anthony was carving the turkey that Hugh mentioned the telephone call, prefacing it with a very brief précis of the dream-story. Anthony looked up, concerned. 'How extraordinary. You're not going?' he said.

'I said I would,' Hugh said. 'What have I got to lose?'

'A lot, if he's a nutter.'

'Didn't sound like one.'

'Nutters usually don't.'

'How many do you number among your acquaintance?' Tilly said.

'Well,' Anthony began, 'there's my agent, for one; our otherwise irreproachable Member of Parliament; more or less the entire lynching mob of *soi-disant* theatre critics; that lollipop lady in Shepherd's Bush . . .'

'Mr Williams,' Sam added.

'Who's Mr Williams?' Tilly said.

'Our maths teacher. He sometimes wears his pyjamas under his trousers.'

'Sounds extremely sensible to me,' Anthony said.

'I think it's a terrible idea,' Siobhan said.

'What, wearing your pyjamas under your trousers?' Hugh said.

Siobhan wasn't smiling. 'You know what I mean.'

'What can possibly happen on a crowded railway station?' Hugh said. 'I'll pop down, see what he's got to say, catch the next train back. Then I won't have to wonder.'

'How can he possibly have known about these dreams?' Anthony said.

'Exactly. That's why I feel I just can't not go.'

'Why's he so keen for you to go on your own?' Siobhan said.

'He said it'd be hard to talk if we were mob-handed. But why don't you come too? Earwig from a safe distance? Rough him up for me if he turns ugly.'

'I said I'd have lunch with Martha on the twenty-ninth.'

'So you did. I'd forgotten.'

'You could ring the local police,' Tilly said. 'Just tell them what's going on.'

'What would I say?' Hugh said. 'What *is* going on? Getting in touch with somebody's hardly a crime, is it?'

'Being called Richard, however, is verging on the suspicious,' Anthony said. 'He might have been named for Mr Nixon.'

'Well, he might equally have been named for Mr

Lionheart,' Hugh said. 'No, I think the thing is just to do it and then . . . you know, it's done.'

On the way home, in the late afternoon, Siobhan tried again to dissuade him. 'I've been thinking about it,' she said. 'I did talk about it at Hester's one night, the dreams. You'd said you didn't mind. And that poor friend of hers, Kate, was there.'

Hugh took her hand. 'So? What could it possibly have to do with that?'

'I don't know. Maybe Kate's told whoever . . . If someone's got her, maybe she told him. I don't know. It just frightens me, Hugh. I think I should cancel Martha and come.'

'Listen,' he said, 'we get tips from punters all the time, hoping to make a few bob or make a name for themselves. The fifteen-minutes-of-fame thing. I'm pretty sure it's nothing at all. All the same I am intrigued. You have a lovely lunch with Martha, I'll schlep down to Kent, we'll get together at the end of the day and I'll give you a ball-by-ball commentary. OK?'

Siobhan gave him a small, unconvinced smile.

That night, and every subsequent night until the twenty-ninth, the dreams acquired a new urgency. The images seemed more powerful than ever, the impression they left more lasting. Hugh could have spent hours each morning recording the details, sure now that the long, painstaking sequence was coming to its end. It was as though a producer, or writer, or anyway their mysterious source had decided the thing needed wrapping up, and that therefore the point of it must be revealed. A sense of anticipation, of intense curiosity, was mixed with an ever sharper edge of apprehension. It was like the excitement of New York, Hugh thought, the dynamic sense of endless possibilities, including the ever-present possibility of some nameless harm veiled by the glamour.

And on the night of the twenty-eighth, the nameless harm began to show its face. For the first time the dream did not feature the dark man, the focus of all the others, in person, and yet so great was the sense of accumulating menace that it pointed in his direction like a pitiless blade.

A rider, bulked with wool and sheepskin, head down against the scouring wind, holds in his right hand the leading rein of a second horse. This riderless animal, the breath from its distended nostrils clouding the raw air, bears fat panniers on its black flanks. Its hoofs sound precise and emphatic. In the distance, against the darkening sky, a tower rises, dwarfing the irregular buildings huddled around it.

From a makeshift shelter at the roadside, picked out from the gloom by a brazier near the opening, a man appears, calling out to the rider. It is not a greeting. It is harsh, peremptory. The man, his face obscured by a thick woollen hood, carries a pike, its blade sharp enough to pierce thick clothing. Alarmed, the rider halts his two horses. The pikeman advances, raising his weapon until its tip is against the rider's throat, making a tiny depression in the flesh, drawing a pearl of blood. As the rider starts to beg for mercy, a second figure emerges from the shelter. This one, his head uncovered, has a lean, unshaven face, with the narrow eyes of a fox. In his hand is a pair of black shears. Without looking at the rider he crosses to the packhorse and, laughing, crops its tail close to the root. As he does so, with a sudden violent lunge his companion drives the tip of the pike deep into the rider's throat. The hot, shocking blood spurts into the killer's face and, in a frenzy of disgust, he tries to wipe it away with the back of his hand. The dead rider falls from his horse, dropping the leading rein, staining the colourless scene with his scarlet life.

The man with the shears slaps the rump of the packhorse. It is reluctant to move. A second slap, harder than the first, accompanied by a yelled curse. Patient, reconciled, the laden animal heads down the cold empty road, towards the tower that proclaims the town.

The image dims, giving way to another fire, much larger than the first, this one the focus of a cavernous hall filled with people. They are happy; flushed in the face and riotous. Servants fill their goblets with red wine, spilling much of it. A dwarf wears a golden crown made of parchment. He makes obscene gestures in a grotesque parody of kinghood. Musicians play unrecognisable instruments. A male singer with the voice of a woman entertains, unheard except by those closest to him. A juggler keeps four apples airborne. Bending to pick one up, he is sent staggering by an uncharitable kick. The eaters howl for him to be punished more.

At the great table, the width of the room at the top, the central figure is notable for the splendour of his garments and the gravity of his demeanour. It is he who shared acrimonious exchanges with the dark man in earlier encounters. As a messenger whispers in his ear, he alone among the assembled company is unsmiling. The hubbub is hushed now as, dismissing the messenger with an abrupt inclination of his head, he turns to the broad, older figure on his right. It is plain that his words are urgent, angry, emphatic. His commanding features betray the quiet rage and desperation of a man who has at last come to recognise the inevitable. All eyes are on him. The courtier to whom he has spoken speaks in turn to his neighbour. Within a short time, all the diners are aware of their leader's apocalyptic cry for a solution.

Recognising the moment, four men rise from the four corners of the hall. They meet at the door, acknowledging their regal host with a deep obeisance. Without any sign of endorsement, he turns away to talk to a striking woman on his left. As the men leave the hall, the dwarf drops to his knees, joins his hands, and rolls his eyes in a mockery of prayer . . .

On Tuesday the twenty-ninth, at twelve fifteen, Siobhan rang Hugh. 'I'm going to be worrying about you,' she said.

'Well, don't, I'll be absolutely fine. What time are you back?'

'Depends on Martha. Four thirtyish?'

'OK. If I'm near a phone I'll give you a ring. If not I'll call the minute I get back.'

'Don't you think it's about time you joined the mobile generation?'

'Hate 'em. Totally unnecessary. Give you cancer. Anyway, go and have a good time. Give Martha a big kiss from me. A few hours from now we'll be having a laugh about it.'

'Look after yourself. I . . . please, Hugh.'

'You too. See you in a bit.'

Fifteen minutes before Hugh's taxi was due, the phone rang again.

'Hello?'

'Mr Severin, it's me. Richard.'

Hugh recognised the voice at once. 'Richard what? Last time you didn't say.'

'Oh, didn't I? It's Bright. Richard Bright. Look, I'm running a little bit late and I was wondering if the cathedral would be OK for you? I mean, I can still get to the station but that'd mean keeping you waiting. And actually, if you've never seen it, it's well worth a look. Would that be OK?'

Hugh cast around for a reason to say no, but couldn't find one. On the contrary, the cathedral, with its dark associations, was one of the many gaps in his patchy historical knowledge. That alone might make the trip worthwhile. 'I can't spend long there,' he said. 'This is all turning out to be a bit of a bloody nuisance.'

'I know. I'm sorry about that. Well, as I say, if you want to hang around at the station . . .'

'I'll go straight to the cathedral,' Hugh said. 'If you're not there when I get there, I'm off. OK? Whereabouts in the building?'

'Er, let's see. How about, say . . . St Benedict's altar? Make it four fifteen? Just to be on the safe side?'

'Where's that?'

'Oh, anyone'll tell you where that is. Just ask anyone. About half-way down on the left-hand side.'

'Right.' This time it was Hugh who put the phone down.

The train to Canterbury was running on time. Hugh's carriage was full of shoppers heading home from the sales. The racks were bulging with bargains they'd persuaded themselves they needed. Children played computer games, isolated by technology. Parents dozed, or chatted, or just gazed at the cheerless landscape. In a corner, four young men were working their way through two six-packs of lager. Every so often they'd break into a chant, punctuated by rhythmic claps. As Hugh watched them he felt a strange sensation, as though he were falling asleep while still awake. His eyes were open, he was still aware of everything around him, but his mind had made an instant adjustment to another time scale; one that insisted on imposing itself.

The dark man is being dressed with reverence by two men in long, rough, woollen garments. Though they are accustomed to the sight of his back, raw from the scourge, they still feel nauseous and full of pity at the perceptible movement of maggots and lice feeding on the wounds. Nevertheless, as they are bidden, they cover his nakedness with a shirt and breeches of goatskin, followed by pants made of cotton. Over their master's head they pull a linen shirt, and then a cowl and two short, soft pelisses, made of lambswool. Next come a habit, of wool, another pelisse of lambskins, a white surplice, and over all a black mantle lined with more lambskins, fastened at the front with a black tassel. On his head they place the round cap of his office.

His heavy shoes sound on the flagstones as he makes a tour of the building he has come to love.

Later, at two o'clock, he dines. Before him are a dish of pheasants and a silver cup of wine. He is then joined by his attendants, but their talk is interrupted by a messenger. This young man, breathless, agitated, is fearful for the first time in his life. The dark man at the centre of the gathering lays a hand on his shoulder, calm and resolute.

At the gateway, the four knights who had left the earlier banquet, dismiss their escort of twelve men and ride into the courtyard, accompanied only by an archer. They dismount under a mulberry tree and enter the hall where the dark man's servants are eating. One of these offers them refreshments. They refuse, ordering a steward to fetch his master.

At three o'clock the four visitors are shown into the dark man's chamber. Ignoring them, he continues to address his entourage. The uninvited visitors sit at his feet. At length the dark man acknowledges them. There is hostility in the air. Voices are raised. Two of the dark man's followers are arrested and taken from the room. His advisers tell him to escape while he can. In reply he says, 'I know what I have to do. In the Lord's battle I will fight hand to hand.'

The twelve knights at the gateway are summoned into the building. The gate is barred behind them. There is uproar. The stone passages are full of fleeing figures, chased by armed soldiers. At last the dark man is persuaded to take to the cellars, which will lead him in safety to his sanctuary.

But in his heart he knows that now, for him, safety is a thing of the past . . .

At the San Remo, the staff made a fuss of Martha Kimmeridge. From the moment she led Siobhan in, like a watermelon chaperoning a sprig of lavender, she energised the room with her warmth and expansiveness. Over her first generous vodka and tonic she talked of the latest political scandal, featuring a high-flying young minister whose social ambitions had laid him low. 'But for *Notting Hill*!' she said. 'Imagine risking all for *Notting Hill*! For a house on the Grand Canal, possibly, though one's neighbours these days would probably be oiks from the City. But to bankrupt oneself for the *haut bourgeois* equivalent of Broadstairs! It's pathetic! Even these creatures' fantasies are mundane.'

Over a balloon of barolo, to accompany her *saltimbocca*, she reminisced about her days in Fleet Street, contrasting their rambunctiousness with the mealy-mouthed keyhole-peeping of the current fourth estate. This brought her round to Hugh, whom she said she loved. He'd lived hard and paid the price, she said, without ever moaning about it. While Siobhan toyed with her half-glass of red wine, Martha told her stories of Hugh's wilder adventures, regretting that he'd never made the most of his talent.

'Well, it's not too late,' Siobhan said.

'Very nearly. Has he been to see Tom Massingberd yet?'

'I think he was waiting for you to say you'd had a word.'

'I'll telephone him this very afternoon.' The waiter refilled Martha's glass. '*Grazie*, Pietro,' she said. 'When Italy lost you, she lost a great artist. Thou art Pietro, and upon this rock I have built my lunch.'

'Signora Marta,' he said.

'Signorina, Pietro. I am, to all intents and purposes, a virgin. One of very few remaining in Pimlico.'

Pietro, who had no idea what she was talking about, bowed and beamed.

Turning back to Siobhan, Martha said, 'So, where is your other half?'

'Funny,' Siobhan said. 'That's exactly what I feel he is. I daren't tell him, though, because I don't want to frighten the poor man.'

'I rather think you'd do exactly the opposite. It's perfectly plain he adores you.'

Siobhan hadn't blushed like this in a long time. After a pause she said, 'He's gone to see someone. In Canterbury.'

'Ah, how very appropriate.'

Siobhan looked up.

'Why?'

'Because it's the twenty-ninth, of course. The great anniversary.'

'I'm not with you. What of?'

'The martyrdom of poor St Thomas Becket. Half past four in the afternoon, December the twenty-ninth, eleven hundred and seventy. Four fat cowards it took to kill him. Sliced off the top of his head. The poor man's blood and brains all over the floor. Some fancy chronicler likened them to roses and lilies. And do you know, when his monks came to undress Thomas, with great reverence, so that they could lay him out in all his archbishop's finery, they found his body raw from the scourge, covered in worms and lice. From the moment he'd begun to serve Christ, having been Henry the Second's pampered favourite, he'd worn a hair shirt and breeches. Imagine, poor soul!' She paused to light a Woodbine. 'Do you know, it's an extraordinary thing but all the important events of Thomas's life, including his appalling death, happened on Tuesdays?' Martha was so carried away with the narrative that she'd failed to notice Siobhan's changed expression. 'Are you all right, my dear? You look frightfully pale.'

Siobhan managed a small nod. 'I'm OK.'

'Reginald fitzUrse was the ringleader,' Martha went on, warming to her theme, 'and the others in the ghastly gang were William de Tracy, Hugh de Morville, and Richard Brito, or le Bret. Foul fiend. He delivered the *coup de grâce*, if *grâce* is the right word.'

Siobhan was rising as she spoke: 'I have to find a phone,' she said, her voice subdued but firm.

At Canterbury, the first indistinct station announcement, calling for a Mr Hugh Severin to go to the information desk, preceded the arrival of Hugh's train by forty-seven minutes. The message had been repeated half an hour and forty-five minutes later.

When he'd woken from his doze, Hugh had at last understood the identity of the dark man in the dreams. If he'd taken more notice of history lessons at school, he thought, he'd have known from the beginning. And the call to Canterbury seemed to confirm it. But rather than answering questions, the revelation asked a great many more. It left unexplained the reason why he'd been haunted by this particular story; had in some bizarre way associated himself with this particular figure when, as far as he knew, they couldn't have less in common. A – what had he been? Twelfth or thirteenth century? Anyway, a medieval saint who'd been murdered in Canterbury cathedral by four thugs because he'd got on the King's nerves, and a twenty-first-century travel writer? Didn't make any sense at all. Hugh couldn't even remember which king it was who'd said he longed to be rid of the turbulent priest.

And where did this Richard Bright fit into the picture? Somehow he must be familiar with the story. Must have made a connection. And now he must feel he had something to add, or contribute. After all, he'd gone to a certain amount of trouble too. He'd taken the time to make the contact, and now he was going out of his way to keep the rendezvous. Not as far out of his way as Hugh, but even so there must be things he'd rather be doing.

With twenty minutes to spare, now the meeting had been delayed, Hugh decided to have a quick cup of tea. Maybe after all he should catch the next train back. Maybe Anthony had been right, and the man he was meeting was a lunatic. Some obsessive, suffering from . . . What was that thing Ian McEwen had written about? De Clerambault's syndrome, where people stalk complete strangers, sometimes for years, convinced they're in love with them. Perhaps this Richard Bright was in love with him. Despite the extraordinary circumstances, Hugh found himself smiling. Don't be daft, he thought. Those cases were as rare as hens' teeth. Things like that didn't happen to blokes like him. That was the funny thing about journalism. Stories never seemed to happen to those who made a living out of them. No. His first thoughts had been the most likely. This was just a young guy who'd somehow spotted a way of getting into print. Hugh would go through with the meeting, keeping a clear head to record the details for later. No looking back now. Be sensible, rational, careful.

But as he raised the cup to his lips, reason gave way once again to a nauseating sense of unease.

It is four o'clock. Sunset. The church is growing dark, the only light coming from constellations of candles on the altars and in the choir. The dark man, Thomas, the Archbishop, is greeted by his monks who are singing vespers. Some run to bar the door, but Thomas reminds them it is a church and not a castle. The four knights burst in, helmeted, armed with axes and unsheathed swords. They shout for the traitor to declare himself, and Thomas asks what they want. All but three of his clerks have now deserted him. One of the knights urges Thomas to escape, threatening death if he remains. Thomas stands his ground. Another knight, fired by tension to insult, tips off the Archbishop's cap with his swordpoint. The knights attempt to drag Thomas away. He will not be moved. The townsfolk begin to arrive for evensong, but are held back. Though present, they will not witness the horror . . .

Ten past four. Hugh looked up from his watch as he came through the archway and got his first glimpse of the cathedral's ancient cream and grey façade. Even the little he knew of that dreadful blasphemy long ago made the building seem timeless with tragedy. A place both cursed and unique in sanctity. But why had he been drawn to it? What purpose was he here to serve? His heart, Siobhan's heart, beat a little faster, responding, it seemed, as much to some obscure recognition as to fear of the unknown.

A group of animated French tourists came up the path towards him. As he passed them his eye was drawn to an extraordinary procession of monk-like figures seeming to head for the main door, but immovable. Some ten feet high, they were made of dun-coloured wicker. Cowled and weary, backs bent under burdens – one bore a cylindrical basket, another a heavy sack – they were frozen in attitudes of hope and humility, at journey's end after a pilgrimage lasting hundreds of years. Hugh looked into the faces of the figures nearest him, but the wicker hollows were blank and enigmatic.

Although he had never been here before, as he entered the nave he felt somehow embraced by the building. It seemed to know him, to claim him, as though prepared for his coming. Now he couldn't be certain where the dream state ended and reality began. His movements were sure, as if his feet were familiar with these flagstones. Every detail of the hushed and vaulted space was sharp-edged in his mind's eye. Facing him, lining the far wall, were pale, ornate tombs. With a sense of purpose that surprised him, he went over to them, noting the inscriptions without effort. *Colonel Bolton . . . Aide-de-camp to Queen Victoria . . . Henry Boswell Bennett, Lieutenant in the 45th Regiment . . . who fell in the strict and manly discharge of his duty . . . 1838 . . . aged 29 years.* The strict and manly discharge of his duty . . . One marble memorial showed two sailors lowering a figure in black armour over the side of his ship. Kneeling below the crests of the waves, his widow, Dame Alice, prayed. *James Hales . . . died of fever and buried at sea. 1589.*

Was it Hugh's imagination or were the other tourists looking at him in a strange way, as though he were somehow significant? A face they had seen before? They seemed to glance as they passed, curious and half recognising. Their movements appeared slowed, gradual, as did his own. When, turning away, they blinked, their eyes seemed to be closed for two or three seconds. Their voices were indistinct; sounds but not identifiable language.

A little further on, a short flight of stone steps. Hugh counted them as he climbed. Seven. At the top, a sign pointing to the left: 'To the Martyrdom'. Without hesitation Hugh turned as it indicated, descending seven more steps. At the bottom, a small stone altar, topped with slate, on which stood a vase of crimson roses and lilies, the red startling against the white. Though he had never been here before, he at once recognised this as the place where Thomas had been butchered for his resistance. Cold, uncompromising, it was electric with ineradicable memories.

Standing before the altar was a slight figure in black trousers and a black anorak. With equal certainty Hugh knew that this was the man he'd come to meet; the man who called himself Richard Bright. As he reached the bottom of the steps, Hugh felt a sudden knot of terror he had never experienced before. Now, too late, it was so clear. He'd been stupid, unimaginative, blind. And there was no going back. The chains binding him to his fate held a power over him as potent as an hallucinogenic drug. By ignoring the obvious warnings he had walked into an inescapable trap. The dark man inside him, the one who suffered in the dreams, was once again being drawn to his savage destiny. At the last, he and Hugh had become inseparable.

Thomas joins his hands in prayer. 'I commend myself to God,' he says, 'to the Blessed Mary, St Denis, and the patron saints of this church . . .'

Hugh longed to cry for help but the panic in his chest stifled the impulse. This was where it was to end, as it had for Thomas. The dreams, all those nights filled with strange, vivid fancies, had formed, piecemeal, an elaborate route to this bare chapel, where the stones had seen unthinkable violence.

Bright turned to face him. As in the main body of the church, all movement appeared measured; time stretched by a slight but appreciable amount. The pale, fair-haired, unremarkable young man, a buttoned white shirt visible under his anorak, spoke in a quiet, unemphatic voice: 'Mr Severin.'

Hugh should have wanted to escape. Turn, head back up the steps, run across the nave and out into the darkening December afternoon. But something in him, his companion from long ago perhaps, made him stand his ground. To come as far as this, after all those weeks, after more than eight hundred years, and not see it through . . . The dreams had not been random, that was obvious now, and therefore neither was their ending. With an effort he calmed his breathing. The transplant operation had been a closer call than this. Having survived that, he was determined not to show fear now.

Whatever the young man represented, however he fitted into this extraordinary re-run of history, Hugh must survive. He thought of Siobhan. He would live for her. And Tilly. And Sam. No deluded obsessive, no vengeful killer on earth was powerful enough to take him away from them.

'How did you find out?' he said.

'A young woman. Catherine.'

'Is that the one who . . . Is that the missing woman?'

Bright nodded. 'She was. She isn't now. I told her she could go at quarter past four.'

'How did she know about the dreams?'

'A friend of a friend told her. Someone she met in Cambridge.'

It was as Siobhan had feared. She must be the link. 'Well, you've dragged me all this way, what is it you want?' Hugh had found the confidence to be peremptory.

The first blow is struck by fitzUrse. Thomas's clerk, Edward Grim, raises his arm to parry. It cuts him to the bone and slices off the top of Thomas's head. The second blow brings Thomas to his knees. Supporting himself for a moment on his hands, he falls forward on his face, the altar of St Benedict to his right. The final blow, severing his cranium, is delivered by Richard Brito, whose blade breaks on impact. A sword is thrust into Thomas's gaping skull, spilling blood and brains on the stone floor . . . roses and lilies.

Though the momentary, terrifying insight had given Hugh the answer he most dreaded, he waited for Bright's interpretation, noticing the wall-plaque in the turbulent silence . . . *this place hallowed by the martyrdom of Thomas Becket 29 December 1170* . . .

'I want an ending,' Bright said.

'To what?'

'To my work.'

Hugh's realisation that Bright was incapable of a rational explanation made him feel stronger. 'What work's that, then?' he said.

'Becket was a priest. You're in touch with him. Priests!' Bright sounded empty, drained of energy or hope. He looked straight into Hugh's eyes, with the intensity of a painter studying his own image in a mirror. 'When it's done it's over,' he said. 'Past and present. They'll have no more power over people.'

'What have they ever done to you?'

'Killed everything I cared for. Poisoned my life.'

'But why me? Why Becket? He was hundreds of years ago. What's he got to do with poisoning your life?'

'Do you know the name of the knight who struck the final blow?'

Hugh shook his head.

'It was Brito. Richard Brito, or le Bret. Ever since I read that I've known the end would be to do with Becket. It was meant.'

'And after? What happens after?'

'I don't care. There's never been an after in my life. Only now.'

All Hugh had to do was walk away. Climb the stone steps and look back at this pathetic, deranged figure with his delusions of destiny. But some unbending impulse, some undeniable resolution or inheritance still made him stand, as Becket, the dark man of the dreams had stood.

'You'd better get on with it, then,' he said, with a courage he didn't know he possessed. 'It was a sword, wasn't it?'

Bright took from the pocket of his anorak a black-handled knife. 'This'll do it,' he said. He held the point of the knife to Hugh's right eye, making a tiny depression in the skin of the lower lid. 'Tell me what you're feeling. I want you to tell me. I want to know how it feels, knowing you're going to die. Talk to me. Confess to me. Tell me what fear is.'

'Is that what this is about? Is that what you get off on?'

The knife pierced the flesh, leaving a single tear of blood.

'Tell me, while there's time,' Bright said.

'I've faced death before. There's nothing to tell.'

Bright registered a flicker of doubt. 'You're lying. I can see it in you. You're like the others. You're feeling sick. You can't control your bowels. I'm the last person you'll ever see . . .'

Hugh heard himself saying, 'I'm not afraid.' Out of the corner of his other eye he was aware of a dark shape at the top of the stone steps.

'I'll kill you anyway. Who's going to miss a priest? They're not fit to live.'

'Do it, then,' Hugh said. 'Stick your pathetic little knife into a journalist and pretend he's a priest. Big deal.'

Hugh could see the growing concern in Bright's

eyes. The indistinct figure was stationary now at the bottom of the steps.

'Do it,' Hugh repeated, his voice loud and hard with anger. 'Go on, you snivelling little runt, bloody do it if you're going to. Do it, you gutless little shit. Do it!'

Bright half turned and now he too was aware of the dark figure in the background. Hugh braced himself. The cornered bull. The sudden gust of wind. The last lunge of a howling soul with nothing left to live for. He saw Siobhan in his mind's eye, shining and hurt, her heart wasted on the cold flagstones. And he saw Thomas, his life spilled; his long, agonising journey ended.

Lowering the knife for the *coup de grâce*, Bright faced Hugh again. For a moment the doubt had paralysed him, but there was still no knowing how he might react. A man with an all-consuming obsession; a man beyond control. His courage, borrowed from Thomas, ebbing away, Hugh clutched at a prayer, and found only an echo of the dream: '*I commend myself to God . . .*'

'This is for my sister and my mother,' Bright said. 'It's what I'll be remembered for.'

'Oh, that's it, is it? Fame? Forget it. It's Thomas they remember,' Hugh said. 'No one remembers the murderers' names. In the day after tomorrow's papers you won't even be a story.'

The knife-point entered Hugh's flesh. He felt the obscene tip centimetres away from penetrating Siobhan's heart. So, after all, this was how his story ended. Thomas's bravery, that had seemed alive again in him, had been a cruel illusion. Steel would overcome resolve, as it had on that tragic afternoon so long ago. Here, on this very spot, men with no compassion in their hearts and with perverted motives in their heads, had massacred their victim. Bright, believing himself one of them, was about to kill again.

Hugh's mind was filled with Siobhan, with her sacrifice and her tenderness. If Bright was without hope, so was he without her. Mesmerised by the dreams that had bound him to a martyr, he was about to lose everything, for nothing. Shock and rage rose in him and with a strength he hadn't felt since he was a young man, he hurled Bright to the floor. The young man fell hard, hitting his head on the flagstones. But at once he raised himself, lunging at Hugh as he regained his feet. Hugh sidestepped the blade, his breathing already heavy with exertion and the knowledge that nothing could save him but his own determination. Looking down he saw a red blotch on his shirt where the first pressure had punctured his flesh. His strength had begun to desert him. He feared that his heart, Siobhan's heart, might not stand the trauma. Bright turned and slashed, slicing through Hugh's coat and into his right arm. Hugh tried to claw Bright's face with his free hand, but Bright was too quick for him. Seeing Hugh's fatigue, the younger man came closer, betraying no emotion. The executioner. Richard Brito. Killing for a cause, unconcerned with the consequences. Hugh's legs felt weak. His own body was defeating him . . . *I commend myself to God* . . . And to Siobhan. I commend myself to Siobhan, whose gift of life is about to be violated on a stone floor in a strange city . . . Movement seemed more dreamlike still. Hugh saw the knife as it came to him across the half-dark. He saw the inexorable blade, closer and closer, about to reopen the long scar on his chest. For some reason beyond his own volition he raised his hands from his sides and cupped the palms . . .

The black-clad arm blurred across his vision with the suddenness of a snake. It disrupted the lazy gradualness of movement with shocking incisiveness. Instead of re-entering his flesh, the blade was falling, had fallen to the floor. Bright scrabbled for it and as he did so a figure in a long black cassock interposed himself between him and Hugh. This, Hugh realised even in his half-dazed state, must be the dark figure who earlier had come down the steps and hovered on the edge of vision. What would Bright do now? Hugh watched transfixed as Bright stared at the stranger, appeared to feint towards him with the knife and then, sudden and decisive, turned the blade on himself, sheathing the steel in his stomach. Half smiling, he fell, and lay still and silent, small and insignificant, in the foetal position, with the table bearing the roses and lilies to his right. Here, in this sacred place, his sacrilege had brought him to the same fate as his hated adversary; the fate he had intended for Hugh.

Hugh felt exhausted. With the stranger solicitous beside him, he leaned on the altar for support, looking at Bright; a martyr to his own delusions. He noticed that something had fallen from the pocket of his black anorak. Bending to identify it, he saw that it was a small plastic crucifix.

Thomas's outer garments are cut away and given to the poor. His spilt blood is collected in a bowl. The body remains unwashed. His monks are astonished at the cruel marks of his penitential suffering. They dress him for burial in the full splendour of his archiepiscopal vestments.

With their cloth of gold, inlaid with precious stones, they resemble a suit of lights.

Chapter Twelve

Hugh had woken with an axing headache. Throughout the journey back from Canterbury he'd felt as though a rogue reactor had been installed in his brain. Images chased each other, collided, faded, leaving faint outlines of themselves. The sensation was so intense that he wondered it didn't show on his face. Perhaps his eyelids were flickering as they might in sleep, or under shock treatment. But the other passengers appeared to be taking no notice, preoccupied with their books or their boredom.

The police had been called by Hugh's saviour in the black cassock, Julian Mason, who had turned out to be on the clerical staff of the cathedral. Mason had also gone to fetch a raincoat to cover Bright's body. At the same time he'd brought Hugh a glass of water and urged him to sit on the steps. He kept saying what a terrible thing it was, and Hugh could see that unspoken, behind his eyes, was a question. Had he seen an unbalanced individual commit suicide, or the ghost of an ancient atrocity? Either way, he'd given as accurate an account as he could to the considerate policemen who'd been first to arrive. Before he disappeared into the recesses of the cathedral, Hugh had difficulty finding the words to thank him enough, though Mason's modesty dismissed any such obligation. They did, however, exchange numbers, and arranged to meet as early as possible in January.

Soon after, when the chapel was filled with police activity, hushed, in spite of its urgency, by the significance of the place, Hugh had asked to borrow a mobile and had called Siobhan from the cathedral porch.

'God, where are you? I've been worried sick,' she'd said.

'I'm OK. I'm fine. I'm still in Canterbury.'

'I tried to call you at the station. What happened? What did he want?'

Tricky one to answer over the phone. Hugh didn't want to frighten her, even now it was over. Later, face to face, he would, of course, tell her everything. 'You and Anthony were right, basically. He was a bit of a nutter,' he said.

'But did he – Are you hurt? For God's sake, tell me, Hugh.'

'No, I'm absolutely fine, honestly. It's all over. Are you going out tonight?'

'Course I'm not!'

'Good. I want to see you. Very much. I'll tell you about it then.'

'Look, are you sure you're safe? You're not just . . .'

'Sure, promise. I'll ring you from the flat the minute I'm in.'

'You'd better. Oh, and Hugh, Hester's friend Kate's

been found! Isn't it fantastic? She'd been kept by this lunatic somewhere in the fens apparently, in an isolated cottage somewhere, and then this afternoon she just opened the door and walked out. She went to the main road and got a lift. Apparently he said he'd kidnapped her because she reminded him of his sister. Said she'd been killed by a priest. Obviously just some lonely crank with a hang-up about religion. Completely barking. The bad news is he's still out there somewhere.'

'I doubt it,' Hugh said.

'How do you mean, you doubt it?'

'I'll tell you later.'

'Don't be so infuriatingly cryptic.'

'I just can't say it all in a few well-chosen words, that's all.'

'I thought journalism was supposed to be about a few well-chosen words.'

'Yes, well, that's why I'm packing it in. Anyway, this is someone else's phone.'

'All right, then. But hurry back. Please.'

'Don't you worry. See you in a bit.'

An investigating detective had wanted him to go down to the police station, but Hugh had made a big thing of being exhausted and had at last persuaded him to take a preliminary statement sitting in the nave. An ambulance-man, seeing the blood on his cheek, though Hugh hadn't revealed the small chest wound, and the obvious fact that he was shaken, had confirmed the wisdom of this. It had taken a considerable effort to précis the bizarre story into some sort of sequential narrative. No point in dwelling on the dreams, though they couldn't be left out. They had, after all, provided the twisted motive for Bright's fatal mission. But Hugh kept his version of them to a minimum, aware that even in this lean form they might make him sound unhinged. He'd surprised himself with the sharpness of the detail he recalled, even confident that his account of the conversation he'd had with Bright was 90 per cent accurate. The detective had congratulated him on his memory, asked a number of questions, then released him, taking down his details and saying they'd be in touch very soon.

On impulse, as he approached the archway where a police car was waiting to take him to the railway station, Hugh had dropped into the bookshop. He'd bought the official guide to the cathedral, and Frank Barlow's substantial biography of Thomas Becket. It was dipping into these on the train that had accelerated the atom-race of his bewildered thoughts. In the guide he soon confirmed the names of the murderers, including Richard Brito, or le Bret, who had struck the death blow. What was he to make of this, Bright's claim to historical imperative? Extraordinary coincidence, or . . .? Or what? Bright had claimed he acted out of revenge against the priesthood. He believed that by killing someone who, to him, represented an arch-priest, he could disable the entire institution. But he also believed that, in some unfathomable way, the murder was his destiny. Maybe Bright wasn't his real name. Maybe, playing his sinister games, he'd decided to add another subtle, convenient, mystical element. The further coincidence of the date, 29 December, might be made to fit that thesis. Hugh could almost imagine Bright plotting the encounter, taking sadistic pleasure in re-creating the pattern. However, this games-playing theory was somewhat undermined when Hugh, reading further, discovered that the only human being who had come to Thomas's aid was a clerk of the cathedral, Edward Grim, whose arm had been cut to the bone by a swordstroke. Hugh's guardian angel, Julian Mason, could not have been party to a Bright plot.

But it was only when he'd browsed through the entire, fascinating biography, focusing on paragraphs at random, that Hugh had begun to feel the tension of real concern. Every single vision in his dreams was mirrored here, in the true story. The christening in the darkened church; the hanged man; the fond friendship with Henry II; the tussle with the teasing King for the red cloak in the road; the monkeys on horseback; the loping wolves with their sure, frightening eyes; the plate of eels; the lonely exile in France; the meetings with Henry, on horseback, in meadows bright with flowers; the return across the Channel; the horse bearing gifts to Canterbury, with its cropped tail; the martyr's death; the shock of the poor, mutilated body; it was all in these pages, this compelling journey he'd made in his sleep. But how, before he'd read it, had it transferred itself wholesale to his imagination? And how, waking, had he seen a reflection of its actual outcome?

There was more. Many of the places Hugh had been to in his recent work matched those on Thomas's route to sanctuary in France and eventual death. In 1158 Thomas had been sent by Henry on an embassy to

Paris. Hugh had been there too, with Gary. Henry had summoned Thomas to a meeting at Northampton. That was the town where Hugh had met the charming explorer, Rupert Kent-Imison. Thomas had landed in France on the broad white sands at Oye, near Boulogne, and had left for home and martyrdom from Wissant, a small fishing village on the same stretch of coast. Hugh and Siobhan had sat in a beach bar there, watching the children fly kites. And later they'd had a happy evening with Gary, Miranda, and Olivia in Pontigny, where, more than eight hundred years before them, Thomas had also found refuge.

By the time the taxi dropped him in Willes Road, Hugh felt ill with fatigue. This was everything Scoular had warned him against: pressure, excitement, worry, over-tiredness. Minutes after he got in, too weary even to pick up the phone, he lay on the bed and slept. When he woke, half an hour later, he was at once aware of two things: the slight soreness in his chest, and the fact that, for the first time in weeks, he'd had no dreams. Or if he had, they were unconnected with Becket. With the ginger, awkward manoeuvre of an old man, he raised himself and looked in the mirror. The face he saw was grey, the colour it had been before the operation. Was that it? Now that the dream had played itself out was it going to claim him, as it had claimed that tragic figure all those years ago? No, he was damned if it was. Take a couple of paracetamol, put a plaster on the tiny chest-cut, ring Siobhan, and get on with living. He owed that to both of them.

Twenty-five minutes later she was sitting beside him

on the red sofa, holding his hand, showing tenderness and concern. First she had insisted on bathing the cut and re-dressing it. Then she made him take his time telling the story, only prompting him when, through tiredness, he lost the thread. Since she was as vague as he had been about Becket's relationship with Henry II, and the reasons why it had turned sour, he had to weave in the facts he'd gleaned from Frank Barlow's book.

The two men, Hugh explained, had been great friends as young bucks, the King lavishing wealth and privilege on his engaging, stammering protégé. Thomas had fought for Henry in France, with great courage and distinction, and the King had rewarded him by making him Chancellor, the second most powerful man in England. But it was when Thomas went to Canterbury as Archbishop that the trouble began. Not content to be an absentee, worldly prelate, Thomas devoted himself to the work with great piety and utter commitment. Unable to accept the King's view of the relative rights of Church and State, he stood firm with stubborn conviction. The result was inevitable exile and the eventual, famous, despairing cry of the King, which Hugh read from the book, to make sure he'd got it right: 'What miserable drones and traitors have I nourished and promoted in my household, who let their lord be treated with such shameful contempt by a low-born clerk!' Overheard by the four knights, this had become a death sentence. Hugh added that, of course, the King, like Becket and all their educated contemporaries, would have spoken French. As he'd suspected, the dreams had somehow given him a tailor-made interpretation.

Siobhan listened, fascinated. 'Amazing stuff, isn't it? "Miserable drones and traitors!" You can see why his thugs thought they'd do him a favour. But why you?' she said. 'Why should the story pick on you? That's what I don't get.'

'Exactly. It'd be a big relief to know that. Anyway, the good news is the dreams seem to have stopped.'

'Brilliant. So this man you met, the nutter?'

'Has to be the one who took your chum's friend, Kate. He said he'd got the idea through a woman called Catherine. Next time you talk to her, ask her if she mentioned the dreams for some reason. Not, you know, accusing her or anything, but just to be sure.'

'Of course.' She paused. 'Well,' she said, 'poor old you. You have been through it, haven't you? And all because I stupidly told Hester in the first place. I'm sorry, Hugh.'

'Don't be daft. Not your fault. I've got a funny feeling it was all meant to happen anyway. God knows why, but I have.'

'So what happens now? How's your head by the way?'

'Fine.'

'Truth?'

'Nearly fine.'

'How about a Vietnamese?'

'Sounds good to me.'

'I'll get a takeaway and we'll have it here. Mmmm?'

'Even better.'

Siobhan turned square to face him. 'Read my lips,' she said.

Hugh looked at her mouth.

'Followed by an early night,' she added, and smiled a slow smile.

In the next two weeks Hugh's life changed. Now that the dreams had left him he slept better than he had for years. For a few days he'd done little except make careful notes about what had happened in the cathedral. He'd filled six black books and felt confident that he had the bones of a story. How to tell it was another matter. Plucking up courage one morning, he'd rung Tom Massingberd. To his surprise the great man said he'd be happy to see him the following afternoon. Martha Kimmeridge, he said, had told him Hugh had a surefire best-seller up his sleeve. Despite this overheated introduction, pure fantasy on Martha's part, on the Tuesday Hugh had taken a taxi to King Street in Covent Garden and made his dry-mouthed pitch. Sitting in shirtsleeves, with his back to the window, eclipsing much of the light, yellow braces and Garrick club tie emphasising the millennium dome of his belly, Massingberd had absorbed every detail. When Hugh had finished, he asked a few pertinent questions in a voice marinated in malt whisky, and leaned back, joining his hands like a cardinal painted by Franz Hals. 'We'll do this,' he said. 'Let me have a letter. Three pages'll do. Just tell me it like you're talking to me. People feel reassured by a piece of paper. Then we'll talk money. It'll probably be derisory, but this is a buyers' market.'

This hadn't been what Hugh had expected. After

Martha's description he'd pictured someone altogether more feline. His first novel! And an extraordinary story to tell. He wanted to phone everyone he knew. He wanted it up in coloured lights in Piccadilly. He wanted to tell the other passengers on the bus, washed out after another grey day with no excitements at all.

Most of all he wanted to tell Siobhan. She'd been through this whole saga with him at second hand. If she'd worried that he was deluded, rather than simply a conduit for dreams, she had never allowed it to show. Throughout she'd been sympathetic, supportive, and now, loving. The day after he'd got back from Canterbury she'd moved in. All his fears, uncertainties, anxieties had been swept away by her simple insistence that she wanted to be with him; needed to be with him, she said. Pre-empting his concern about the age gap, she'd set what she'd called ground rules. For them there was no for ever, she'd said. At best they'd have ten years, and now that she'd mentioned the figure, it must never be quoted again. At the same time it mustn't be like a contract of doom. It wasn't a contract at all. It was two people staying together for as long as they loved each other. Hugh had wanted to say that, in his case, that would mean to the end of the line, but realised that wasn't what she wanted to hear.

They decided to have a party to celebrate. Gary came with Miranda; Martha arrived in her crash helmet, parking her scooter on the path; Dacre turned up with six bottles of Perrier Jouet; Charlie, Miles, and a dozen others from Hugh's journalistic past were there; Tilly and Anthony, with Sam, who had a special dispensation to stay up late; and, from Cambridge, Hester and Kate, with Gareth. Though there wasn't time to talk for as long as they would have liked, Kate confirmed that she had described the dreams to Bright, and that she felt terrible guilt about the frightening result. Hugh said she shouldn't give it another thought. In any case, he said, if she hadn't provided the link, he'd have had a story with a beginning and a middle but no end. Kate sketched for him the brief course of Bright's persistence; his disconcerting mixture of aggression, charm, vulnerability, and inner torment. She recounted as much as she could remember of the chilling soliloquy in the white room, when Bright had unlocked his dreadful secret. If Hugh wanted to know more, Kate said, she'd leave her number and he could give her a call.

Later Hester had told him that, according to Corcoran, new evidence, including Gilbert's, had established undeniable links between Bright and the hit-and-run killing of Martin Taylor in Cambridge, the murder in Southwold, and the one on Midsummer Common, as well as four earlier deaths elsewhere. Corcoran had called him a madman with a mission.

There had been no need for Hugh and Siobhan to make any announcement about their new togetherness. It had been obvious to everyone in the room. Dacre had taken Hugh aside and told him there was still plenty of work if he needed it. Hugh had thanked him, filled his glass, and told him he was sure now that he wanted to go it alone, even if it meant a pauper's funeral. Dacre had said doubtless it would mean that, and that Hugh wanted his bumps feeling. Nevertheless he wished him luck, and asked for first refusal on the serialisation rights. Hugh had also invited the Canterbury cleric who had saved his life, Julian Mason, but the self-effacing hero had said he'd promised to join a walking party in Snowdonia.

The next morning, as Hugh and Siobhan were washing the glasses and clearing up the debris after a late start, the mail arrived. Breaking off, Siobhan picked it up and brought it through to the kitchen. Two bills, theatre tickets from the Almeida, Barclays wanting to lend Hugh money he'd never be able to repay, and a letter from Siobhan's father, forwarded, after some delay, from the flat in Hampstead. She sat down to read it. Five pages of thin air-mail paper, written in black ink in a handsome, regular script. Often it was her way to comment as she went along, but now she was silent, a slight furrow in her brow.

'What's up?' Hugh said. 'Bad news?'

Siobhan didn't answer.

'Problems?'

Siobhan looked up. 'You'd better sit,' she said.

Hugh put down the tea towel and sat opposite her.

'This is weird,' she said.

'Go on, then.'

'Apparently my father bought this job-lot of books. Dealers often do that. To get the couple you want you have to take the rest of the bundle. Anyway, in among them was a very old one . . . eighteenth . . .' she glanced again at the page '. . . no, sorry, seventeenth century, badly foxed and the binding gone and everything. But it was about various families, including our lot.'

'And?'

'The thing is, whoever wrote it, this book, Geoffrey something, apparently puts forward this theory that my dad had never come across before.'

'Don't tell me. You're the rightful heir to the throne.'

Siobhan looked at him. 'It's about Becket, Hugh.'

It was Hugh's turn to frown.

'Evidently this Geoffrey somebody says there was a rumour that when Becket was young, having a good time with the King like you said, he had a bit of a thing with this young woman he met at court, Agnes Foliot.'

'Sounds reasonable. Power's sexy.'

'According to this rumour, Agnes conceived a child by Thomas, Stephen.'

'Kept that very quiet, didn't he, crafty old so-and-so?'

'The point is, Hugh, according to Dad, very soon afterwards Agnes Foliot married a Herbert. That makes her an ancestor. Incredibly remote but it's there all the same.' Siobhan let this sink in before she went on, 'More intriguingly, of course, it also makes her son, Stephen, who took the Herbert name, an ancestor. Presumably Agnes managed to pass him off as her husband's. So, theoretically, there could be a drop of Becket's blood in me. In which case since, you know, Papworth . . .'

Hugh was quite still. He saw the dark figure standing in the prow of the small boat; the vast white beach; the great church, which Hugh now knew was at Vézelay, in Burgundy, where Thomas excommunicated a number of his English enemies and issued a stern warning to

Henry II; that other magnificent church, at Canterbury, lit only by clustered candles; the upraised sword in the hand of a murderous knight crazed with loyalty, ambition, and the rage to strike. He saw the pathetic, foetal figure lying on the flagstones, and heard again an ambulance siren.

Heredity. How to explain a child's ear-lobes being identical to his father's. Or a family talent for music passing from generation to generation. Or an inherited tendency to certain types of cancer. Though science put these wonders down to genes, they remained mysterious. So why not an inheritance of dreams, even if, in Hugh's case, it had come as a gift, rather than in direct line? Siobhan's unique gift, bringing with it extraordinary visions, as well as life itself. No gift ever given could match it. Even Bright's insane opportunism had been unable to destroy it. And Hugh knew that by recording the gathered images as he wrote, he could share his visions with others.

'So that practically makes this incest,' Siobhan said. 'Me and that heart of ours, sharing a bed!'

Smiling, Hugh reached across the table and took her hand. As he did so his eye was drawn to the first page of her father's letter. Thanks to the bold script in which it was written, the date was plain: Tuesday, 29 December.

'Just keeping it in the family,' Hugh said.

CHRIS KELLY

TAKING LEAVE

'Tom, we haven't seen Helen for two days now . . .'

Tom Bellman is daydreaming about joining his wife at their cottage in France when he gets the alarming phone call. He knows Helen wouldn't just disappear without telling anyone. And when he hears that an American heiress has been kidnapped from a nearby village, Tom is deeply concerned.

It seems obvious that the kidnappers have taken Helen as well. They are not admitting it, however, and the kidnapped girl's father, fearful of reprisals, is reluctant to bring in the gendarmerie. Torn apart by fears for his wife, memories of their years together and a desperate desire to do something – anything – to find her, Tom joins forces with his friend, ex-policeman Robert Ryaux. Suddenly, what should have been a golden summer in the ancient stone-built towns of Burgundy, drinking wine and sharing meals with good neighbours, has become a frantic race against time.

HODDER AND STOUGHTON PAPERBACKS